PAXTON PRIDE

Shana Carrol

A JOVE BOOK

PAXTON PRIDE

A Jove Book / published by arrangement with
the author

PRINTING HISTORY
Three previous printings
Jove edition / April 1982

ISBN: 0-515-06324-X

Jove books are published by Jove Publications, Inc., 200 Madison Avenue,
New York, N.Y. 10016. The words ''A JOVE BOOK'' and the ''J'' with
sunburst are trademarks belonging to Jove Publications, Inc.

PRINTED IN THE UNITED STATES OF AMERICA

RAVEN

From the Caribbean's sultry rain forests to England's gracious country estates, over the Atlantic's stormy waters to America's vast frontier came the blackhaired voluptuous beauty known as Raven. A plantation heiress turned pirate, she becomes the first of the dazzling Paxton women...

YELLOW ROSE

The one small bit of beauty in a Pennsylvania town, torn from the earth to take root in distant Texas where the family fortunes lay. YELLOW ROSE, the story of the pioneer spitfire, Elizabeth Michaelson, and lean, hard-riding True Paxton, is a prairie-fire saga of love and the war for independence in the raw new West...

AND THEN, PAXTON PRIDE

The tempestuous novel of ravishing Karen Hampton and Vance Paxton—an elegant, city-bred woman, a proud, unyielding man, a love welded by passion and wedded to the brawling new turf of TEXAS!

Books by Shana Carrol from Jove

PAXTON PRIDE
RAVEN
YELLOW ROSE

PART I

CHAPTER I

The young woman in the mirror struggled with one obstinate, delicate strawberry curl. She twisted it about, pressed it against her creamy white temple. The curl held for a moment and then defiantly sprang askew. The girl in the mirror pouted, stamped one small foot in protest and resumed the struggle.

"Baby, now I jes don' know what to do with you. Your momma and papa are waitin' for you at de table, and your papa is one man who don' like to be kept waitin'. You lookin' jes fine, Baby. Now hurry along."

Karen Hampton whirled from the mirror, her emerald green eyes flashing all the more brilliantly as her temper rose. "I am twenty years old, and not a baby. I will not be hurried and I will not look fine until I look as I please. That will be *all*, Retta."

Retta shook her head in amusement. "Honey, you sure have your daddy's temper. Oo . . . weee . . . you sure do. But he's more 'sperienced at it than you, an' if I was you I'd hurry along, fine or no." The black woman opened the door to Karen's bedroom and held it, waiting. Karen's outbursts perturbed her not at all.

Karen twisted back to the mirror, grabbed a slim pair of scissors from the dressing table and clipped the traitorous curl from her head. Then in a swirl of taffeta and petticoats, she strode through the door, not deigning to glance once at Retta's bemused face.

She traversed the hallway and descended the grand, curving staircase with petulant grace, one hand lightly touching the dark luster of the maple railing, the other peevishly snapping open and closed an ornate fan. She stopped at the bottom of the stairs and paused before turning to the dining room. Her mother and father were in the midst of some dreadful conversation and their voices, rising heat-

7

edly, carried through the thick, closed double doors. Karen knew the subject well, for she had suffered for the last three days as her parents hammered at each other in a furious clash of wills and personalities. The sole purpose of the countless words—oh, destiny, Karen thought sarcastically—was to determine whether the three would stay in Washington for the Secretary of State's formal ball or absent themselves from the city to travel to New York for business reasons. The ball was a prestigious affair, a near requirement for those of the inner circle, and Iantha, Karen's mother, was indignantly and adamantly in favor of attending. The trip to New York, because it involved foreign trade concerns unknown to Iantha but highly critical to her inclusion in the inner circle she valued so highly, was as equally espoused by Barrett, Karen's father.

The decision to be made was awesome, one for which Karen felt little or no concern. Two years ago as a girl of eighteen she had been entranced at the prospect of attending the many social functions continually held in the nation's capital. The war had ended in a Union victory and the Republican exuberance manifested itself in gala after gala, party after party, each grander than the next and all overshadowing the boring New York scene, to which she had become so accustomed. Now they all seemed to run together. The ubiquitous and corpulent, power hungry politicians sickened her. The similarly inane chatter of the capital wives drove her to distraction. The identically handsome and debonair youthful rakes, nodding sagely to each other, eyes ever roving over the low cut gowns, infuriated her. The same silly and tittering girls, their one concern the capture of a suitable male, embarrassed her completely.

More galling still, Karen had once been the most proficient of the lot, and in the process, garnered the favors of Alfred Randol Whitaker II, the most sought after, up and coming junior representative in Washington. Everyone knew he was destined for a wonderful future. He had money, influence and raffish good looks to accompany undeniable and winning charm. For all his sophistication and urbanity, though, he had turned to putty under the assault of green eyes and golden hair. Karen had captured him completely. But now they were finally betrothed, the game had soured. Karen was acutely aware that the arrangement was an empty one, based on mere coquetry and flirtation, the result of boredom and crushing ennui. Her father, delighted at the prospects of a wedding, had bestowed his unconditional blessing on the match. In his entirely pragmatic view, such a fortuitous union would join two families to the distinct advantage of both. And while she could surely cast off Alfred Randol with the same casual arrogance with which she had won him, she bore no illusions about her father's reaction, nor about how miserable both he and her mother would make her life if she so disappointed them. Sighing, she snapped the fan closed in a weary gesture of resignation, and steeling herself against the unpleasantness of the scene she was about to join, opened the doors and entered the dining room.

Barrett Hampton rose to his full, magnificent height and as the door opened, delivered the parting shot. "Your perception of the world is distorted. I assure you, Madam, power is based on wealth and its proper management, not upon the ostentatious display of finery and incessant, empty flattery." He turned, dazzled by his own virtuosity, and moved to the door to escort his daughter to the table. "Good evening, Karen, I'm glad you . . ."

"Karen, darling, how lovely you look," Iantha interrupted, a dissimulating smile frozen on her face. "I'm so glad we bought that dress. Doesn't she look simply wonderful, Barrett?"

Iantha's interruptive ploy notwithstanding, Barrett had to agree. "My daughter is a beautiful woman," he said gallantly.

"You flatter me, sir," Karen answered, curtseying deeply in mock deference.

"Not at all." Worldly wise, he still found himself discomforted when his daughter, displaying more skin than he thought necessary, swept into a room. He couldn't help but notice the cut of her gown. The icy blue fabric accentuated the outline of her breasts and revealed to all their perfection. Damn, but he hated the thought of rapacious eyes feasting on her! In spite of himself, Barrett Hampton flushed darkly, his scarlet cheeks the more vivid in contrast to his white puffy sideburns and the starched glaring white of shirt and tie tucked under his jowls.

"Oh, Daddy," Karen laughed, rising and taking his arm. "You simply must learn not to blush. You look simply too, too silly when you do so."

9

"Young lady, you are inordinately tardy. You have kept your mother and me waiting. In addition, you have sorely grieved the kitchen help who have been trying, unsuccessfully I'm sure, to keep our dinner warm and palatable. What do you have to say for yourself?"

Karen sat demurely in her chair at the middle of the long table, allowing her father to seat her properly. "You should have started without me."

Barrett, speechless despite himself, glared at the back of his daughter's head and retreated to the end of the table opposite Iantha. Iantha came to his rescue. "Don't be common, Karen, dear. If you wish to be treated as a lady, you must behave as one. A lady does not keep people waiting like so many servants, especially her parents. Which you know full well." She sighed deeply, the signal for the next speech, one given at least once a week. "Sometimes I wish we *had* sent you to England for your education, rather than that . . . that place in New York."

"That place is Vassar, Mother, and it is very highly thought of."

"I could care less about the name. And I could care less what others think. It is an American institution."

"As American as money can buy. I can't imagine why anyone should deprecate it. Dorothy Edwards is attending Vassar, and certainly, Ambassador Edwards wouldn't allow the apple of his eye to go anywhere he considers inferior. Even he, stodgy as he is, recognizes quality when he sees it." Karen had hit a sore spot. Anglophile that her mother was, Ambassador Edwards was the ultimate in Washington society and could do no wrong. It was at this point in the weekly discussion that Karen always prevailed and her mother knew it.

Fuming, Iantha reached for the crystal dinner bell and changed the subject. "Your father is talking again of a trip to New York next month." The bell punctuated the sentence clearly and concisely. "We shall luckily have the evening to ourselves, and since I have not been able to convince him we should stay here for Ambassador Edwards' ball, I trust you will attempt to do so."

Ross, the butler, appeared from the kitchen. Karen was saved for the moment.

"We are ready to start, Ross. You may bring the wine."

"Very good, Madam." Ross turned to the side table and

10

with one fluid, graceful movement extracted the bottle from the ice bucket, twirled and wiped it dry. Karen watched her mother out of the corner of one eye. The older woman sat primly, haughtily. Ross was the one servant in the house of whom she approved. He was English, of course, and for that Karen hated him.

"Will Miss Hampton have some wine?"

Karen nodded a touch too curtly, startled by the sudden appearance of the cadaverous butler at her side. Such surprises were another reason for her hate. The man never made a sound when he moved, appearing and disappearing seemingly from nowhere. Earlier he had stalked her dreams, and even now, years later, a perfect memory of the nightmares haunted her occasionally. Hiding a brief shudder she tensed imperceptibly as Ross leaned over her shoulder to fill the crystal goblet with colorless, sparkling liquid.

"This is a very light Rhine, Barrett. One glass won't hurt you, will it? You really ought to try some." Iantha kept the mockery well-concealed, her voice purring in a bright masquerade of solicitude.

Barrett Hampton paused only the briefest of a second and decided not to play the game. A slight smile flickered across his face, drawing his lips tight in an even white line. "You may serve dinner, Ross. Now that my daughter has deigned to sit with us, I suppose we might as well see how cold the lamb has grown." The well-bred butler seemed not to react as he silently disappeared into the kitchen.

Karen sighed. The evening was definitely, irrevocably off to a bad start. She would be forced to take sides again, no matter how noncommittal she tried to be. And once committed, flaring tempers and harsh, unkind words would intensify the loathing for her parents, the two people in the world she should most love. She was determined not to live a life of bickering, open argument and divisiveness. She would not be a captive to a marriage of convenience, as her parents were, but rather a slave to love and passion, a happy, passionate, giving wife of a loving, understanding husband. Such dreams were interrupted by the arrival of the lamb and, once again, the cat-footed Ross.

If there were only some distraction, even a dull party to which she might take herself. This would be one of the few evenings, though, that the Hamptons would not be entertaining. Nor was anyone entertaining them. They would

11

pass the evening together at home, pleasantly, delicately and elegantly carving each other into ribbons recognizable only to themselves, then taking themselves off to bed to count points won and points lost, and dreaming of brilliant ripostes and deft parries, intricate conceits and eloquent replies, drift off to a troubled, conniving sleep. Karen wished otherwise. She had hoped to draw her father into a level-headed, calm, serene discussion concerning her growing disenchantment with the idea of becoming Mrs. Alfred Randol Whitaker II, but all hope for such a conversation was lost, at least for this night.

To make matters worse, the lamb, although daintily prepared, was overdone.

Vance Paxton avoided the mirror. He felt terrible enough without going out of his way to look at what he knew he'd see. Bleary blue eyes against a sea of crimson. Pouched eyelids. Puffy lower lip and right cheek. The very picture of debauchery. "Christ," he said to the floor, "you'd think I'd know better."

The water pitcher was before him and he reached for it, his hand knocking the empty bottle in front of it from the bureau onto the chair. He caught it before it rolled off and smashed to the floor, then steadied himself against the bureau. Rather than look at the mirror, so close to him now, he stared into the vast emptiness of the bottle. The heady, stale bourbon aroma swelled into his face and he gagged and dropped the bottle anyway. It didn't break.

He made his way across the bedroom and sat heavily on the bed. "Reckon I gave Texas a bad name last night," he groaned, the groan fading into a low chuckle as he looked down at his bruised knuckles.

There were two of them, two large-boned young dandies who swaggered into Robin's Tavern as if they owned the place. Robin's was the one nightspot Vance had discovered where he could get away from it all and escape the continual political conversations springing from every corner of Washington. Unaware of a brewing storm, he was drinking heavily and immersed in self-pity, trying to forget the fact he might be stuck in this damned city for another month before he would be free to pack his bags, get on a boat and return to the spacious freedom of Texas and his beloved ranch.

The two dandies, already half drunk, posed in front of

12

the fireplace. Casting about for some excitement, one remarked about Vance's less than proper dress, mimicked his Texas drawl and called him Rebel trash. But it wasn't until they began to make insinuations about his forebears that he lost his temper.

He had sprung from sturdy stock. Pirates, pioneers and trail blazers. Determined folk who fought the British at Kings Mountain and won again at New Orleans, saving the newly-born nation its pride at the close of the War of 1812. The first Paxtons had emigrated to the Mexican Territory of Texas in 1834. A Paxton had died with Travis, Bowie and Crockett on the sun-and blood-drenched walls of the beleaguered Alamo. Vance's own father had charged to glory with Sam Houston at San Jacinto and lived to carve a hundred square miles of raw wilderness into one of the largest ranches in the new state. And Vance, like his resolute and freedom-minded forefathers, had taken a stand in the War between the States and captained a troop of Texas Volunteers at the battles of Galveston and Sabine Pass.

The Paxton pride ran deep indeed. The Washingtonian ne'er-do-well had barely begun his own version of Vance's cherished lineage when he found himself lying on his back, spitting up teeth and wondering how the rustic could possibly have struck him from twelve feet away. When his eyes cleared, he saw how. The Texan toward over him, his eyes tight, his face white with rage.

His partner made a better showing, having studied fisticuffs at Harvard. He danced about the room, bloodying Vance's face with an assortment of left and right jabs until Vance tired of the game. A steel-like hand grabbed one fist in the middle of a jab, held and spun the brawler about on tip-toe. The dandy, squalling in protest, felt himself picked up by the seat of his pants and the back of his jacket and ignominiously hurled through the window to the horror of the other gentlemen and ladies present.

Vance laughed aloud, his voice hollow in the quiet bedroom, then cursed as the gesture sent stinging currents of pain through his cheeks and into his head. Good God, nothing was that funny.

A soft knock sounded on the door to his room. He groaned and pushed himself from the bed, issuing a weak ''Just a minute' as he shakily crossed the room. He leaned against the wall for a moment, forcing himself to breathe deeply in an attempt to clear the fog from his head. Slowly, he opened the door. The light from the hall was blinding and he winced, jerking back from it and closing the door abruptly, leaving but a crack through which he could talk but not see.

He could smell the perfume. And recognize it from the night before. One of the spectators had come to call. Who was she? Ah, yes. Leighton's wife, the one he'd turned down, with too much whiskey as an excuse. But not bad for a hangover, he thought. Just what the doctor ordered. Shielding his eyes, he let her in and closed the door quickly behind her.

She was dressed in white, a wide-brimmed hat cocked to the side in the latest fashion. Long ringlets of black curls against pale skin brushed his shoulder as she entered. A full, womanly figure, pressing taut the clothes she wore. And only in the right places, Vance mused.

"I knocked earlier. You didn't answer."

"I wasn't able to."

She sat on the bed and removed her hat, dropping it languidly to the floor. The black hair draped about her shoulders and shimmered in the full light. "It's stuffy in here."

"I'll open the window." Vance crossed to the windows, a trifle more sure of himself and his feet now.

The woman watched as he walked past her, clad only in trousers. Her eyes roved over his powerful back, the naked muscles bunching under his shoulders and cording down his back. Her voice was soft, beckoning. "Don't bother, Vance. I wouldn't want you to catch a chill."

Vance halted. He hated middle-age coquettes. But Angie Leighton exuded a rich aura of passion and her full, ripe figure and smoldering eyes promised an obvious knowledge of the art of exciting men. He found himself aroused in spite of the coquetry. His hangover forgotten, he turned back from the window.

"What of Mr. Leighton this morning?"

"The House is hard at work today. He is otherwise occupied." A small smile played about her face, inviting him to her. When the man in front of her made no move, the smile disappeared and her eyes brightened in anticipation. Vance Paxton was not to be led about like a mere boy. He

14

had forced her to make the first move. That she had done and had come to him gladly. Now he was forcing her to make the second as well. Few men could get away with so playing with Angie Leighton's favors. But this Texan . . .

Slowly, languidly, she ran her hands through her hair, shaking it out. The action accentuated the ripeness of her full breasts, giving the impression they sought rather the touch of hands than the impersonal restraint of fabric. Her hands, as if in answer to the unspoken desire, moved to the buttons of her blouse and casually opened the top two, revealing the beginning curve of the swelling orbs.

"You are a hard man, Mr. Paxton." The voice was lazy, full of promise.

"Which is why you are here, Mrs. Leighton."

She held out a hand and he walked toward her, stopping only when the open palm touched his thigh, then advancing again when the hand, as though burned, withdrew. His strong, calloused fingers played along her lips and the line of her jaw to her ear, then dropped to bestow a tantalizing caress on her shoulder and weave in and out of the rich, luxuriant hair. Angie's eyes filled with desire, gazed up at him, then faltered and lowered. She caught her breath at the sight of his mounting desire, so close to her now, as it strained to be free, strained, too, for the touch of flesh. Trembling, she lay back on the bed as his lips sought the rising mounds of her breasts and his tongue explored the deep crevice between them. His fingers deftly undid the rest of her blouse and pulled it aside, then unlaced the chemise under it, freeing the glorious, pouting aureoles. His tongue, fire now, caressed them to greater rigidity, then suddenly left as he stood.

Her eyes glazed, she rolled to her side as he stepped out of his trousers. She gasped at the lean hard lines of his body, the white scars deep in his brown flesh. And then she could see but one thing, and her hand reached out to stroke the quivering, tumescent flesh, close gently on it and draw it to her lips.

Somehow she lost the rest of her clothes then, and lay open to the lean body kneeling on the bed next to her. Her body was rigid with desire, aching for fulfillment. "Come to me," she moaned, "Come to me, Vance. . . ."

"You're a whore, Angie Leighton."

"Don't say that. Just come. . . ."

15

Suddenly he was on her, his manhood seeking her, driving deep within her, filling her, drawing her higher and higher with him.

"You're a sweet-voiced, lovely, hot-blooded, high-browed whore. Good as gold, but a whore just the same."

She hated him for saying it, but not enough.

CHAPTER II

Spring came to Washington in early April. By May the winding banks of Rock Creek near Georgetown were dyed a lush green. Foliage thick with birds shot forth tender runners in all directions. Tiny irregular fronds poked tremulously through moist, dark soil, eager to be born into summer. Wisteria and azaleas splashed great dabs of white, pink, red and purple across the landscape. The flowing creek, ruffled by puffs of spring wind, bubbled and chuckled softly in pleasant anticipation of its imminent mating with the Potomac. A moist spring breeze captured floating seed pods and drove them along, spinning and swirling in unchoreographed acrobatics, bobbing and dancing in an ancient ritual of rebirth until they settled on fertile soil or in the racing shallows themselves. One such wayward seed puff narrowly skipped a watery death, flirted with smooth stones, skimmed over the low bank and alighted softly on a delicate silken-skinned foot. Karen gave a soft, delighted laugh as crystal clear and tinkling as the water itself before lying back and kicking her foot high overhead. The puff flew into the air once again and drifted off among the trees as if too shy to linger so near the delicate curve of ankle and sheen of glowing skin.

Karen sat up to watch the floating seed dart among tall reeds. A gust of air swept it along and dramatically whirled it out of sight among the budding drapery of a nearby willow. Karen sighed softly to herself, lay back down and yawned lazily and most unladylike, stretching lithe arms toward the patch of blue overhead. Her long unbraided hair splayed out like random sunbeams to cover the clover and rain-sweet grass with softly curling tresses, bright gold in the thousand dancing shadows breaking the afternoon sun.

A cardinal fluttered among the branches directly overhead and crimson feathers flashed against a backdrop of blue sky, golden sun, brown wood and soft green leaves completing spring's palette. The male was joined by a female of the species, dull brown with a spot of vibrant orange on its beak only. The two chirrupped and scolded each other as lovers will, then bolted upward in a tightening spiral to a high branch, there to remain chattering side by side, lord and lady of their immediate domain. Karen closed her eyes and pretended she was a fairy princess. A crown of violets and lilies-of-the-valley adorned her head. A multitude of birds filled the air about her with sweet music and her ministers, the squirrels, bustled about chattering of state affairs. A chipmunk, her jester, appeared for a moment on the gnarled root of a fallen elm. His eyes, bright with laughter, twinkled their own little joke. His tail flicked once, twice, and he was gone again, as silently as he had come. A pleasant way to spend an afternoon, she thought, a bit surprised at how glad she was to have been so rudely inconvenienced earlier on.

The day had begun as usual. Karen awoke early and lay in the giant maple bed, half drowned in sleep and the fluffy feather quilt. Only the occasional rustle of sheets destroyed the still silence of the house. Half dreaming, she heard the splash of water from the next room. Her bath would be ready soon, steaming hot and with fragrantly perfumed towels piled nearby. It was a matter of custom in the Hampton household that Karen rose long before Barrett and Iantha and attended to her toilet in the early morning calm.

Karen looked on the day with a certain amount of dread. She was to meet Alfred at noon and lunch with him. Alfred would undoubtedly discuss at great length the morning's politics; the debates, the compromises and deals, shady and otherwise, the decisions made and the others left for a long line of indeterminate tomorrows. He would go on and on about how cleverly he had manipulated X, convinced Y and seen through the diabolical machinations of Z. Karen was expected to ooh and ahh in the right places at the right times, no matter how bored she might be. It wasn't that she hated politics, Karen reflected as she rose from the bed and walked sleepily to the next room, but rather the way Alfred

18

played at them. Like a kitten with a newly-found ball of yarn. Alfred a kitten? Oh, dear.

She dropped the subject with her robe and sank into the hot reaches of the giant ceramic tub. The water would relax her, soothe the troubled thoughts away. Morning baths were the most delicious, she thought, running the rough sponge filled with perfumed soap over her legs. They got a day off to a decent start. The water was just deep enough to support her breasts. She sighed and lay back, running the sponge under and around those twin badges of femininity, proud of their fullness, intensely aware of the emotions they could rouse in men. She dozed, surrounded by the warm depths of her bath.

Retta poked her head in the door, startled Karen awake then bobbed out again. On her way for tea, no doubt. Karen sighed and rose from the tub, the water streaming down her naked body. She stepped to the towel on the floor and wrapped herself in another, tucking it between her breasts to keep it in place. Thus attired she made her way back to her bedroom.

Golden early morning light tinged with new green of budding trees streamed through the sheer curtains on the east window and left flowing patches on floor and wall as Karen stood in front of the full-length mirror and dropped the towel to the floor. The Queen of Sheba awaiting her lover, she thought, posing unconsciously, shoulders back, head held high. A slight frown crossed her face as she leaned forward to inspect the small mole on her right hip, then the larger dark one on her right breast. She tossed her head imperiously. Not moles! Such an ugly word. Beauty spots, rather, to set off flawless skin. A wisp of golden hair twined across her breast. She rearranged it so the mole, the beauty spot, peeked through. Much more alluring, she told herself, satisfied now with what she saw. "And how much, sirs, would you pay for this handsome wench?" she asked the mirror, demurely covering herself with crossed hands.

"Honey, you ain't gonna get no prettier starin' at yo'self lak dat, fillin' up yer own eyes wid what's meant for a man to stare at. C'mon, now. Here's yo' tea and biscuits."

Karen padded from the mirror to the dressing table, quickly donning the chemise Retta handed her as she went, then sat to write in her diary and drink tea while Retta brushed out her hair. It was that nice time of day when all was right, all quiet. Thank God Papa didn't insist on a family breakfast, with everyone half awake and still listless and grumpy. She much preferred her hour alone, blissfully relaxed with her tea and biscuits, her diary and Retta brushing her hair.

"Honey, your hair is gonna be the light in Mistah Whitaker's eyes. You mark my word. Pretty hair and pretty eyes done trap more men than, well, I doan know what. Der's nothin' to compare dem to, I reckin."

The brush sank into the tresses, traveled their length without binding, repeated itself in unvarying rhythm as it would for over a hundred more strokes. Karen looked up at the black woman reflected in the mirror. "Love shouldn't be a game of trap and catch, should it, Retta? It sounds so cold. Like a fox hunt."

"Tha's what it is, chile. You hunts for the man you wants and you grabs him and lets him know it's high time for settlin' down. If you don't do it, no one else will." Retta laughed aloud at Karen's worried expression.

"You're horrid, Retta. Absolutely horrid. You have a soul of ice."

"Honey, I'se got the hottes' soul nawth of Souf Carolina. But facts is facts. You wants you man, you hunts him down. Ain't no diffrint fo' whites or coloreds, rich or po'."

"Perhaps so. But I'll marry for love, Retta. You mark my word."

"Missy," Retta answered sternly, "you been readin' too many of dem books your mama tellin' you to keep away from. Ain't no Hampton never married for no love."

Karen's eyes flashed. She loved Retta dearly, but the black woman had gone a little too far. "I think that will be enough for my hair now, Retta. I should like to dress, please."

Retta placed the brush on the dresser, paying no attention whatsoever to her mistress' implied admonition. She had known her too long to worry about Karen's moods. She turned and waddled across the room. "What you want to wear today, honey?"

"The light green, I believe."

Retta paused, raised an eyebrow, then continued to the huge armoire in the corner of the room. As always, she ran her fingers over the shining surface where dull red inlaid cherry flowers lay entwined in wreaths and garlands of carved black walnut. She pulled the doors open and reached for the article indicated, a daring light green spring dress with form-fitting bodice and flaring skirt. "Ooo-weee, honey. Don' let you momma see you in dis. She already think you should dress up accordin' to her way of thinkin'."

"I shall dress as I please, Retta. Anyway, that was a gift from Count Milano when he was here from Italy visiting Daddy. If it's good enough for the Count, it's good enough for Momma."

"Noooo, missy. Tha's even worse. Your momma thinks dem Italians is worse dan anybody else. Now I *know* you better use the back door."

"I live in this house and have as much right to use the front door as anyone. And I most certainly will use it today." Karen stood as Retta carried the dress to her and helped the young woman into it. "Anyway," she continued, giggling lightly as Retta pulled the bodice tight and fastened it, "I'll be leaving before Momma comes downstairs. So there." Both of them laughed together at that, Retta shaking her head in mock despair as Karen smoothed the skirt over her hips and adjusted her breasts to better fit the bodice. Count Milano had excellent taste.

The carriage was ready and waiting with Hermann, the dour coachman, listlessly standing by. Hermann had been with the Hamptons for nineteen of Karen's twenty years. Tall, rawboned and lanky to the point of emaciation, he made a singular picture as he stood by the front wheel. He seemed to have four elbows, each jutting at a different angle from his body. His great, bulbous, pockmarked nose drew stares and wry comments. A huge, bobbing Adam's apple attracted its own attention. But ugly as he was, Karen would have no other driver, for the man was entirely devoted to her. And ugly or no, he could handle a team as no one else, became, indeed, a flowing, graceful extension of horses and carriage when perched on the driver's seat.

"Good morning, Miss."

"Good morning, Hermann. The Capitol, please. But not too fast. I'm not due until nearly noon."

"I'll go by the Washington Monument, Miss. It's another twenty feet higher since we last passed."

"That would be nice."

21

The door closed behind her, followed by a brief rocking motion as Hermann ascended to the driver's seat. The pleasant, musky odor of horse and oiled leather filled the carriage as it rolled off smoothly. Karen leaned back and closed her eyes. I'm not even going to look today, she thought, just smell and listen.

Mockingbirds paved her way. Mockingbirds and blue-jays. A cardinal whistled the same piercing note over and over, fading out behind as the coach made its way through the streets. Children laughed. One cried. Fresh bread here. A peddler there, his call of "Fresh fish, fresh fish caught this mo'nin'!" backed up by the reek of sea and salt.

She could always tell when drawing nigh the mall and the last part of the trip to the landmark structure housing both the Senate and the House of Representatives. The curses of carpenters, stonemasons, draymen and ironwork-ers, and the raucous clashing noise of construction on the new Washington Monument drowned out all other, more mellifluous noises. Soon after, the fetid stench from the canal running through the mall defeated the smell of the dust from the construction. Karen closed her eyes even tighter and wrinkled her nose in disgust until the carriage passed onto Pennsylvania Avenue and clattered up to the Capitol where the smell of wisteria once again became pre-dominant. She opened her eyes to the sight of the awesome white-washed Capitol, its dome jutting dramatically into the sky and capped with the soul-stirring statue of Free-dom. Completed only seven years ago, the magnificent building never failed to take the breath away from even the most callous visitor.

Karen alighted, told Hermann to wait and made her way up the broad, lengthy flight of stairs into the rotunda. As always it was alive with activity. Senators and representa-tives, lobbyists and aides blended together in indistinguish-able patterns of bustling self-importance. The honorable Sen-ator Duffy of New York recognized Karen, interrupted a conversation and approached her. "My dear Karen. Your lovely presence graces these all too hallowed halls." The elder statesman bowed before her, his white-fringed side-burns and sunburned, balding pate provoking a stifled chuckle from Karen. Duffy took her hand and gave it the mandatory kiss of courtesy, lingering slightly longer than necessary.

"It's nice to see you, Senator Duffy. I'm sorry I missed you Saturday evening."

"Business, business, my dear. And your father? How is Barrett enjoying Washington this time?"

"Well enough, Senator. Business agrees with him whether it be here or in New York."

"He'll be heading back to the city soon enough, my dear. His work with the trade commission lobby has been invaluable."

"My father has always been very efficient at whatever he does, Senator. Business is his life, and Washington is a city of business, *par excellence*. He finds it very stimulating."

"I quite agree. There is no better calling for a man than to devote his life to business. Keeps the country growing. Expansion! That's the key. Yes, I've entertained the notion of dabbling in business myself. After my work here is finished, to be sure. Of course, men like your father keep telling me to consider the executive office, but I can't see me in the White House. No . . . too much trouble. I'd rather leave that kind of pressure to the generals." He chuckled, pleased with his wit and condescension. "In any case, the Senate . . . now there's where the real work gets done. But listen to me, how I carry on. The presence of youth and beauty, my dear, sets my old tongue to wagging. You must be here to see young Alfred. Fine boy. Known the Whitakers a long time. Good family. Wish he'd get that silly notion about the House out of his head. Still, one has to start somewhere."

Senator Duffy's voice trailed off as he realized Karen's attention had been diverted. He turned to follow her gaze. The man he saw was an enigma to the many frock-coated, wing-collared politicos making their way across the rotunda floor, hurrying from one meeting to another. He was a Texan, taller than most of the others present and clean shaven except for a smooth brown mustache curving down across the corners of his mouth. Unlike the stiff, almost funereal wear of those around him, this man wore an open-throated coarse linen shirt under a sackcoat of brushed buckskin which fell to hip level and soft, well-worn cream nankeen trousers fitting tight in the legs. A thick leather belt with a richly worked silver buckle circled his waist and a gaudy scarf was tied about his neck, adding dash to his already unusual appearance. Soft leather boots rode high

23

on his calf, bulging in the rear where the muscles stood ou in relief. His flesh was almost copperish beside the pale Washingtonians, some of whom tagged along beside him in heated discussion. He carried a large, floppy-brimmed hat in his hand. A mane of light brown, almost shoulder-length hair surrounded a hard, high-caste face.

"Who is that?" Karen asked in a voice soft and thick with sudden emotion. Her breath quickened and she was acutely aware of a soft blush creeping up her cheeks.

"Oh, him," Duffy scoffed. "He's an upstart Texan who's been stirring up the House. Just 'cause the southern rabble got their state back and the provisional reconstruction period is over with, they think they can come up here and make demands as if they were as equal as all the loyal Union states. As if the War never happened. Hrrumph! Equal, indeed!"

"He *is* different," Karen remarked softly. The Texan's eyes met hers for a brief moment, then, as he was pulled away by an importuning hand, winked at her. It was over with before she knew what happened. The Texan was escorted past them and out the massive doors, the chattering voices dying out rapidly.

"Different. Hrrumph. A clown, a renegade and a barbarian if you ask me. No respect for the seat of government. He's evidently caught the fancy of some of the members of the House, though I dare say he'll be less successful in the Senate where older, wiser heads hold sway."

Karen watched without listening as the cluster of politicians vanished down the stairs, Senator Duffy's remarks so much babble in her ears.

The peal of church bells rang over the city to announce the noon hour. The sound triggered a change in tempo in the rotunda. Quiet, purposeful activity disappeared in the suddenly charged atmosphere as the men around her moved rapidly on unseen random paths, hurriedly greeting each other, passing messages and rushing off to keep appointments. One of Alfred's aides appeared at her side. The congressman had an emergency meeting and would be held up for some time. If Miss Hampton would be so kind as to wait in her carriage. . . .

Karen fumed inwardly but smiled in acquiescence as the aide hurried off and Senator Duffy launched into a discussion of the reconstruction problem. Ten minutes turned to

24

fifteen. Finally she could take no more, and excusing herself graciously, escaped just in time to avoid an elaborate dissection of the unmentionable behavior of the "treacherous" French.

Normally Karen would have been outraged at having been left waiting by a young man, but today she felt unashamedly free, released from an afternoon she dreaded. She bade Hermann follow a meandering course through the city, so beautiful in spring. She visited a favorite dressmaker, lunched with an artist friend and called at the British Embassy for tea with Emily Edwards, who was nowhere to be found. With little else left to do, she told Hermann to head back to Georgetown and stop just below the heights at the foot of Rock Creek Bridge. Once there, she instructed him to travel on to the house without her. Hermann, more disgruntled than ever, urged her to come on in the carriage, but Karen would have nothing to do with the idea. She was more than capable of walking back through the park and sent the man packing. That had been two hours ago and she had long since lost track of time.

Karen slid her bare feet along the smooth moist silt fringe along the burbling stream. She dug her toes into the mud, feeling ever so much the child. A child . . . no . . . not any longer. Her hands pressed against her cheeks, then traveled down her shoulders to cup each breast, full and rounded and unconfined beneath chemise and partially unlaced bodice. Her mind flashed on the stranger at the rotunda, how he towered above the others, the brief, conspiratorial wink, the tightness of his trousers leaving little to the imagination. Her nipples hardened beneath the fabric and she pictured him standing over her, legs partially spread, his shirt undone, hands on hips. He would stare at her, his eyes flashing with lust, stare at her barely concealed breasts. His eyes would travel down her body, undressing her, then back to her face as he knelt at her side, his hands reaching for her.

Karen's hands traveled the path his imaginary hands must take, touching lightly her cheeks, lifting a curl from her shoulder, touching her breasts, with fingers inscribing small circles around the taut, distended nipples. And then the hands alive and of their own volition traveled down,

down to brush lightly over mons and stroke aching thighs...her warmth, his hands....

She bolted upright at the voice. A man's voice, clear and strong, deep and melodious, singing softly, evidently to no one in particular. Karen jumped to her feet and with fumbling fingers quickly laced the bodice. Sweat beaded her forehead and she glanced around. Had someone been watching her? She could see no one. She wanted to hide, to run, but couldn't decide where to or in what direction. The singing drew closer. Someone was walking up the stream. She could make out the splashing steps. If she could only find her shoes . . . but there was no time. The owner of the voice stepped from around a hillock and stopped short, but fifteen paces from her. "So beat the drum slowly, and play the pipes . . ." The singer halted in mid-song, startled by her presence. Karen stood unmoving, shocked. The man before her was none other than the Texan she had seen at the Capitol. He stood ankle deep in water, boots in hand, and doffed his flop-brimmed hat.

"Pardon me, ma'am. I never figured on running into anyone out here."

Karen forced her eyes from the bronzed, brown fur-matted muscular chest and the gold, strangely shaped amulet that nestled there. "I . . . I come here quite often," she finally answered defensively. "I live near by."

Vance's eyes roved approvingly over her lithe figure, stopped at swelling breasts and tiny waist, then strayed back to the shock of unruly honey gold hair. With a grin he stepped from the water. Karen stepped as quickly back from the bank. "Begging your pardon, ma'am," he assured her, "but I just realized the water is mighty cold."

Karen was determined not to let him sense her discomfort. He's even taller, close up, she reflected. She attempted to assume her most aristocratic pose, despite her muddy feet.

"I don't mean to be forward," the Texan said, "but don't I know you?" Vance was very close now and his voice was quiet, soothing, as if directed for her ears only, so even the trees wouldn't overhear.

"Why . . . no . . . I don't think . . ."

"Of course. This morning at the Capitol. You were in the rotunda. I remember well."

"Why, yes . . . I suppose you're correct, but I don't

26

seem to remember you," she lied, her breath coming a little too quickly.

The Texan smiled, displaying two even rows of white teeth. "Well, you did look kind of busy."

"I think I remember . . ." Why was she talking so rapidly? "I was conversing with Senator Duffy."

"I didn't have time to pay my respects, but I certainly intend to do so this moment, Miss . . . ?"

"Hampton. Karen Hampton."

"I'm Vance Paxton. And most pleased to meet you." The lanky Texan squatted down where Karen had been lying and looked up at her. His eyes, blue and deep, flashed innocently. "Care to join me, Miss Hampton?"

Karen considered. Proper etiquette required her to leave immediately, but curiosity and an adventuresome spirit insisted she stay. The scales tipped to the latter as the innocent look in the Texan's eyes gave way to one of daring. Karen was willfully confident she could handle any dare.

She sat next to him, arranging the full skirt daintily. Vance smiled, his eyes narrowing as he squinted up at the receding late afternoon sun. "I didn't think Washington ladies ventured into the forest unescorted," he said, his voice faintly mocking.

"This is a park, Mr. Paxton. They don't have parks in Texas?"

Vance chuckled aloud. "Ma'am, all of Texas is a park." He paused a moment. "You know where I'm from."

Karen started, embarrassed at being caught in the lie. To cover her embarrassment she picked up a handful of pebbles and tossed them one by one into the creek, the plink plink of each stone interrupting the uncomfortable quiet. Vance appreciatively studied the curve of her back, partially hidden by thick golden cascades of hair. Now that her eyes were averted, he could examine her profile. A wave of hair couldn't disguise completely the high forehead. Her nose was slightly upturned, a nose bespeaking curiosity and impishness. Lips a little too tight, a little too dry, parted and hinted of secret, hidden sensuality as her tongue flicked nervously over them. The chin not weak, not too strong; argumentative perhaps but not intransigent. Her skin was creamy white, but not the sickly pale of the rest of the northerners. Rather a healthy, glowing ivory. Green eyes, into which one might wish to dive, to be willingly lost forever, glowed with an inner light and hinted of the woman hidden beneath the child-like innocence of her face.

Karen sensed his perusal and despite her efforts a soft flush crept up her cheeks. "I . . . I come here often . . . to be alone," she said, her voice giving further evidence of her discomfort.

"Miss Hampton. It would be ungracious of me if I did not say you are a very lovely woman."

Karen felt his hand touch hers, grasping it in his own sun-browned, calloused fingers, lifting it to his lips, kissing it softly. She withdrew her hand from his grasp and rose abruptly, head swimming and legs weak. She had to clear her throat before speaking. "As you are a visitor to Washington, sir, perhaps I might take it upon myself to guide you through Rock Creek Park. It's a lovely place. Much that is special and beautiful about Washington is to be found here."

"So I have discovered." Vance rose and gave a slight bow. "Ma'am, following you would be one of the few pleasurable experiences of my entire stay here in the capital."

"Is that what they call 'southern cordiality,' Mr. Paxton?"

"Only the truth, simply stated, Miss Hampton."

Karen flashed a smile, put on her slippers and stepped off down the trail. Vance fell in behind her, watching the gentle sway of her hips. He wondered to himself whether or not to reveal to the ravishing woman in front of him how he had been so struck by her beauty he had spent the afternoon following her all over Washington to the foot of Rock Creek Bridge, how he had watched her from afar, desperately pondering the best way to make her acquaintance. It was a game he was unused to playing. Karen turned, smiled back at him. The path was wide enough for two now and she held out her hand. He took it and joined her and they started off together. The clean, heady scent of spring clover and newly-budded flowers clung to her shapely form. If it was a game, Vance thought, it was well worth the playing.

Karen and Vance followed the path as it led from tiny glade to high brushed knoll and down again to creek side. From there it sloped gently up again through dogwood, white blossoms blazing in dappled golden afternoon light, to pause on the fringe of an expansive meadow. An old blockhouse had fallen to ruin near the wooded fringe, leaving behind only half a vine-choked wall and a length of stone fence along which a host of berry bushes clung. Having cooled themselves with water from the creek, the couple meandered through the high growth toward the blockhouse.

"This is a famous spot in Georgetown."

"Famous for what?"

"Fighting. People call it the Dueling Wall. It hasn't been used for ages. Dueling is illegal, of course. Still, if a couple of senators or congressmen want to have it out and settle their differences violently, there would be no one to stop them. The police are too busy catching pickpockets and lawless Negroes to worry about enforcing the law when it comes to politicians."

"You are too young and beautiful to be so cynical, Miss Hampton," Vance chuckled.

"My father is too wealthy for me to be anything but cynical, Mr. Paxton," Karen retorted, playfully darting out of sight among the vines. Her voice came from behind the wall. "I used to play here as a child."

"What did you play?" Vance asked, plunging in after her.

She waited by the wall until he appeared, her delicate features set off by the dark, rough-hewn stones. "Why, house, of course. What do little boys play in Texas?"

Vance stopped in front of her, suddenly serious. "I never got around to playing much. As soon as I could walk Pa had me out tending to any chore I could manage. And some I couldn't. When I got so's I could ride the local trail boss took me on as a button on a drive to Kansas."

"A button?"

"Yep. That's what they call the fellow who gets all the jobs nobody wants. And the first one everybody kicks when the going gets rough."

"Goodness," Karen said excitedly.

Vance sighed before continuing. "Pa always figured a man's got to earn his lumps before taking on the responsibilities of a ranch. It's the only way he can figure out if he's right or wrong for the job. Try it on for size, so to speak." Vance drew closer to Karen who stepped back, stopped by the wall behind her blocking her retreat. "A man . . . and a woman . . . ought to try the thing out before deciding whether it's right or wrong, too. Makes sense, doesn't it?"

Vance's face was only inches from Karen. She wanted to flutter her eyelids, laugh and spin away flirtatiously, keeping her beauty out of reach. All she could manage was a weak, "No." The protest was cut short as Vance brought his lips to hers and slowly, slowly forced her head back against the wall. I should be fighting, calling for help, anything but this, Karen thought, but her arms, as if with a will and mind of their own, encircled his neck. He felt even stronger than he looked, she reflected as her hands ranged the length of his back. Her breasts tightened, strained against the bodice so cruelly holding them in, so cruelly interceding between flesh and flesh. His left hand pressed along her throat, then down to her right breast, the fingers probing gently under the bodice and chemise, hungrily seeking the taut nipple and touching it with fire. Karen's lips parted greedily to accept the tongue that entered. Dazed and afire, wildly seeking to fulfill the newfound hunger, she arched feverishly to him, moaning as she felt the hardness of his manhood pressed to her thigh, straining, as her breasts, to be free and find the flesh it so desperately sought.

My God, she suddenly thought, I am Karen Hampton, not some street hussy or Texas bar queen. A sharp cry of protest broke from her and with a surprising show of strength she pushed Vance away, tears springing to her eyes. "No . . . no! You have no right . . . you forget yourself, sir. They were right . . ." Her voice caught and she sobbed. "You . . . you're a barbarian. Worse. A . . . a . . . Texan!" And with that worst of all epithets, she broke from him and ran from the blockhouse, scrambled through a gap in the fence and tore across the meadow toward the distant palatial homes.

Vance, taken totally unaware by Karen's outburst, watched helplessly as the diminishing figure of the young woman fled. Even when her body was no longer in sight he could see the flashing of her golden hair in the dying light of the sun. He watched spellbound until even that disappeared before turning back to the woods and thoughtfully heading back for his carriage. Karen Hampton . . . Karen Hampton . . . Karen Hampton. The name echoed through his mind over and over again, accompanied by the ache in his loins and the disturbing, haunting image of flashing green eyes, cascading golden hair and warm breasts.

CHAPTER III

Karen paused behind the row of hedges marking the farthest boundary of Iantha's garden. She sank to her knees, choking on the sobs that refused to stop. "Damn him," she cried, "he had no right . . . no right at all . . . to be there." She tore a bit of cloth from her petticoat and dabbed the tears from her eyes and face, fighting for control, for breath until the sobbing finally subsided. Trembling fingers laced the front of her dress for the third time that day as she made her way to the ornamental pool. The last bare glimmer of light showed a red and puffy face and eyes, and hair beyond any hope of order. There was nothing to be done about the hair so she didn't try. Her face was another matter though, so she ripped a larger strip off her petticoat and set to work. Fifteen minutes later the cool water had done its work and, her composure recovered, she began the brief walk to the front of the house.

She drove the images of the afternoon's experience, the confused array of thoughts that endangered her self-control, from her mind. As she rounded the corner of the house she noticed a carriage drawn up before the front porch. Alfred's! That was all she needed. *Oh, God! What could he possibly be doing here at such an hour?* She hesitated for a moment, then struck out boldly in the realization his presence would be an advantage; Barrett would hardly make a scene in front of the young congressman. She thrust the afternoon from her and concentrated on the confrontation to come.

Ross was there to let her in. Cold and efficient as ever, he allowed not the slightest expression of surprise to cross his face. "Shall I announce you, Miss Hampton?"

"That won't be necessary," Karen answered curtly, breezing past him imperiously.

Ross' voice halted her in mid-stride at the bottom of the

32

great staircase. "Your father and Mr. Whitaker are in the library."

"I'll go up and change first, Ross. I'm afraid I'm quite a mess. If you'll be so kind as to tell Retta I'm here."

"Karen!" Alfred Randol Whitaker II exclaimed from the doorway of the library. Karen's face soured with resignation, but by the time she turned to greet her intended the scowl had turned into a demure smile, somewhat at odds with her disheveled appearance.

Barrett Hampton appeared behind Alfred. "This waiting is simply inexcusable . . . Dear God! What ever has happened to you?"

Karen shrugged, her eyes wide in an expression of total innocence. "Nothing, Father. I spent some time in the park. As I was walking in I fell. I'm afraid I must appear a trifle scruffy. Perhaps I'd better continue upstairs and change."

"And you may come right back down and join us. It's a good thing your mother isn't here to see you. I only hope none of the neighbors . . . "

"I came in the back way, Papa."

"Very well. Alfred has been here the better part of two hours, and while we've enjoyed our visit, he undoubtedly came to see you. I think you owe him an apology."

Karen was already partway up the curving stairs. She stopped and turned, her hand resting lightly on the railing. The dim light from the lantern behind her backlit her hair and formed a halo of gold against a dark portrait. The lights from below in the hall lit her face unevenly, dropping her eyes in deep shadow and giving her the appearance of a beautiful, mysterious priestess, the effect heightened by the ominous hiss from the lantern. She paused for a moment, fully aware of the spell she cast on the two men below, paused as they stared up at her. There was no hint of apology when she spoke. Instead her voice was low and heady, full of promises yet unfulfilled. "I'll be right down, Alfred. Will you wait in the parlor for me?"

Alfred nodded, his jaw dropping slightly. So glib and masterful in the presence of the most powerful men in the country, he was reduced by the girl above him to a stuttering schoolboy.

Karen flashed a final smile, gathered her skirts and continued up the staircase, rounded the top and disappeared down the hall. Retta stood in the open door to her room, three doors to her right. The black woman took one look and shook her head in disbelief. "Land o' Goshen, look at you. What you been into dis time dat your momma ain't gonna lak? Chile, you looks lak a storm dat's done been played out, lak the rag-a-muffin end to a bad day."

"Not a *bad* day, Retta," Karen quickly corrected as she entered the room, pulling at the laces on the bodice. She stopped in front of the mirror. She didn't look any different. Still Karen Hampton. Retta bustled around behind her, mumbling incoherently, then started undoing the back of her dress. "A strange day, perhaps," Karen said with as much brightness as she could muster. "But not a bad one."

She chose a simple dress with little flair to the skirt but a bodice of daring Parisian cut revealing dangerously much too much of herself. The dress was of pale green silk overlaid on a darker green velvet. *Green again. Green for the grass I lay on. Green for spring. Green for my eyes. Green for Alfred's envy.* Retta worked on her hair, pulling the tangles from it with hard, swift strokes of the brush while Karen applied just enough blush to accent her cheeks. Nothing more. That, and the eyes framed by her long dusky-blonde lashes ought to make apologies hardly necessary.

Her appearance in the parlor had its desired effect. Alfred was alone, nursing his third brandy when she entered. His eyes grew wide with obvious appreciation and he stammered her name. Why does he look so fragile and pale? she wondered silently, unaware of the comparison she was making to the Texan now consciously forced from her memory. Alfred crossed the room and escorted her back to the double cushioned love seat.

"Karen, I searched all over for you but no one had seen you. Someone finally said you'd driven off. I must admit I was worried."

"I decided not to wait, Alfred. Senator Duffy droned on and on, and when he started telling me for the fortieth time how terrible the French are, I couldn't take it any longer. It was such a lovely day I took the opportunity to visit friends and take a stroll. Surely you understand, don't you?" Her eyes lowered in calculated contrition.

"But I told you . . . that is I asked you to wait. The

Speaker asked to talk to me and I simply couldn't get away."

"Alfred Randol Whitaker. I had no intention of standing alone in the rotunda like some lost puppy, nor sitting in my carriage as do some men's mistresses."

"Karen . . . !" Alfred's voice rose alarmingly in shock.

"They do and you know it, Alfred. We've both seen them, pretending to be that which they're not."

"You could have gone to the library and left word with John."

"John is a fool. And I had no desire to wait in a stuffy library full of law books for the conclusion of a meeting that might have taken fifteen minutes or all day. I think it was most rude of you to have expected me to do so."

She allowed Alfred to take her hand. He held it gratefully, as one accepts a favor one doesn't deserve. "You're right, Karen," he agreed a little too rapidly. "I apologize. It was unforgivable of me."

A cringing puppy. Nothing more than a cringing puppy, showing the whites of his eyes. "Oh, Alfred, not unforgivable, please. I'm just explaining why I left. Your work is so important and you do get so involved with it . . . and someone is always demanding your time, asking your opinion, seeking your advice. Sometimes I feel so left out, so unimportant . . ."

"Karen, you are more important to me than . . . than . . ." His voice filled with emotion. "Will you forgive me?"

His total surrender took her off guard. She had expected a better showing somehow. The question popped unbidden in her mind. Would Vance Paxton have given in so easily? She doubted it. Alfred was simply too easily led about. Amused, she leaned a little closer to him, coyly drawing his attention to the top of her bodice and the swelling breasts, laughing inwardly as his eyes lowered unconsciously and the color came to his face. There would be no unpleasantry.

Suddenly aware of the growing silence, Alfred jerked guiltily to his feet and crossed to a tasselled cord hanging against the wall near a large oil painting. He studied the painting for a brief moment before pulling on the cord. Scant seconds later Ross appeared, giving his usual curt bow.

"A brandy for the lady, Ross. And I'll have another one too," Alfred ordered curtly. Giving an order seemed to reassure him, and instantly more at ease, he rocked back on his heels and ignored the butler, studying the painting as Ross bowed to his back and left the room. Alfred wanted more than anything else to look at Karen again but refused himself the pleasure, made himself wait in an abortive attempt to force Karen to take the initiative. When she didn't say anything he was compelled to give in himself. He turned and posed with the painting at his back, his head cocked to the right to present his best profile. A confident smile lit his face. "Your father and I get on famously, you know. He and I understand each other quite well. We had a pleasant chat."

Karen watched demurely, once again and in spite of herself comparing him to the stranger she had met that afternoon. Alfred didn't present an unhandsome picture. His sandy hair neatly combed and one eyebrow arched a little higher than the other, he exuded, at the moment at least, the confidence she had seen him display at work on the floor of the House so many times before. Only three inches taller than Karen, his smallish frame was trim and of pleasing proportions, set under a rounded boyish face that would later run to jowls. He was far from being a weakling but his hands were delicate and he walked with feminine grace. And though he sported the traditional somber garb of black tail coat and trousers, his clothes were better tailored than most and he wore them with undeniable flair. When he added his tophat and ever-present ivory-knobbed cane he cut quite a dashing figure. One could do worse. *And yet he is so easily manipulated. I feel so safe with him.*

Ross appeared carrying two crystal snifters on a silver tray. Again the bow. Karen wondered if he could physically manage entering a room without bowing. If only he'd forego the convention once. Her mind wandered, trying to remember if he ever had. He hadn't. Alfred quickly crossed to the door, took the snifters from the tray and carried them to Karen. Ross, with the appearance of one who had been in the room the whole time, unerringly headed for Alfred's empty snifter half hidden behind the candelabra on the side table, placed it on the tray and started for the door. He stood there and announced, "Mr. Hampton bids you his apologies. He has work to do in preparation for an important meeting tomorrow, and will retire directly upon finishing. He trusts you'll forgive him not wishing you good-night in person."

"Of course," Alfred replied, his eyes wandering over the delightful cut of Karen's gown. "That will be all, then, I think." Ross nodded and left. Karen raised the snifter, cutting off Alfred's view. He raised his eyes to find her gazing at him, a secret smile lighting her eyes. Alfred smiled back and raised his glass. "To us, my dear," he said, his voice nearly a whisper.

Karen nodded and took a sip of the brandy. It tasted of peaches and reminded her of earlier days, of summers spent along the coast of Maine. Of a grandmother too old and too kind. It reminded her of warm New Hampshire summers. Even her mother loved New Hampshire and for a time the Hamptons had been happy there. A bit of England in the colonies, as Iantha put it. Barrett Hampton kept spending less and less time with them and more in New York, though. His shipping firm expanded and by the end of the war Iantha and Karen had joined him in New York City and the Hamptons had become extremely well-to-do. From New York it was but a small step to Washington, and as the business trips to the capital increased in frequency, Barrett decided they needed a place there, too. There were drawbacks. The early, easy happiness dissolved the wealthier her father became. And the more time they spent in Washington, the more they associated themselves with power and the requirements of prestige, the more Karen ceased to be a daughter, becoming instead a marketable commodity, a high-priced piece of trading material. At least that's how Karen felt.

Alfred's lips against her neck broke the train of thought. His kisses trailed up along her neck behind her ear. His left arm encircled her as his right hand turned her face toward his. "Karen . . . my love . . ." he whispered, then kissed her deeply. The pressure of his left arm increased as he held her tightly. His breath came faster and faster. His right hand stroked the creamy flesh of her shoulders then inched down to the top of the deeply scooped bodice, forcing the fabric away from her breasts. Karen submitted to the touch with a coldly analytical mind, amazed at how little she felt, at how differently Vance's touch had affected her. Alfred's fingers felt clinically impersonal as they poked and pinched, pawed and plucked at her. *Disgusting, disgusting!* The thought shattered when Alfred groaned passionately and his hand cupped her full breast. Karen dropped her still full brandy snifter in his lap.

"Christ!" Alfred shrieked brittlely. He jumped from the couch, his voice breaking into a higher register with his frightened yelp. A large brown stain spread across the lower part of his shirt. The bulging crotch of his trousers, now thoroughly soaked by the brandy, flattened itself as his obvious arousal shriveled with noticeable speed.

Karen rose quickly in sympathy. "Oh, Alfred, I'm so sorry. I forgot I had it in my hand," she said innocently as she straightened her dress.

"Tha . . . that's all right," Alfred stuttered, managing as best he could an indignant tone to his still breaking voice.

"Can I get you a wet cloth?"

"No. No. I'm fine. I had to be going anyway. I can take . . . care of it on returning home."

"Well, if you're certain there's nothing I can do," she insisted, moving toward him.

Alfred was already heading for the door. "No. Please, Karen, you've done . . . uh . . . I'm fine, really. A little brandy never hurt anyone." His laugh was brief and totally devoid of mirth.

They entered the main foyer. Ross appeared, seemingly out of thin air, carrying Alfred's top hat and cane. The butler allowed his forehead to wrinkle momentarily, his eyebrows arched high in disapproval. Alfred, all composure gone now, blushed under the English butler's icy stare and accepted his cane and hat without a sound. Ross muttered a polite, "Good-night, Sir," his mouth moving almost imperceptively, bidding Alfred farewell with as much sincerity as a man with vinegar on his tongue.

"I hope you're not angry with me, Alfred," Karen said with a pleading tone, afraid she had gone too far.

"No . . . no. Of course not. Perhaps you'll join me at the House tomorrow. We're expecting an interesting session. You might find it entertaining. After that we might dine. I have an important announcement."

"Can't you tell me now?"

Alfred scowled. "I hardly think it's the time, considering the circumstances. May I expect you?"

Karen would have declined but she decided Alfred had had enough setbacks for one night. "Yes. I'll meet you," she managed to say without sighing. It was little enough.

"Splendid. I'll see you then. No later than two, please. Our visitor addresses us then." Alfred bowed stiffly and traversed the long stone path leading to the carriage circle. He walked with an unusual flourish, as if trying to keep his flesh from touching the clothes on his body.

"Poor Alfred," Karen said quietly, finally allowing herself a sigh of relief at his departure. She pushed the door to and watched the distorted image of the lighted carriage through the leaded windows. Ross stood silently behind her, waiting for her to go upstairs. "I'll close up, if you don't mind, Ross. You may leave now."

"Yes, ma'am," Ross answered, retiring through the swinging doors to the back of the house.

Karen locked the door and turned down the lantern over the umbrella stand. For a moment she stood quietly, the day running in confused circles through her head. The day? Not the day. The afternoon. Twenty minutes of it with Vance Paxton of Texas. Her head whirled and she forced herself to stop and look at objects around her. The hall became a reference frame, soothing the torment of images clouding her mind.

The umbrella stand. Only one cane, now. Papa's ironwood with the ivory grip. Two umbrellas and one parasol, the latter hers, a gift from Alfred the day they had gone to the races and her old one had got torn on the fence. The matching Talbert leather-seated chairs at the sides of the library and parlor doors glowed with a rich luster, adding warmth to the generally austere setting. Karen walked slowly toward the parlor. Poor Alfred. He looked so . . . she couldn't go back in there.

The library door was ajar so she crossed the hall and entered, closing the heavy oak door behind her. The lantern on Barrett's desk was burning, the hiss of the escaping gas filling the room with a sibilant, sinister note. She moved to it and turned it off, plunging the room into darkness and silence, then stood quietly for a moment until the room came to her again. Smell, first; three walls of books exuded the perfumes of a thousand mysteries. Leather from the hides of beasts from around the world. What had once given form to flesh and bone and blood now lived on protecting words by the thousands. A cow from England, a lamb that had once frolicked in the plunging mountains of Spain. The noble sheep once king of an icy promontory now nestled snugly in a bank of thoughts, ideas, visions, facts and conceits. A noble beast for noble words. Perhaps it was a fitting end.

Karen walked slowly along the south wall, fingers trailing over the bindings. One she recognized, and as she pulled it partway from the shelf the odor of the Nile leaped out at her. "Early Phoenician Trade Routes." She remembered her father poring over the maps, remembered him telling her as a child how one could learn from the ancients. She shoved it back in place.

The east window in front of her suddenly erupted in a blaze of white light as a bank of clouds cleared the full moon. Dark shadows jutted into the corners behind her, transforming them into dark pits hiding a thousand ghosts, all of which she remembered well as frightening apparitions of the unknown when first the Hamptons took the great house when Barrett's business required they have a residence in Washington. A whole world, literally and figuratively, lay in those shadows, for in addition to the books a huge globe rested on a stand of mahogany inlaid with ivory. But Karen wasn't really interested in the whole world. It was enough that she sort out the day she had spent in her little corner of it. She pulled the large leather reading chair around to face the window and curled up in it. No sooner was she comfortable than another cloud scudded across the moon, leaving only the bright silver edge of the cloud visible. It soon disappeared and the room was dark again.

Washington lay before her. Distant, dotted with pinpoints of light, the city glowed and sparkled like a scene from a fairy tale book. There the hub of the nation slowly turned while untitled princes wove invisible but unbreakable webs of destiny. Out there men and women ate and slept, worried and anguished over the thousand trivialities of their own private worlds. Out there lovers met and caressed, murmured sweet words of endearment and sated the ravening hungers of burning passion. Out there a carriage carried a handsome, frustrated young man pulling his soaked trousers away from his body as he wound his uncomfortable way home. And out there a disturbingly provocative stranger, an enigmatic outsider to this cultured center of politics and society, walked the streets with devil-may-care fashion or lay deep in sleep, his body hard and oblivious to the luxury of soft sheets, his face nobly framed by flowing earth-brown hair. The images blurred and blended, melted softly, and Karen slept. In her dream a disembodied face surrounded by dogwood and blackber-ries—strange combination—turned cruel and hard, then soft and tender, shifting back and forth at a moment's no-tice. She lay huddled against a huge wall of stone. Fasci-nated, fearful, unsure, unsafe. . . .

"Karen . . ." Her mother's voice startled her awake. It was still dark, but Iantha carried a coal oil lamp, the flame turned up high enough to send a thin column of oily smoke drifting toward the ceiling. Iantha wore a floor-length dressing gown, pink and padded against the night spring chill. Her hair was unpinned and hung down past her shoul-ders, giving evidence that Karen's own golden coloring came from Iantha's side of the family.

"Mother. Are you just getting in?" Karen asked with a yawn.

Iantha sat in a chair near Karen. She lowered the flame and set the lamp on a nearby table. "Don't be silly. I've been home all evening."

"Papa said you were out."

"Your father pays little attention to whether I'm in or out. I went in to greet Alfred and, after your father let me know in no uncertain terms I wasn't needed, returned to my room. I suppose I must have dozed, for I didn't hear Alfred leave. When I awoke I went to your room to say good night but you weren't there," she said with a thinly disguised hint of disapproval.

"I'm sorry, Mother. Alfred left and I came in here to watch the city. It's so beautiful. I fell asleep."

"We provided you with a bedroom for the sole purpose of affording you a place to sleep, my dear. It comes as a shock to think you've given up such a comfortable chamber for the dubious benefits of the library. But I suppose it is to be expected, as you have been behaving somewhat unrea-sonably of late."

"Oh, Mother . . ."

"Karen, it isn't polite to interrupt, especially when I'm

41

scolding you. I suppose I should find some small satisfaction in the fact you are at least alone down here."

"Mother!" Karen managed, her voice appropriately shocked.

"Now don't be offended. Your father and I both know how you two feel about each other. And I shouldn't for one second believe you immune to the temptations of the flesh."

"I have never allowed Alfred even the slightest indiscretion, Mother, and I don't . . ."

"I know. I know. Alfred is a gentleman. But a young man withall. And I hardly need point out to you that young men have, from time to time, attempted . . . indiscretions, as you say . . . with young ladies."

Karen sat up, her ire aroused by her mother's condescension. "I suppose," she began frostily, "it would be different if he were a loyal subject of Her Majesty's."

"There is no need to be impertinent. I am more than aware of Alfred's antecedents. His grandfather was in Parliament and his family is vastly important even if he was, as were you, poor child, born in America." She paused once again, no doubt relishing the misery of the true anglophile. Karen sighed in exasperation. The sound drew Iantha from her reverie and the older woman leaned toward the younger. "Karen," she asked, "do promise me dear, that you will at least visit England on your wedding trip. Alfred could do so well over there. Both our families have no small amount of interest with the British Empire."

Karen bit her lip in frustration and she stifled her rising anger over the way her parents had her life so patently formulated for her. "Mother . . . Alfred and I haven't set any plans. I don't know where you get the idea we are even thinking of anything so definite as an actual wedding."

Iantha laughed softly. A suspiciously knowing kind of laugh. "Why, from your father, of course. We *do* speak from time to time."

Karen felt a chill stealing through her veins. "What does Papa have to do with it?"

"Really, Karen. Alfred certainly has more to do with it than your father. And I do wish you wouldn't play games with me. I find it most distressing."

Karen stiffened, her knuckles white from grasping the arms of the chair. She stared at Iantha.

Iantha reacted with confusion. Never had she seen Karen so. . . . "Alfred did tell you, did he not?" she asked.

Karen was very awake now. "Alfred had to leave rather suddenly," she said shakily. "It was a rather brief visit. Nothing much was said. Of any importance."

Now it was Iantha's turn to stare. Whatever could have happened? Could their plans have changed? No. Alfred would not be easily swayed. It wasn't his manner. He must have waited for . . . "Oh, my." Her hand went to her mouth in a tiny gesture of suppressed mirth. "Oh, my," she repeated, "I hate to spoil Alfred's fun, but I suppose I should go ahead and tell you."

"Mother, tell me what?" Karen asked, her voice trembling.

Iantha sat back regally, enjoying the role thrust upon her, the bearer of such happy tidings. "Your father stopped by my room before he retired. He was in such good spirits, even smiling. He told me he had a lengthy visit with Alfred during your absence—I trust, my dear, you will be so kind as to let me know just how you spent the afternoon—and they decided . . . well, obviously you were not with them, but. . . ."

"Will you please get to the point!"

"Alfred and your father have set the date for your wedding." Karen stood abruptly, the blood rushing from her head. "It's to be in July, on the fourth, of course—a nice touch, I thought—and will be officially announced at a gala we will hold here a week from Saturday." She rose from her seat and embraced Karen. "I'm so happy for you, my dear," she managed to finish, making a conspicuous show of dabbing at her eyes and stifling a sob.

Karen was stunned. She stood totally mute and unbelieving. In a little less than two months' time she would be Mrs. Alfred Randol Whitaker II. It was set. The trap had finally been sprung. Up until now her relationship to Alfred had taken on the aspects of a game. A complicated game to be sure, but a game one could stop playing whenever one wished. Now reality loomed over her. The game was nearly over. She had played too well, and had lost.

Iantha picked up the lantern and turned the flame higher. "It's late, dear. Much too late for proper young ladies to be up. And much, much too late for proper *old*

43

ladies such as I." She chuckled briefly, started to leave, then stepped quickly to Karen and embraced her again. "I know you're happy. Your father and I are too. Come along."

Karen followed more through shock than obedience. Her mother chattered ahead of her, hardly aware of the silence that hung over Karen like a dark cloud. "I'm so excited. I think we shall have the wedding right here on the grounds. The formal garden is a bit scruffy, but we shall have plenty of time to make it presentable. There is so much to be decided. Guests, flowers, your gown—I'm sure we shall have Mrs. Peachman for your gown don't you think?—refreshments. I shall have our family china sent down from New York, I think. And your grandmother's carriage. Repainted and resprung it will be magnificent. And Hermann must get the bays in shape. Oh, you shall be a picture, I'm sure. . . ."

They stopped at Karen's door and Karen allowed her mother to hug her once more. "Good night, dear," Iantha said tenderly. "Sweet . . ." She stopped and held Karen at arm's length. "My heavens! Whatever are you wearing? You are positively bare. No wonder Alfred forgot to tell you. The poor boy was probably half out of his mind. Why you insist on wearing those . . . those . . . French garments! It's very naughty of you, even if it is effective."

"Mother. Please. Good night? Just good night?" she pleaded, tears welling in her eyes.

Iantha enfolded her in yards of chiffon. "I'm so happy, Karen. The marriage will be a good one. The Hamptons and the Whitakers! We have come a long way, my dear. We will go farther."

Karen pushed herself back from her mother. "How far is farther, Mother?"

Iantha's gaze turned cold. Her words were measured, as if she had been waiting a long, long time to say them. "Wealth and power are not to be sneered at, my dear. Nor is position. We shall have all three in abundance. I will allow nothing to stand in my way."

Karen could find no answer. Afraid of giving away her true feelings should she speak, she leaned forward and meekly kissed her mother on the cheek, then turned and entered her room. Behind her, Iantha watched as the door

44

closed, then slowly walked down the hall, her head held high in triumph.

Inside her room, Karen walked to her bed as if in a dream. She kicked off her slippers and sat on the edge of the mattress. The lantern burned brightly in front of her and she stared at it a long, empty time, seeing only the light and nothing more. Finally her gaze slipped down to the table. The forbidden Zola lay there. *Les Rougon-Masquart.* She picked it up and stared at it, seeing it for the first time in its entirety. It was about the decay of a family through alcoholism and a number of other vices. "I could write a book about the decay of the Hamptons, Monsieur Zola," Karen told the book, her voice choked with emotion. "Not through vice and corruption, but ambition and greed." Sobbing now, she lay back and drew her knees to her chest. The tears streamed down her face and wet the pillow. "I could write such a book, sir, but I should not like to read it. I should not at all like to read it. . . ."

CHAPTER IV

Retta found her in the morning, eyes puffed and red from crying, still asleep, still fully dressed in her rumpled Parisian finery. The black servant stood over her for a long moment. Her little girl had cried herself to sleep. She looked so small, so fragile. Retta remembered the little girl she had watched and served and cared for over the years. Now the little girl was a big girl. How fast they grow, she thought, how rapidly the little bodies turned into big bodies. And yet how long it took for the inside to learn how to handle the hard parts of life without letting it show on the outside. She leaned over the girl and touched her tenderly. Almost her mother, she thought, I know her better than her mother. "Karen, honey? Time to wake up, chile."

Karen's eyes came open slowly, struggling against the puffiness and red, then closed again. Morning. A new day. She glanced out the window. Clouds. Dark rain clouds, gloomy and threatening. Thank God Retta was there. She stretched, pushing and pulling the cramped muscles taut. "Retta?"

"It's me all right, honey. Yo' sure looks a sight this mornin'. If I was you I'd forgit today and try again tomorro'. You want to talk about it?"

"No," Karen answered a bit hesitantly. "I have to figure out this one alone, Retta. I'm a big girl, now." The Hampton determination flared in her eyes. "I'm fine, Retta. I'll just take my bath as usual. That ought to wake me up. You needn't worry about tea. I'll eat with Papa this morning." She slid out of the bed and shrugged out of the disheveled dress, dropping it to the floor behind her as she pulled on the gown Retta handed her. She stepped into the hall, grateful for the silence surrounding her. Neither Retta nor Karen spoke until they entered the bathroom and Retta

47

busied herself with the towels and one last jug of steaming water.

"Lawd, it's hot this mornin'. Yo' watches yo' step or dat tub water'll near scald yo' pretty hide, chile."

"Thank you, Retta."

The black woman left the room and went about her chores. Karen disrobed and put one leg in the steaming water. Retta had spoken the truth and Karen winced as she stepped completely into the tub and sat all the way down, gritting her teeth until the water became bearable. *Burn, burn. There's much to be done today.*

She stayed longer than usual, letting the heat soak away her tiredness, ease the stiffness from her limbs. When she was finally out and toweled dry, her skin pink and shining with the healthy glow of youth, she padded back down the empty hall toward her room, barely missing her father as he descended for breakfast. Retta was waiting, ready to brush her hair and help her dress. She chose a pink gown of very proper cut by anyone's standards, quite suitable for a visit to the House later in the day. A small bustle from which hung yards of draped taffeta in a small train, rode just above the swell of her hips. She chose a cameo throat piece given her by her grandmother as her only jewelry. Retta helped her pile her hair into a broad sweep of curls. A Dolly Varden hat trimmed with white roses would later perfectly complement the pink taffeta and the natural warm red of her lips, for today she especially wanted to please her father and hopefully ameliorate his ire when she set about breaking the news of her unhappiness with the arrangements made the night before.

Barrett was seated at the spacious table, an empty breakfast plate shoved away from him. He still wore a bib cloth tucked into his collar to cover the front of his shirt. A steaming cup of coffee filled the air with its heavy aroma. Barrett was intently studying his paper. The sound of her approach broke his concentration. He rose from his seat and offered his hand to her. "Aah, Karen. Sit down. Sit down. Ross, bring my daughter's tea. And find her some breakfast. Something to stick to her ribs."

"No thank you, Father. Just tea will do."

Barrett held the seat for her. "I don't understand why you women won't eat a decent breakfast. What do you live on during the day? Why, I don't know what I'd do if I

48

missed a meal." He patted his growing paunch with affection and sat again as Ross entered with a china tea pot and a cup and saucer for Karen. "And take this damn dish out of here," Barrett continued. "I keep getting yolk on the paper."

Ross grimaced at Barrett's tone, but removed the offending plate, even if with obvious distaste.

"Now," Barrett said. "Tell me about you and Alfred. So it's set, hmmm? That makes your mother and me very happy."

Karen smiled and sipped her tea. The smile would have curdled milk had Barrett taken the time to notice. "I'm glad you're happy, Papa. That everyone is happy."

"Yessir," Barrett continued, lost in a fabrication of his own design, "the Whitaker influence in England and on the Continent and the Hampton enterprises in America. Plus Alfred in politics, of course. A fine combination. Daughter, this is the beginning of a financial empire, mark my words."

"I'm sure it is, Papa."

"Oh, by the way. Alfred invited us to attend the meeting of the House today. Some bumpkin from Texas will be addressing them. It should be most entertaining if you want to go along."

Karen experienced a moment of panic. A bumpkin from Texas? She shivered slightly at the memory of his hand on her breast, his hardness pressed against her. Could she face him without blushing? Would anyone suspect? There was little to do but acquiesce. "Alfred's already asked me. I said I would be there," she answered quietly.

"Fine. Fine. We'll have Hermann drive us down a little early. Pick up something to eat at the Senate Club. Father and daughter, eh?"

"That will be lovely, Papa." She paused as he picked up his paper again, hating to begin yet knowing she must before it was too late. "Papa. . . ."

"Damn!" Barrett exploded, shaking the paper angrily. "The fools don't understand the first thing about international finance. I've told them and told them. But do you think they'd listen? Of course not. An ignorant lot hardly fit to govern the backside of. . . ."

"Papa!" Karen tried again, her voice pleading.

Barrett glanced up. "Oh, yes. Sorry," and went back to his paper.

It was too late already. Barrett Hampton was totally engrossed again, miles from the daughter who sat so near across the table.

They left before noon in plenty of time for a leisurely luncheon at the Club before continuing on to the House. Hermann guided their carriage down Massachusetts Avenue and along a garden- and shop-lined street running parallel to Pennsylvania. They passed a small French cafe and after a moment's pleading, Barrett agreed to Karen's wishes that they dine there instead of at the Club. Karen often visited the cafe. To her a wistful reminder of Europe, the Dog, for short, was a colorful spot where artists, poets and clever wits came to argue endlessly over innumerable cups of coffee and tea. Barrett gazed suspiciously at the crudely lettered sign above the door where faded blue paint announced the Dog in more complimentary terms as *"Le Chien Commendable."*

Inside the place was all but deserted save for three or four silent, shabbily dressed fellows and the proprietors, a middle-aged Frenchman and his wife. The Frenchman, Clement by name, hurried to greet his new customers, recognized Karen and gave a stiff bow, elegantly kissing her proffered hand. "Ah, Madamoiselle Hampton. Such a pleasure to see you again," he said in a voice that carried only a slight trace of accent.

"This is my father, Monsieur Clement."

"I am honored, sir," Clement nodded exuberantly, extending his hand.

"I trust you have something suitable for an American stomach, Mr. Clement," Barrett said officiously. "We're in somewhat of a hurry."

"Mais oui, but who in Washington isn't in a hurry these days, *ça va?* It is very bad for the digestion." Clement's eyes twinkled as he chuckled to himself and led his guests to a prominent table near one of the front windows and assured them he would bring their food quite rapidly. The Frenchman clucked to his wife and the pair hurried off to the kitchen.

Barrett was ill at ease in the unfamiliar surroundings so obviously far below his standards. Had he been in Europe

50

he would have thought *Le Chien Commendable* quaint and amusing, would have assumed the food to be above average and more than prepared to accept it as superior. But this was Washington. The United States of America. Such a place would not be visited by anyone he knew or cared to know. He hoped no one saw him. "He seemed to know you quite well," he observed brittlely.

"I come here often, Papa."

"It would seem a young lady of your upbringing might frequent establishments of a more proper nature."

"This is a perfectly proper place, Papa. And the people are most pleasant, gracious and cultivated. And talented. The young man by the door is writing a novel. The elderly gentleman is a painter whose works are hung in museums in Europe. Clement's grandparents were chefs for the French court. On the contrary, what better place to spend one's time? Why, the entire place is less a cafe and more an education."

Barrett grudgingly gave up the argument. There was no point in carrying on a discussion with anyone who catered to artists, even if the anyone involved was a daughter. She would be neither convinced nor swayed by logic. Should he tell her he had no use for artists of any sort, Karen would only become embarrassingly upset. But such was the way of women. The way they should be, probably. Kept them busy and out of the way. Not one in a thousand realized the world turned on the marketplace and in the halls of state, not on some artist's canvas or writer's romantic blather.

Clement brought them their lunch, paper thin slices of rare beef smothered in a combination of gravy and sauce in which floated the button heads of tiny, succulent mushrooms. Small young potatoes boiled and spread with fresh butter lay surrounded by tender spring-sweet green English peas. Tiny loaves of white bread, brown and hard on the outside, sweet and soft on the inside, filled a wooden bowl, next to which lay a platter of thinly sliced fresh cucumbers, grown God-only-knew-where at that time of the year. Karen had a light Bordeaux while her father, refusing to be seduced by the delicious meal in front of him, declared himself unconvinced any wine bought in a cafe named the Dog could be anything other than vile and settled for coffee.

51

Barrett, his eye on the lowering clouds, hurried through his meal and urged Karen to finish hers much more rapidly than she wished. It was obvious he was anxious to be out of there and to the Capitol before the storm broke. Karen sensed his discomfort and mischievously lingered over her meal, sipping the wine with infuriating slowness as the interior of the cafe rattled to the reverberation of distant thunder.

Outside the gray clouds grew suddenly ominous and black and the wind stopped, leaving an expectant and weighty hush over the city. Swallows swooped low, an indication of a sinking barometer and the imminent approach of a storm. Brilliant streaks of lightning darted in and out of the boiling clouds, stitching them together with blue-silver fire. Each flash increased Barrett's discomfort until finally, his face livid with growing anger, he snatched the glass from Karen's hand and finished it himself, flinging change enough to cover their bill twice over on the table even as he drank. As they stood to leave, the Piper entered. The Piper was a huge burly fellow, a street musician earning pennies as best he could. His beard and hair were long and ragged, his clothes in such a state of disrepair it seemed they might fall off him at any moment, leaving him dressed in no more than his flute. Barrett hustled Karen around the disreputable fellow as if he had the plague, snorting in disgust as Karen greeted him affably.

"My God in Heaven, Karen! I hope Alfred doesn't have to put up with such behavior. It would drive me to distraction."

"But the food was good, wasn't it, Papa?"

"Food is as good as the surroundings in which it is enjoyed." He held the door for her as they exited. "I did not enjoy it."

"And you must admit the price was reasonable."

"Had we eaten at the Club, as I intended, I could have signed for it as usual. Further, we would be where we were going, instead of a half mile away and threatened by a storm."

His words might have served as a cue, for suddenly large fat drops of rain began to splatter the ground around them, leaving wet, saucer-sized stains on the stone path. They ran to the carriage. Hermann quickly wrapped his cheese in its cloth and jumped to the door, opening it just as Karen reached the carriage and holding it while she climbed in. A bolt of lightning struck somewhere nearby and the horses started, forcing Hermann to leave the door to go to their heads and calm them, leaving Barrett to enter the coach unassisted. Just as the older man climbed to the running board, however, a gust of wind snapped the hat from his head and sent it tumbling past the horses, startling them anew. Barrett cursed and gave chase, nearly bowling over Hermann, hard at work now holding the plunging beasts. Karen couldn't help but laugh at her father's victimization at the hands of nature as Barrett finally managed to trap his wayward hat, jamming it to the ground with his cane. He scooped it up and hastily returned to the carriage, his face furiously crimson, more from anger than exertion.

Hermann crooned to the horses and worked his way back to the steps to the coachman's seat, holding the reins tightly all the while. He freed one hand to shut the door after his employer and quickly climbed onto the high seat, at the same time lightly touching the backs of the nervous horses with the carriage whip. The animals broke into a quick, crabbed gait through the increasingly heavy rain, splashing water and mud to all sides.

Karen decided abject silence was the better part of valor and turned her attention to the Washingtonians scurrying along in search of cover. On one corner an irate fruit seller screamed useless epithets at a cluster of ragged Negroes huddled beneath the cloth awning protecting his racks of fruit. So closely were they packed together there was not even room for the owner to re-enter his shop. Karen caught a final glimpse as the carriage rounded the corner. Several of the children were beaming happily, cheeks puffed out and jaws chewing, obviously delighted and thoroughly enjoying their pilfered gains.

The carriage increased in speed as the rain fell faster. Lightning flashed in dramatic bursts of brilliance. Suddenly they swerved violently to the right and skidded. Karen had time for a brief, muffled scream as the carriage teetered crazily to one side then partially righted itself and settled at a drunken angle to the road. Hermann looped the reins around the brake lever and leaped from his seat into the ankle-deep mud and water. The trouble was readily apparent. The right rear wheel had hit a pothole and sunk axle deep, leaving the left rear wheel in the air. The coachman knew he'd never be able to get them out alone. He sloshed to the carriage door and knocked. Barrett's face, appearing for all the world like an angry ghost, peered through the fogged-up glass.

"I'll be needing to find some help, sir. I'm afraid we're stuck."

The face shook sideways, indicating Barrett couldn't hear, then disappeared. A moment later the door opened and Barrett, misjudging the steepness of the angle of the coach, almost fell onto Hermann, who had put out a hand to steady him and unceremoniously shove him back into the carriage. "What's that?" he yelled at Hermann.

"We're stuck. I'll have to get some help." As close as he was, the steady hiss of rain and the driving wind, accompanied by an almost constant rumble of thunder, plucked the words from his mouth and made them nearly incomprehensible.

Barrett shouted back, "Damn it, man. Hurry up. Do what you must, but hurry up."

Hermann, his drawn-out face especially morose in the dim light, touched his fingers to his hat in a small salute. The gesture loosed from the brim of his hat a small torrent of water which cascaded down his startled face and disappeared under his slicker. He shook his head woefully, slammed the door and started out for a nearby tavern, pushed by the wind at his back and soon hidden by a thick curtain of rain.

Karen looked out her window. The wind, full force, howled around the side of the carriage and drove streaming sheets of water against the pane. A sudden curiosity to see what the storm really looked like seized her and she released the latch and pushed the door slightly ajar. The fiercely driving water stung her fingers and cheek and she released her hold, allowing the wind to slam the door shut again.

"Damn it, what are you doing?" Barrett grumbled at her furiously. "Leave the door shut."

"I was just. . . ."

"Don't 'I was just' me, young lady. I've eaten at your cafe, ruined my hat, broken my carriage, probably, and gotten wet in the bargain, to say nothing of the delay. We could have been safe and dry, quietly and serenely sitting at the bar over a decent glass of port had I not been so affable. Now I am beyond affability. Leave the door shut," he roared, striking his cane on the floor in emphasis.

The carriage soon grew quite stuffy. Barrett suffered the most for he refused to shed his coat. Karen's dress was light so she suffered to a lesser degree. Indeed, the wait was more boring than uncomfortable, the only diversion being a glance cast now and again toward her father who was desperately trying to sit up straight in spite of the angle of the seat. There was one consolation: the delay would keep them from the House, hopefully until too late. Seen in those terms, the ordeal became more than bearable.

A rap on the door broke the stiff silence. Barrett opened it again to find Hermann, quite drenched to the skin. The driver touched his hat carefully and bowed slightly. "I've brought help, Mr. Hampton. We'll have the wheel free momentarily."

"Be quick about it, man."

"Yes, sir." The door slammed again and directly the carriage began to rock to and fro as Hermann and the men he had found tried to push it loose. Muffled curses and shouts sounded through the steady drum of rain and drone of wind. The whinny of excited horses cut through everything. Karen held on as best she could, rocking violently against Barrett at one moment and the side of the carriage the next. Finally the rocking and cursing stopped. Silence, followed by another rap on the door.

Barrett flung the door open for the third time. "Well, what is it?"

"Yes, sir. Begging your pardon, sir. The carriage needs to be a bit lighter. It's sunk pretty deep."

"Damn it, man, are you asking me to help?"

"Not actually, sir. Only if you'll be so good as to step out while we try again, and if you could stand at the horses' heads, sir. They're a bit spooky, what with the thunder and all. . . ." He paused apologetically. "There's but three of us, sir."

Barrett flustered. He started to tell the lanky servant to go straight back and get more help but there would be little use to that. Only hold them up longer. The best thing to do would be get out from the damned mess they'd found themselves in before they all drowned in the mud. Barrett sighed deeply, the picture of sacrifice and resignation. "Must my daughter get out too?"

"No, sir. I don't think so."

Barrett pulled a rain slicker from the trunk under the seat, donned it, placed his already ruined hat on his head, his cane in hand and stepped nobly into the torrent. A rush of rain swirled in behind him before the door could be closed, spattering Karen's dress.

She could hear an assortment of male voices shouting back and forth.

"If you've got their heads, sir, we'll give her a push."

"Push, then, damn it, push."

"Aye, sir. Put your backs to it, men!"

"Together, now. Heave! Heave!"

The carriage rocked forward then settled back into the rut, rocked forward again, almost righted itself and then settled back. The horses whinnied and strained at their bits, terrified of the storm, more so of the flapping slicker under their noses. The curses started anew, fierce and hard against the rain, wind and rolling thunder. A whip cracked and the horses screamed in protest as their bodies strained against the harness.

"Heave . . . heave . . . heave!" The carriage bolted upright, free of the rut at last, hovered on solid ground for a second, then lurched forward a foot or two and held.

Barrett relaxed his hold slightly just as the air sizzled with a bolt of cobalt blue. A pine tree to the immediate rear of the carriage and team exploded with a fearsome clap and an awesome cannonade of thunder roared through the man-made valley of low buildings and shops. The team, panicked by the lightning and sent into a frenzy by the thunderous retort, broke free of Barrett's grasp, knocked him aside and surged into a terrified, mindless gallop. Hermann was clipped by the right rear wheel and sent sprawling face forward into the mud. Barrett stood rooted to the spot, his hand reaching for emptiness, his mouth gaping open in horrified surprise at being left behind, unable to realize that what was an inconvenience for him was an extremely real danger for his daughter.

The inside of the carriage was transformed into a violent maelstrom, the air filled with flying objects. Karen was first slammed against the back of the seat then jolted about viciously, flung to one side then the other in a nightmare of unpredictable motion. She managed to grip the right door latch, pull her way over to the side and force the door open. Store fronts and staring faces, trees and parked carriages blurred together as the carriage careened past, ever managing to increase its speed. She wanted desperately to jump, for sooner or later the carriage must strike another rut, quagmire or tree and destroy itself and her in the process, yet she didn't dare for fear of broken bones. Or worse. Visions of her body dashed to the ground and run over by the flashing wheels, broken and lying in the mud. . . . The door was torn from her grasp by the howling wind and slammed back against the carriage siding, leaving nothing between her and a disastrous fall but rain, wind and a screen of flying mud thrown from the horses' hooves and the wheels. The fear-maddened horses lurched left and just as abruptly back to the right. Karen's fingers dug with the strength of desperation into the doorway. She screamed, her voice a tiny, insignificant addition to the murderous cacaphony of rushing wind and pounding hoofbeats.

Suddenly a figure ran down a boarded walkway from a tavern and leaped at the carriage as it sped by. A hand accompanied by a flashing form slammed into her and knocked her sprawling back against the other side. Her eyes widened in new fear, for whoever had attempted the dare-devil leap was only halfway into the carriage. His lower half dangled into the stream of mud and water outside, inches from the rear wheels of the coach. The figure heaved itself forward, grasped a new hand hold and hauled itself into the doorway, and just as immediately leaped forward and up toward the driver's seat, gone before Karen could say a word or recover from her surprise. But in that instant when the face darted across her line of vision, Karen had recognized Vance Paxton.

She crawled to the doorway again in time to see Vance maneuver himself onto the carriage just behind the upsweep of wood construction capped by the driver's seat. Vance grabbed the back of the seat, hauled himself up and over, almost losing his balance as he dragged his leg over the top. For a moment it appeared he would topple over and down under the slashing hooves of the frenzied team, but his left hand shot out and he steadied himself and managed to secure his perch. He reached down to unloop the reins and gradually began to exert pressure on the guide lines and brake. Karen could hear him calling to the animals in soothing tones. Slowly the horses responded to the pressure on the lines and brake, responded to the strength in the voice above and behind them. The team's speed decreased slowly into a controllable gallop, then a canter, a trot, and finally stopped. It was over. Less than three minutes had elapsed since the bolt of lightning had stampeded the team. Karen sat back in the seat, her face white, hands and body trembling with relief.

Vance leaped from the driver's seat. He still did not know the occupant of the carriage. He had seen but a flash of a helpless figure leaning from the runaway carriage and that had been enough to warrant his action. And what the hell, he figured silently, this was as good a way as any to avoid that infernal speech. His breath came slowly as he talked to the horses and led them to a nearby hitching post. He tied the reins and stroked the beasts' necks, calming them farther before leaving them.

Hermann, in a carriage borrowed from one of the occupants of the tavern, sped down the road in hasty pursuit and hauled the trembling team to a halt when he saw the carriage safely tied to the post. Barrett flung open the door and jumped out the second they stopped, for once unconcerned about the sea of mud around him. Expecting to encounter only shattered remains of coach and daughter, it took him a few seconds to comprehend what he saw; his team stopped, carriage in one piece and his daughter's face framed in the open doorway. A mud-drenched man sloshed toward the compartment. The shock on Barrett's face was nothing compared to the expression that crossed Vance's when he leaned in the door to check on his passenger and came face to face with Karen Hampton.

"Are you all right, Karen?" Barrett forced his way past Vance and climbed in.

"I . . . I think so."

"My God, we thought something terrible had happened to you. I don't know what we expected to find." He turned back to Vance, still standing in the doorway. "Who is this?"

"He saved my life, Papa. He jumped on the carriage and stopped the team. He . . ."

"Climb in, man. I would not have you drown now after having been of such service."

Karen adjusted her hat and offered Vance an amused smile. Vance hesitated but a moment before stepping into the carriage and sitting on the jump seat facing Karen and Barrett.

Barrett extended a hand to Vance. "My name is Hampton, sir. Barrett Hampton. And this is my daughter Karen."

Vance looked across at the woman whose life he had probably saved. A tenuous strand of gold had come undone from her coiffure and fell from under her hat. It framed her cheek, coiled down across her bosom and curled up provocatively at the tip. She was as beautiful now as she had been the day before.

Karen extended her hand. "Thank you, Mr. . . ."

"Paxton, ma'am," he answered, wondering why she should choose not to admit their acquaintanceship. Could she be ashamed? Spoken for? Or was this merely a social game to be played on a mere whim? "Vance Paxton from Texas." Very well. He would play. Again.

"Paxton. . . ." Barrett's forehead knotted in thought. Then he brightened. "You're not the fellow who was to speak this afternoon?"

"Yes, sir. I'm afraid so." *Afraid* was the correct word. He had sought out information about the Hamptons only that morning and discovered Barrett had an intense dislike of southerners. Texans were southerners, were traitors. The relationship would not be a happy one.

"Well, then. I suppose you ought to be riding with us if you want to make it there in time to clean up. You're a frightful mess, if you don't mind my saying so. We'll be on our way directly." He ducked his head out the door to confer with Hermann and pay the man who had loaned them his carriage.

Vance glanced boldly across at Karen whose eyes dropped demurely away from his. After an uncomfortable silence, Vance was the first to speak. "Miss Hampton, it seems we've met before. A lady lovely as yourself would be difficult to forget."

Karen returned his appraisal more boldly. "You are very gracious, Mr. Paxton, but I doubt it."

"Possibly at a party?"

"Possibly, though I think not. I should imagine we travel in different circles." Karen smiled again for him. Her voice was one of pleasant formality but her eyes told him a different story. *Two can play at this game, Mr. Paxton, and I would suspect I'm more adept at it than you.* The door

59

slammed closed and the carriage jerked forward. Vance gave up the point and gazed out the window, a slow anger beginning to grow inside him.

The remainder of the trip was brief and passed silently. They stopped at the base of the Capitol steps within minutes. "We'll go on in. Karen, you might as well return home," Barrett decreed. "You're a bit mud-spattered."

"I'm not nearly as soaked as you two, and Alfred is expecting me," Karen replied. "Besides, if Mr. Paxton is going to speak, I should like to see if his words are as heroic as his actions."

Barrett frowned and started to contest the issue, but as the downpour slacked abruptly, he gave up without a murmur, shrugged and said, "Suit yourself."

Vance, wondering at this new turn of events, managed to back his lanky frame out of the coach without cracking his skull on the door frame. Barrett followed and waited to one side as the Texan offered his hand to Karen. *Hot one minute, cold the next. A man should stick to cattle and business, land and politics. I'm damned if I understand them.* Karen's hand touched his lightly as she stepped down. The contact startled them both. She withdrew the hand as if it had been burned and moved toward her father to take his arm. Barrett was oblivious to her, though, now the danger was past, and hurried up the steps ahead of her.

Karen frowned and turned back to Vance. "My father is a man of the moment, Mr. Paxton, little given to the niceties of life. Now that he has given you the use of his carriage he's probably decided the favor you paid me has been returned. You risked life and limb and he graciously allowed you to ride in the Hampton carriage. I wouldn't expect anything like a verbal expression of his appreciation, were I you. He never expresses gratitude. Such a gesture would be entirely out of character. I suppose he feels any service rendered him was due him in the first place."

"Many people feel similarly, Miss Hampton."

Karen looked at him inquisitively. "Yes. I suppose they do." She hesitated a brief second. "I hope you will accept my thanks, if nothing else."

"I'll try hard not to expect . . . anything else," he answered slowly, the innuendo only half meant.

Karen blanched. The memory of the scene at the Dueling Wall flooded through her again. She flushed with embarrassment, realizing what an impossible tease she must have seemed. "I'm sorry about yesterday in the park," she said quietly. "I'm afraid I was unseemingly forward. I should prefer we forget the whole episode if you don't mind."

The anger returned. She would forget it? Not damned likely. Not if he could help it. But perhaps it was his turn. "Why, Miss Hampton, what on earth are you talking about? What woods? I should imagine we travel in different circles."

Karen blushed with an awkward mixture of embarrassment and anger. She had tried to apologize, only to have sarcasm flung back in her face. She felt Vance's eyes boring into her, eyes flashing with bold insolence. *I will not allow this. I will not allow this.* She drew herself up to her full height and stared back at him. "Father doesn't like southerners," she said coldly before stalking away from him. "I don't think I do either."

She found herself momentarily alone inside the Rotunda, her footsteps echoing hollowly through the empty hall. Why did he do this to her? Why did she always become so upset after seeing him, speaking to him? Why did she make such a fool of herself? If only she could undo what had happened in the park. . . .

"Karen!" Alfred came running over to her just as Vance entered through the great doors behind her. "Karen, your father told us what happened. Good Lord, you're lucky you weren't killed," Alfred blurted.

"I'm all right, Alfred, really. Please don't fuss." Whether or not she loved Alfred she was vastly happy to see him at the moment. She stole a glance behind her.

Vance stood to the side and watched as Alfred Whitaker rushed to Karen. He knew Alfred only as one of the junior members of the House, one who supposedly stood in favor of the requests for aid Vance carried from Texas. Still, Vance had to fight the urge to intervene when the youthful representative, a mere dandy, embraced the Hampton beauty. *But why should I care?* The thought troubled him more than anything had in some time. He forced it from his mind and started for the cloakroom to clean up.

Karen noted the movement. A small look of Hampton determination crossed her face. She wouldn't let him get away that easily. "Oh, Mr. Paxton," she called with a slight lilt brightening her voice, "I know you need to clean up, but I would like you to met my fiancé."

Vance stopped and turned with a slight scowl of preoccupation. "Ma'am?"

"Alfred, this is the gentleman who proved to be of such service. Mr. Paxton, Alfred Whitaker."

Alfred rushed to Vance and grasped the Texan's hand. "Sir, I must shake your hand in gratitude. You have saved me a lifetime of grief."

Vance fabricated a smile. "Well now, I'm certainly glad of that, Mr. Whitaker."

Karen regretted her decision immediately. Seeing the two men face to face made her wish she had never left the carriage, much less introduced the two. Alfred's sophisticated handsomeness appeared more a case of masculine prettiness and his posture and studied movements almost girlish in comparison to Vance's rough-hewn, country manner. *More like an animal. A wild beast with a veneer of civilization.* But it was too late to do anything but smile amiably and join them.

"I can assure you, Mr. Paxton," Alfred went on smoothly, "that when word gets around of the service you have performed, I'd wager ten to one odds the House will vote in favor of the Texas resolution."

"Alfred," Karen interrupted, "we're already late. Shouldn't we retire to the chamber and allow Mr. Paxton to . . . clean up . . . before he has to speak?"

Alfred laughed easily. "Oh, I'm terribly sorry, Mr. Paxton. The session . . . I forgot to tell you. That infernal downpour caught most of us completely unprepared. The agenda has been changed in order to allow my colleagues to dry out. I'm afraid your speech had to be rescheduled for next week. It's a devil of an inconvenience, I know, but there's hardly a soul present and there's but little sense in talking to empty seats."

Vance shrugged. One day was as good as the next. Now that was odd. Only two days ago he had been anxious to get the damned speech over with and the vote on the resolution out of the way. One way or the other he'd have been able to leave the place and return to Texas where he belonged. Now it seemed he was almost happy at the delay. It didn't make any sense.

Voices drifted from the entrance to the House and Barrett appeared in the doorway accompanied by a congressman. One of them had just told a joke and both were laughing politely. Karen noticed her father was in exceptional spirits. Perhaps it was because the speech had been cancelled and there were few to see him in such a disheveled state.

Barrett noticed Karen standing with Alfred and led his companion in their direction. A slight expression of distaste crossed his face at seeing Vance still there. Taking advantage, no doubt. Couldn't trust a Texan. Too damned little breeding and no sense whatsoever of common manners, even if he had saved Karen and Barrett's English carriage.

"Ah, Karen, there you are. I want to be the first to congratulate you," the congressman called out as he approached.

Karen curtsied and allowed the speaker to kiss her hand before answering. "Thank you, Mr. Leighton."

Vance's interest peaked anew at the mention of the man's name. *So that's what he looks like. No wonder Angie's so desperate.*

"Alfred," Barrett broke in, "I've taken the liberty to invite Earnest and his lovely wife Angela to the gala. I've already told him the purpose of the event, as you can see."

"Angie dearly loves parties," Earnest replied. "I remember announcing our engagement at one party, setting the date at a second and finding time for a third before the wedding. What the purpose of the third one was I'll never know, but Angie certainly had a good time. That's the way to keep a woman, Alfred. Partying. Women love partying, right, Karen?"

Karen looked up at Earnest Leighton. What she saw was a tall, well-proportioned man falling gracelessly into age. His hair was graying and combed to conceal a spreading bald spot. He was developing a paunch and his shoulders remained perpetually stooped. His pock-marked face showed evidence of face powder, little bits of which glinted obscenely from the scars of that distant illness. The stories concerning Angie Leighton's indiscretions were legion among the Washington social set, and from the look and attitude of Earnest Leighton they were probably true. Nevertheless, Karen spoke as pleasantly as possible. "If you say so, Mr. Leighton."

"And this is Mr. Paxton. From Texas," Barrett said.

63

"Of course." Earnest Leighton pumped Vance's hand. "Brave thing you did, young man. Paxton, eh? My wife spoke of you. You were kind enough to give a talk on the Wild West to her children's study group. She tells me you held that squalling bunch of youngsters enraptured with your stories. Said you were quite talented. You must tell some of them at Karen and Alfred's announcement party."

Karen glanced at her father, her expression as bland as she could manage. Alfred coughed nervously.

Vance spoke first, for the first time since Karen had known him at a loss for words. "I . . . hadn't . . . didn't know I was. . . ."

Barrett interjected in a booming voice, saving face as best he could. "I hadn't got around yet to inviting you, Paxton. Of course, hadn't met you until this afternoon, but I do hope you'll do us the honor of accepting. It's the, uh, least we can do. I'm certain Karen will be upset if you don't allow us to show our, uh, appreciation and gratitude by considering this an invitation to our party."

Vance ran his fingers through his hair and nodded curtly in Karen's direction. "If Miss Hampton wishes me to attend. . . ."

Their eyes met, Vance's and Karen's, each daring the other to break away first. Karen was not to be outdone by this westerner. Returning his stare she took the greater dare. "I would be offended should you not attend. I look forward to your amusing stories, Mr. Paxton." *Parry, riposte and thrust home, Mr. Paxton. It will be a most amusing evening.* She turned to Alfred, who offered his arm. "Alfred will see me home, Father. Good day, Mr. Leighton. Good day, and thank you again, Mr. Paxton."

"Certainly, ma'am," Vance answered, his voice subdued.

Karen could not help but feel a sense of self-satisfaction at leaving the Capitol with her aristocratic pride intact. She was not there, though, to overhear when Earnest Leighton discovered he'd had his dates mixed up and was committed to attend an important business meeting on the afternoon and evening of the gala. Nor was she there when Earnest suggested Vance escort Angie to the Hampton affair in his place. Angie did so love the Texan's stories. Nor was Karen there to hear when Vance, with diabolical pleasure, accepted Leighton's invitation.

CHAPTER V

The razor traveled down from the sideburns in sure swift strokes. Tiny, precise strokes with the tip of the blade were necessary above the curving mustache. Long cuts along the jaw preceded a flurry of small movements on the chin. Long, smooth strokes floated down from the jaw, then up and out from the Adam's apple. The razor, delicate as a feather in the calloused, raw-boned hands, cut cleanly, stripped the wiry beard from wind- and sun-toughened hide. Vance had been in an ill temper for the last ten days. He mused as he shaved, his hands moving unconsciously, face contorting to fit the razor's demands. The brush beat the soap to a white, full-bodied lather as he prepared for the second pass over the stubborn beard. The razor flip-flopped on the leather strop, soft cowhide smoothing the hard steel, honing the already flawless edge.

Why such a foul humor? Too many reasons. The damned food, to begin with. Too fancy and far too rich. The stifling air caustically pungent with the odor of too many horses in a too small a space. The mosquitos swarming in clouds from the canals and ditches. The crowding people jarring a man whichever way he turned. The sour water unfit for man or beast, but invariably used to vilify good whiskey. The constant damned jawing, bickering, backbiting carried on in the countless halls and offices of government and business by men whose handshakes were as reliable as a horsethief's, which they probably were anyways, or would be, given half a chance. That damned hot-crotched Angie Leighton, never able to get enough, pushing for more and more and him fool enough to try to oblige her in the face of all sense and reason.

"Damn!" The razor sliced a sliver of skin out from under his jaw, the red blood welling quickly, spreading through the white lather. "Having to shave every God damned day, that's why!" he said fiercely, glaring at himself in the mirror. But that wasn't the reason either, for Vance Paxton couldn't yet admit the single insurmountable fact that had governed his mood for the last week and a half. He wiped the blade carefully and flipped it into the carved bone handle, dried it and slipped the razor back in the leather pouch. The bleeding had stopped so he rinsed his face one last time, dried and pulled on the fancy Mexican shirt. *Black tie, hell. No Paxton wore a tail yet, and I'm damned if I'll be the first one. They can throw me out first. If they can.* The neckerchief tied, he shrugged into the buckskin coat. There was nothing left to do.

Vance sauntered down to the lobby of the hotel. A bellboy old enough to be his father doffed his cap as the Texan approached. "Afternoon, Mr. Paxton."

"Afternoon, Grover."

"Mighty nice Saturday. Gonna be nice and cool this evening, too."

"I hope so."

Grover looked the tall westerner over, wondering about the brush-brown buckskin coat, the coarsely woven Mexican dress shirt with the thickly ruffled facing, the scarlet and black kerchief about the man's throat. "Woo-ee. Dressed fit to kill. You Texas boys wear the damndest party clothes I ever seen." He jumped to continue, "Meanin' no offense, sir."

The old man's bobbing head barely came to mid-chest on the Texan. Vance thought of a fragile, weary old derelict wild stallion he'd dragged from a sinkhole once. Cowed and beaten by his narrow escape, left behind by the herd that had finally rejected him, he stood trembling as Vance undid the rope from around his neck, unable to comprehend he was free to roam again, free to follow the sun and wind. Vance had understood why he didn't when some of the mud dripped from his left rear leg. It was bent and swollen, a wreck unable to stand any weight, probably painful as hell to boot. The decision was easy. He had taken out his rifle and shot him where he stood, leaving the once noble beast for the vultures and coyotes to pick clean. *But what of Grover? Who will show him compassion? Not a damned soul, that's who. He'll be left to sink slowly, without even a shred of decency left to cover him.*

Vance grinned down at the old man. "No offense taken,

Grover. And most folks I like call me Vance. It sits more comfortable than Mr. Paxton."

The old man's eyes lit up and his face split with a broad, toothless grin. "I'll sure do that, sir."

Vance looked about the lobby. All the chairs were filled with other old men and women sitting out the afternoon without a thing to do. He growled angrily and headed for the hotel bar, shoulders hunched with a tension for which he couldn't account. "If I gotta kill a couple hours, I might as well do it without realizing I'm doing it," he muttered.

A nickel bought him a foaming jack of beer. He sat in a dark corner out of the way of an unusual afternoon crowd. The cold beer went down smoothly, tasted good enough to follow with another. And then another. The bartender left a bowl of peanuts on his table along with the fourth mug. Vance lifted the brew to his lips, wishing he were back home on the ranch drinking with True, his father, and the rest of the boys. He took only a shallow sip, then checked his pocket watch. Another hour yet. He'd better take it easy. He mulled over the fourth one, taking his time with it, consuming it slowly, chomping on the peanuts and savoring the bitter chill of hops, malt and barley.

Karen's image floated in unbidden during the sixth mug. Karen Hampton. . . . no. He had drunk away that haunting memory, that image of sensuality. A party to announce her wedding? What did he care? Hell, tonight there would be Angie . . . another man's wife, to be sure, but if Earnest wasn't man enough to hold her . . . but he had no right, even so. What had his Washington sojourn done to him? Filled him with anger, irritation and frustration, that's what. The anger, if nothing else, had been useful. It had fueled his speech before the House the day before, firing an arrogant, devil-may-care, audacious delivery that had left the conservatives foaming at the mouth and brought cheers from the progressives. Now the matter went into debate and committee meetings. There was nothing he could do about the final vote, so these could well be his last few days in Washington. Only one more meeting, one more brief lecture on Texas' need for federal money and his task would be complete. He'd be on the boat and on his way back. Galveston, the stage to San Antonio and his own horse from there to the ranch. Marcelina would be waiting. Marcelina could make a man forget a lot of things.

67

So why not a party tonight? He'd saved her pretty neck, hadn't he? He hadn't asked for favors or rewards. A Paxton never asked for any favors. Nor were they beholden to any man. They had worked and fought for and built what was theirs. Alfred Randol Whitaker II? What the hell kind of moniker was that for a man? Sounded like a damned Bloody Newton gambler, someone who'd take an honest cowboy for his last piece of silver, maybe his saddle and pony to boot. Now, *Paxton*. Short and to the point. Clean sounding. A name you could say without twisting your tongue through a damned cactus patch.

Damn. What was he saying now? Nothing. It was the beer talking in his head. *Karen Hampton. . . . Here's to your wedding, Miss Hampton. My very best wishes. . . .*

Back in Texas, that's where a man needs to be, with real work to do, not just talk and smile and shake hands. Uncrowded and free, a man can live a lot of things out of his system. The prairie swallows his past. The wind and rain and sun and snow leach it out of him, if a bullet doesn't steal it first. A man can forget parks and girls with hair gold as a conquistador's treasure and eyes that promise . . . promised. . . . "Dammit!"

He drained the mug and slammed it down on the table top.

Iantha had spent ten feverish days in preparation. Now all was impeccably ready, nothing left to do but dress and wait for the guests. She sat in her tub, soaking and relaxing, anticipating her triumph even as she ran through all the details for the thousandth time and mentally inspected the house.

The drive was adorned with candles stuck on metal poles, each flame protected by glass globes. A man had been hired to light them a half hour before dusk and the planned arrival of the guests, then tend each candle, replacing them as need be. The two hundred pinpoints of light would glitter dramatically as they lit the way to the columned entrance.

The front porch was manned by two huge blacks dressed in formal livery, coached to swing open the great oak doors with the stained glass windows as the guests walked toward them. The foyer was done simply but elegantly. Two extra chandeliers had been hung and three maids had spent the week waxing and shining every piece of wood and leather in sight. Visitors entering would be treated to a thousand reflections of candles sparkling on glass and glowing in the soft, warm sheen of wood and leather. To complete the quiet statement of aristocratic taste, the great white stairs at the end of the hall swept up and out of sight in the upper reaches of the house.

The front parlor to the right was set aside as a cloak room to be managed by a reliable little English servant girl borrowed from the Edwardses. The one to the left was done in lilacs—white and pink only—and reserved as a sitting room for the ladies. A small table with sterling tea service and delicate, light blue Spode china cups and saucers given to Iantha by her mother graced one corner of the room. Another corner held a table laden with tiny cakes, delicately iced in white and pink. The room was impeccably staffed by two more of the Edwardses' maids.

Down the hall on the right the library was open. More somber, there were no flowers or other decorations, only an extra long table set with bottles of whiskey, rum, brandy, liqueurs and boxes of cigars. Harold, their New York butler, would handle this room. He had the quiet good sense and dependability needed for a man's room. Nothing would go wrong there.

· The dining room opened off from the hall across the library. The great doors had been removed, leaving ample access from the hall and, from many places in the room, even a partial view of the stairs. Here was the heart of Iantha's party, where the quiet good taste of the hall and front rooms exploded in gaiety. The ten-piece orchestra, without a cellist still—there was never a cellist in this dismal country when one needed one—was set in the northwest corner near the French doors. A huge board at the south side of the room near the entrance to the kitchen would soon be groaning under the weight of countless dishes and platters. Hams, beeves, legs of lamb, venison, ears of steaming corn—when the time was right—and salads would lie ready throughout the evening. In the center of this table and outside on the lawn on another table sat the twin-cut crystal punch bowls surrounded by cup after cup arranged in neat lines. Hundreds of daintily iced cinnamon and sugar cakes lay on silver platters flanking the punch bowls. Iantha frowned. The room was too small—

69

only thirty feet by sixty feet—and there wouldn't be as much room as she would like for dancing. But the time would soon come for rectification of that particular drawback. Their next house would have a ballroom as befitted their place.

But there was nothing of which Iantha needed to be ashamed. The room would be sumptuously decorated with countless candles shining brightly amid the yards of white streamers. Cherry, peach and apple blossoms already filled the corners, lay in great, flowing arrangements around the meats and other foods, festooned the orchestra's platform and piled in a bower over the French doors leading to the side lawn. The lawn itself would twinkle and shine almost like daytime. Lanterns hung from trees and shrubs and a special chandelier brought down from New York hung suspended between the matching, age-old oaks which formed the basis of the garden arrangement. Iantha had yet to see such an outside chandelier in Washington and was well pleased with the sensation she knew it would create.

All in all, Iantha was pleased. The evening would be perfect, a heady step nearer to the goals she had sought for years. She smiled secretly. There was no doubt the wedding was a coup. Next year the Edwardses would borrow some of her people for their annual party. At that point no one would question the Hamptons' arrival.

Down the hall, Retta fluttered about in animated nervousness. Karen had already fitted herself into a full formal gown of sheerest sky blue silk and deeper-hued taffeta. White satin slippers were lost beneath the voluminous folds of her skirt. Retta had bound her hair back and then fashioned it in thick long curls draping down across her left shoulder. The gown left her shoulders and a generous expanse of back and front quite bare. Her breasts, bound by a bodice stiffened with whale bone, swelled with breathtaking beauty above their tight restraint.

Karen looked up from her cloth-bound diary and saw Retta's beaming face framed in the gilt-edged mirror. She wished she felt the same way, wished she could generate the same enthusiasm for the night ahead, indeed for the days and months and years that so frightened her. *A tool, a slave, a bauble and no more. Meant to be pretty, meant to be gracious, meant to be charming. I do not want this. I do not want to marry Alfred.*

She had searched, these past two weeks, for a way out. Surely Alfred had not been serious. But alas, he had never been more so. In fact, he had become unbearably cocky now their nuptial ceremony was to be announced at last. So sure of himself and smug to the extreme. Karen shuddered at the thought of Alfred assuming the role of domineering husband, of lord and master, as he surely would. Of Alfred herding her about to all the right social functions, using her as that most necessary of all the successful politician's necessary accoutrements—the dazzling, pliable, forgotten wife. Of Alfred planting his seed in her, using her to breed further specimens of the line that so sickened her. Of Alfred and his world eventually wearing her down, convincing her, changing her into the social creature her mother already was. Of Alfred. . . . Karen Olivia Hampton would not be dominated nor used by Alfred or any other man. Not even a Texan.

How were women treated in Texas? The same as in Washington and New York? She leaned back in her chair, closing her eyes and shutting out the final pre-party sounds, daydreaming of a strange land a thousand miles away. The land was flat, sere, bounded by a sky as lonely and empty as the miles falling away from her on all sides. A single man loomed on the horizon and strode toward her. It was Vance Paxton. *If all the men in the world were like him, I'm sure I'd . . . I'd . . . just hate it*

The clatter of rapid footsteps accompanied by Iantha's admonishing voice broke her uncomfortable reverie. She opened her eyes to see Retta fashioning a tiny bouquet of flowers, twining an assortment of dainty ribbons among the blossoms. Retta fitted them into Karen's already elegant coiffure, her nimble fingers darting among Karen's yellow gold ringlets to adjust a pale blue ribbon here, fasten a stray blossom there. When she finished, Karen was transformed from a ravishingly pretty young woman to a goddess of myth, a Helen whose beauty had caused the toppling of distant Troy, a siren luring men from their course, dashing their hearts upon the cruel whims of her caprice. Aphrodite herself.

Retta stood back and admired her handiwork. Karen stared, more than a little bewildered by her own reflection. She had always known she was pretty. She accepted the fact as natural, seldom giving the matter much thought.

But now. . . . Every part complimented every other part. Lustrous hair touched by Midas himself. The green of eyes set off by the gold of the hair. The nose, not pert and cute any more, but regal and bold without being outlandish. Perfect lips sculpted of ruby, gentle against ivory skin. *It's not me. It's not me.* She leaned forward slightly, hand covering her mouth in surprise. "Oh, Retta. Don't you think it's a little too much?"

"Honey, yore beauty done come from de Lawd," Retta answered firmly. "Dey's no shame in showin' it off. Dem flowers is from de garden an' dey's de Lawd's too, and he doan mind you wearin' them 'cause it's obvious to him, an' me too, dat dem flowers and you was made for each other."

Karen gazed back into the mirror. Suddenly she felt very powerful. The feeling surged through her. *Something important is going to happen tonight. I don't know what it is yet, but something important is going to happen.* And suddenly, too, she was glad for the party. Her whole being tingled with anticipation and she felt more alive than ever before. She settled back in the chair and dipped her pen into the ink well and sat poised with the tip against the page. Unmoving and lost in a confused welter of thoughts and excited expectations, Karen dreamed again while the deep blue stain on the page spread and spread. . . .

The carriage let him off at the customary iron grill gate. Vance walked only a trifle unsteadily up to the Leighton house, there to be admitted by their Castilian butler and guided into the drawing room. The butler gave Vance a knowing smirk and excused himself after the Texan declined an offer of anything stronger than coffee. A moment later Earnest Leighton made a hurried entrance, stepping back in surprise when he saw his visitor.

"Why, Paxton! I'm . . . well . . . I didn't even hear you come in. I swear that goddam butler never tells me anything. That's the trouble with help these days, you know. You take them in, give 'em a job and they think they own the place. Have you got a drink?"

"I told your man just coffee, thank you."

"That's all? I thought you Texans were drinking men." He paused, staring curiously at Vance, then turning abruptly to the window behind him. "There was an influx of

72

foreign servants and the like after Richmond fell. Virginia gentry always were fond of Europeans. Gave them a feeling of class. But a lot of them were put out of work by the war. Left to wander, as it were. Washington got more than its fair share, and we're burdened with them even if we have managed to keep their salaries within reason. That's how we came across Modero. Not a bad boy as these people go. Angie so dearly loved Spain when we were there. A lovely country. Lovely country. . . ."

Vance stood unmoving as the congressman paced nervously back and forth in front of the window, his hands jerking spasmodically, his words spilling rapidly. *A man who doesn't dare or can't stop talking. Something wrong with that man. Something bad wrong.*

Modero entered the room bearing a small silver tray on which rested a white china cup and saucer. Vance gratefully accepted the proffered cup and sipped the steaming, deep brown liquid, savoring its taste and waiting for the man he had cuckolded to continue.

"Angie isn't even dressed yet," Earnest went on, his pace finally slowing. "You know women. They spend hours on their hair and face and a minute to dress. All that preparation. . . ." He sucked in a deep breath, imposing control on himself with an effort. The tension was gone when he turned back to Vance. His delivery was easily normal, businesslike and sincere. "I'm awfully sorry I won't be able to join you tonight, but this damned meeting just can't be postponed. Still, I hope to get away and possibly arrive late. It shouldn't matter to a party of that sort. People seldom notice who's come and gone."

"We'll keep an eye out for you, Earnest."

"Do that. I appreciate you escorting Angela. She'd be heartbroken if she had to miss Alfred and Karen's party. And you certainly ought to attract attention in that outfit. Angie dearly loves attention. Thrives on it. Couldn't wear such a getup myself, of course. Wouldn't fit my personality." A strand of graying hair fell away from his head and hung over his ear, revealing a chalky streak of scalp. He combed the lick of hair back into place with fingers in a slow, old man's gesture. Another hole in the conversation stretched out lamely and Earnest Leighton fumbled awkwardly for his pocket watch, hauling it out and glancing at it too rapidly to read what time it said. "Damn it. Rude of me, but I've got to get going."

"I'll make do until Mrs. Leighton is ready to leave."

"Fine."

As if on cue, Modero appeared in the doorway holding Earnest's hat and walking stick. "Your carriage is ready, sir."

"Thank you, Modero. Take good care of Mr. Paxton here, please. See that he gets whatever he wants. I should be back sometime tonight." Earnest took the trappings from the butler and turned in the doorway to face the Texan once again. "Until later, Mr. Paxton?"

"Yes, later. Thanks for your hospitality and the use of your carriage."

"Yes. My carriage." An almost sinister or sickly clever smile flashed across Leighton's face. He turned and left quickly.

He knows why I'm here, Vance thought. Knows damn well. And it's almost as if he approves, even enjoys the idea of having another man mount his wife. Vance began to feel very tired of the city. He was weary of the intrigue, the clandestine debauchery hidden behind the venerable veneer of aristocracy and formal trappings of state. Worse yet, he was getting tired of himself, tired of the way he'd let the city influence him, slowly affect him, twist him to its inanimate will.

Modero re-entered, bowed, announced that Mrs. Leighton wished to speak with him in her sitting room and walked out again. Vance's immediate reaction was to leave immediately, to get as far away from Washington, from the teeming cities of the North, as soon as possible. The anger swelled in him. *Damn them. Damn them all.* He stalked out of the library to the hall, grabbed his hat from the rack and started out the front door, stopped only by a tiny noise from Modero. The butler stood partway up the stairs, waiting for him with a small, nearly invisible smile, more perhaps implied than expressed, frozen on his face.

What thoughts raced through Vance's head then? He didn't mind lying with Angie Leighton. Not in the slightest. She was an exciting woman. Her body was full, tough, responsive, ready to accept his slightest mood or whim, ready to reciprocate with unabashed sensuality. They had been together four times now and each time had been better.

74

Each time they had used the memory of the time and times before as they tortured each other with the secret touches, the secret caresses they knew would please beyond pleasure. But this was something different. They had met before in his hotel room. Old Grover knew, of course, and possibly others, but the liaisons were essentially private. Now he was involved in a group affair. Earnest Leighton certainly knew, must have given his blessing. Modero had to be in on it—why else the supercilious smirk? Why was Angie allowing this to happen? Was he a pawn in some political game played beyond his knowledge or skill? Or merely an instrument to fulfill the strange sexual desires of an effete class for which he had no liking? And what of the gala? Was he expected to play the hired stud, pleasure the man's wife and then lead her to a party where everyone would undoubtedly read the sleepy residue of passion so evident in Angie's eyes?

And what would Karen think? Karen! Would she care, really? A cold-hearted little bitch, one who'd play with a man, lead him on only to clamp her legs closed and leave him hanging, empty and seething. One who'd marry an Alfred Whitaker for money and prestige and power. Well, the hell with her, he thought angrily. By God, he'd swive the lady waiting for him upstairs, swive her well and to the hilt and parade her forth for all their fancy world to gape at. The rumor mill would spin dizzily, fueled by giggles and hushed asides, gasps and innuendos enough to last until the next scandal thankfully reared its exciting head, relieving them of the boredom of the past so soon sucked dry by countless wagging tongues. Miss Fancy Hampton would puff and swell with indignation, but 'twould serve her right. Give her some notion of what a real man was, even if only through the look in Angie's smouldering eyes.

The decision was made in seconds. He tossed the flop-brimmed hat on the stand. Modero smiled knowingly, turned and led the way into the dark at the top of the stairs. Only one area of the hall was illuminated and this was spillover glow from their destination, Angie Leighton's sitting room. "First damn time I had to have a damn butler show me the way," Vance muttered aloud.

"Sir?"

"Nothing."

Modero bowed and gestured Vance toward the door.

Vance moved with sure purpose and entered the room, one hand indicating to Modero he could leave. The door shut behind him softly.

A low chandelier lit the empty room evenly. A French dressing table with a marble top held scattered and sundry female accessories doubled by the mirror behind them. A deep leather chair to one side held a gown of red velvet. Two more mirrors. Three in all. He watched all three of him take a deep breath and savor the fragrant scent of a woman's perfume lingering in the air. Across the room a door led off and into what had to be her bedroom. Vance grinned determinedly. Angie Leighton waited in her den.

His coat slid from his shoulders, his soft buckskin boots from his feet. He shed his neckerchief, shirt and trousers, leaving all lie where they fell and strode naked across the room to the invitational door.

The soft yellow glow of a dim lamp highlighted his powerfully muscled form and gave him a god-like appearance. Like some larger than life statuary, a homage to what man once was and should be, his body was hard and lean, forged by fire, hammer and anvil, tempered in the boiling cauldron of time and empty space, left glowing with the slightest trace of copper, burned there by the sun. A primeval deity come to life. A man who had faced the elements, survived the rigors of a harsh pioneer upbringing and existence, and lived life to its fullest.

Angie lay on the bed. She was swathed in a shimmering gown of transparent silk. She gasped at the sight of the man her body hungered for and his latent animal sensuality swept over her, left her trembling with anticipation of the rapacious sexual feast to come. She unloosed the single bow holding the clinging silk across her breasts. It fell away as she lay back on the satin coverlet, her thighs, warm and inviting, parted beneath the sheer covering.

For a moment the two stared at each other, the mere sight of their naked bodies arousing them. No touch was needed between these two. Angie felt the throbbing ache awaken in her loins as the animal before her hardened, rose tumescent and pulsing to its full height. Her hand went down to sweep the remaining piece of silk from across her thighs, revealing the soft, moist lips so eager to be stroked, parted, entered and ravaged. Eyes burning and lips parted, she threw wide her arms to greet the carnal god as he approached. There would be no more waiting.

The sound of the party drifted upstairs, filtered down the hall and into her room. Karen sat alone, brooding over whether or not to return to the festivities. The evening had started off as well as could be expected. She swept down the stairs just at the right moment, paused near the bottom so those in the dining room could see her and managed to divert every eager male and jealous female eye in sight. Alfred ascended the stairs and escorted her the rest of the way down. He was totally enraptured by her beauty and after their first dance, allowed her to convince him they should put off the announcement of the wedding date until later in the evening when everyone had arrived. Business quickly intervened and they were soon separated, Karen to demurely accept compliments and return jealous barbs, Alfred to bask in the envious glow of his colleagues.

An hour passed and Karen found herself wandering the entire lower floor from dining room to reception room, from parlor to library, seeking the Texan. When she didn't find him she retreated up the stairs to the safety of her bedroom. *All right. I was looking for him. But only to let him see just who I am.* A tiny doubt assailed her. *Karen Hampton, of course. Soon to be Mrs. Alfred Randol Whitaker II. No. I shan't be! I'm Karen Hampton. I . . . I'm a fairy princess.* She swirled her skirts before the mirror. *Oh, I'll show him. But why isn't he here? Texans are so rude. He said he'd be here.*

A knock sounded on the door. "Who is it?"

"It's me, honey. . . ."

"Come in, Retta."

The black woman entered and sat down on a nearby chair, fanning herself violently with her hand. "All dem people, all dem purty dressed people and none of dem can hold a candle to my baby. And where is my little girl? She up here by herself so's no one can see her."

"I was just tired, Retta. That's all. All those people get so boring at times. They all talk about the same things, even dress the same, when all's said and done. It's no fun anymore."

"Well now, Missy Hampton, I don't know how's you can say dat. Sit up. Lemme check yo' hair." She reached over and dabbed at a tiny blossom. "No, suh. I can't see dat at all," she said grinning, taking her time with the news she knew Karen wanted to hear. "You should see dat fella jus' made his entrance. Oo-whee, my oh my. Big as sin and twice as purty. Dressed like I never seed in dese here parts."

Karen jumped off the bed and ran out of the room, leaving a laughing Retta behind. The bright lights and chatter from below stopped her at the top of the stairs. *Calm down. Compose yourself. The barbarian must be shown a regal princess, not a rushing silly girl tripping over her own skirts.* Head high, she descended haughtily. She was halfway down when she stopped abruptly. He was there, his presence a certainty beyond proof of sight. She turned automatically to where she knew he stood, eyes drawn to him of their own volition.

Vance knew she was looking at him. The sure knowledge of her presence behind him interrupted the conversation he was having with Edward Fox, a large burly lumber and mining man from the Montana Territory. Fox, an old friend of Barrett back East on business, was saying something important but Vance heard not a word, for all sound was blocked out by the sudden roaring noise in his head. She was there, incontrovertibly there, and he turned automatically, his muscles taught by some unconscious force. Vance Paxton, knowing the truth now, looked up to meet the gaze of the princess on the stairway.

For the first time in his life he was totally surprised. She was heartbreakingly beautiful. More beautiful than he remembered. A radiant sunburst in a city choked with darkness he felt had cast its shadow over even him. Purity she was, obviously worth far and above more than all the others pressing around him. In the island universe formed by their looks, he bowed to her, bowed deeply in deference to her beauty, her worth, her very person.

Karen's face went cold and she felt her heart turn bitter as brine, for from behind Vance's muscular shoulders Angie Leighton's eyes burned up toward her, oh so catty, ominous and daring. Karen steeled herself against any display of surprise, any indication of perturbation. Instead she forced herself to look nonchalantly away from them and continued down the stairs as if nothing had happened, smiling and calling gaily to the first person she saw.

Vance disengaged himself from Angie as the Hampton lovely made her way across the hall. He intercepted her before she could escape into the ballroom. Karen feigned surprise. "Why, Mr. Paxton. We had assumed you weren't coming. I'm delighted you were able to join our festivities, even if tardily."

"I'm sorry I'm late," he answered, his tongue slow and awkward. "You are more beautiful than I had remembered."

"You flatter me unnecessarily, sir." She tried to sound bright and gay but somehow knew the words hadn't come out that way.

Angie hurried up and re-attached herself possessively to Vance's arm. He appeared embarrassed, almost sorry she was there yet obligated to put a good face on the situation. "You know Mrs. Leighton, of course."

"Of course," Angie broke in, her voice sultry and confident. "Earnest was terribly sorry he couldn't make it. Mr. Paxton was good enough to escort me."

"Yes, I see. I'm sorry Earnest was busy." Something was dreadfully wrong. The world was rushing at her too fast. Events piled pell-mell on each other, surrounding her in a confusing welter beyond comprehension. Her head whirled giddily and she felt faint, but had to make the effort. "I'm afraid I shall soon have to learn how to cope with being a congressman's wife myself. So often alone, bored and with little to do save grow another day older." Angie's face, bright and with a slight sheen of perspiration, swelled and shrunk in front of her like some monstrous, macabre mask.

"Ah, but one manages to amuse oneself if one tries hard enough," Angie smiled, teeth and lips bloated horribly out of proportion. Her voice echoed hollowly in Karen's ears, receding as if the speaker were falling away, away. . . .

"I'm afraid I would find such a frantic search rather tiring," Karen returned, functioning now on instinct and training alone. "It must, after all, become more and more difficult as time goes on."

Angie's smile froze momentarily, froze in a hideous parody of courtesy and friendliness. Karen tried to go on but couldn't. Angie was speaking, a delightfully camouflaged malicious retaliation, no doubt, but Karen couldn't hear her any more. The thunder of a thousand waterfalls filled her ears, blotting out all intelligible sound. Suddenly the

79

entire exercise seemed petty and paltry, unimportant in the extreme. But why were his eyes so blue? To match the blue of Texas skies? To mimic the cool sweet depths of a hidden, secret pool where lovers were wont to meet?

"I'm sorry, but you'll have to excuse me," Karen managed in a breaking voice. She turned and broke away from them, skirts swirling in a flurry of blues and whites, traces of shocking pink. The garden lay only yards away through the dining room and French doors. There she would find fresh air, air she could breathe without choking, without crying out in rage or fainting.

A whirlwind of flower petals gusting across a garden, Vance thought as he watched her disappear among the crowd choking the entire downstairs and spilling out onto the yard. He felt like a sheepish school boy caught with his hand in the cookie jar. The conversation had flowed around him too rapidly for his muddled state of mind. He had understood little, so intent had he been on watching Karen. That the two women had been throwing barbs at each other he had no doubt. But neither did he really care. He was more concerned with what he felt, what he finally knew he should have known, should have admitted to himself, days ago. He dredged his memory. . . .

He was eleven and his little boy's heart quivered and shook at the sight of Jo Leann. Jo-Jo attended the same prairie school house as he, and he could still remember her richly freckled face and flame-colored hair. After an initial period of pigtail-dunking and placing horny toads on her bonnet, the two grew quite close and even made plans as children will. She was an innocent, sweet child and would have grown to womanly beauty had she not died of cholera. Her oak board grave marker was inscribed "Jo Leann Parker. Age 13. Our little girl is with the Angels." Vance could remember reading the words over and over again, wondering, trying to understand why they had to be there, trying and failing. Even as a man of thirty he could not understand. . . .

He passed his hand across his face, rubbing his eyes in the manner of one who has just awakened from a deep sleep. He looked about. Angie had led him into the dining room just as the little orchestra broke into a slow waltz. Several couples took to the floor around them. Angie was immediately surrounded by a trio of young dandies who vied for her attention. She giggled flirtatiously and countered their ribald remarks with more of her own. Vance backed off a few paces. Whatever spell the seductress had woven over him, it was over now, dissipated, no more binding than a dream from which one awakens and leaves behind in the clear morning light. Vance dodged a number of swaying, spinning dancers and crossed the dance floor, searching for Karen amid the throng. She wasn't dancing. She wasn't at the banquet table. He stood there, suddenly ravenously hungry but not caring what he ate. Piles of neatly stacked sandwiches, slabs of meat and bowls brimful of punch held his attention only long enough for him to quiet the growling in the pit of his stomach. And still no Karen. He wandered from the table.

He found Alfred standing in the center of a large group of congressmen and holding forth on some legal point or other, vehemently disputing each of his colleagues' opinions, basking in the light of their approval. Vance, his face wrapped in a puzzled frown, turned away from the self-impressed knot of men and surveyed the entire room. She wasn't there. Had she been, he would have found her. There was no way she could help but stand out in the middle of such a crowd of bland faces. The frown was displaced by a look of determination. He would search the house. And he would find her. Ignoring the reactions of the dancers he bumped into, unaware even of their existence and totally indifferent to their irritated grumbling, he started for the first open door he saw.

Karen walked the length of the garden and crossed the spring-fed pond on a line of stepping stones. She paused beneath a wisteria arbor to breathe the silent, fragrant air and clear her muddled thoughts. A laugh broke through the night air to break her concentration and she moved yet farther away from the noisome party until the empty stillness of the garden reduced the sounds to a barely audible undercurrent. Without realizing it she had come to the final border of lilac trees separating the garden from the meadow, across which lay the ruins of the old blockhouse and crumbled Duelling Wall. In the night the pinks and lavender blooms of lilac were mere dark patches against the limbs. Those that bloomed white turned silver in the pale light of the sliver of moon left to the sky. The sky itself was as clear as a city sky could be in spring, crowded with stars that disappeared near the horizon where the glow of man-made lights overwhelmed them.

Everything had gone wrong. Karen felt tired. So tired. There were just too many people, too many mouths, too many faces, too much to do in too little time. She hadn't been able to convince Barrett she didn't want to go through with the wedding, hadn't been able to make him listen to her when she tried to talk to him. Her mother was even more difficult. Committed body and soul to a social coup, she worked from dawn to midnight, making herself unavailable most of the time, chattering incessant inanities the few moments they did manage together and never imagining for a moment—because it never occurred to her to imagine—Karen could possibly be anything less than ecstatic. Alfred had been totally impossible. His goal achieved, all timidity fled. The Alfred she was used to seeing at work as a politician replaced the bumbling, awkward schoolboy who courted her. This . . . obnoxious Alfred was so busy strutting about feeling smug and complacent, spent so much time acting as if he were already married, she hadn't even seen him except in the presence of two or three others. There was no possible way to discuss postponing a wedding under those circumstances.

All the noise, all the fuss, all the lonesomeness in the midst of all the people left Karen confused and disoriented. A pawn in a game she didn't want to play but had to play because she was in the game by breeding, birth and custom. Only Retta would listen to her, but Retta didn't count. Beyond the confusion was a further factor of shock. Karen couldn't quite bring herself to believe she would soon belong to Alfred, belong to him alone, be his to do with as he pleased. If only she loved him, she thought over and over again. But no. She had tried but couldn't. And she would consequently wed and bed and gradually grow chilled and contemptuous, ambitious and frustrated like her mother. Perhaps even become another Angie Leighton, weaving spells to capture man after man with the promise of illicit sexual titillation with the wife of a powerful man, wantonly reaping a harvest of lust and deceit, and forever and forever unfulfilled.

She stared out across the moonlit meadow. If she looked

long enough she could make out the blockhouse against the darker outline of trees beyond. She thought back on that moment less than two weeks ago, relived each breathless, daring second. So long ago, so many ages past. The pressure of his lips. The naughty eager way her body responded to his touch. *That's what love should be like . . . love? . . . Oh, my . . . no!* . . . The thought struck her like a thunderbolt. Her heart was suddenly full, nearly bursting with excitement beyond bounds. Surely she didn't . . . couldn't . . . be in love with him? Not him. Why, she wasn't even . . . wasn't anything like the people who. . . . Her hands went to her face, fingers white-tipped against her temples to press the notion away. But it was useless to try. Tears welled, crested and ran scalding down her cheeks.

"Karen."

She spun about, stifling a scream. He stood in the open, legs slightly apart, tall and wide in the dim light. His hat was held in his left hand and a slight breeze stirred the shock of brown hair, blew it back away from his moonlit, sculptured face.

"I've been looking for you everywhere." His voice was soft and rich with resonant strength, softer for the slight accent, a slight twang reminiscent of sultry nights under open skies. He seemed so less frightening to her now, but she trembled all the same as he walked toward her. His hand reached out and touched her cheek tentatively, tenderly. *Almost as if he can't believe it either.*

Suddenly she was in his arms. His kisses traced a searing path along her neck and his body pressed hungrily against hers. Their lips unerringly sought each other's as Vance and Karen lost themselves in the love which had waited so long it had to explode when finally realized and admitted. Vance lifted her off her feet and held her in his arms. She buried her face in his neck, clung to him tightly as the man she had searched for all her life carried her a few steps past the top of a small hillock which promised to block their view of the house. He sank to his knees and laid her gently on the grass, easing down beside her, his lips once again seeking, finding, provocatively enticing. The heady scent of lilac mingled with that of clover from the meadow below them and the crushed grass underneath them.

"Karen . . . Karen. . . ." Her name floated in the nebulous void, an impression thought but not spoken.

Vance rose to his knees. "They're calling you. We'd better go back."

"Karen . . . Karen. . . ."

"I thought it was you. Saying my name in your mind."

Vance smiled gently. "Your father. And Alfred. They'll . . ."

"Please. I don't want to go back."

"Are you sure?"

"Yes," she nodded, more sure of herself than ever before in her life.

"They'll be worried."

"Only for themselves. Not for me."

Vance looked down at her, studied her flawless face and flashing emerald eyes lit with fires of a dare taken, a decision made, a love found.

"Mr. Paxton. I had thought a true Texan would be more bold," Karen said, her voice pitched just above a whisper, gently mocking as she brushed, then touched more boldly his chin.

Vance grinned, sinking down again beside her. "Ma'am, when the situation calls for boldness, you'll find a Texan more than happy to oblige."

Her fingers touched the amulet hanging at his neck. The gold glinted, like his eyes, in the moonlight. A tree and brambles. A singular configuration. "And so you find the Washington ladies scandalously willing?" she asked.

"There's only one Washington lady and she's in my arms right now. Too pretty for Washington." He lay back, his arm under her back, holding her close. "A long time ago I can remember a story about a princess who lived in a castle in a deep forest. Because she was the most beautiful princess in the world, her father the King kept her there rather than let anyone see her. I never really believed she existed until I saw you that day in the Rotunda. Even then I found it hard to believe until I'd followed you all afternoon and finally got enough nerve to catch up with you there by the creek. The only time in my life a fairy tale came true." His eyes searched for hers, found them and wondered at their beauty. "Now the princess is here with me, and I find that hard to believe."

"Do you need convincing still"

"I don't know."

Karen eagerly met his kiss, her arms clasped tight around him. Her breasts swelled, strained against their cruel confines. She felt his hands against the small of her back. One strayed up to her bodice, fumbled there and loosed the catches at the back. Her breath came in heated spasms. A moan began deep within her and slowly rose to her throat, caught there unvoiced as she felt her breasts freed from the bodice. His hand stroked one nipple until it rose taut. He lowered his head to this sentinel of her desire, his tongue sliding across and around it, his lips nibbling, teasing unbearably, driving her mad with frenzy. Part of her dress had been pushed aside and only a thin petticoat separated the smooth skin of her leg from the pressure of his manhood straining to be loose from its own constraint. She could feel it throbbing with a will of its own as he shifted his weight to bring the prisoned organ in closer contact with her thigh, then higher and higher, seeking its ultimate goal, held back by so little, touching her now through the light fabric where no man had touched her before.

A tide of sexual exultation swept over her, swept over them both, leading them toward an inevitable inundation of uncontrollable passion. She wanted to yield, wanted to strip the last vestiges of restraint from her mind and body and be carried away on the flood, yet she resisted. This was her father's garden. This was a man she hardly knew. *But I want to know him. I want to know everything about the man to whom I shall give my maidenhood.* And while she had not said these words aloud it was as if Vance understood, heard her thoughts and relented from leading her past a point both of them might regret. His kisses became more subdued, less arousing yet comforting and deliciously gentle. Vance understood how she felt. She knew it. *This is the way love has to be, each knowing the other's thoughts. He knows I want him as much as he wants me.*

"I can wait, Miss Hampton," he said softly. "When it's the right time, both of us will know. And then there won't have to be any holding back. When I can have all of you, heart and mind and body. I can wait, my love."

She drew his face to her lips, kissing him tenderly. His words echoed in the very fiber of her being. "My love, my love, my love. . . ."

85

Time passes. The merest fleeting second in continual progression miraculously becomes a moment, becomes an hour and then two. Such is the timelessness of love ever and anon. The world spins for itself, not for man nor woman. Distant and remote; the stars signal each other with a myriad dancing flames from across the stygian void, their secrets unshared with an audience that loves and weeps and lives beneath their fragile glow.

A sparkle against an infinity of shadow and vacuum. A song in the face of immortal quiet and hollow peace. A shifting yet immutable tale whispered on the breath of ages by uncountable numbers of hearts and minds.

Karen awoke abruptly. Warm and soothed, his shoulder her pillow, she had fallen asleep in Vance's arms. He was breathing quietly, also asleep she thought. His moustache tickled her cheek. Everything was so still. *This is happiness. Serenity and quietude.* But something had caused her to wake so suddenly. She listened, heard nothing, sighed aloud. Whatever had bothered her certainly wasn't there now. And what possible threat could exist within the tranquil borders of her father's garden? The world was indeed as it should be. The grounds were still and peaceful, the house dark and quiet. Karen bolted upright. "Oh, my! Vance!"

The Texan had not been asleep, but rather lying as quietly as possible in order not to disturb her. Still, her outburst brought him almost to his feet. "What is it?"

"Oh, Vance, the party's over. Papa will be furious. And Alfred . . . oh . . . everyone. What shall we do?"

"Well, I guess we'd better start by getting you home. I imagine they'll be worried."

Karen scrambled to her feet, awkwardly hooked the catches on the back of her bodice and brushed the twigs and lilac blossoms from her gown. "Worried, but not for me. For themselves. I wonder what happened. If Alfred announced . . . but surely not without me there. He would have been too embarrassed. He must have been . . . after bragging to all his friends. Oh, God, he'll kill me!"

Vance's eyes narrowed ominously. "I don't reckon he'd better try," he said coldly, his words chillingly hard and brittle.

Karen laughed. "Oh, silly. I don't mean really." She took Vance's hand and the two started toward the house.

"Karen, you're . . . you're not going to go through with that thing, are you? I mean with Alfred?"

Vance's question stopped Karen in mid-stride. She turned to him, her eyes glinting with amusement as Vance stumbled over his words. "Why, Mr. Paxton, are you so timid at last? Whatever does it matter whom I wed?"

Vance ran his fingers through his long hair, pausing to scratch his head, wincing at her words. Finally he shook his head and gave a low, throaty chuckle. "Ma'am, I know Mr. Whitaker has a lot of money and a real good background. In fact, he'd probably make some girl a real nice husband. But not you."

"Aren't you being presumptuous, Mr. Paxton?"

Vance suddenly reached out and drew her close to him. He leaned down to kiss her, his tongue parting her lips, darting inside her eager mouth. When he broke away she was breathing heavily, aroused by the ardor of the kiss. "I'm being me, Miss Hampton."

Karen snuggled to his chest, holding on to him until the whirring in her head stopped. "Vance, what shall we do?"

"First of all I'd better get you inside. We can meet tomorrow. I want to tell you about Texas. I want you to know something about it before I ask you to go there with me. Can you be at the Duelling Wall? Say the middle of the morning?"

"I'll be there." She looked up at him, eyes glowing in happiness. "I'll be there, my love."

"Miss Karen? Honey, is dat you?" Retta called *sotto voce* from the back of the house.

Karen jumped, frightened. Vance whirled in a deadly crouching blur. "Who's that?" he whispered, ready to spring at the slightest indication of danger to Karen.

Karen heaved a sigh of relief. "Retta. My maid. Don't worry about her." She called softly into the night, matching Retta's delivery. "Over here, Retta. By the gazebo."

It took but a moment for the dusky figure to appear from the direction of the house. Karen ran to her, embracing her happily. The black woman held her tightly, glaring at Vance over her shoulder. "You all right, honey?" she asked, menace clouding her voice.

"Oh, Retta. I'm fine. I'm finer than I've ever been in all my life."

The black woman held her at arm's length, peering intently into her face. "Well, I'm glad *you* is fine, 'cause nobody else in dis whole house is. Dey's madder'n hornets dat had a rock chunked at 'em. Lawdy, yore papa's gonna tan yore hide de minute he see you. I doan know what you been up to, an' I doan care, but if you is gonna face Mistah Hampton, it better be in de mornin', 'cause right now he's got the conniptions and de meanest fit I ever seed. Now come in heah an' git up to bed. I'll go in 'fore too long and tell him you done ben in de bed fo' some time, dat you was asleep on de couch in yo' dressin' room an' I didn't see you. Dat way he'll go on to bed an' sleep some a' dat bad temper off."

Vance shrugged his shoulders. "I don't mind facing him now, if you think I should."

Karen shuddered at the thought. "It's best we do it Retta's way. She can handle Papa tonight and I can in the morning. We're used to him."

"But. . . ."

"Don't worry. He'll rant and rave but it will be nothing I haven't seen before. Please. I'll meet you tomorrow. We'll talk then."

Vance nodded, kissed her again, then disappeared around the corner of the house. Karen turned to the grinning black woman. "Well," she said a little self-consciously, "are you ready or are we just going to stand here?"

Retta shook her head and laughed low and quietly. "Honey, yo' eyes is lahk a book fo' ol' Retta to read. Lawdy, dis ol' black woman seein' her little girl fell plumb in love. An' ain't you de lucky one! Ooo-wee!" She grasped Karen by the arms and gazed long and fondly at her, then abruptly enfolded her in the great black arms, rocking her slowly. "Honey," she said tenderly, "I'se glad for you. I'se glad and I'se sad an' I feels lak cryin' but I ain't goin' to."

Karen hugged the old woman who had raised her. More mother than servant, more friend than anything else. She looked up into the dark kind eyes. "I'm glad too, Retta. I'm very, very glad," she whispered.

The two women gazed a moment longer until Retta suddenly grinned hugely and looked about. "Sho' . . . here I is talkin' an' you standin' out here in de chill. You follow me now, girl, an' be quiet whiles I gets you past yo' daddy." She took Karen's hand and led her through the dark to the back door and into the kitchen, still swimming with sweet, pleasant odors from the party. The night lantern by the sink glowed eerily in the dark, casting huge shadows of pots and pans on the front wall from where they hung over the table in the middle of the room. Copper and brass gleamed in the feeble light, cast their reflected glow on the huge iron pots black with the soot of a thousand fires. Retta led Karen unerringly through the piles of litter on the floor, led to the hall doorway. At the door she turned and put her finger to her lips, peeked out to check the hall and motioned for Karen to follow. The two women crossed the hall carefully. Karen kept away from the glow coming from the library door, ajar and obviously open to afford Barrett an immediate view and entry out of the smoke-filled room. They rounded the ornate newel post, stepping over more litter piled in random stacks and ready to be taken out early in the morning. Seconds later they were up the stairs and safely in her room where they could move freely and relax. Retta helped Karen undress.

"Where you been to all dis time?" she whispered hoarsely.

"In the garden by the meadow."

"Din' you hear 'em callin'?"

"Yes."

"Honey," Retta stopped suddenly, staring into Karen's eyes. "You din' . . . well, I means, you ain't gone and . . ."

Karen giggled. "No." Retta sighed with relief. Karen hurried on. "Oh, Retta, I wanted to. I wanted to so badly but we didn't. I'm in love, Retta. Really in love. It's as wonderful as I thought it would be."

Retta hung the rumpled gown on a hanger to be put away. "Honey, you sho' gets yo' timin' mixed up all which a way. Sweet baby Jesus, Lawd a mercy, you sure a messy little girl. Imagine, fallin' in love wid a big strappin' boy lahk dat an' on de nite you is announcin' yo' weddin' to Mistah Whitaker. Dat is de spice which takes de cake. Pore Mistah Hampton doan even know half of de reasons why he so upset. I ain't gonna be de one to tell him, neither. No, suh, missy. Not me."

Retta closed the door to the armoir and turned back to

Karen. The girl was already in bed. The black woman stood by her a moment, grinning conspiratorially at her. A work-hardened hand reached down and stroked the golden curls lying on the pillow. "You sleep purty tonight, honey. I'll make yo' daddy glad enuf you is safe and sound he gonna keep away from you till de mornin'." The black woman turned down the lamp and started out of the room.

"Retta?" Karen called softly.

"Yes, honey," she answered, looking back.

"Will you kiss me goodnight like when I was a little girl?"

Retta stood unmoving while the tears welled in her eyes in spite of the clenched smile on her face. She finally moved back to the side of the bed and leaned down to kiss the forehead of the little girl she remembered and would never, never forget. "Good night, princess," she whispered huskily.

"Good night, Retta."

The black woman stood, her eyes focused blindly somewhere in the past as she walked to the door and out.

Ten minutes later Karen heard Barrett come up the stairs and pause outside her door. She rolled over and feigned sleep, but the footsteps went on and she was left alone. But sleep, chased by a thousand images of Vance, wouldn't come. She rose from the bed, finally, washed her face in the cool water in the basin, stripped the chemise from her and climbed back in bed. The sheets felt cool against her still burning skin, cool and delicious. Suddenly she was tired and yawned mightily. Her life had changed this night. She knew it well and good. She dreamt a girlish dream. Of sleepy fairylands and radiant princes and damsels rescued from their fathers' castles. . . .

Love was with her.

CHAPTER VI

The morning storm broke furiously within the Hampton house. Karen started from a deep and dreamless sleep to hear the pounding of a fist on her door. A moment of confusion and disorientation ended abruptly as the pounding stopped and Barrett's voice boomed through the panelling. "Karen! You will see me in the library, young woman. You will be there in fifteen minutes and not a second later." Karen listened as his loud deliberate footsteps receded from the door. The storm would be violent. But brief, she hoped. She sighed in relief. The waiting was the worst part. Now it would be over.

She sat up in bed, turned about and hung her legs over the side, her feet searching for her slippers. She was naked, having slept sans gown. Her hands crisscrossed and she hugged her shoulders, yawning sleepily. Suddenly the memory of the night before leaped full-blown in her mind, vividly in focus, nearly palpable. She lay back on the bed, relishing the newly discovered sense of direction to her life, the contentment of resolution in place of a vague and ambiguous limbo in which she had heretofore merely existed. Vance Paxton. She loved him. Yes, admitted it freely now. A fleeting image of Angie Leighton crossed her mind. She frowned. So he had been Angie's escort. An unwilled image of Angie's smouldering eyes taunted her, but she quickly forced it from her. *At least he didn't leave with her. Nor will he ever again. I'll see to that.*

Vance was so unlike anyone Karen had ever met. Strong yet gentle. Powerful yet considerate. Masculine without being overbearing. The perfect mate. And the Texan felt the same way about her. Hadn't he said she was the only woman in Washington? Hadn't he almost proposed to her? She had wanted him to take her, yet had been so afraid at the same time. She had never given herself to any man,

91

never even let any man touch her where he had, much less with . . . but when the time was right she knew there would be no holding back. She tried to imagine what it would finally be like. She had never seen a man undressed, knew only vaguely what he must look like, what he might feel like. Inside her . . . inside her . . . how big was a man when he . . . how deep would he go? Would he hurt her? Would he simply use her, take her for pleasure as men were said to do, then discard her, soiled and tainted?

She rejected the thought. The fact he had controlled himself, respected her virtue, wasn't that ample demonstration of his love? She rose quickly from the bed and found a dressing gown, slipped into it, stepped to the dresser and brushed her hair until it hung in soft curling waves covering the twin mounds of her breasts. It was time. She smiled boldly at herself in the mirror, left the room and headed downstairs.

The library smelled of cigar smoke already. Barrett Hampton sat behind his broad desk, cigar firmly clamped between clenched teeth. Ross, impeccable as ever despite the earliness of the hour, held the door for her before carrying a cup of coffee on a tray to the desk. "Will that be all, sir?"

"Yeah. Get the hell out of here," Barrett mumbled angrily.

"Will Miss Hampton. . . ?"

"No. I said get the hell out."

"Yes, sir." Ross paid no attention to his employer's mood, merely took all in stride and vanished as silently as he had appeared.

Karen stood mute and unmoving before Barrett's unwavering stare. He blew a cloud of blue-gray smoke into the air, bringing the coffee cup to his lips as soon as the cigar left his mouth, draining the entire cup without taking his eyes from her. Karen returned his stare, grateful for inheriting that one quality from him. Nothing was said. Father and daughter locked in a contest of the eyes, each trying to wear the other down, neither successful.

Barrett certainly looked his fiercest. Karen decided she might as well make the first move and start him off. The longer she waited the more the pressure would build and the more difficult her father would be. "The doctor said cigars and coffee in the morning are bad for your health, Papa."

92

"The hell with my health. I have a daughter who is bad for my health. I want to hear where you were and who you were with. And I hope to hell it was just one, or have you taken to it like a mare in heat, servicing all the studs who come around?"

Karen's face drained. Somehow she managed to find the strength to control herself. "That is a vile, horrible accusation, Father, a base canard devised by an evil, degenerate mind. You have no right to speak that way."

"I have every right. Your actions of last night give me every right. Can you imagine how embarrassing it is to give a party announcing the wedding date of your own daughter and not be able to find that daughter, not be able to announce anything? To have Alfred so insulted he leaves without so much as a good evening, stalking out in a rage and slamming the door behind him in full view of over a hundred delighted guests? The humiliation to your mother after spending so much time and energy in an attempt to make this the most talked-of party in Washington? Talked-of . . . ? Laughing stock is more like it."

"That's the trouble, Father. Your party. Mother's party. Alfred's party. What the wedding means to you, to Mother, to Afred. What about me? Why hasn't someone asked me, 'Do you want a party, Karen?' Or 'Do you love Alfred, Karen? Do you want to marry him?' No one has asked me at all."

Barrett erupted, rising to his feet so fast he sent his chair crashing back against the bookcase. His face turned crimson, his sideburns stood almost straight out from his head. He did not look funny. "Just what the hell are you trying to say?" he asked in a voice low and horribly calm, like the eye of a hurricane.

"What I have been trying to tell you for weeks, Father. That I do not love Alfred Whitaker, that I will not marry him, not for the advancement of your all-consuming financial empire nor Mother's precious social aspirations. And as far as *your* party is concerned, I left it. I was with Vance Paxton in the garden."

The outburst surprised even her. But it was said now and so much the better. Barrett spoke not a word. He crossed around the desk and stood before his daughter, staring intently into her eyes, his face blotched with fury, hands trembling uncontrollably. Without warning one hand

93

lashed out and slapped her across the jaw and cheek. The impact spun her around, knocked her against the globe in the corner and sent her reeling into the bookcase. She staggered wildly trying to regain her balance and managed to whirl around facing him in expectation of another attack. The violent movement was so sudden her gown fell open as she crouched like a devil at bay, her breath hissing from between clenched teeth, her eyes blazing.

Barrett glared at her, panting with fury. "Slut!"

"Slut!?" Karen spit back. Her voice was low, barely audible in the heavy silence. "Is that how you see your daughter? As a slut?" The two faced each other in timeless attitudes of belligerence until Karen straightened herself, stood regally, boldly before him, her gown falling away to her sides to reveal her naked body, the perfect breasts rising and falling slowly, the thick light brown patch of pubic hair exposed between finely sculpted thighs. "Do I look like a *slut* to you?"

It had been a long time since Barrett had seen his daughter naked. Not since she was a little sandy-haired tomboy swimming in a New Hampshire stream. But this was no little girl. His eyes raked over her and he was unable to stop them. Karen watched her father's line of vision and made no attempt to cover herself. Contemptuously aware of the power her body could wield over a man, any man, even her father, she stood still as a statue blatantly displayed to he who should not look. Barrett, his momentum shattered, suddenly aware of his licentious reaction, staggered back, shocked by his obvious and less than fatherly interest in his daughter's body. He coughed drily and turned away, his face ashen. Karen slowly fastened the gown again. "I'm decent now. You may hit me again if you like."

Barrett Hampton stood before the window, staring out at the scattered, white-bellied cumulus clouds. It would be a nice day, clear and warm. To the east, under the rising sun, Washington began its blighted sprawl, each year uglier and more pronounced in contrast to the still safe, still beautiful Georgetown. The unfinished skeleton of the monument for President Washington stood out in stark, geometric relief against the white clapboard sides of a cheap, soon-to-be-torn-down hotel. The government was full of damned fools who knew only how to waste funds better earmarked for trade and commerce. But all to no avail. A nation of monument builders. He scowled. Try and spend a monument, he told them. Try to pay your bills with a damnable monument. The nation was heading for a depression and all those idiots on Capitol Hill could find to do was siphon off funds for another monument. Deficit. A man can't run his house on a deficit. A business can't run on a deficit. A people can't run a nation on a deficit. The economy needed a boost, not another monument. New markets must be developed, new avenues of trade. This was the first year his corporate figures had dropped. His corporation . . . an empire he had built with his own two hands, with his own sweat and blood, scrambling, pushing, pulling with all the daring, knowledge and relentless ambition he could dredge up from the innermost corners of his soul. . . .

Too much was at stake. He had to expand or sink. The Whitakers' influence was now the key to expansion, especially in Europe. If Karen didn't marry Alfred, he, Barrett Hampton, would be labelled a fool, unable to control his family, therefore suspect in business. If the wedding were called off it would be a direct slap in Alfred Whitaker Sr.'s face and doors would consequently slam in Barrett Hampton's face. What might have been easy would become close to impossible. The marriage was vital. The two families must be joined. He felt the achievements of twenty years' dogged determination slipping uncontrollably away, floundering in spite of all effort. He was losing ground while his own daughter looked callously on, the lifeline in her hands and refusing to throw it. He mustered his forces to bring himself under control and brought as much parental inflection to his words as he could bring to bear. "Karen. I apologize for striking you. I know you are a woman who likes to feel she has a will of her own. Very well. I can understand that. But this is the real world, a world forged and run by men and women who see their duty, understand it quite clearly and hew to it no matter what may fall. You are a member of a considerably wealthy, powerful family, a woman destined to be a member of an even wealthier, more powerful family. As such, you have, as have I, an obligation not lightly dismissed. I do not resent you falling in love with this Paxton fellow. He is a handsome enough man, I suppose, and—as much as I hate saying so to my own daughter—undoubtedly considerably attractive physically. Such infatuations are more common than any of us wish to acknowledge. They are to be expected—permitted even—as long as you do not become emotionally involved, as long as you conduct such affairs at the correct time and absolutely discreetly." He paused, wiped his forehead with his handkerchief.

"But last night you did neither, and in the process embarrassed everyone concerned. I hope it is not too late. I am to meet with Alfred and his father at ten o'clock this morning. At that meeting I will tell them you were under great pressure from your mother and I, have been feeling ill—I will hint of female trouble and the moon, no doubt— and, as Retta lied to me last night, fell asleep in your dressing room. This afternoon, I trust and expect, you will meet with Alfred privately and apologize. You will do so graciously and sincerely. Once he has accepted your apology, and I have every reason to expect he will, you will make plans to be married at an early date. You *will* marry Alfred Randol Whitaker. Is that understood?"

Karen did not reply.

"Is that understood?" he repeated, turning to add the emphasis of his sternest countenance to the question that was more a command.

The room was empty. The door open, the hall outside was devoid of life. Listening intently he heard the faint echo of her footsteps in the hallway above. He strode to the bottom of the stairs and bellowed, "You *will* marry Alfred Whitaker." Upstairs, a door slammed in belligerent punctuation to his fiery command.

To Vance's way of thinking, mid-morning meant eight o'clock. But he figured adding another couple of hours would be more like mid-morning for city folks. Still, just to be on the safe side, he arrived at nine, hobbled his horse at the edge of the creek below and walked to the blockhouse to spend whatever time need be dozing in the shadow of the wall covered with the thick stand of blackberries. Hidden from all but the birds and the countless insects, he bided his time patiently, confident she would appear.

It was almost eleven when he saw Karen's distant figure the length of the meadow away. She was running lightly, her radiant gold hair flowing loose behind her like spun sunshine, her white dress pressed against her legs to reveal the perfect form of which he was so enamored. Vance tensed imperceptibly, sensing the constriction of his heart and the renewed tingle of his flesh. He would remember this image of her always, come what may. Karen of the meadow. Karen of the flowering fields. Karen of the tall and wavering pale green and purple thistles, stirred by the wake of her passage.

She rounded the wall and within seconds was in his arms, the short hours of separation, so long for new lovers, finally ended. Vance held her tightly, thirstily kissing her until she winced in pain. His brows knotted in concern and anger. "You're hurt. What happened?"

"Father and I had our little talk early this morning. I'm afraid it got a trifle difficult, physically speaking."

"That son of a. . . ."

"No, Vance," she interrupted. "He's my father. He's upset and disappointed. He doesn't understand what's happening. He feels as if he's losing control and he can't function unless he controls all he considers his. His business, Mother . . . me. I'm afraid what I said came as quite a shock to him."

"I should have been with you." Karen could feel his muscles tense and bunch under the linen shirt. His large bony hand clenched into a fist which he smashed down on the top of the wall.

Karen covered his hand with hers, held it gently until the clenched muscles relaxed, then raised it slowly until the fingers touched the purple bruise. "That *is* silly," she said with a conciliatory smile. "Physical retaliation would solve nothing. I hate to think what would have happened had you been there. No, it was better for me to face him alone. I understand him."

"I don't understand this," Vance said in reference to the bruise.

"The union of the Hamptons and the Whitakers is very important to my father. What I feel is unimportant. I'm merely a small piece in a large transaction. That I should have feelings is incomprehensible. That I should contradict his wishes is intolerable, and he . . . lost control of himself. He's never hit me before. Not even when I was a little girl. Of course, he wasn't around all that much. I feel sorry for him. And just a little afraid, but not very. He told me—bellowed at me, really—I was to stay in the house until he got home, so I had to wait until the carriage left before coming to meet you. I could hear Mother in her room. I think she was crying. I called to her but she wouldn't let me in."

Vance led her into the shadows of the blockhouse ruins where they might be hidden from view. Karen embraced him again, coming to him eagerly. She marveled at the change in herself, how she had recoiled from his touch such a short time ago, how she was now so wantonly pleased when he pulled her close and held her. Love would be sudden, she had known, and yet she was breathless with the realization of how quickly she had succumbed to the heady emotion. She giggled beneath his lightly caressing lips as they traced a teasing path across her forehead, down her unbruised cheek and along her neck. She twisted around and leaned back against him, held his hands clasped around her waist. "Tell me about Texas."

Vance chuckled aloud. "What would you like to know?"

"I don't know. Tell me everything."

"Miss Hampton, you have a lot to learn. Didn't you know can't any one person tell you everything about Texas? It's too big. Why, Texas is so big it would take two hundred men talking for a hundred years each to tell you everything there is to tell."

Karen squirmed teasingly against him, intensely aware of the immediate effect of her movement as she felt his manhood stiffen and press against her bottom. "Braggart. Tell me *anything*, then," she said, looking up at him.

Vance's whole body tensed. "You're making it awful hard . . . to even talk," he said between clenched teeth.

"I'm sorry," she said contritely, moving from him and sitting on the grass, trying not to giggle again. "I won't do that again."

"Well, I don't know as you shouldn't. Sort of enjoyed . . ."

"You said, sir," Karen interrupted with mock authority, "you would tell me about Texas."

"Yes, ma'am," he answered ruefully. Karen watched intently as he pulled at the corners of his moustache, first the left and then the right. She noticed he always repeated the gesture when thinking of a suitable response. "Well," he started, "from our ranch house, if you look to the north, you can see a line of low sandstone cliffs with a funny shape like a man lyin' on his back. Kind of purplish at sunset. Real pretty, too. We call them Sleeping Giant, from the Comanche. The Comanche believe the line of cliffs really is a giant. One of their gods. And one day he's gonna wake up and drive the whites out of Texas and stomp on all the forts and towns and anything else the whites built to mess up the land. Then there'll be a period of five years when life gets real good. The giant will lie back down again, but he'll only be dozing because the laughter of the people, the powwows and the drums will wake him up again and he'll decide it's time to dance the last war dance. He'll destroy everyone but the Comanche because they're the chosen people. Them he'll lead to his hogan where all the great chiefs from all the dim yesterdays feast and smoke their pipes.''

"That's wonderful," Karen said, her eyes wide and dreamy with visions of savages and thunderous gods. "What do you see to the south?"

"The valley. And past that, nothing."

"Nothing?"

"Nope. Nothing but prairie. Raw, lonely land with tall yellow grass waving in the breeze. Silent. Peaceful hillocks. A mesquite tree now and again. To the south it's mostly flat. Lots of wild flowers, though. Bluebonnets. Indian paint-brushes. Daisies. Cactus. Plenty of them.''

"Blue bonnets. Indian paint brushes. What nice names.''

"And to the west the land dries out. Gets rocky and mean. The farther west, the meaner it gets. The dirt turns red and sandy and it's hot. There's a mesa way off there. We call it the sit-a-spell mesa because it looks like a great big wide stool left there for someone to sit on and rest when they pass that way. And a stone needle pokes up at the sky a little bit away to the north. The sun sets right between them along about June and September. West is no place to pick flowers 'cept in the early spring when the cactus blooms, but it's a good place to find a thought or two. I ride it sometimes just to be alone, but it doesn't pay to go there often. The whole area is sacred to the Comanche.

"Now the east is different. What we call hill country. Actually the hill country sort of peters out there. Low rolling hills, lots of mesquite and oaks. Cottonwoods and gums. There's more water there it's greener. Better farm land than ranch land. San Antonio is back east, too. You'll like

San Antonio. People, music, dancing and fiestas—even our own brand of society for when you get lonely.

"I'm not going to tell you about the ranch, the hacienda. You have to see it yourself. When we ride out there we'll go by Horse Belly Creek and the bluff. Arrive about four in the afternoon when the sun hits it from behind and you can see the mesa outlined behind it. You'll see why I don't want to tell you about it. I guess it's the most beautiful place in the world."

Neither spoke for some minutes, rather listened to their own thoughts and the myriad bees and insects humming in the noonday sun. "It all sounds so marvelous," Karen finally said quietly. "Like visions in a dream. There's nothing like that here." She leaned on the wall, her back to Vance. The words came carefully, almost as if she was afraid to ask them, as if she still wasn't quite sure Vance meant to take her. "When are you going back?"

Vance moved to her, placed his hands on her shoulders and turned her around to face him. His eyes traveled the length of her body and stopped at hers. No longer was there a question. He was committed, body and soul. "That depends on you, Karen."

Karen found herself holding her breath. The tension was too great, the happiness too much for her, too much to handle seriously else she would break into tears. She spun coyly from the wall so she wouldn't have to look him in the eye. "Why, whatever do you mean, Mr. Paxton?"

"Plain and simple," he answered matter-of-factly from behind her. "I'm not leaving Washington without you." He swept her into his arms and she thrilled to the heat of his nearness, the rising ferment of her own passion. *"Love beckons, and one must go, for it will not tarry."* A line from one of Gabriel's sonnets. *How true, how terribly, wondrously true. One must go. Quickly. Quickly.*

"Then we'd better make plans soon, my darling," was all Karen said.

Karen floated across the meadow toward the garden and house. She felt weightless, light and ephemeral, her body translucent and glowing. The lilac border, fragrant perfume in the sun, streamed past to either side of her in pastel clusters of pink, white, lilac and green. The pool sent the friendly, smiling sky back to her from below, increasing the floating sensation. To her right an old gnarled cedar bestowed the wisdom of its years on her, bestowed its blessing. A wood duck exploded from the foliage in front of her and beat its sudden way past her to disappear beyond the lilacs, sobering her instantly, bringing her back to earth. *It's one of the last times I'll see the house from here. One of the last times. And then I'll be gone.*

The kitchen was hot and full of the smell of freshly-cooked pie. Ravenous after her rendezvous with Vance, Karen snitched a piece of crust and slowly nibbled at it as she walked from the kitchen toward the front hall. Retta's pie, she could tell. The black woman would have scolded her more from bemusement than anger had she been there to see her pie disfigured. As it was, Karen found the treat slightly less enjoyable without Retta's chidings. She pushed open the door to the hall.

Iantha was waiting for her, standing for all the world like a queen by the door to the front parlor. "Karen," she called imperiously, "may I speak with you for a moment, please."

Karen let the kitchen door swing closed behind her, stood quietly while she finished the piece of crust. Two women, mother and daughter, staring at each other from opposite ends of the hall, symbol of the greater distance between them. The last crumb gone, Karen impudently licked her fingers and moved up the hall to follow her mother into the parlor and wait in the doorway while Iantha primly seated herself in one of the high-backed chairs. The older woman dabbed at an eye from time to time lest Karen forget the indignity and pain she had caused.

"Hello, Mother," Karen said, her thoughts wandering to Vance, wondering where he was, where he went after leaving her in the meadow.

"Sit down please."

Karen sat. Perhaps he was preparing for their departure. *Our departure. Our departure.*

". . . and it was monstrously rude of you to disappear from your own party without saying a single word. After all, the evening was planned in your honor. Alfred was upset and I, for one, can't say I blame him."

"I'm sorry, Mother," Karen answered automatically, wondering how much of her mother's sentence she had missed. "I'm sorry if I've made you unhappy."

Iantha brightened. The prospect of a swift victory and a suitable act of contrition loomed as a distinct possibility. "Now, Karen. Your father has talked to Alfred and his father. He has sent word you won't even have to go there in person. A nice letter will do."

"What letter?"

"Why to Alfred, of course, apologizing and indicating you have been ill of late, repeating what your father told him and begging him to continue with the wedding plans."

Karen shuddered, took a deep breath. "I'll do nothing of the sort, Mother. Am I to grovel to him, give him something else about which he can strut and brag like a drummer boy home from the war? No indeed. Should he choose to pay a visit, I'll apologize for losing track of time. And I'll explain why I can't and won't marry him, but that's all," she finished, steeling herself for her mother's outburst.

Iantha paled. She sat upright, quivering with indignation. "I was told you and your father had settled . . ."

"We have, Mother, only he doesn't realize exactly *what* we settled because he no more listened to me this morning than he has at any other time in my life. I am getting married, as I told him, but not to Alfred."

Iantha stiffened, her voice cutting, mocking. "Surely you're not intending to start seeing that mindless French would-be poet again? I had thought you were quite over him. After all, a youthful romance is a youthful romance, but this is . . ."

Karen sprang to her feet, anger flashing from her eyes, her voice harsh with tension. "Mother. There never was a youthful romance with Gabriel. We were friends, nothing more. A shy boy and a shy girl who talked to each other because no one else would ever talk with us. Had you ever listened to me you would know there was no 'romance'."

"You needn't shout in my presence. We are in the same room." Iantha's voice was calm now, all pretense of tears gone behind a foreboding matriarchal mask. "Of course there has never been a romance. Why else would a silly girl flutter and giggle and carry on like a Fleet Street whore for every eligible male in two cities? Don't presume too much with your mother, Karen."

"I shall have to presume too much with my mother if she can't tell the difference between flirtation as an accepted, highly desirable mode of social behavior and 'romance,' as you put it, no doubt in stable imagery."

Iantha rose to her full height. "Sit down this instant and shut your foul mouth." Karen resisted for a moment, then gave way to the older woman's commanding presence and did as she was told. "Very well." Iantha continued, collecting herself. "I see the child I bore is now a woman. Aware, of course, as is a full-grown woman, of her own needs, her own desires. Not an unusual occurrence, I would think, since every woman has gone through the same process of growing up. However, if you wish to be treated as a grown woman, I suggest you put away your childish thoughts and dwell more on the obligations all of us have to ourselves and our parents." She stopped her pacing in front of a bouquet on the tea table, unconsciously started rearranging it. "It is," she continued in as worldly a tone as possible, "entirely natural for any high-spirited woman to have her little romances, but . . ."

"Mother," Karen interrupted, her voice strained, "I want you to listen to me for once in your life. I want you to try to understand. I *am* in love. Really in love."

"Of course you are, dear." The fingers pinched and plucked, rearranged the dying flowers. "Who is it this time?"

"Vance Paxton."

Iantha paused, one eye cocked, considering an out-of-place fern. She relaxed. Thank God, she thought, it was nothing serious. Another infatuation and purely physical at that. A final one, hopefully, if she had sunk so low as to pick the uncouth barbarian this Texan was said to be. And to think he had *wheedled* an invitation to the party. Thank God Alfred had his little peccadillos, too. At least he would understand . . . Karen was talking again.

". . . has been decided. Vance and I will be leaving. I'm going with him to Texas."

Iantha glanced understandingly at her daughter. "Karen, dear. Alfred won't wait forever. And there are plenty of girls who would just love to marry the Whitakers. So if you must have this final . . . fling . . . please be so kind as to conduct it discreetly. The sooner you patch things up with Alfred, the better for all of us. Perhaps I'll invite him over for dinner Tuesday night. You may even wear that daring bit of finery you had on the other night. . . ."

"Mother, stop it. Please stop it! I'm serious. I love Vance Paxton. I'm leaving with him for Texas within the next week or so. Why won't you listen to me?"

"Of course, dear," Iantha said knowingly, stepping back from the bouquet, arranged now to her total satisfaction. "Now don't you think you ought to write your letter to Alfred? Be sure to invite him for Tuesday night."

"Mother . . ." Karen started, the frustration almost too much to bear, "won't you please . . ."

"Karen. There is much to be arranged. Now run along. We haven't lost Alfred yet."

Karen stood and stalked from the parlor, left her mother still plotting, still trying to shape Karen's life. *Let her plot. Let her shape all she will. I will not be a bouquet to be arranged at the whim of others until I'm old and brittle and dry.* The girl-now-woman felt a sadness steal over her. They would never understand, not until her room was empty and she was gone from the house forever. *Oh, Papa, Mama, I said goodby to you today, goodby to you both, and neither of you heard.*

CHAPTER VII

The stream began its course with no thought of turning back. Eddies, swirling currents, foam-capped rocks with inverted v's trailing from their white heads, leaves, helpless as lovers caught in the ever increasing flow and borne to what destination only love itself could tell. Which is to say time passed. Time. A week. Days caught in the prism of a water bead to be split and fractured into component parts of hours, minutes, seconds, each dragging solemnly into tediousness and ennui. Empty mornings, emptier nights alone. Emptiest of all, dawn, when lovers should sit enfolded in warmth and watch the sun mother rise through pewter, pink and egg-blue eastern sky. But Karen missed these sunrises, missed them because she hadn't yet seen them with Vance, had only seen them in loneliness. How she wished time would hurry, get itself over with.

Then a rendezvous with Vance. A picnic or a meeting for an innocent tea. And what then of treacherous time? Did the hours, minutes, seconds drag then? Of course not. They flew. Many she never noticed, so quickly did they disappear into the past. Others she glimpsed only briefly, like the flash of a redwing blackbird bursting from a patch of cattails, gone before fully realized. Karen, in a strange turn of logic, begrudged those fleeting instants she had so sought but hours earlier, begrudged the moments leading to the end of each tryst with the man she loved.

Karen sat in her room overlooking the garden. She could see the very spot where Vance found her the night of the party. Their night. Had the intervening lifetime been only four days? Already she felt there was nothing more to be learned about Vance. She knew everything possible about him, for what unseen, unsuspected aspect of himself could he reveal that her heart had not already seen? *I love him. What more could I wish to know?* She remembered the poem and scribbled a line into her diary, pursing her lips from force of habit, looking quite like a child at her numbers. "How do I love thee, let me count the ways. . . ."

Retta soundlessly opened the door, hesitated and decided not to speak. Her little girl looked so intent. Karen was leaving. Retta knew it for a fact though Mr. and Mrs. Hampton had so far refused to take their daughter seriously, figuring the best way to handle this insane whim, this crazed infatuation, was to ignore it completely. But Retta knew, for she had helped pack the secret bags and the great trunk, then stood watch as Hermann carried them down the stairs at night to stow them in the coach. Had either Barrett or Iantha caught them at their task, the fireworks would have flown high enough for all Washington to see. Retta was frightened, but persevered.

The black woman couldn't decide whether she was happy or sad. Love. A powerful notion neither man nor beast might ever hope to restrain. Retta certainly wasn't about to attempt it. If Karen loved her man and was determined to follow him to Texas, all the powers that be wouldn't hold a candle to stopping her. That was the way love worked. For a moment Retta relived her own memories of the strong, free, dark-skinned man who had wooed and bedded her—even bought her so she would be his very own, then freed her, still his own—and then went off to die at Chickamauga like so many others. Retta and Charlie had been married twenty years and worked for the Hamptons all that time. Charlie was too old to fight for the Union cause, but had taken it into his hard head and couldn't be swayed. The war raged to free other black men and women from bondage and he would do his share.

Oh, they had had some times. Good and bad, harsh and easy. Friends, dancing, babies, fights, love-making in the tiny shack. Retta remembered Charlie's hands stirring her soul, his body probing, spitting life into her, his sweet smell as they lay exhausted side by side, sweat streaming from their naked bodies . . . ah, *that* was love. But Charlie was dead now, dead and lost in a nameless grave. Retta had known no other man like him. That, too, was the way of love.

Karen stirred, put her pen down and stretched her arms out, little fists clenched tightly. She yawned lazily and rose to go to the window and stare out. Retta's eyes grew moist and she dabbed at them with her apron. *You live yo' love, honey. Dat's what it all about. Live yo' love, live it long and good. Yo' ain't gonna get but one of 'em, de good Lawd knows.* The servant shut the door quietly and stepped off down the hall.

Vance walked from the Rotunda, his body stiff and aching from the drawn-out meeting, boring as the one the day before. He hailed a carriage and walked to meet it. Things weren't going well. Whitaker's faction had withdrawn its support. Barrett Hampton's weight had been thrown into the debate against the Texas cause. More and more he realized how little politics depended on the needs of the people who did the voting. The powerful assuaged, the powerful denied. There was the key. The system was a nightmare in which beady-eyed compromises nestled comfortably side by side with wide-mouthed, yawning accommodations. Fragile promises balanced precariously on jagged, upthrusting threats, held in place by cleverly spun webs of cajolery. Well, there'd be little more of it. The vote would come Monday and he would be gone Tuesday, win or lose.

A knot of congressmen halted in mid-conversation to stare unabashedly at the Texan as he passed by. More of Alfred's friends, Vance mused. Word certainly traveled. Well, it was no worse than back home. Gossip was the sweetening of prairie life, perhaps more accurately the spice. Loneliness bred an intense desire for news of people and so news, as if in deference to the great need, ran like wildlife, leaping ten-, fifty-, even hundred-mile gaps with a rapidity hard to explain. The frontier was a tiny village spread over thousands of square miles of basically empty territory, and what happened here was soon heard of there. Every rider was a compendium of gossip and news. The most important were those who traveled constantly. The blacksmith carried tales in his wagon, stories as hard and real as the metal he wrought. The peddlar's wagon was a cornucopia. News of marriages, births, death both natural and unnatural, catastrophes, triumphs went with each piece of cloth, each bow, each trinket and each pot and pan. Gossip old or new was the newspaper of the prairie, published by everyone, avidly consumed by everyone, edited by no one. Vance was used to it so ignored the cluster of eyes peering at his back until he was settled in the carriage, only then turning in their direction and flashing his broadest leer. The men raised hands to mouths in feigned coughs and refocused their attention elsewhere.

Vance settled back, let the swaying carriage lull him as it carried him across the city. Tuesday. The morning tide, to be confirmed by the captain in the morning. Tomorrow, when he knew for sure, he'd tell Karen they would be going home. Home. He hadn't thought of home very much recently. He tried in vain to imagine the look on True's face when his son showed up at the gates of the hacienda with a new wife. A Washington lady, an elegant northern beauty—but still a Yankee, no doubt, in True's eyes—come to live as Mrs. Vance Paxton, come to carry on the name. True would be suspicious at first. The old man was cautious when it came to strangers, especially Yankees. But he'd warm up, right enough. What man wouldn't after meeting Karen? His rough, taciturn ways would soften slowly so he wouldn't have to admit he was giving in to her charm.

Perhaps Elizabeth would be well by the time they got there. Vance's mother, taken ill just before he left, had been hopefully improving, or so True's last letter had led him to believe. Elizabeth would glow and fuss and carry on like a mother hen.

And Maruja. Maruja would be overjoyed. Always after Vance to marry, she'd be delighted with Karen. She'd retire to the kitchen in a fit of handwringing embarrassment and come out later with a wide grin and a table full of the best food for a hundred miles in any direction—*Cabrito* barbecued to a turn, the meat brown on the outside, light on the inside, the sweet juices waiting to drip down grinning chins.

The hands would give him a good ribbing, snickering behind raw-skinned fists and hoo-rahing openly whenever they thought they could get away with it. For sure there'd be a chivaree, one loud enough to wake every cow in the whole state. Ted Morning Sky would approve, no doubt of that. Comanches, even half breeds, had a streak in them for golden-haired women that bordered on the religious. All their women dark of hair, Karen would be held in high esteem.

There might be some problem with Marcelina, Maruja's daughter. Vance chuckled to himself. He and Marcelina.

Now there could have been a pair if she'd only been a few years older. Only fifteen, she was fast becoming a woman and was already a regular wildcat when she chose. No telling how she'd react to Karen.

The coach stopped at the stable and Vance got out, paid the driver and went in to get the buggy he'd hired for the afternoon. There was just enough time. . . .

Another interminable morning had passed and Karen was on her way to keep an assignation with Vance. They met not quite in secret, not quite for public scrutiny. Hesitating to display their affection for each other so publicly, Karen had insisted they meet in places less frequently visited by the socialite friends with whom she was once more closely associated. Vance proclaimed he didn't give a hoot in hell who knew about their seeing each other. Karen laughed to herself over the cute way he fumed and chafed when it came to a question of doing things his way. She loved to provoke his frontier-born independence, found an attraction in his distaste for any social graces save his own. She thrilled to the way he gentled before her, let her lead him through the wily games of courtship. And such a game! Each day brought new pleasures, new sensations. His moustache tickled her ears and neck, sent delicious tingles up and down her spine. His caresses brought an aching weakness to her stomach and loins, yet never led her farther than she wished to be led.

The steam donkey whistle blasted nearby. One o'clock. Nearly time. She glanced out the window to see the workers on the new Pennsylvania Railrod station slowly head back to their jobs They would be hard at work while she and her love dallied in the country.

Soon they were out of the city and on the high road. Trees to either side of the road shaded them from the sun. Vance had told her to enjoy them while she could. Precious few trees stood on the ranch. Texas . . . she still couldn't picture it, couldn't imagine mile after mile of treeless prairie. She watched a Baltimore oriole's nest as the carriage passed. The dark, hanging bulb swayed gently and elegantly in the breeze. There would be no Baltimore orioles in Texas. A shadow of doubt grew in her. After all, what did she know of Texas? He'd said it was hot. He'd said it was dry. He'd said it was lonely, sometimes only the wind for company. He'd said it was harsh. He'd said, he'd said, and everything he'd said was different from everything she'd known all her life. The thought was frightening when she let it be. All her father's money, all the Hampton prestige wouldn't mean a cup of water where they were going. Was she capable of living in such a place? Was the wind companion enough? But no. She would have Vance. And she would be in the midst of a great journey of love and adventure, the very stuff of which dreams are made.

The carriage came to a halt sometime later, the rasp of brakes shattering her current reverie with the present. She stepped from the carriage, accepting Hermann's helping hand. They had traveled the pike west and stopped atop a scenic bluff overlooking the Potomac. Washington was hidden from view. Civilization was gone. Only the breeze remained . . . Karen brightened. The wind wasn't such a bad companion after all.

Close at hand and just below her the river flowed imperceptibly, its surface covered with tiny ripples which shifted capriciously from place to place with the breeze. Overhead the sky was like a Wedgewood plate, dark blue and gleaming with sculpted white clouds held motionless, independent of the zephyr which ruffled her hair and the water's surface. Vance was nowhere to be seen. *Curse these politicians and their committees and meetings and delays. Curse them for a pox.*

"Miss Hampton, perhaps I'd better stay," Hermann said from behind her, breaking the stillness.

"If you wish, Hermann. I appreciate your company." She turned to see him standing hat in hand by the door to the carriage. Sudden concern flooded through her. "I hope Father isn't too displeased when you return without me."

"Yes'm. I don't figure to go back just yet. I thought it might be a good idea if I sort of waited in the old drive. Then I could bring you on to the house."

"Hermann, you're a dear. Perhaps that would be a good idea." She frowned. "Oh, dear. I know Mr. Paxton won't agree."

Hermann blushed, lowered his coarsely featured face. "Miss Hampton, I been meanin' to say somethin' about you leavin'."

110

"There's been no date set, Hermann. I won't be for a little while yet."

"Yes'm," he said, his face reddening with embarrassment, "I know. But I just wanted to say it'll be a loss. I'll be mighty sorry to see you go. You always been nice to me, and I always had a kind of soft spot for you. Things won't be the same no more. The house'll be awful empty, and . . . well, I just wanted you to know."

Suddenly Karen realized how much Hermann and Retta meant to her. The realization was overwhelming, accompanied by a sense of impending loss of two of the dearest friends she had. It was fortunate Vance arrived before this increasing wave of homesickness completely submerged her, shattering her composure in a fit of girlish tears.

Hermann climbed onto the carriage and guided the bays around Vance's buggy, returned the Texan's gesture of greeting and headed the team back toward Georgetown.

Karen ran to Vance, burying herself in his embrace.

"Is something wrong, Karen?"

"No. Just . . . just . . . oh, silliness. Hold me, darling."

Eons passed. They didn't notice. Lovers never do. The sun glided grudgingly into the west, sending up a spray of pale gold against which fields and gleaming farms settled, grateful for the coming coolness. Vance and Karen finished the last of the wine, and working together, repacked the picnic basket and folded the blanket. "This was so much more pleasant than last night's supper."

Vance looked questioningly at her. "So he came after all?"

"And on his best behavior. Unctuous as usual." She recalled the shock of entering the dining room, dreading the evening before it started. Alfred was already there, a glass of wine in hand, his face as sour as if the wine had been gall. The stiff formal greetings over, the junior congressman waited silently, obviously expecting Karen's apology. The acknowledgement of wrong never came. Idle, meaningless chatter soon disintegrated into longer and longer embarrassing silence and the four finally fled to the table, there to sit like so many megaliths carefully set by some barbaric tribe of old at the four corners of the compass.

Before soup was finished, and just as Ross snuck into the room with the entree, Karen fled in tears to her room. "It was dreadful. Retta told me Alfred stayed a few moments longer and then ordered his hat and cane, leaving without touching his meal and with barely a good evening. Mama dissolved in tears. Papa was furious and threw a tantrum. I thought he would break into my room but Mother talked him out of it. She's so certain we're in the midst of a lovers' spat and I'll come back to my senses. As if I'm the one who'd lost them."

They loaded the buggy without speaking further, each lost in a tiny private reverie. Karen was blissfully happy and once again dreamed of the day they would leave. Vance helped Karen into the buggy and walked around to the other side, pausing to gaze pensively over the water. An old premonition stiffened his shoulders. Something was wrong with this place. No doubt about it now. It was time to get out. Tuesday wouldn't be any too soon. He ambled to the buggy and climbed in, keeping to himself the sudden, nagging apprehension.

Alfred kept the spyglass centered on the buggy until it was completely lost from view. He rolled over on his side, put the glass down and opened a thin silver flask, tilting it to his lips and taking a long swallow. He had followed the Texan's buggy from town, keeping far enough back to avoid being seen. On horseback he had ridden across a neighboring field to the west and come out on a hillock sweeping up from the bluff. He did not enjoy horseback riding and it put him in a foul, irascible mood. He did not enjoy lying in grass and staining his waistcoat and trousers. But clothes were cheap. His honor, on the other hand, was dear. The Whitaker name was not to be taken lightly. Not to be smeared by some bawdy upstart from far-off Texas. Alfred's name and bearing demanded satisfaction. He was determined to have it.

Oh, how his friends—friends, ha!—had enjoyed his humiliation at the Hampton party. How they had laughed and presumed to take advantage of his embarrassment. They had presumed too much. He smiled crookedly. Damn them all. They would see. He would show them.

"Call the ruffian out," they taunted. "We saw your intended arm-in-arm with Paxton," they whispered discreetly. "Strange occurrence. Just happened to see the Hampton girl with the Texan," they sympathized, smiles hidden until he turned his back. Bah. They spoke like forked tongue in cheek, Alfred told himself, the pulp metaphor muddied by too much bourbon whiskey. They'd love to see him call Paxton out, of course, the bastards. He put the bottle to his mouth and drank until it was empty. Too soon. In a rage he threw the silver flask as far as he could, watched it arc in a glittering path through the air and land partway down the slope, caught in a shrub, there to catch the last fading rays of the sun and glitter malevolently back at him.

Karen would be his one way or other. She would scorn him no more. She had led and used him, she had trapped his affections, and like a damned fool he had let her. He had been the envy of his fellows and now they laughed. Damn them. Damn her. He wanted her more than ever, now. Not out of love. Not anymore. Never out of love, by God. He would see her grovel and crawl and plead for forgiveness. He would stride about her as she called him lord and master. She would humbly and contritely submit to his chastisement.

Alfred half ran, half fell down the hill to his mount, tripping and stumbling into the horse's right side at the last moment. The mare reared in surprise and fear, would have bolted had she not been tethered to a log. The same with women, he thought drunkenly. Tether them. Hobble them. He crossed under her head, tearing the reins free. The horse reared again as the bit pinched her mouth, but Alfred quickly settled that with a blow to the nose. The animal stood still, quivering, while Alfred mounted awkwardly, clawing his drunken way up her side more as if she were a mountain than a beast. "Damn you. Damn you! Hold still!"

He mustn't lose control. Mustn't lose control. He sat stiffly in the saddle, thinking muddy, dire thoughts. He needed to be shrewd, to bring all his faculties to bear. A situation like this called for help. And he knew just where to find it, by God. Edgar had been appropriating funds from the old man for the last year. Edgar would help him. No question about it. Edgar would be glad to help him. Alfred giggled. There. It was all arranged. Or would be.

113

He drove his heels into the skittish mare's flanks, laughing aloud now. Oh, the joke would be on Vance Paxton, all right. With the Whitaker fortune available, Alfred could afford lots of jokes. Funny ones. Jokes to keep the Paxton fool in stitches.

CHAPTER VIII

The woman's hand traveled only a short distance. Back, then forward and across. The nails were long, tapered, polished and very, very sharp. Like talons of some dreadful bird of prey they slashed out to seek flesh and blood, raked down to strike the cheek before them and carve bleeding grooves from the tanned skin. Vance grinned and caught Angie's hand in midair before it struck, then twisted it around behind her back. Angie reddened with fury and began to scream, howling a surprising stream of epithets strong enough to make even a longshoreman blanch.

Vance yanked the thrashing woman to his bed and forced her face down into the pillow. The time for delicacy was long past. Gentility forgotten, he piled on top of her, forcing her face deeper into the pillow and successfully muffling the outraged woman beneath him. Still she struggled, buttocks squirming and grinding as if to rouse the flesh pressed down on them. The taut, heaving body carried a singular message of pleasure and Vance, resolution swaying, teetering on the edge of desire, felt his loins harden in heated expectation of one last sexual foray beneath Angie's ruffled skirts. Then he cursed himself for an adolescent fool and drove the thought from his mind, concentrating anew on keeping the thrashing wildcat under him as still as possible.

Finally, nearly suffocated, the fury ebbed and the woman sagged. Confident spirit would be as weak as flesh now, Vance rolled quickly off the bed and out of reach. Angie raised her head and gasped for air, trying to replenish her starved lungs. "You . . . bastard . . . you tried to kill me." she managed to gulp between breaths.

"Sorry, Angie," he answered, pillow in hand and ready for more action, "I may not be the handsomest fella to ever come down the pike, I know, but I've kind of grown fond of this ol' face. Used to it, you might say. I'd hate to see it striped bloody, courtesy of a fire-thighed Washington lady like yourself. Now if you can promise to behave yourself and keep your voice down to where I can hear without having to share what you say with every other soul in the hotel, maybe we can get some things said that need to be said."

Angie scowled at him, rolled over and brushed a strand of hair from her face. "You . . ." she brayed, stopping immediately as Vance gestured threateningly with the pillow. She lowered her voice to complete the sentence. ". . . are a bastard."

"If calling me names settles anything, I'll let it go. For my part I'm sorry I've given you grief. I could chalk it up to your being an attractive woman and me being a long way from home and pretty damn lonely, but I have to admit it's my fault. I acted like a buck in rut and I apologize."

Angie dabbed at her eyes with a corner of the sheet. "You led me on. I loved you. And now you've broken my heart."

Vance tossed the pillow on the bed, picked up his coat from the chair and shrugged it on. "Aw, come on, Angie. Admit it yourself. All you wanted from me was a good roll in the hay. That's as deep as the river ran."

"You left me alone at the party and didn't even come around to apologize. I had to sneak into your room like some street tramp. Who have you spent the week with? The Hampton bitch, no doubt. I'll bet she's cooled the urge below your belt. It's common knowledge she's a . . ."

Two hands snaked out and grabbed her before she could finish the sentence. Iron fingers bit deeply into her soft shoulders and hauled her off the bed. Angie gave a startled cry and her eyes widened in fear. The look on Vance's face made her afraid of him for the first time since she had known him. She had thought the Texan completely malleable but now read a hardness of purpose and coldness of manner beyond any previous experience. Strange and explosive emotions lurked in the hard eyes glittering in the dim light of the room. Pent-up fury crouched ready to leap and destroy her.

The tableau shattered when the door to Vance's room swung open violently. Earnest Leighton stood in the hall, looking into the room. He took three deliberate steps and stopped, eyes focused on Vance. "I believe you've said all you came to say, Angela. I'm sure Mr. Paxton has appointments he needs to keep. A busy schedule before he returns to Texas."

Angie shrugged away from Vance's already loosened grasp. She picked up her hat and parasol from the floor, straightened her skirt and blouse and flounced from the room without a word, brushing carelessly past her husband on her way out.

Earnest and Vance stood without moving, staring at each other in silence. Earnest spoke first, his voice a little sing-songy. "Ah, Mr. Paxton. Here we are. The trysting place. How very elegant of you both." He appeared impassive as he looked about the room. "No answer, eh? Very good. A lawyer's sense," he chuckled lowly. "In Texas, I suppose, the proper protocol would demand the outraged husband invite his wife's paramour into the street." He paused, smiled wanly. "But this isn't Texas, is it? Besides," he said, reaching abruptly into his pocket and producing a small derringer which he pointed at Vance, "I find this setting more apropos."

Vance eyed the derringer, assessing the danger it posed. A .25, it was heavy enough to cause substantial damage at short range. "You knew what was happening, Mr. Leighton. I could see that Saturday night. You even set it up for us, knew Angie was waiting even as you walked out the door and knew I'd be in that bedroom ten minutes after you left."

"Six minutes, to be exact." Vance's eyebrows shot up in surprise. Earnest laughed hollowly. "Modero is very clever. Standing in my room I could see perfectly well through cleverly concealed holes in the wall. Modero is experienced, you see. He was responsible for a similar arrangement for another wealthy patron in Spain. You are lucky, however. I have no dungeons in my house."

Vance didn't move, tried not to show the disgust welling up in him. A ruthless, cold glint shone in his eyes. "Did you enjoy it, Congressman?"

Earnest sighed and cocked the derringer. His madness more and more apparent, he relaxed. His manner unconcerned, his tone one of gentle sophistication, he allowed the derringer to wave about as he spoke. "As a matter of fact, I

117

did. Not, perhaps, with as much relish as the . . . participants, but nevertheless enough. Found it fascinating, of course. Always interesting to watch one's wife perform with an agile, strong partner. Stimulating, even. I didn't know she was so . . . inventive, shall we say? The little trick with the . . ."

"Shut up. Shut your filthy mouth." Vance's words were low, barely heard but menacing enough to stop Leighton.

The gun lowered, seemingly forgotten for the moment as Leighton bowed slightly, mockingly. "Angela's mouth is filthier, wouldn't you say? After all, to put . . ."

Vance took a step toward Leighton, stopping when the gun steadied immediately on his stomach. "You are undoubtedly better with a gun than am I, Mr. Paxton, but I assure you I am quite adequate at this distance. You took your pleasure with my wife, it is now my pleasure to discuss the matter with you."

Vance stared at Leighton in disbelief. A man of the frontier, he was used to the obvious in man and nature. If a man hated you, he'd let you know he was coming or simply hide and shoot you from the back. But to spew his hate in your face and then shoot, never. Nature could be kind or cruel, but always gave advance notice. If it was going to storm the clouds told you. Nature was not given to intrigue and deviation. The man before him was beyond his experience with either man or nature. Vance reached into his belt and withdrew the pocket watch his father had given him. "Mr. Leighton. Anything you want to discuss you may discuss with yourself. Anything you want settled, begin it here, in the street, anywhere you like, only hurry up because I'm already late for a very special appointment."

"Ah," Leighton laughed, a rough edge of nervousness now tinging his voice, "but there is no appointment you could possibly have more important than the one you are keeping right now."

"Perhaps so. Nevertheless, I'm leaving. You do what you will."

The gun waved jerkily. "You're not afraid, are you?"

"Nobody likes to get killed, Mr. Leighton. Nobody likes to die. But if you came here to shoot that thing you'd have done it long ago. I've seen enough dying and death in my day to know how it works and recognize it for what it is. When it happens, it happens. When my time comes I in-

118

tend to be doing what I've always done, living my life the best I can, and for myself. I haven't done such a good job of that here in this damned city, I admit. Not until recently, anyway. And I guess, if it makes you feel any better, I'm sorry. But that's all past. Lock the door behind you when you leave, please." Vance walked to the dresser, picked up his hat, gave Earnest a curt nod and walked past him into the hall.

Leighton stood without moving, his shoulders squared, his eyes staring into nowhere. After a moment his whole body began to tremble slightly, then more and more violently. Finally the trembling stopped and his shoulders slumped, the gun hanging limply at his side. "Outrage doesn't become me, Mr. Paxton," he said to the empty room. "Not after all this time." He uncocked the derringer and placed it back in his pocket, turned and walked out the door and started down the hall. Halfway to the stairs he stopped and after only a moment's indecision, turned and walked back to Vance's room. Earnest Leighton closed and locked the door behind him.

The coachman, under the abusive admonitions of his lone passenger, lost little time in hurrying through the quiet afternoon, hitting as many chuck holes as he managed to avoid, cursing with each jolt his carriage was forced to sustain. The coach slid to a halt before *Le Chien Commendable* even as Vance leaped into the street, tossed the appropriate coinage to the driver and hurried into the cafe.

Inside, Clement broke away from a heated discussion with one of his regular customers and approached the Texan, staring with obvious curiosity at the stranger's clothes. "May I be of service, *monsieur?* A table for one?"

Vance anxiously searched the interior of the low-ceilinged room from the doorway. "I'm supposed to join a Miss Hampton here. Have you seen her?"

"Ah, *monsieur,*" Clement exclaimed, his face lighting up with joy, "so you are the one who has stolen our little flower's heart!" He rushed to Vance and shook his hand with typical European abruptness. "She has spoken of you, of course. Glowingly. I am Clement and this is my wife Marie. We are very pleased to make your acquaintance, *monsieur.*" Marie curtseyed shyly from across the room.

Vance, a little ill at ease, removed his hat and bowed to

119

the lady. "Yes, sir. I'm pleased to make your acquaintance, too. Now if you could tell me . . ."

Clement threw his arms wide in a gesture of sorrow. "*Monsieur*, I am too sorry to tell you. Miss Hampton is no longer here. You are only a tiny moment too late. Perhaps you can still catch her, no?"

"Did she leave in a coach?"

"*Sacre bleu*, I am so sorry. I did not notice. I was in the kitchen preparing a little something for our friend the Piper. He has sent word he was blessed with a gold coin and wishes . . ."

Vance broke in to thank him, touched his hat in deference to the diminutive Marie and darted back outside. Damn the Leightons anyway, he thought. Karen had planned to meet him at *Le Chien Commendable* at one o'clock. The time was now well after two. He was more than an hour late, and if there was anything he had learned about Karen Hampton, she wasn't one to be kept waiting. The coach in which he arrived was long gone, happy to be quit of the frantic Texan. He looked up and down the empty avenue, realizing the futility of finding another conveyance. He considered walking back to the hotel stable to hire a horse but dismissed such a plan as self-defeating. It would take too long. The only reasonable course of action was to walk, as much as he hated the idea. Perhaps a coach would come along.

Three swarthy roustabouts lounged sleepily in the back of a wagon loaded with barrels. Parked only a few yards down the avenue, Vance looked them over with the possibility of hiring them in mind, but when he walked toward them one snored and another pulled his cap over his face. They were obviously more interested in sleep than work. He turned away from the trio, a small frown of half-guessed recognition clouding his face. They weren't complete strangers, he felt. He grasped at the wisp of memory and caught it. He had seen them recently. Yes. At his hotel, shooting dice in the alley across the street the morning before. And that morning, too, the dice put away and occupied with steaming cups of coffee. And now here they were again. . . .

He had more to worry about and dismissed them from his mind. If he could only find a coach, a carriage, even a wagon. He passed a millinery shop and, farther down the road, a rich sweet aroma of a bakery beckoned with yeasty fingers and started his stomach growling in protestation over having been denied lunch. The Leightons' fault, too. He should have eaten with Karen. The door to the bakery was open and the heady smells of pastry and bread made him think of Maruja, the Mexican house servant, cook and second mother to him. Maruja's kitchen was almost legendary among the neighboring ranches, not a one of which didn't want and hadn't tried to get Maruja. But she was more than just another Paxton employee. She was family to the Paxtons and the Paxtons were family to her. There was never any question of her leaving. . . . A thick slice of hot fresh bread sounded mighty good, would hold him until he could get some real food under his belt.

The sound of pounding hooves and rumbling wheels caught his attention just as he started up the walkway. He glanced along the avenue in time to see a carriage round the corner onto Georgetown Boulevard. Karen's carriage! He forgot the promise of bread and broke into a run as the carriage disappeared around a corner without apparent notice from either Hermann or Karen. The street empty of vehicles of any description, he ran on, oblivious to the pedestrians who stopped to stare at the outlandish figure calling after the long-gone coach.

He rounded the corner only to see the Hampton coach disappear again, this time around a tree-shaded bend in the road leading out of the city proper to the secluded and stately manors of Georgetown. To call out would be useless. There was nothing left to do but follow. He might not be able to overtake the carriage but he'd be damned if he would let the day go by without seeing Karen, even if he had to follow her right up to Barrett Hampton's wrathful door and risk a confrontation with the irate businessman. He settled into a smooth, distance-eating fast walk, a gait he'd learned from the Comanche. And if he cut up Rock Creek and across country, he'd not miss her arrival by much.

Washington was soon out of sight to the rear, as were the last shops and cottages. The boulevard continued alone through a delightfully wooded parkway following the capricious meanderings of hill and valley. Before a half hour passed, Vance came to Rock Creek, his favorite creek since the day he had followed and met Karen for the first time.

The banks here looked tended, for the grassy slopes angled gently to the water's edge some twenty feet below the level of the roadway. An inviting scene. Clear, cool water gurgled pleasantly through woods. Vance heard the clatter of horse and wagon overtaking him from the rear just as he started to descend to the path leading to the meadow behind the Hampton residence. He stopped and turned, his hand raised to hail the driver, and saw the motley trio for the fourth time that day. The barrel-laden wagon—moving too fast, perhaps?—slowed as it approached. Suspicion dug tiny heels into him but he continued to hold his hand high. A ride was a ride, he decided, and called out to the driver. "Ho, there!"

The wagon drew abreast, the driver pulling back on the reins. Two of them rode on the wagon seat, the third sat on a barrel in the back. For the first time Vance had a chance to look them over carefully. The driver was an average-looking fellow though his eyes were set mean and close. He wore a pair of filthy canvas trousers bunched with a rope at the waist and a graying linen shirt. Next to him sat a rather good-natured-looking Negro, younger than Vance and built like an ox. His nose was pushed obscenely flat against his babyish face to give him the look of a simpleton. His mouth gaped open. No doubt he had to breathe through it. A roustabout fit for doing what he was told and little more. In the back a short, fat bully sat with legs spread for balance, a Yankee forage cap pushed back on his head to reveal a shining bald pate. He stared at Vance, a little grin on his face.

The driver spoke. "Can I he'p ya?"

"Your horses seem to be movin' faster than my feet. Mind if I ride with you a piece?"

The driver grinned, revealing a row of black stumpy teeth. "Sure. Climb in back with Horace."

"Much obliged." Vance stepped to the running board of the wagon and hoisted himself up. The fat man, Horace, rose to offer a hand, and when Vance took it, jerked violently to throw him off balance. Taken by surprise and acting on instinct alone, Vance tried to fall to the side, only to find himself held upright and wide open to Horace's booted foot which swung up and rammed into his right side. A whoosh of air exploded from the Texan's lungs as pain ripped through him. He didn't even see the big Negro twist in his seat and send a ham-sized fist into the side of his head with a blow hard enough to tear him from Horace's grasp.

Only thinly aware of what he was doing, Vance pushed himself from the wagon and fell back onto the side of the road, slammed into the incline and started rolling down to the creek. Barely conscious and fighting for air he let himself tumble all the way down to the water, rolling into the rushing current. Before his head sank for the first time he managed a fuzzy picture of the Negro and Horace descending from the wagon and starting down the slope after him. The shock of the cold water hauled him back to consciousness. He raised his head as best he could, gulped another lungful of air and let himself fall back into the shallows, expelling the air and rising again, continuing the process. To the approaching attackers it appeared their victim was floundering helplessly, badly hurt and so much beaten meat to be pounded even further into submission.

The black man reached Vance first, grabbed a handful of the Texan's matted hair and brutally yanked him upright. Vance rose with the momentum, slamming a fistful of silt and mud into the giant's face. The black man howled and released his hold on Vance, bringing his hands up to claw the filth from his blinded eyes. Horace clumsily sloshed through the water and swung a knotty fist which bloodied Vance's lip and sent him reeling backward to trip over a rounded, loose stone and fall, twisting in order to land face first. It was an unfortunate tactic, Vance realized, as he rolled against the blinded black man. How unfortunate he soon learned, for suddenly the weight of the Negro dropped on him. By the time he figured out what had happened it was too late. He was caught in a strangle hold from behind.

His right side numb, his head still spinning crazily from the original fall, Vance strove mightily but to no avail to free himself. He thrashed and squirmed desperately trying to slip out of the iron grip but the black was too strong, his arms locked into place and immovable. Something dug into the flesh of Vance's leg. He reached down with his left hand and found a jutting length of tree limb which crumbled when he tugged on it. His hand, fingers rapidly growing numb to the point of uselessness, reached again and closed, this time upon a water-smoothed stone, the one on which he'd tripped. His lungs burning with lack of oxygen, his mind striving for a consciousness gradually slipping away, he clawed for the stone and finally grasped it just before the Negro lifted him from the water, his massive black forearm still locked around Vance's throat. "You tries to blind Rufe?" he panted. "Well, it do you no good. Rufe don'ts need ta see ta squeeze."

"Git him, Rufe. Break his damn Rebel neck!" the fat man screamed.

It felt like an eternity, the time it took to whip his left arm up and smash the smooth round stone into the black man's face. And then suddenly there was air. As much as he wanted. Vance dropped to his knees, his mouth wide open, his body heaving with each gasp. The Negro sat in the stream, bawling out like a stricken calf. "O, lawd, ma' po' nose agin. Horace, he hit ma' nose."

The fat man lost precious few seconds in covering the short distance to the downed Texan. He aimed a kick at Vance who slid to the side and rammed the rock up into the fat man's groin. Horace shrieked, doubling over and falling back into the creek, moaning and scrambling awkwardly toward the bank. Vance rose and staggered over to the Negro. Rufe had regained his footing but still held his hands to his pulped nose, blood darkening further his dusky face.

The hamlike fist swung out wildly, but Vance blocked it with his weak right arm. He slapped his left fist, still holding the rock, across the side of the Negro's jaw and grimaced with diabolical pleasure as he heard the sound of bone crushing. Rufe collapsed. Felled like a tree, he landed on his face in the water. The creek was only a foot deep, unconscious as he was, deep enough for drowning. But Vance didn't want him to drown. He wanted him to enjoy the full range of pain the next week would bring. He propped the Negro's head up on a nearby jumble of branches and stones and left him blissfully unaware of the excruciating delights the future held in store.

Horace was getting away. The fat man was halfway up the slope, bent and struggling, cupping his injured groin with one hand and pulling himself up with the other. To his immediate dismay the driver, seeing Vance in close pursuit, urged the team forward, turned the wagon in a wide spot on the road and galloped off toward Washington. Horace crawled and cursed him with each breath.

Vance reached him near the top. The terrified ruffian spun about and threw a punch. Vance caught the arm in midswing and twisted it around behind the fat man's back. Horace struggled but without result, gradually ceasing as the hand crept closer and closer to the shoulderblade. Horace screamed.

"Who paid you?" Vance asked.

Horace shook his head. Vance twisted the flopping hand, lifted it higher, forcing the squealing fat man into a little tip-toe dance. "Edgar . . . Edgar did. Oh, God, you're breakin' my arm."

"Who is Edgar?"

"I don't know. Jesus, I swear on my pa's grave, may his soul fry in hell. I don't know."

Vance wrenched the arm higher. Horace screamed. "Tell me something else, Horace."

"Wha . . . what . . . ? I swear. I'm tellin' . . . Oh, God . . . I know. Edgar, he's . . . he works in the stables."

"What stables?"

"I don't know. . . ."

The arm twisted tighter, nearly touching his neck. "Last chance, Horace. What stables?"

"The Whitakers'! Horace screamed just before his arm popped, the bone broken neatly at the shoulder. The wounded man's eyes bulged from his head, only the whites showing. His mouth fought for another scream but couldn't find it, could find only a rasping gasp of pain.

"Rufe needs help, Horace." Vance planted his foot in Horace's back and shoved. The fat man tumbled down the slope and splashed into the creek, his broken arm flopping back and forth as he fell, ending up awkwardly behind his back. He struggled fiercely to get his head on the muddy bank and succeeded before fainting.

Vance walked down the slope, and ignoring the two who had so grossly underestimated him, washed the blood from his swollen lip and cleaned his clothes as well as possible before continuing to the Hampton house. A little shakily at first, then growing more determined with each step, he didn't hurry. He wanted to be dry by the time he got there. Maybe Alfred, full of fond expectations, would be there. Visiting. Vance hoped he would be. He wiped the blood from his lip again, feeling the warm sun bake into his bruised neck and shoulder. Only a mile and a half to go. He rubbed his right side, wincing in pain which he drove from his mind the second he realized no ribs were broken. Only a mile and a half. He'd be ready by then. For anything.

Karen leaned out the window and ordered Hermann to drive on around to the stables and carriage house. Having missed her afternoon with Vance she was in a foul mood. Visions of Angie—though she knew they couldn't be true—drifted uninvited through her head. The stables and carriage house would calm her. Karen loved the smell of leather and oiled wood that permeated the carriage house. The smell was intensely masculine, still soft and luxurious. Collars and hackamores and traces and shining polished reins. Horses and hay and straw and grains. A restful smell. A peaceful smell. A smell certain to bring back childhood memories of riding with her father when he was a father and not the chief stockholder and executive of Hampton Trading of New York. A smell to soothe and calm the angry breast. A smell to heal hurt feelings and smooth out frustration. A balm. *Why didn't he come when he said he would?*

The carriage clattered through the gates and up the curving drive, then swung abruptly to a stop at the front of the house. Karen drew back the curtain from the window. "Didn't you hear what I said, Hermann?"

"Yes, ma'am, I did." He gestured to the turnaround in front of the house. Karen looked, her mood instantly changing to one tinged with worry and indecision. Alfred's carriage was pulled up, the big grays standing quietly in the afternoon shade. "I thought they'd probably want you to go inside, Miss, seeing as Mr. Whitaker is here."

Karen sighed and gathered her purse and parasol as she felt Hermann jump down from the driver's seat. She had avoided meeting Alfred since Tuesday night's abortive dinner attempt in spite of numerous protestations and grinding pressure from Barrett and Iantha who day by day became more and more frustrated, more and more angry with her. The door opened and Hermann held out his knobby hand to help her down. "Thank you, Hermann. I suppose you're right. Whatever he wants, I'd better go on in and get it over with."

Hermann grinned wanly, for he more than anyone save Retta knew what was going through Karen's head. It was Hermann, after all, who had driven her hither and yon for nearly a week of assignations with Vance. "Yes, ma'am. If I may say so, ma'am?"

Karen stopped and turned back to him. "Yes, Hermann?"

"Good luck," he said, jerking his head toward the house.

"Thank you, Hermann," she answered warmly. She turned again and walked to the front of the house, her head high in a show of defiance and determination not at all matching her new mood. With Vance beside her she would have faced any confrontation gladly. But she was alone. Vance had not kept their appointment. He had let her down. Perhaps he was preoccupied with business. Well, what could be more important than her and the love they shared? Didn't he realize she was tired of the constant tension she faced in her father's house? He got off easily. He didn't have to contend with the stares, the silent, interminable, pained recriminations.

Retta greeted her at the front door, duster and polish rag in hand. Her eyes rolled toward the back of the house when she saw it was Karen. "Where you been, chile? Mistah Whitaker here to see you," she said in a loud whisper. "He done been here an hour already."

"I saw his carriage. Where is he?"

"He said fo' me to send you out in de side garden."

Karen sighed deeply, removed her hat and placed it and her purse on the stand. "Are you going to wish me luck too, Retta?" she asked.

Retta grinned broadly and her head bobbed up and down in a silent answer of "yes." Her words indicated the opposite. "No, missy," she said, gesturing with her eyes toward the library. "Mr. Hampton, he pay me and he de boss man. Dis ol' black lady, she gets in trouble she wish you luck."

Karen almost laughed, instead reached out and briefly hugged the massive woman in front of her. Retta and Hermann. What an improbable pair of conspirators! "I understand, Retta. Thank you."

Her spirits revived, she paused for a moment, took a deep breath and marched resolutely to the dining room doors and through them, taking care not to look to the right and risk catching a glimpse of her father in the li-

127

brary. The French doors stood open. She stopped by them for a second to check her hair in the glass, then swept through onto the porch and into the garden.

Alfred was under one of the massive old oaks, hands folded behind his back, eyes cast downward, intently studying the lilies-of-the-valley planted under the ornamental grapevine running down the small fence which led to the back of the house. Each tiny white bell blossom trembled in the light afternoon breeze and nodded to and fro as if sharing whispered secrets forever unknowable to man or beast. His mind on other matters, Alfred failed to notice Karen as she approached, her steps muffled by the soft green grass.

For a moment she said nothing, only watched him, the man she had almost married. Comparisons were inevitable. Karen shuddered. All those categories at which Alfred excelled she realized she had come to abhor. Sophistication, cunning, intrigue, deviousness. A courtier of old, a sycophant by design, he sought to climb to such heights as to command his own retinue of flattering, fawning admirers. How different Vance was. Direct, bold, audacious to the point of impudence. As for his dress, he redefined *distingué*. Karen sighed. Poor Vance. Almost a bad choice for an emissary. Too proud to flatter, Alfred and Barrett would claw his cause to shreds with a multitude of whispered promises and send him home empty-handed. But Vance would learn, of that she had no doubt. No, there was really little to compare. She snapped open her parasol. "Good afternoon, Alfred."

He jumped, startled. "Karen. Why, I didn't hear you come up."

"The lilies-of-the-valley are lovely, aren't they."

"Oh . . . yes. The lilies-of-the-valley. I hadn't noticed." Alfred cleared his throat, began to speak and then offered his arm instead. They strolled through the garden around the back of the house and into the large formal gardens bordering the meadow, eventually reaching the garden pond across which floated a dozen water lilies like triremes of old, flowery barges fit for the fairie queen of naiads. Once out of sight of the house, Alfred became more bold, placing his bowler hat and cane at the foot of a sturdy elm. He took Karen's hand and brought it to his lips. "Karen, I . . ."

"I'm sorry I caused you any embarrassment, Alfred," Karen interrupted rapidly before he could say anything he'd later regret. "I know you had great expectations for the party, as did my parents. You're terribly . . . sweet, and . . . I know a dozen girls who would be enthralled at the chance to marry Alfred Randol Whitaker. . . ."

Alfred's face clouded. "You're mine," he said hoarsely. "We're engaged. You had no right to humiliate me before my colleagues."

"It wasn't and isn't a question of right, Alfred. Don't you see? Our wedding wouldn't be a marriage. It would be a merger. A financial arrangement blessed by the gods of industry and state. But that's not what I want from life."

Alfred stared at her, his eyes widening with amazement. "I find it difficult to understand you, Karen. Don't you enjoy the finery with which you've been blessed? This house? The parties, your carriage, servants, clothes? They are the rewards of your father's labor and come directly from his position in the world of business and politics."

"I would rather have had a father," Karen said bitterly. "I did, for a short time when I was a little girl. And I liked it. Wealth is not all there is to life."

Alfred shrugged, his eyes taking on a detestable paternal glow. "What else is there, Karen?"

"Love. Love! A man and a woman sharing, blissfully merged in the rapture of being together."

"Really, Karen, isn't that naive? Who do we know who is," his voice rose in mocking imitation, " 'blissfully merged in the rapture of being together'? Aren't you being a trifle immature? Unrealistic in the extreme? You sound like a child."

"And you sound disgustingly condescending. I have such a love. If you find the concept impossible to understand or accept, you have my pity. I only expect you to have the grace to leave me alone," she retorted angrily, turning on her heel.

Alfred gripped her arm and spun her about. His face flamed with anger. "Who? Who is your great love? The Texas stud? The southern trash who's made you the laughingstock of all Washington while you blithely follow in Angie Leighton's footsteps? Don't think the word hasn't gotten around. Poor Angie pining away for the lover who spiked her and spurned her. Everybody weeps to her face and laughs behind her back at how the Texas bumpkin in his fool's clothes set the pants of Washington's prima donna afire." He stopped for breath, his face red, his eyes black pinpoints boring into her. "Has he dipped his wick in you yet, Karen dear, or are you stringing him along as you did me?"

Karen's hand shot out, exploding in a hollow-sounding pop on his cheek. Alfred's face darkened with fury and he backhanded her, striking her across the right side of her face and knocking her to the ground. "Now you listen to me. I am a Whitaker. I am not to be slapped like a commoner, dallied with, bandied about by any frivolous piece of Itching Jenny who comes down the pike. I was in love with you at one time, wanted desperately to marry you. Not for money, not for power, not for position. Perhaps I was naive. I am no longer so.

"My father and your father are powerful men. They need each other and I need them. Our wedding is a perfect excuse for certain manipulations and changes, certain combinations of benefit to them and, as ought to be as plain as the itch between your legs, for me. I cannot afford to be made the laughingstock of my district, as I have been assured I will be if there is no wedding. I am determined to strengthen the political base from which I started. Whether or not you like it, you are part and parcel of the deal. That's the way the world works. And it's just quite simply too bad if you don't like it.

"As for your barbarian, forget him. He's had an accident." Karen blanched. "A terrible accident which should convince him he's no longer wanted and will not be tolerated around here or around you for one moment longer."

"What did you . . . ?" Karen tried to speak.

"Shut up. You wanted a barbarian? Very well. I'll play the part for you. Perhaps I should have done this long ago." Standing over her, his hand drew back and started down again, but only traveled a fraction of an inch. His arm was caught, his wrist enveloped in a fist. A perplexed look crossed his face and he turned his head in an attempt to see what was wrong.

Vance Paxton was there towering over him, his grip like steel, his face like stone hewn from a solid piece of granite. "Washington is full of slappers," Vance said contemptuously, jerking Alfred around. "Perhaps I should have done *this* a long time ago." Vance's fist started from his waist and grew and grew, blotting out everything until Alfred could see no more. Suddenly pain exploded in his face and he went sailing across the lawn, slamming into the elm tree and sliding down it to sit on top of his bowler hat.

Karen stifled a scream of terror as the hulking form bent over her. "Karen, it's me. It's me," Vance said gently. Nearly unconscious, she took the two hands held out to her, then saw his face, his eyes, so strong and wilful. Panic left her and she pulled herself up and threw herself recklessly into his arms, clasping his lips tightly to hers. Vance pushed her back gently. "Ouch," he said.

Karen noticed the dried blood on his lips and chin, the abrasions and the swollen lower lip. "Oh, my dear, what on earth . . . ?"

"Just a fat lip. A bruise or so. I've had 'em before. Probably have 'em again."

"He said he'd . . . he said he'd. . . ."

"Naw . . . he just thought he did."

Alfred groaned, braced himself against the tree and staggered to his feet. A large blue-yellow bruise started to swell across his face and a thin trickle of blood ran from one corner of his mouth. Vance turned to him. Alfred managed to pick up his cane and face Vance, his eyes blazing with hatred, his voice incongruously murderous. "I have friends. . . ." he managed to mumble, wincing as he spoke.

"So I heard. But they tried already. I've met them. Nice fellas. One of 'em ran off as fast as his horses would take him, the other two you can pick up along the road, just under the bridge over Rock Creek. I suspect they're still there and would be grateful for a little help. You can kiss your money good-bye. They'll have to spend it on a surgeon."

The revelation took the fire out of Alfred's eyes. His shoulders sagged in defeat. But not for long. Drawing himself up as tall as he could, he gave Karen a final glance and adjusted his coat and tie. The familiar gestures helped and his haughty mein returned. He laughed contemptuously and walked away, leaving his crumpled bowler where it lay.

Vance watched as Alfred stalked off, keeping an eye on him until he heard a ripping sound behind him. He turned

131

to see Karen let her skirt down. She held a piece of petti-coat which she dipped in the pool and, having wrung it out, stood on tiptoes and started washing his face. "You were so gallant," she said. "I've heard of southern gallantry, but I never thought it would come to my rescue."

"I don't think Alfred would have done much else to you."

"Why, sir, he would have ravished me," Karen cried in mock horror. Then she snickered in spite of herself. "Well, maybe not ravished. Not Alfred, anyway. Nevertheless, he was most unpleasant and you did come to my rescue. Like a chivalrous knight of ages past. Whatever did they do to you?"

"Your old boyfriend paid them to get rid of me. They didn't, is all. We went 'round and 'round . . . ouch, careful . . . a little, and they agreed to leave me alone."

"A little?"

"Well, maybe more than a little. At any rate, they convinced me about one thing. It's time to get out of here. How soon can you be ready?"

Karen dropped the piece of fabric and stood unmoving. A single tear formed in her eye, spilled onto her cheek.

"I leave for Galveston in three days, Karen. It isn't much time. I want you on that boat with me."

"Vance, we . . . I . . . oh, God, yes, I'll be there. I'll be there with you. . . ." she sobbed happily, throwing herself into his arms, clinging to him, tears of joy and exultation flowing freely now. Suddenly she stopped crying and thrust herself back from him. "We'll have to be married first."

Vance shook his head slowly. "Nope."

Karen's face fell, then brightened with the thought he must be playing a joke. "Surely, sir," she teased, "you wouldn't ask a maiden to travel unmarried?"

Vance reached out and put his hands on her shoulders. "Little lady, if I get married up here in this heathen country, old True will never let me hear the end of it. Don't worry. We're gonna get married all right. But in Texas. We'll have a wedding like you've never seen before. Not one of your stodgy old Washington affairs with *petit fours* and dainty cakes and tea, but a real Texas wedding right on our ranch with a whole cow cooked up and lots of music and dancing. Even have a shivaree, probably. No way to keep the boys from having their fun. Now, I don't know what your folks'll think about that, but they're welcome if they want to come."

"Not hardly," Barrett said, stepping from the garden path. Vance and Karen spun to face him. "Alfred stopped by the library. He was furious, of course, and I don't blame him. For your sake, Karen, I convinced him not to have the police apprehend Mr. Paxton for his spurious and contemptible assault on one of Washington's finest gentlemen." His eyes fastened malevolently on Vance. "Mr. Paxton. I do commend your decision to take the next boat to Texas. Your absence will be keenly felt, but I assure you we'll bear up. Now I suggest you leave these grounds immediately. Hermann will drive you to wherever you wish to be taken. Hotel, saloon, bordello, whatever. Karen, if you will be so kind as to follow me. . . ."

"Father, stop it!" Karen said, her tone one of complete defiance. "I *am* going to Texas. Vance and I will be married there. I will leave with him." Her unwavering gaze bore into the older man as she took Vance's hand and stood at his side.

"That is your decision?"

"Yes, Papa. It is. Freely made."

Barrett Hampton stood unflinching. Every trace of emotion drained from his face. When he spoke his voice was as cold and devoid of feeling as a wind blowing through an empty house. "Very well. Then it is over. You are no longer a member of this family. You are free to follow your Mr. Paxton and join his tribe of barbarians."

Karen forced herself to stand straight, helped by Vance's arm which stole around her to give her support. "Papa, I didn't want it this way. Won't you please . . ."

"The decision was yours." He laughed sardonically, brought himself under control. "Freely made, as you said. You are no longer welcome in this house or on this property."

"Papa . . ."

"There is," Barrett concluded, turning his back on them and starting for the house, "nothing left to be said."

And there wasn't.

PART II

CHAPTER I

Texas . . . from the earliest days, men followed their dreams to Texas. Cabeza de Vaca, Coronado, LaSalle, and later Englishmen, Germans, Poles, Irishmen and more. Men large of stature and small. Men riding from the past and men riding toward the future. Men of all faiths, all ideologies, men of great wealth and of none. Some perished in the swamplands to the east where the Sabine undulated like the water vipers traversing its tributaries. Some perished on the wide, empty plains where the untrammeled earth stretched as far as eyes could see and the heavy lid of heaven, an infinite dome of blue dotted by wayward clouds, sloped down to fasten on the wind-whipped grasses, a joining toward which one could ever travel but never reach. Some perished on the brutal lances of the Comanche, Apache, Chiricahua, Kickapoo and Tejas, which meant friend. Not all survived, for not every seed takes root, but those who did flourished and were made strong, raised strong children who stayed to tame the land. Here was the true promise, more valuable by far than the ephemeral gold. Here was birth, both literal and figurative, of men, values and a way of life destined to survive and more, to build a nation.

The ship skirted Matagorda and, sails full of the strong southerly wind from her port side, darted by Galveston, following the curve of the Gulf of Mexico to Corpus Christi Bay. Vance Paxton, his dream at his side, was returning to Texas. Gulls like ancient Viking craft caught in the maelstrom of the sky whirled, dipped close, winged upward, ever circling, their cries echoing over sea and swell, carrying beyond the salt flats of the Nueces River, beyond the ramshackle false-front buildings of Corpus Christi, to be swallowed by the quiet vastness of the coastal plain. Corpus Christi . . .

"Dammit!" Vance cursed aloud. He rested his brawny forearms on the rail of the schooner, took the makings from the side slit pocket of his ruffled Mexican shirt and rolled a cigarette. He stared down at the muddy shallows and cursed again

This was a hell of a sight for Karen's first glimpse of Texas. Oh, he had nothing against the town personally, but Galveston, with its hotels, theaters and fine restaurants, now there was the Lone Star State he wanted his intended to first experience so she could see Texas was more than some rawbone frontier, uncouth and unpolished. But Captain Beeman had pointedly avoided Galveston. Vance couldn't blame him, had even concurred in the decision. With a yellow fever epidemic ravaging the town, only a fool would have docked, much less spent time there. Yellow fever . . . of all the damnable luck.

He glanced wistfully down the ship toward Karen's door. She would still be asleep, warm, snug and good to hold in his arms, the kind of woman to make a man curse the morning hours alone, driven from bed to a day's work.

Or so he imagined, for Karen slept alone as she had the entire trip. Separated by nothing more than a bulkhead of wooden planking, he had honored her wish that they wait to consummate their love until their wedding night. For seventeen long days, interminable to Vance, they had talked of Washington and their pasts, of Texas and their future, held hands at the rail as they passed down the churning Atlantic, through the blissfully peaceful Straits of Florida and into the quiet Gulf of Mexico. In the evenings they had eaten with Captain Beeman and spent long hours in conversation, Karen mostly listening while Vance and the old seadog swapped stories. Later Vance would walk her to her cabin, kiss her gently—she had found, on the first night out, how dangerously seductive a more lingering touch could be—and leave her, his footsteps fading quickly into the creak of line and wood, the murmur of wind in the rigging. After a final smoke with the old man he would retire to his own cabin and quietly pace the floor. Talk was all well and good, but the woman he loved was near . . . so very near . . . near enough to drive him into a rage of vexatious frustration. Damn Washington morality!—a laugh if the Leightons were any example. Still, Karen wanted to wait. He loved her and so he would, damning the hours and the thin plank wall between them. For seventeen nights he slept alone, wrapped in solitude and plagued by dreams. But finally the voyage was over, and behind him the door to his empty cabin swung open and closed as the schooner rocked gently to and fro on the slight chop as the wind kicked up a notch. He inhaled the tobacco, relishing its strong earthy flavor and blowing a cloud of pale smoke into the sea-warmed air.

"Corpus Christi sunrise," Captain Beeman said as he approached the tall, ruggedly handsome young man leaning on the rail amidships. "Glass is goin' down. That and the water and the swell buildin' up behind us when we came through Aransas Pass . . . must be a storm brewin' out in the Gulf. Sorry about havin' to pass by Galveston. We'll dock in about twenty minutes."

"Nothing to be done, Captain. There's a stage line running from here, and it's closer by eighty miles to San Antonio. I imagine we'll get there all right. Maybe even in time for the Fourth." Vance shoved away from the rail and sauntered back toward his cabin, tossing the smouldering remains of his cigarette into the bay. The cabin was illuminated by the faint morning light, the air cooler with the door open behind him. The shallow bunk was rumpled and unkempt, the emptiness symbolic of the empty feeling in his loins. Placing his two carpetbags on the mattress, he opened one and reached beneath the folded shirts, removed a belt and a handgun snugly fitted into a worn leather holster. He untied the leather thong and took the pistol, a .44 caliber army Colt, in his hand and spun the cylinder to check the load, then replaced the weapon in its holster and swung the belt around his narrow hips.

How long? How many days since he'd felt the reassuring weight at his side? Three months? His hand fitted the hard bois d'arc grip comfortably and the gun slid out effortlessly, smoothly. A sixth sense told him eyes were watching and he glanced over his shoulder in time to see Captain Beeman standing near the ship's rail and studying him. For a moment their eyes locked in silent communication, then Beeman averted his gaze, shouted an order to the first mate and went on his way. Vance dropped the weapon into the worn leather, pulled it out again and again, his

139

hand moving faster and faster each time until it was a blur, the pistol leaping free of the leather and into his palm, ready to fire at imaginary targets. Finally satisfied, he left the weapon in the holster and shrugged on his traveling coat, the front opening in a wide slash to either side, allowing him instant and deadly access to the .44. When the carpetbags were repacked and closed he left them on the bunk and went back out on deck, glancing at the dark line under the door to Karen's cabin. The thought came unbidden to his mind, how she must look at that moment, all sleepy and tousled, her gown, perhaps, pulled up in sleep to reveal the curve of her legs, the . . .

Desire welled in him. The very thought of her was a heady narcotic. More than any woman he'd known, he wanted Karen Hampton. He found his hand raised to knock on her door but thought better of it and pushed away to walk toward the bow where Beeman and the other two passengers were clustered, watching as the boat glided softly toward the mouth of the Neuces River and her dock.

The sharp cries of the crew awakened her. Karen yawned, thrusting her arms into the air. She sat up slowly, thinking of her bath, then realized where she was. There would be no bath this morning. There would be no Retta. Not ever again. The thought struck her suddenly, an almost savage realization.

The Captain said they would be in port come morning. It *was* morning. Golden shimmering streams of reflected sunshine sifted through the shuttered porthole over her head, filling the air with softspun light. The room was stuffy. She rose, attired herself in a dressing gown and threw back the shutters. She could see the long line of graying wooden shacks that ran along the featureless shore. Good heavens! The harbor was a veritable slum. Vainly she raised her eyes to see the inland part of town. More shacks, a dusty street and falsefront stores, none over a story tall. Just like in the magazines. She sighed with relief. A faint line of bluffs, no more than twenty feet high, stood back a quarter mile from the docks. The town proper must be back from the edge of the bluffs, back where she couldn't see it. No doubt a carriage would meet them and they would ride to their hotel before spending a day sightseeing.

As she watched, the schooner pulled nearer and nearer

to the dock, bumped softly into the piering and stopped, barely rocking on the remnants of a tidal swell which ran upriver from the bay, there to dissipate in the shallow salt flats lining the lower banks of the Nueces. Lines from the ship flew through the air and men on shore grabbed them and looped them around huge posts, hurried about to set up a gangplank and prepare for unloading. Soon it would be time to disembark. Good heavens, she had to dress!

"Karen!" She jumped in alarm. Vance pounded on her door. "Karen, time to go." She could see the shadow of his feet at the bottom of the door as they turned and left. What would have happened if he'd come in and seen her as she stood there? The fantasy swelled to life. She pressed the sponge between her breasts, ran it down along her stomach, trying to imagine what it would be like if he were there with her to guide the sponge with delicious bathing strokes over her flesh. She shuddered with arousal, opened her eyes and stepped back quickly from the basin, toweling herself vigorously. There would be time for all such intimacies. Soon, now . . . soon.

She selected a corset and traveling gown from the trunk and dressed rapidly in the quiet island stillness of the cabin as the ship gently rocked back and forth to the tune of tiny wavelets lapping against the hull. Outside she was dimly aware of the shouting, boisterous crew as they set to work unloading the vessel. The voyage was over for them too. Their work would soon be done and they would have a night in port, some of them, perhaps, with their families. . . .

The homesickness hit her again, harder than before. She sat dully on her bed, remembering home then forcing herself up and about the business of doing her hair. As she worked she listened intently, studying each sound not out of any particular interest in the sound itself, but rather to keep from thinking. Why now? Why today, this morning, had these feelings beset her? Because she was to disembark? Because from now on she would be in Texas, a bride with responsibilities, obligated to learn all the ways of a strange land? Her family. . . . Her family was in Washington, lost to her forever, her father immersed in his world of finance and politics, her mother preoccupied with the whims of social prestige and both tied to the irrevocable past. Unbidden, the image of her father on that fatal afternoon sprung to mind and suddenly she wanted to find Vance, needed to be near his reassuring strength. She fitted herself into the dress as rapidly as possible.

Vance was standing near the bow of the ship, speaking to Captain Beeman. He turned as the door closed quietly behind her, mysteriously aware of her presence without seeing or hearing her. She watched him excuse himself from the Captain, turn and start toward her. But there was something different about him. As he walked a hint of a breeze sprung up and caught the corner of his coat. *My God! He's wearing a gun! Whatever . . .? Why . . .?*

Returned to his native soil, the change in Vance's appearance was due to more than the wearing of a gun. He was near home now. He could smell and see Texas, feel it in his bones. Every nerve was strung tight, every muscle on edge in anticipation. He was all too aware of the way Karen's eyes were drawn to the weapon resting at his thigh, but decided to wait until she said something. "Darling," he said in a near whisper. "We're home. This is Texas."

She continued to stare. "Vance. That's a gun. You have a gun."

"Of course. Don't look so horrified. Your father had an entire wall rack full of guns."

"But he never . . . carried one around on the street."

"The streets we'll be walking, where there are any, it's best to *always* carry one."

"Really, Vance, you exaggerate."

His eyes narrowed and his tone became deadly serious. "There is one thing you have to realize, Karen. Life here is different than in Washington. There will be no police standing one to a corner. Away from the major towns a person is on his own. There are bad men here. And Indians. If the good men didn't wear guns, they wouldn't stay alive. I love you too much not to want to be able to protect you."

Karen smiled demurely. She had heard the stories over and over again, but like many an Easterner born to wealth she simply didn't believe half of what she'd heard. "I think you're being much too serious. But what you say is very sweet." Her face drew close to his. The faint odor of lilac of the first night they had kissed, made him yearn to hold her again, kiss her deeply and drink in the very passion of her nearness.

"You'd best get your bags ready," Vance said gruffly.

"We'll be off in a few moments." His voice was harder than necessary, and for a moment Karen's eyes clouded.

"I'm almost ready. A few more things."

"Get them ready. A man will take them shortly."

She paused briefly then returned to her cabin, perplexed at his sudden change of mood. Behind her, Vance's face set in a determined frown. Her reaction to the gun bothered him. They'd discussed this many times before and he had been sure she understood. Good grief, had she agreed solely for the sake of agreement? Had she learned nothing, listened not at all to his stories of the frontier?

His thought was interrupted by a sailor. "Ready to take the lady's duffel off, sir. And yours, if you will."

"Mine is on my bunk," Vance told him shortly. "I'll check on the lady myself, then let you know."

The sailor touched his cap lightly. "Aye, sir."

Vance strode to Karen's cabin, knocked gently. "We're about ready, Karen."

The door opened and she stood there, face serious for a moment until she could assess his mood, then brightening when he smiled at her. "Everything is packed."

"Good." He offered her his arm and turned toward amidships, calling over his shoulder to the sailor who was emerging from his cabin. "You may get the lady's duffel now."

Captain Beeman watched them coming and marveled anew at the girl. By Neptune, she was a beauty! A face and body to set the blood of an old sea dog roiling. He hid the twinge of jealousy. "Your trunks are already off and on the way to the stage depot," he said, meeting them at the forward gangplank and nodding slightly to Karen. "You may go ashore any time." He looked closely at Vance. The two men had spent many a late hour during the voyage and he had grown to like the tall, spare Texan. He wished him well and was glad to see him wearing the gun, gladder yet to have caught a glimpse of him as he handled it, for stories of violence were rife all up and down the seaboard. Reconstruction, as elsewhere in the south, was a harsh and emotional time, a time during which the voice of anger and gunfire too often drowned out that of good will and reason. By now news of Vance's speech before the Congress would have gotten back home. Vance was a known man and his stance would not be looked upon with favor, at least not by the scalawags and carpetbaggers who still retained control of the state government. Governor Davis' hated State Police had been dissolved during his absence, but still men went armed and feelings ran high. He held out his hand and Vance took it with a sure, strong grip. "Luck," he said.

Vance grinned. "Hope I don't need it, but thanks. You too."

"Aye. When I need a good man I'll know where to look. Even if he be a lubber." He turned to Karen. "Miss Hampton . . ." he cleared his throat before continuing. "Your charming presence has lent a certain grace to this poor vessel. We will miss you." He wanted to warn her again but thought better. She was in good hands, and more words now would be a waste of time.

Karen offered him her hand. "Thank you, Captain," she said. "Thank you very much." Vance took her arm and the couple gingerly traversed the gangplank to the pier. Behind them Captain Beeman doffed his cap in silent farewell.

They crossed the splintered planks of the dock and passed between the storage sheds where men toiled in the already terrible heat. Corpus Christi lay before them. Karen glanced along the beach. "But where is the carriage?" she asked.

"What carriage?"

"The carriage to take us wherever we're to go? To town. . . ."

Vance continued walking. "We're in town and it's only a couple of minutes to walk to the depot." He chuckled softly. "I doubt there's a carriage anywhere in the whole place."

Karen stopped abruptly. "This is . . . this . . ." she gestured dramatically, ". . . is Corpus Christi? All of it?"

"I know it isn't much," Vance began apologetically.

"I thought it was just the waterfront. Good Lord, this . . . *slum* . . . is the whole town? I can't believe it."

Vance coaxed her into the street separating a handful of clapboard buildings to either side. "Texas is still frontier. You can't expect the finery . . ."

"I'm not talking of finery. Just some visible aspects of civilization."

"Wait. Wait until we reach San Antonio. You'll love it, I promise. With luck we'll be there by the Fourth. It will be *fiesta* time, in spite of the bad feelings. Everyone will come to town for a big party—any party. The Rebs'll be there too, even if they aren't so sympathetic. A party is a party. You'll see." He guided her along the street and to the depot. A weather-beaten clapboard sign hung from rusted chains, "Matherson Stage Line" scrawled across the planks in large black letters. Karen recognized her trunks stacked on the porchway as she accompanied Vance inside.

The interior was more bleak than the exterior, if that were possible. A single counter ran the length of the back wall. A huge iron stove, black with age and smoke, stood to one side and the walls were hung with old sheets of newspaper, the faded headlines screaming worn tales of battles won and lost, death, mayhem and tragedy. Crates and parcels, most covered with a heavy layer of sandy dust, cluttered every corner and stood in tall haphazard stacks. Behind the counter, a grizzled character of indeterminate age sat, laboriously writing in a ledger. "I want to purchase fares for two to San Antonio," Vance said.

The man behind the desk spoke without looking up from the ledger. "No point in payin' now. Y'all can if yah want, but no point to it."

Karen's apprehension grew. She desperately wanted to get out and away from the dingy room, from the whole town. She started as Vance dropped her arm and reached across the counter and closed the ledger, sending up a small cloud of dust. The old man looked up angrily. "Say, what the . . . oh. Pardon me, ma'am." He adjusted his glasses and squinted at Vance. "Now look here, mister. . ."

"I'll need two fares to San Antonio. When will the stage be leaving?"

"That's what I'm tellin' yah, if y'all weren't in such a consarned rush. She ain't leavin' 'cause she ain't got here yet. Ain't due for another three days. Only had two coaches an' one a' them got busted up runnin' from a bunch a' outlaw Mescans. Mr. Matherson ain't put another'n on the line yet. They's a hotel jes' across the street. I reckin y'all can put up there."

Karen went pale. *Three days. No. Not here. Not in this Godforsaken . . .*

As if reading her thoughts, Vance headed for the door. "Wait here," he instructed briefly, and was gone. Karen started to protest but there was no one to whom she might.

She felt the stageman's eyes on her and drew herself up to her full height. She looked about for a place to sit, but found naught but trunks. Choosing the cleanest looking, she slapped at the grimy surface with her handkerchief and sat down, haughtily returning the old man's gaze. He immediately averted his eyes and returned to the ledger.

Beads of perspiration began to form on her forehead and she dabbed at the moisture with the silk handkerchief, then gave up when she felt the first drop run down her neck and chest, another run down her side. She glanced ruefully at the stove, wondered whatever it might be used for in such a climate. A large dusty clock on the wall ticked heavily, each interminable minute passing more slowly than the one before, each adding to her sense of despondency.

The clatter of harness and the sound of a wagon drawing up before the depot jerked her from her reverie. The door swung open and Vance entered hurriedly, closing the door behind him and pulling a tiny blue parasol from under his coat. "This is for you. I had to hide it, else the boys in town would have given me a time." Vance crossed to the old man behind the counter, who looked up from his ledger without any assistance from the lanky Texan. "The hosteler told me you had a rifle for sale."

"I got one. Don't know as it's fer sale. A Henry .44. Shoots sweet an' straight." He glanced pointedly at the weapon on Vance's thigh and knew he could make a good trade, for with the Henry, Vance would need to carry but one kind of ammunition.

Vance nodded at Karen and she left the room and the men to their haggling. She walked outside and looked at the buildings around her. A slight breeze kicked up little eddies of dust along the street but did little to dissipate the mid-morning heat. She opened the parasol to take advantage of the shade it offered. The wagon Vance had driven up was a simple outfit, a wooden seat over a long rickety-looking flat bed half filled with an odd assortment of boxes and sacks. Two melancholy mules were hitched to the tongue, the reins draped loosely over the rail in front of them. Karen thought of Hermann and the carriages at home, the care he gave to each polished piece of wood, leather and brass. She imagined herself standing once again in the cool dark stables, surrounded by the smell of leather and hay, by her father's magnificent horses, sorrels and bays alike animals for the coach of a king. With a handful of carrots stolen from the kitchen she would draw close. Oh, they knew her. Each would whinny for attention, hooves stomping impatiently on the straw-covered planks, ears pricked forward and eyes rolling. Each received a carrot, a soft pat on the neck and a gently, playful tug on his luxuriant, combed and ribboned mane.

The door opened behind her. Vance and the stageman stepped out, each carrying a pair of carpetbags which they dropped on the porch and left while they loaded the trunks. The old man packed the carpetbags into the wagon bed, wedging them between the trunks and the seat, while Vance returned briefly to the door, reached inside and came back out with a rifle and spare cartridge belt. The stageman stepped back onto the porch, wiping his face with a soiled red kerchief. "That Crawford's buckboard?"

"Was," Vance nodded as he stashed the rifle under the seat and shucked his coat.

"It'd make more sense to wait fer that stage. Three days ain't so long when it comes to keepin' yer hair. Them Mescans an' Apaches causin' all kinda hell, beggin' your pardon, ma'am. They come up from Mexico at Eagle Pass an' disappear into the countryside. A band a' one of 'em between here an' San Antone, fer sure. I wouldn't be chancin' gettin' there on my lonesome, especially escortin' a fine-lookin' lady."

Vance offered Karen his hand and helped her onto the seat. "We won't be alone," he replied as he took up the reins and climbed into the seat. "And you can tell that to anyone you want."

"If yer thinkin' a' the train, better think again. A bunch a' renegades hit the last two, tore 'em to pieces."

"We'll take our chances," Vance answered coldly, angered at the talk he knew would upset Karen.

"Well, don't say I didn't tell you."

Vance clucked and snapped the reins sharply on the mules' backs and they ambled away from the depot. Karen was more than glad to be away and for the time being rode silently, reflecting Vance's mood and trying fruitlessly to fully comprehend the vast space around. *It's like the ocean, only solid . . . hot. . . .* Some half a mile ahead a small grove of trees poked out of the emptiness and it was for these they headed and there sought respite amid the dappled shade. Vance applied the brake, jumped down and circled the wagon to assist her. She leapt to the ground, supported by his strong arms. Neither had spoken for the last hour and she was full of questions, forgotten when his arms enfolded her and held her close. Her lips eagerly went to his and the plaguing fears left her, driven from mind and heart by the feverish embrace. Their bodies felt right, matched by love's own cunning, each made to fulfill the desire of the other. A bee buzzed low, its hum underscoring the serenity of the moment.

"Sit here," he said gently. He looked around them, out onto the fiery plain surrounding the tiny grove of mesquite and live oak. "Don't talk. Just sit and let it all soak in. You'll need a while. I'll rustle us up some food." He pulled down one of his carpetbags and set it on the blanket for her to lean against.

"Vance?" she asked, suddenly afraid.

"Yes?"

"You said we wouldn't be traveling alone."

He gestured back toward town in answer. Coming over the small bluff, barely visible, she saw a cloud of dust. "What is it?"

"A wagon train with supplies for San Antonio," he answered. "They were to be unloaded in Galveston, but couldn't because of the fever. It's a shorter trip this way but the trail isn't as good and they have to go through wilder country and the danger of surprise is greater. With luck, though, there'll be no problems. Seven wagons and three outriders, we shouldn't have too much trouble." He paused. "It's not the way I wanted to introduce you to Texas, to bring you to San Antonio. Not at all. But we will get there. They'll be here in another fifteen minutes, half an hour." He stood and took her hand, pulled her to her feet and placed his hands on her shoulders. "Karen, I don't believe you really believe all the stories you heard. Not yet, no matter how earnestly I told you. I'm sure you think them too fantastic to be true. But they are, and you will believe, before too many more days have passed. Perhaps even hours, for one never knows."

He paused, frowning. "You were at home in Washington. Here you are what we call a tenderfoot. You'll have to learn a great many things. I only ask you do learn, not reject what you see simply because it differs from what you have known. The men who will ride with us are rough—they have been through a great deal."

His voice went on but Karen paid no attention to the words, only looked up at the man she had loved enough to leave a world behind. His clear blue eyes, the long brown hair beneath the broad-brimmed hat, the purposeful line of jaw. She could not help herself and drew close to him, her arms circling around his waist, her mouth seeking his. She could feel the hardness of his flesh beneath his shirt. His wide, strong hands slipped down her back, one continuing on until it rested deliciously near her hip. Enough to leave a world behind? *Yes . . . yes! A world and more. . . .*

CHAPTER II

Around them stretched the vast table of the coastal plain, emptier, wider and more vast than anything she had ever seen save the ocean. At wide intervals a dry creekbed running to the Nueces broke the land and along these a few mesquite and cottonwoods grew. The land rolled gently, barely enough to make a difference, and from the tops of the small rises one could see for miles. At the bottoms, only the sky. The image of the ocean kept returning to her, burned in further by the barely waving sun-yellowed bunch grass, brown and parched in most spots and miraculously green in others.

Karen looked wistfully to the west. There, some hundreds of yards away, lay the flowing waters of the meandering Nueces, whose winding course they followed. "And I thought it was warm on the ship," she sighed aloud, dabbing at her face with the soaked kerchief. "Thank God for the parasol. I would simply perish without it."

Vance tried his most reassuring look. "We might pick up a little breeze before too long, from the look of those clouds. Be thankful we're at the front of this freight line instead of the rear."

Karen glanced at the seven wagons in line behind them, the farthermost hidden in a choking cloud of dust raised by the ones before. They had been traveling for the greater part of the day. *Oh, for a breeze. For anything to alleviate this heat.*

The sun finally completed its brassy passage across the sky, and as it lay partially over the horizon, one of the horsemen she had seen rode up to the wagon and touched his hat in deference to her. "We'll be pullin' in to Sandy Bend fer the night. I done scouted it out. Looks good."

Vance nodded as the man rode off, and a few hundred yards farther turned the team from the tracks they followed

151

and headed toward the line of green to the west. Each yard they went the air grew cooler.

"Why didn't we travel closer to the trees?" Karen asked. "It seems cooler."

"Too dangerous. Out here, there's time to see someone coming at you." He stopped the wagon a couple of hundred yards away from the trees and spent a long five minutes studying them. Finally, satisfied with what he saw—or didn't see—he clucked to the team and headed toward a large cottonwood.

Vance pulled the buckboard up close to the river and within a half hour the other wagons were moving into position, forming a loose protective half circle around the buckboard. Karen stood to one side and watched as the men leaped from the wagons and stretched. The drivers unhitched their teams and led them to water, then strung ropes between four trees and left the animals to roll and eat. She felt helpless in the quiet bustle. Vance unhitched their team, watered them and put them in with the others, took some of the trunks from the buckboard and made, using the wagon for one side, a small three-sided partition around her own private campfire. Within moments the smell of food filled the air, and when she looked around she saw a larger fire had been built, over which hung a huge iron pot. To one side of the fire a coffee pot, squat and black, sent out a tiny plume of steam.

Vance spread out a blanket for her and left to go to the fire. When he returned he carried a cup of coffee for himself and a pair of tin plates heaped with beans and bacon. Surprised at her hunger, Karen attacked the smoke-flavored simple fare with relish. In no way comparable to the food at Captain Beeman's table, much less what she was used to at her father's house, she finished it off gladly, for the food was wholesome and filling.

The rest of the light disappeared while they ate. The heat, oppressive during the day, faded and a slight breeze from across the river cooled the night and left her at ease and comfortable for the first time since morning. Night sounds filled the air with pleasant harmonies and she relaxed, enjoying the rustle of leaves in the cottonwood, the crackling of the fire, the quiet rumble of masculine voices beyond her circle of trunks. Vance kept up a steady stream of talk, explaining first this sound and then that, pointing out how the fire had been laid and why it was kept small, how she could tell from the stars what time it was. An hour passed and the men at the fire lazed around, now and again one going into the night to check the mules.

Karen was getting tired and Vance could tell it. "You'd better get some sleep," he said. "Maybe think about what you're going to wear tomorrow. Going to be hot again." He stood and stretched his legs.

Karen sat up, suddenly a little afraid. "Where are you going?"

"Just out to scout around. The boys know their business, but I'll feel better if I look around for myself. Don't worry. I'll be back, and sleep right on the other side of the trunk from you."

Karen smiled, reassured. "I'll stay awake until you get back."

"No need." And he was gone, slipping away from the wagons toward the water. She didn't hear a sound, couldn't catch a glimpse of him. She stretched lazily, and suddenly realizing she was alone, undid some of the buttons on her dress and managed to wriggle out of the corset. Relief was immediate. She left the sweat-dampened article out to dry and sank down to the blankets, bones and muscles weary from the long day and jolting ride. *I can't remember being this tired. Everything is so strange, so new.*

A low laugh from around the fire drew her attention and she turned to see what was happening, studied the men gathered about the flames. They were a scruffy lot, all right. Ten grizzled, rough countenances. They talked little, some of them still eating, dipping full ladles of beans and bacon into their tin plates. Deep-throated voices, curt and to the point, talked of the weather, Indians, the epidemic and how far west it might have come, of gunfighters Karen had read of in the papers and dime novels her artist friends used to leave around on the tables of *Le Chien*. If only those friends could see her now. Now? No. Grimy and bedraggled, hiding behind a trunk and listening to the coarse voices of western men gathered around a campfire.

A thrill went through her. She had never been afraid of any man. Intimidated by men such as these? Not likely! She was Karen Hampton, was she not? The belle of Washington society, the most sought after young lady in a town full of beautiful women.

She buttoned her dress, brushed back her hair and strode haughtily from the barrier of trunks into the very center of the camp. Immediately all conversation stopped. A rugged looking man with a patch over one eye stood and removed his hat. A gun was thrust into the top of his trousers next to where his suspenders fastened to the cloth. She recognized him as one of the men on horseback who rode ahead of the wagons. Vance had called them outriders, whose job it was to check the countryside for any possible sign of trouble.

"Evenin', ma'am. Hope us boys ain't disturbin' you none."

"Yes'm," a portly man who drove the wagon immediately behind hers added. "You jus' say the word an' me an' the boys'll turn in."

Karen turned to face the new speaker. "That's quite all right, Mister . . . ?" She paused.

"Uh . . . Considine. Jersey Considine," the portly man answered, blushing furiously. All the others stared in envy. She had asked his name, the lucky galoot, each man silently reflected.

"Actually, I thought I might impose on you for a little coffee."

There was a near riot to see who would pour her a cup. The youngest of the lot produced a clean cup from his gear, but the burly man with the eyepatch, the one who had first spoken to her, unwisely grabbed the pot with his bare hand, wincing at the searing heat. The youngster grudgingly handed him the cup. Every eye watched as the coffee was poured and the cup handed to Karen, who smiled sweetly. "Thank you."

"My name is Roscoe Bodine," the burly man said. He touched the patch over his eye. "I lost this at Chickamauga. Yer the prettiest little gal the other one's ever seen."

Karen flashed a most entrancing smile. "That's very gallant of you, Mister Bodine. Thank you all for the coffee." She curtsied slightly and returned to her wagon. Only when she was safely obscured by the trunks and kneeling by the fire did she allow an impish, naughty smile to cross her face. Tough, stolid westeners, indeed! They had all but fallen over themselves to fulfill her slightest wish. She did not feel so bedraggled now, rather more self-assured, for she had captivated them on the instant.

At that moment Vance rounded the wagon, appearing silently and carrying an armload of firewood. He squatted near her and dropped the wood, tossed a few pieces onto the guttering flames.

"Vance," she whispered, touching his arm. He turned to her and she set the coffee cup down and leaned toward him, her lips moist and eager, burning with the hunger of the flames. Vance was caught totally unprepared by the unabashed display of emotion, felt reason and control swept away by the fervent ardor of her embrace. Her body melted against his, her tongue a teasing dart of love, their lips bruised with the moment's passion. She felt his hands drawing her close. She did love him, loved him more than he could ever know. Moaning, she welcomed his hand stroking her thigh as they sank to the ground by the fire. Karen's breath came in hard, shallow gasps. Her resolve weakened by the exhaustion of travel and her body driven on by the aphrodisiac of the primitive land surrounding her, she pressed hungrily to him. Through the clothes separating their hungry flesh she could feel the throbbing strength of his manhood, found herself yearning for it sheathed inside her, thrusting fiercely again and again. Her whole body aching, she reached for his groin, sought the probing, pulsing flesh. . . .

Suddenly he was away from her, rolling back against the trunks, his eyes open and staring into the night, his breath ragged, his fingers clutching the blanket.

"Vance?" she whispered, feeling empty and afraid, embarrassed by her forwardness and unable to understand why he had left her. "I want you. I don't want to wait any longer." She crawled to him, lay her head on his chest.

For a long moment neither spoke. When he did, his voice was low and hoarse, carrying no further than her ear. "Two reasons. First, I agreed to wait, and though I want you badly, I'll not break an agreement lightly." He paused. "Listen."

"I don't hear anything."

"That's the other reason. You think they don't hear every sound in the night? I'll not leave you open for sly, winking looks from any man. And if we went on, they'd have cause enough."

155

There was nothing to be said in protest. The moment was past. Karen sat up, stared with empty eyes into the fire. Behind her Vance stood. "I'll get you set for the night," he said, loud enough for all in the camp behind him to hear. Vance made a bed for Karen on the ground, the soft blankets cushioning the hard packed earth. Sleeping out was a great adventure for her, for this was the first night since she was a child she had not slept in a bed. Adding a few twigs to the fire, Vance came upon the coffee cup. "What's this?"

"Oh, I forgot. One of the men gave me some coffee."

Vance's face clouded. "You mean someone came over here?"

"No, silly. I went out and asked for some. For such an intemperate looking group of men I must say they were extremely polite." She took the cup and sipped some of the still warm dark liquid, almost gagging on the first swallow. Having tasted her father's coffee, Karen thought herself prepared for anything. But not this brew. "Good heavens, it tastes like . . . like bitter mud."

Vance grinned and took the cup. "Serves you right. A lady shouldn't go wandering off to other men."

"I am perfectly capable of taking care of myself in my social endeavors. I have had ample practice."

"But not out here."

"Men are essentially the same everywhere, Mr. Paxton," she said, shrugging her shoulders. "If you would like to join your friends I think I'd like to sleep now." Paying no attention to him, she lay down and pulled the rough blanket up to her chin, turning her back to him and looking into the remains of the fire. For a moment all was silent, then she heard Vance sigh perplexedly and leave. She stifled a little laugh and told herself she should be ashamed of carrying on so. But she simply had to make up for her earlier wanton behavior. She had literally flung herself at him, and his rejection, no matter what the stated reason, stung her to the quick.

She curled up in a little ball, wishing he were with her. Something had happened in that moment when he returned to the fire. She had known desire before, but never had love's ardor burned so brightly in her, never had she allowed mere physical passion to override all caution. She rolled over onto her back, staring at the stars and glad for the blanket, for the night had grown cool. Why had her resolve crumbled so? Somehow she seemed powerless to hold herself back. Why? Excitement coursed through her and she shivered despite the blanket. The day had started poorly but the night brought with it a renewed sense of adventure and romance. The fire, the stars above her and the feel of earth beneath her all contributed to the sense of being at one with nature. As never before she realized she was the female of the species, prey to the need for fulfillment, hungrily anticipating the ultimate act of an all consuming love. She fell asleep, missing the stupendous display of a full moon coursing through towering clouds which came from the south.

Bodine and another man were the only two left around the campfire. With one man on guard, slowly riding the perimeter of their camp, the others had turned in. Vance squatted by the coffee pot and poured himself a cup of the strong hot brew. He rolled a smoke and sat quietly, savoring the complementary tastes of tobacco and good range coffee, black, boiled and bitter. The guard came in from the night, sacking out immediately, and the man beside Bodine got up and left, disappearing around the nearest wagon.

Vance relaxed, sipping his coffee and staring across the fire at the burly one-eyed man. The two had ridden together on a couple of cattle drives to Kansas and had known each other during the war. Not quite friends, they had shared work, danger and food and bore a grudgingly mutual respect for each other. "Made good time, Roscoe," Vance remarked quietly.

The one-eyed man nodded, sitting back against his saddle and stretching his legs. He looked at Vance warily for a moment, then relaxed. "Ain't much of a job." He spat to one side. "Hell, who can't run a wagon down a stage line?"

"Surprised to see you riding guard for a freight line. You're too good a cattleman. Last I heard, you were taking a herd up Kansas way."

Bodine scowled, sat up and refilled his cup. "Lost it to a band a' murderin' Comancheros up on the Red. Bad country up that way. Worse'n before the war. Real bad. I was lucky to get out with the hair on my head. Come back down to San Antone figurin' on tyin' up with another outfit, but nobody wants a man who's lost a herd, even if it wasn't his fault. Knocked around a while 'til I run outta cash. When I heard about the fever over Galveston way, an' that they'd be sendin' wagons up from Corpus, figured I'd try to make an easy dollar."

"You see any trouble sign out there at all, Roscoe?"

"Nothin'. Not a damned thing, which bothers me, even if I am glad enough. Lot can happen 'tween here an' San Antone. I figger we'll make camp at Three Rivers come tomorrow night. The way station's there and the lady can sleep inside, if she's a mind. Mighty lonesome country out here."

Vance studied the man's face, trying to read the motive behind his final remark, then inwardly cursing himself for a suspicious fool, drained the contents of his cup. "I'm turning in." He rose, paused a few steps from the fire, half turned and said to Bodine, "Roscoe, we can always use a good hand on the ranch. If something doesn't break for you in San Antone, come on out."

Bodine looked at him questioningly, evidently decided to accept the offer at face value. "Maybe I'll do that," he answered as he lay back on the saddle and closed his eyes.

Vance peered over the trunks, checking on Karen. Satisfied all was well, he flipped open his bedroll. For a long while he lay there listening to the night sounds and questioning the wisdom of bringing her to Texas with him. Right or wrong, he knew only one thing for a certainty: he could not have left Washington without her. No woman had ever excited him so completely, ever so disturbed him, brought his blood to fever pitch and raging through his veins. Her seeming inability to understand she was living under a totally different set of conditions bothered him, but he was willing to give her time. Deep down he felt sure she was a woman fit for the frontier, a woman for Texas. She would harden to life on the ranch and in so doing add immeasurably to his life. She was a beauty fit for the Paxton ranch and the Paxton line. He dozed fitfully, senses alert to the nuances of the night. Finally he slept, but restlessly, his dreams marred by premonitions, of what, he did not know.

Morning came early for the camp. Karen woke to the strange sounds, only dimly aware of where she was. The snort of a mule brought her to her senses and she peeked over the trunks to see where Vance was, only to catch a glimpse of him leaving the fire and heading for the rope corral and their mules. He had told her the night before to remain near camp, but she was used to a morning bath and decided a short trip to the river couldn't hurt. Unnoticed by all, she slipped away from the protective ring of trunks, past the cottonwood and down a short, steep bank. The river flowed sluggishly, its waters brown with silt near midstream though clear where it ran over a stretch of shallow rocky bottom in front of her. She unfastened the first three buttons of her bodice, dipped a handkerchief into the water and bathed her neck and face. The water felt luxuriously cool and refreshing and she longed to change her dress for another but dared not disrobe so far, even under the blankets. Vance had promised her they would be stopping at an overnight station somewhere and that she would be given the chance to bathe and change.

A horse whinnied up river from her. She glanced to the sound. Roscoe Bodine sat astride his big bay gelding, staring at her, his coarse manly features impassive. She smiled and lifted a hand, innocently waved to him, then scrambled back up the bank and walked to her campsite. When she looked back, horse and rider were gone.

Vance had the team hitched and was obviously concerned with her disappearance. "Where were you?"

"In the bushes, *if* you don't mind," she answered shortly, irritated by his tone. *He could at least have said "Good morning."* "And down to the river to wash my face."

Vance looked closely at her, stared toward the river. "Well, don't wander off like that again."

"Mr. Paxton, I am a grown woman and shall walk where I please."

"You don't understand," he began exasperatedly, rolling her blankets as he talked.

"I understand all too well. Ever since we've gotten off that ship you've been behaving just like Papa. And if I had done everything *he* told me to do, I would not have met you, nor would I be here now." She turned her head and stalked off a few paces. *He's treating me like a child. I don't care what he says, I won't put up with it.*

Behind her Vance busied himself with breaking camp and loading the buckboard. Somewhere in the trees to her left a blue jay squawked raucously. To the east the sun, already a brassy hot ball of fire, was breaking over the horizon. She studied the activity around her. No one moved rapidly but she marveled at their efficiency. She looked to the north and the direction they would take. Ahead there was nothing but more rolling land and grass stretching, it seemed, forever. The memory of the day before caught at her, left her suddenly tiny and insignificant, once again alone in the face of the unknown. She glanced at the sun, over the horizon now and starting its upward climb. In another hour it would beat down on her with incredible ferocity, sucking the moisture from her body, burning her . . . burning her. . . .

She turned and ran back to the wagon. Vance was checking the harness, grumbling impatiently as he tugged and tightened the stiff leather. His hands looked so strong, so competent, so utterly capable of caring for her. She smiled tightly. She had won a tiny victory, she knew, and satisfying as that was, she knew she wouldn't try to take any more advantage. *What would I do if I were here alone? How would I cope with the sun? The distance?* As he straightened from his task and walked toward her, she took an acquiescent step in his direction and held out her hands to him. "I'm sorry, Vance."

He looked into her eyes, trying to read the message behind the words. "No need to be sorry. There's a lot to learn, is all."

They continued on their northwest by north heading all that morning. Enormous white clouds piled high overhead and scudded along on a high river of wind from the south, patches of shade racing below them to give thankful relief from the harsh bright sun and shield them for all too brief moments from the sun's fierce, intemperate rays. The day rolled along at the pace of a slow mule's walk, slow and agonizing, each moment a groggy hour. Karen dozed, stuporous from the heat, until a chuck hole on the trail jarred the wagon and disrupted her daydream. She had been reliving a moment of her past, the coming out party Barrett had held for her on her sixteenth birthday. She had danced the entire evening, and with a different partner for every dance. Had anyone told her then that in four years she would be riding at a snail's pace across the Texas wilderness with a handsome, dashing cowboy at her side. . . . The jolt caused her to open her eyes and utter a tiny "oh" in surprise, gripping Vance to keep her balance.

"Sorry," Vance said.

Karen only sighed quietly and clung to his muscular arm. How long she had dozed she didn't know. The sun hung halfway in the western sky so it must have been for an hour or two. She looked up as Vance stiffened briefly.

"What?"

He pointed.

"I don't see anything."

"Dust. Just to the left of that mesquite."

She stared into the shimmering heat waves and finally located what she sought, a barely discernible plume just above the horizon. A few seconds later a horse thundered up to their left and Vance stopped the wagon. Roscoe and one of the other outriders reined in and they and Vance held a hurried conference. "Anybody else on the trail?" Vance asked.

"Haven't heard. Shouldn't be. Not over there," Roscoe said. "I sent Billy out for a look."

Karen followed his gesture and saw a man on horseback riding hard to the northeast, his rifle out of the scabbard and lying across his saddle horn.

"Well," Vance asked, "we keep on?"

Roscoe stood in the saddle, looked about. "I reckin. Don't see the dust any more, so they must be headin' away from us." The two men looked back at the dust the wagon train had generated. The cloud lingered on the air. "If they didn't see us I don't guess they'll come lookin'. Hell, I hate to lose the rest of the day." He looked briefly at Karen. "Don't want to keep the lady in the sun all day. We'll make Three Rivers." At that he touched his horse's flank and, turning sharply, rode back and started the wagons moving again.

Another hour passed and Billy rode back in to confer with Roscoe. The two men stopped to one side, talking and gesturing toward the east and north. Finally Roscoe galloped off due north and Billy came to the buckboard and rode slowly alongside. "Six of 'em," he said, his youthful voice forced to a dubious bass. "Three shod, three not. They was headin' east, so I don't reckin we got to worry too much. Roscoe says to tell you he's going to check on the way station."

"Thanks, Billy."

The young man, barely more than a boy, kept his pace by the wagon, his eyes straight ahead.

Vance chuckled to himself, looked enigmatically at Karen, then back to Billy. "Billy, like you to meet the future Mrs. Paxton."

The boy flushed red as he touched his hat to Karen then dashed off on the horse, cutting the gelding sharply to ride back along the train.

Karen giggled. "He's cute."

Vance kept his eyes straight ahead. His voice was flat but hard. "If you need help, you'll be sure to get it. Just don't ever take advantage."

Karen looked at him with surprise. "I don't . . ."

"Ever. Because you'll never live it down."

"Really, Vance, you sound like . . ." she broke off with a shriek as an old mossy-horned bull broke from a clump of mesquite and headed for them. Lean and huge, with horns a full seven feet from tip to tip, he trotted toward the buckboard, stopped and glowered at them, lowering his head threateningly as Vance steered past.

"Oh, by God, Vance, he's going to charge us! He's. . . ."

The sound of pounding hooves cut her off. Billy came from the rear of the train and cut across in front of the old bull, on whose domain they had trespassed. Wheeling his horse, he took off his hat and waved it in the old mossy horn's face. The bull snorted and turned toward him. In a flash Billy cut the horse behind the bull and gave him a swat on the rump with his quirt, sending the old fellow back to the mesquite, there to stand and snort indignantly as the rest of the train passed by. Billy, proud as punch, cantered past the buckboard, careful not to look at Karen. His back was straight and his head held high. Karen gazed after him in astonishment while Vance hid his laughter.

A few moments later Roscoe Bodine came riding in from the north. He reined up near the buckboard. "Three River's way station ahead. I checked it out. You can ride on if you want."

"Thanks," Vance answered, slapping the mules with the reins.

The heat was getting to her, that and the hours of sitting and riding with nothing to do but look at empty land. He told himself perhaps he was being a little stiff, perhaps

162

making too much of nothing. But it did bother him that he might be jealous. He had never been so with any other woman. But then, there never had been a woman quite like Karen Hampton. Never had been . . . she was one of a kind . . . his kind.

CHAPTER III

Three Rivers way station was a simple two-room log and adobe cabin. The large main room was for feeding the hungry stage passengers and, if there was a layover, the long wooden tables could be placed against the wall and used as sleeping quarters for the menfolk. A huge fireplace and cooking area filled one end of the room, and from great iron hooks on the facing beam, cast iron cooking utensils threw shadows over the low ceilinged room. The back room served as quarters for the stagekeeper and his wife, though the hosteler was used to sleeping out in the main room whenever the stage brought an infrequent woman for an overnight stay.

The way station was run by Ed and Cathy Carter, a friendly couple of indeterminate middle age who hid well their surprise at finding a lady like Karen accompanying the freight drivers. Beyond her surprise, Cathy was excited and obviously thrilled to have another woman to talk to, even for a single night. While the men took care of the mules and settled them for the night, Cathy busied herself about the stove. Hair flying, she was a bundle of energy, cooking beef and beans, sourdough bread and, as a special festive treat in honor of Karen's presence, a huge bowl of custard which used up most of her milk and all of the few eggs her ten hens had laid in the last two days. As she worked she bombarded Karen with questions and kept her busy relating the latest news of life of Washington society and the latest fashions. Touched by the woman's loneliness, Karen searched through her carpetbag and found an ornate tortoise shell comb given to her by the French ambassador and during a lull in the cooking made a present of it to Cathy, whose eyes brimmed with tears and sent her running to the back room, calling for Karen to follow. A fragment of mirror sat on a shelf and the older woman, laughing through her tears, forced her hair into a suggestion of a bun held up and ornamented by the new gift.

The mules watered and fed and the wagons in place, the men, washed and with hair slicked down, gathered around the tables for dinner. Karen put on a good face and tried to help as best she could. But she lacked training. Used to being served, she moved slowly, once almost spilling a whole platter of beef when the metal proved too hot for her tender hands. Cathy finally shooed her away as gently as possible, ameliorating the sting of her words with the promise that Karen would all too soon have her share of cooking and serving and she should spend what little time she could enjoying her freedom. Once given a free rein, the hosteler's wife bustled about, seemingly everywhere at once, now setting out another platter of beef, now taking another loaf of bread out of the stove top oven. All the while she walked proudly, taking every chance to show off her new comb.

Karen found a seat next to Vance and picked at her food. She couldn't find anything of consequence to say, and used to conversation at dinner, the silence oppressed her and left her feeling lost and ill at ease. There should be talk at a meal, discussion of politics and friends, she thought sourly. At least the weather. But the only sounds were the scrape of knives on tin plates and the grunts of men as they indicated with their heads what they wanted passed.

Karen tried to take comfort from her physical proximity to Vance but soon gave up. They were supposed to be in love but she felt only an empty closeness, a bare indication of acquaintanceship and no display of endearment or affection. Karen fidgeted through the meal, wishing she were outdoors around the campfire.

Dinner over, the men rose as one and went outside. Karen and Cathy were left alone to clean up and ready the room for the night. Karen was unused to such manual labor, but when Cathy started with hardly a break from the cooking and serving, Karen insisted on helping. Cathy moved quickly, efficiently, with no wasted motion nor energy. Karen felt all thumbs. She dropped a plate, and bending to pick it up, sharply struck her shoulder against the edge of a table.

"Don't feel right," Cathy remonstrated. "Only one time

166

before when a woman came through did she help me. The others wouldn't turn a hand. And you a finer lady than the lot of them."

Karen protested. "It wouldn't seem fair if I didn't help. You work hard. You'd think the least they could do is thank you."

Cathy's laugh was rich and warm. "Thanks is where you find it. Ed don't expect me to thank him for catchin' up the horses. It's the extra things you get and give thanks for. Like the comb." She touched the ornate figures lightly with her soapy hands, quickly gave a cry of alarm and jerked the comb from her hair, dried it carefully and set it aside high on a shelf and out of harm's way. "Now look at me. A fine gift and I'm sloppin' soap and grease on it." She shook her head despairingly.

Karen suppressed the urge to tell her it didn't matter. For it did. To the simple woman before her the comb was of more value than anything she had seen in some time.

"You take those men," Cathy went on. "The way they tell you they like what you've cooked is to eat lots and not waste time talkin'. A strong man reachin' for his third helpin' is thanks enough, although I admit it took me some time to realize. Ed an' me come out here from Pennsylvania four years ago when times were bad. We were sure-enough Yankees and almost everyone we met hated us for carpetbaggers. And that was without even askin' us why we came or what we thought."

Her hands stilled and she leaned back against the sink, her voice full of tenderness. "One day Ed got shot by a man. Ed defended himself and the man died, but Ed was sick for a long time. When he got some better we left San Antonio." She looked around her fondly, each niche, each cranny, each beam and board familiar and imbued with special meaning. "And we took this job.

"Before he got shot we used to say 'thank you' a lot. That an' 'please' an' a bunch of other words. But watching that man lie there day after day, tendin' him an' wonderin' if he was goin' to live, watchin' the thanks in his eyes even if he didn't like bein' dependent on a woman . . . well, that was enough. When we got out here we just naturally didn't think to stop an' say them words any more. Didn't have to. We both knew what we was thankful for."

The door opened behind them and the women glanced

back. Ed Carter entered and went to the cupboard, reached into the coffee box and pulled out a handful, dropping the whole beans into the grinder. While he ground the coffee Cathy took a cup from one of the hooks and filled it with sugar. "This'll please 'em," she said. "They been ridin' an' workin' hard." The man nodded, took grounds and sugar and went to the door, pausing to look at his wife, the trace of a smile turning up the corners of his mouth. Karen watched the exchange silently.

"'Law, they'll sit an' yarn until ten o'clock, likely. Men are always talkin' about how women gab, but I noticed they do their share, sittin' around an' tellin' tales when they should be asleep."

The dishes done and the front room ready for the men to sleep, Karen asked where she could bathe. Cathy called out the front door. "Ed, we're goin' down to take a bath. You keep them rowdies away, now."

Karen gratefully stripped out of the sweat- and dust-caked dress and pulled on her dressing gown. Cathy was waiting by the back door, a shotgun casually tucked under her arm. Karen started at the sight, but said nothing. They crossed some fifty yards of open ground and plunged into a twisting, overgrown path—more nearly a tunnel—which led to the muted roar of the river.

The water was cool and invigorating and she luxuriated in scrubbing away the dust and grime of the past two days. Cathy bathed quickly, in and out of the water within scant moments. Toweling rapidly, she dressed and picked up the shotgun again, retreating to the shadows to stand watch over the pale form splashing in the moonlight. By the time Karen climbed out of the water, hair and body scrubbed clean and glowing, she could contain her curiosity no longer. "Why do you carry the gun?"

"Ed wouldn't let me come down here if I didn't. You never can tell, especially at night. We'd best get back. He'll worry." Karen quickly pulled on her dressing gown and followed the hosteler's wife back to the cabin.

Inside, the two women talked, mostly of the east and the life they had known. Karen let her hair hang free, toweled each section briskly until her scalp tingled and then brushed vigorously over and over again until the golden waves flowed with a life of their own. Cathy carefully wrapped the comb in a piece of silk cloth and stored it with the few simple treasures she had gathered in a box kept under her bed. A hosteler's wife had little finery, and Karen's generous gift would be well cared for, cherished deeply. Guiltily, she recalled all the pieces of jewelry she had forgotten, lost or given away as useless over the years. And what wouldn't this woman, whom a simple gift had moved to tears, have given for even a tenth of them?

The hour was late. Outside the door in the front room the men came in, rustled about and fell silent again. The faint sound of a snore carried through the wall. Karen cleaned the oil from her face and fiddled with her hair, trying to arrive at some semblance of a coiffure. Nothing would work. She sighed in exasperation and started to say something to Cathy, then realized the older woman was sound asleep. Settling for a simple bun she could wrap with a kerchief in the morning, she blew out the lantern, stripped off her dressing gown and tried to lie down to sleep.

But sleep wouldn't come. Quietly she rose and crossed to the window to look out. Behind the cabin the dark thicket masked the river sound until only a soft whisper reached her. Three Rivers . . . Cathy had named them for her. The Nueces, the Leona and the Aransas, all converging within a few hundred yards of each other and running cold and pure, excellent for bathing, especially during the warm summer months. Above, the stars. . . .

A form moved in the moonlight. Someone was walking across the clearing. The moon cast a pale light upon the figure, outlining him for a moment before he disappeared into the river path. She recognized Vance and started to call his name, instead, hurried from the window to the door. Silently she lifted the bar and impetuously stepped out into the night. The evening was warm and alive with the raucous music of cicadas and crickets, and in the dark shadows left by the pale moonlight, fireflies flickered, dancing all aglow like tiny, tremulous dryads beckoning her.

Vance was nowhere to be seen. The brush was thickly choked with prickly scrub trees and the trail, more mysterious and frightening now she traveled alone, swerved and twisted through the fastness. The only path Vance could have taken, she knew it must eventually lead her to him. She toyed with the notion of turning back to the house, then dismissed the idea. If Vance became upset when he found she had ventured outside her stuffy room, that was just too bad. She was not a child to be scolded nor a servant to be chided and ordered about. Deftly she picked her way along the trail, the noise of her passing blotted out by the insect songs and the muted roar of the churning river ahead.

Abruptly the foliage parted. From where Karen stood a stretch of clear ground cut a sandy swath some ten feet in width, forming a pleasant little beach. To her right, upstream, large rocks protruded from the water and on the western bank a twenty-foot bluff reared darkly into the night, forming a sequestered cove screened by the tangle of willows and junipers skirting the bank. A pile of clothes lay sprawled at the edge of the water, barely visible as a cloud touched the moon.

She took a wary step out of the covering foliage, then drew back as a pale shape rose ghostlike from the water. The wayward cloud, passing on, released the captive moon and a shimmering curtain of silver dappled the surface of the river with twinkling diamonds. The sand at her feet glowed in the pale light.

The form was of a man. Without even seeing his face Karen knew he was Vance, could only be him. The water level dropped from his chest to his waist, to his thighs, calves and ankles . . . she wanted to run yet did not, held in place by the sight of the primeval, glistening form, naked and powerful.

Her eyes roved down past the ridged muscles of his chest and flat stomach, lingered spellbound at the patch of dark curls and length of flesh and muscle protruding there. Karen blushed yet could not draw her eyes away. She had never seen a man. Not . . . like this . . . all of him. Vance had stopped, stood motionless. Karen realized he was watching her and she stepped out onto the sand, drawn by the magnetism of his eyes. She stepped closer, past the pile of clothes, her breath ragged and the sound of her heart beating wildly in her ears.

And then she was within reach. Vance shook his head and drops of water flew into the night. His eyes bored into her, drove deeply to force open her heart of hearts. She lowered her eyes, not wanting nor able to stare into his, only to find her attention drawn again to the forbidden

170

place where his manhood, prompted by virile hunger, swelled and rose as she watched.

She gasped sharply. *So big . . . I didn't know. So big . . . in me . . .* The very air bristled with the energy sparking between them. Her hand reached out to touch the quivering organ and her fingertips traced along his length that grew harder and more erect, rigid with expectancy. Vance shuddered as her hand explored him, as his own hands caressed her tear-streaked cheeks then floated gently down to the ribbons that fastened her dressing gown.

For the first time she realized how tight her nipples had grown. Her breasts felt full and eager, ripe for his teasing lips. He slid the gown over her shoulders, letting the fabric drop until it caught at her waist where a last bow held firmly. His hands cupped each breast, his fingers provoking their taunt pink crowns and forcing a shameless moan from her throat before they slid down her sides, stopping at the swell of her hips where the gown still clung and moving across her stomach to tug briefly at the ribbon. Karen started to protest but the gown instantly dropped free. She stifled a second, more abrupt exclamation. No man had ever seen her like this, naked and in the voluptuous bloom of womanhood. She drew her hands away from him and tried to cover herself, but Vance caught her wrists and held them gently but firmly away from her body.

She was beautiful. Utterly so. A woman of classic mold. He kissed her lightly along the cheek, neck and shoulders, down between the luscious swells of her naked breasts, twin mounds of perfection swollen with the ache of desire. His knees struck sand as his lips journeyed randomly across her stomach and lower abdomen, lower still to tease the triangle of tight honeygold ringlets. Then lower still. He released her wrists which promptly fell and tried to push him from her.

"No, Vance. . . ." she said, her voice breaking. Her legs felt weak and she feared she might faint. The palms of his hands slid up the backs of her thighs, spreading and kneading her buttocks, forcing her forward into his kisses. His fingers stroking from behind brought an ecstasy never before experienced, never even imagined in her wildest dreams. Her mind awhirl, she felt her maidenhood flush warm and moist with a desire that drove her hands away and parted her thighs to let his tongue flit across that most secret kernel of her mounting passion, gently, deeply probe the soft membranous confirmation of her virginity and travel back to tease the swollen bud of her desire.

He can't . . . I can't let him . . . ! Her fingers clawed at the tangled brown mane below and the breath whistled in her throat. Deep within her the pain of ecstasy built, throbbing blindly, overwhelmingly as his tongue brought her to a shuddering climax. Sobbing and openly moaning, her legs buckled and she sagged to the moist sand, her back arched, caught in the uncontrollable waves of the slow, rolling explosion.

Now was the time. Now was the place. Beneath the night's starry vault she whispered, "Now! Oh, Vance, now. Please . . . please. . . ."

Her legs parted, the musky sweetness beckoning him. Vance tried to calm his own raging passion as her hand sought him and her small fingers enfolded the engorged, impatient member. His chest pressed against her rigid nipples and his mouth covered hers as his manhood stood poised and touching the treasured gate of her body. *Be gentle. This is her first time. Be gentle . . .* he repeated over and over to himself lest he succumb to the tempest of the moment.

And then he heard the soft splash of a horse entering the water downstream. Several horses, almost inaudible save for one whose wilderness-honed hearing could pick the slightest unnatural sound from the roar of the rushing river. *What the hell!* His head lifted and his body stiffened, his ardor at once cool, the passion draining from him instantly. A second passed before Karen realized something was wrong, realized there was an unexpected and unaccountable lull in their love-making. He brought his mouth to her ear. "Take your gown and get to the bushes. Don't make a sound."

"Vance . . . what? It's all right. I want to. . . ."

"Dammit, do like I said," he whispered abruptly and harshly. He rolled off her and to his clothes. Karen's face went livid with anger but before she could speak he returned and dragged her by the arm into the concealing foliage.

"Of all the . . ."

Vance roughly clamped his hand over her mouth. "Shut

up and get dressed," he said, more out of anger at himself than her, though she could not know that.

In a moment he was into his hat and jeans, had his gunbelt around his waist and was stepping into a pair of moccasins. He slipped a knife into a sheath on his belt. Karen, embarrassed now by her nakedness, drew the dressing gown about her, fastening it haphazardly while Vance searched the river bank for signs of life. Karen sighed aloud and in return received a furious glance from the man who only a moment before had been so arduously making love to her.

She was no sooner dressed than Vance pointed toward the path leading to the house and nudged her gently. "Move. Now." She grudgingly entered the trail, still unconvinced of danger for she had heard nothing. It was dark under the trees. Heavy shadows hung over her. Something rustled in the brush to her left. What? A footstep . . . ? Suddenly she was filled with fear. Supposing there were Indians . . . or renegades, as she had heard the men discussing? Vance must have heard something, some sound to which her ears weren't attuned. If she could only reach Cathy. There she would be safe within the impregnable adobe walls. . . . *Oh, my God! The door to Cathy's room . . . The back door!*

There had been no way to lower the bar from the outside and she could picture the door swung open and inviting, the woman inside, asleep and unsuspecting. A new and colder wave of malicious prickling fear added impetus to her movement and she found herself in headlong flight down the path. Thorny fingers reached out to pluck at her gown, catching and tearing at sleeve and skirt as she ran. . . .

At least three. No less. Who? Who!? Vance checked the river bank one last time, spun about at the noise of Karen's hasty passage through the woods and quickly changed position, concealing himself behind the trunk of a cottonwood at the mouth of the path. He cursed silently. Every broken twig and stumbling step served to pinpoint her location. Downstream he heard the soft sound of a twig or branch rubbing against cloth, then the muffled pounding of hooves along the bank. Whoever they were, he could only hope they didn't know of the path. Even as the thought passed

173

through his mind he knew himself for a fool. They would know. Of course they would know. The sound of their horses gave them away. They were heading directly for his position at the head of the path, the quickest and easiest way through the thicket.

He could hear the horses clearly now. Soberly, he considered the next few minutes. He was squatted low in the brush, partially concealed by the tree trunk. He didn't want a fight until he could be sure Karen was safely inside, yet was willing to stand and give battle should trouble come his way.

At least he could no longer hear Karen. *She must be near the cabin by this time. Unless. . . .* No, he dared not think so. Twenty-five yards away, and still the brush intervened. He couldn't consider shooting before he had a clear shot. A bird took flight from a willow and the men on horseback froze suddenly, looked around. A hoarse whisper of reassurance and they moved on again. Vance's aim never wavered from the spot where the first rider would clear the brush.

There would be time for only one or two shots before his enemies were off their horses and well-hidden. The way station would be alerted, but every gun along the river would know his whereabouts, know he was entrenched across the mouth of the trail. The only way they could approach the way station from the rear and in any kind of time would be through Vance. So they would kill him. It didn't seem fair. To have found a woman, a fine proper lady around whom he might build a life, to come all the way from Washington only to find death. *Death never is fair. It simply is.* And wouldn't go away without its bounty, without its due. Vance cursed the thoughts. Since when had he ever given a damn? His way was always the reckless, the unexpected. To meet the devil head on and kick him in the teeth. The first man would clear the brush and come into his field of fire in seconds. The time was at hand.

Karen hurtled across the open ground and into the room to find the cabin quiet and undisturbed, with Cathy still sound asleep. She rushed to the older woman's bed and startled her awake. The two of them alerted the men in the outer room where there was an instantaneous, maddened scramble for hats, boots and guns. Billy ran outside to alert

174

the men on guard around the corral and wagons. Freight drivers silently took up previously but unconsciously planned positions, dividing their number between the wagons and the firing ports in the walls of the way station. Karen returned to the bedroom, hastily garbed herself in her dress. Feeling not quite so naked, her confidence returned. *Vance!*

She stumbled into Roscoe Bodine as he entered behind her. His hands gripped her briefly as he brushed past her. "Beggin' your pardon, ma'am, but I'd better check that back door." He released her and strode across the room.

"Vance! Vance is out there. Down by the river alone."

Roscoe checked the bar on the door, dropped a chair under the knob. "Paxton's salty enough. Rode with him durin' the war. He can take care of himself."

Ed Carter stuck his head into the room. "Hey, Roscoe, come out here. You oughta see this."

Bodine gave one last telling look at Karen then checked the action on his rifle and walked into the outer room. Karen followed, noticing immediately the front door stood open and the men were gone. The leader went on outside but Karen stayed, content to watch from the doorway. The freight drivers were standing bunched around a small group of mounted horsemen. As she watched, they dismounted, joking with the drivers. Suddenly Cathy came into the room. "Karen, there you are. Come help me with coffee and sandwiches."

"I don't understand. Who's out there? Where's Vance?"

Cathy laughed good-naturedly. "Dear, you certainly had us worried. Mr. Paxton is out front with the soldiers he brought in. Seems he nigh came close to shootin' one before he realized who they were. Sergeant Dekker and his men have put in some hard hours. I'm sure they could use a bit of food."

She turned at the sound of footsteps. Vance entered the room followed by a short, broad-shouldered man who immediately on seeing Karen doffed his cap. She pointedly avoided looking at Vance, but smiled at the stranger in uniform.

"Sergeant Luther Dekker at your service, ma'am."

Karen nodded. "Thank you, Sergeant."

"This is Karen Hampton, my intended, Sergeant," Vance said.

Dekker beamed at her, his eyes registering good-natured, unabashed envy. "You're a lucky man, Paxton. Wish you all the best, Miss Hampton." He unbuttoned his army coat and a look of pure relief crossed his face. "Ma'am, it was fortunate for me your husband-to-be here don't like to shoot at strangers. He had me dead to rights."

"Pure dumb luck I saw the chevron. You gave me a scare."

"I give a whistle. Figgered anyone there who was supposed to be there would answer. Surprised a fella with your trail savvy didn't hear it." He shot a wary look at Vance.

Vance almost blushed, turned aside to one of the tables, already pulled out from the wall and loaded with coffee cups. "Too busy washin' up, I guess," he said uncomfortably. "Looks like coffee's ready."

The sergeant poured himself a cup as his men came through the door and headed for the table. Karen, seeing Cathy had managed quite well without her, excused herself and retired to the back room, not wishing to face the verbal jibes of the drivers and soldiers for her part in the false warning. Vance followed her. "Karen . . ."

"I have nothing to say to you, Mr. Paxton."

"Karen, I. . . ."

"Washing up!" she mimicked, the words icy with sarcasm. "There wasn't any danger. There was *never* any danger. I think you knew that all along. I suppose this was just another lesson to be learned. You let me. . . . Oh! I don't want to talk about it. Now everyone thinks how silly I am. All those stories about danger and guns and Indians. . . . I've never been so humiliated in my. . . . Don't touch me! Go eat a sandwich or something with your friends. I'm tired."

"Karen, I admit I made a mistake, but I. . . ."

"Please go, Vance. Please?" Her voice choking, she turned away from him and sat on the edge of the bed.

Vance, utterly perplexed and unable to cope with tears, stared at her a moment longer, then shrugged uncertainly and left the room. Things weren't working the way he'd planned. If only they'd been able to disembark in Galveston. He shouldn't have let himself get carried away down at the river's edge. Shouldn't have—wouldn't have, if he'd kept his wits about him—missed the signal. They could have moved into the shrubbery and stayed hidden. No.

176

They would have missed her at the house and still the harm would have been done. He was damned if he did and damned if he didn't.

Been better to wait in any case. But how was a man to wait? Seeing her there and sensing her willingness . . . his nakedness . . . the moon and all those stars . . . Her breasts and thighs, the magic of her hands. . . . What the hell was a man supposed to do? He loved her, dammit. He wanted her. The moment had been right, there beneath the Texas night sky, the broad expanse of stars and the music of the river to lull them into a magic unreality where only the two of them lived and loved. The union would have been so perfect, would have been something for both of them to remember and cherish forever. Not some hotel room or the ranch house, with people all around. Just the two of them and the night.

If only the damned soldiers hadn't ridden in. Damn! Let them look for Jaco—or whoever the hell else they wanted—at some other time. After all he'd told her of Texas, only to end up behind a pair of mules for four days. First the Galveston bypass, then the arrival at Corpus Christi, and then this. For the fates to have chosen that one moment! He scowled at the thought. And Dekker had said he was lucky.

CHAPTER IV

Karen looked back and watched Three Rivers way station gradually disappear in the dim morning light. The lack of wind and the brassy ball of sun rising over the horizon presaged a day similar to the last two, the only kind she had known on Texas soil. Ahead of them the land assumed the look of a darkly-knobbed prairie, gradually rising. Other than themselves and three does standing quietly with a buck at their side on the top of a small knoll there was no sign of life on the featureless landscape. A few morning birds called, but they soon left the empty air alone.

The depot became a tiny speck and was then suddenly lost behind a mesquite, leaving naught but a thin trail of smoke barely visible against the brightening sky. She was not so angry at Vance as she had been, for after a tearful, hushed session with Cathy, the older woman had explained briefly he had been better off erring on the side of safety than taking chances. Men, she had said, died in this country if they weren't careful. *They all believe the stories they've made up. Even Cathy. Like a bunch of children playing at make believe.* But looking around she could see why. Any normal person would have to do something to relieve the boredom of the Godforsaken place, and when all was said and done, those she'd met in Texas probably weren't much different than the men and women she had known in Washington and New York. All made up their roles and played them to the hilt. She had to admit the incessant game playing made life more bearable. Even exciting. She smiled secretly, and deciding to keep Vance guessing, assumed an aloof posture despite the bumping, jostling progress of the wagon and the extreme heat. Her back stiff and unrelenting, she soon succumbed to the lulling pace of the mules, and before two hours had passed her resolve had withered and she found herself caught inextricably in a lethargic web of boredom, woven helpfully by the slow, lazy circles of distant carrion-eating vultures, their somber, stately forms outlined against the sky.

Vance decided any attempt at explanation was useless. Karen had been disappointed, he felt sure, but no more than he had. She would simply have to resolve the issue in her own mind. She had heard enough of this country to know there had been danger, and real danger at that. He was ashamed of his lame-brained excuse for missing the signal from Dekker, but couldn't for the life of him think of what else he might have said. He'd been caught in an unfortunate situation stemming from his own lust and had to live with the results. His course now was to concentrate on the mules and the path they traveled. Time would heal such a tiny wound.

Before long she was asleep, her head on his shoulder and one hand on his thigh. They were following the Aransas River north, having left the westward-bound Nueces far behind. Karen dozed fitfully, more than once jolted half awake by the lurching buckboard. When they stopped for the nooning she was left alone at the buckboard, barely able to choke down the dry bread and beef which passed for sandwiches. She ignored the men who gathered to one side of the wagons to talk with Roscoe and Billy when they rode in, their horses lathered and blowing hard.

The pace picked up. Roscoe and Billy seemed worried, and no sooner had they eaten and changed horses than they rode out again, Bodine across the river to the west and Billy ranging far ahead. Vance reflected their concern, growing more taciturn with every passing mile.

The wagon swerved sharply and Karen clutched at the seat, her eyes open and her mind grasping for the present, startled by the sudden movement. The sun was low in the sky and the ground released its heat to dance in shimmering curtains under the frail tops of the mesquites.

"Did you sleep?" Vance inquired, his voice soft as the rustle of leaves.

"No . . . yes. I was daydreaming. It was Christmas a few years ago. A party. I was remembering the annual Christmas gala given by Ambassador Stone. He loved a party more than anyone."

"There'll be parties here, Karen. Why, the shindig we'll throw for the . . . for *our* wedding. . . ."

"The what?"

"Shindig. You haven't seen a party until. . . ."

"Shindig. How funny."

"A *fiesta*, the Mexicans call them. We do too, sometimes."

"*Fiesta* is a pretty word. I like it better than shindig."

"Whatever name you use it means a good time. Tomorrow night we'll be in San Antonio and stay over the Fourth. You'll see what a real *fiesta* is like. Texas style."

The freight wagons circled once again for the night. Vance kept up a steady flow of speech, describing again the ranch, his father, mother and friends. Karen had never known him to carry on so. It was a change in him she had not expected. But conversation made the time pass quickly and night fell rapidly. At peace again with the world, she relaxed and let the night sounds wash over her and cleanse from her soul the remaining shreds of frustration left from the night before.

The freight drivers squatted around a bare mention of a fire and spoke in hushed tones. Karen noticed Vance had arranged her trunks further from the river and closer to the main campfire. They too spoke in whispers and gradually she realized something was out of sorts, a notion which gradually undermined her sense of euphoria and made her distinctly uneasy.

The men had finished their dinner when Bodine and Billy hailed the camp, rode in from the darkness and dismounted to sink to the ground by the fire, obviously near exhaustion. Two of the men led their horses off to be rubbed down and fed while the rest of the drivers sat quietly, waiting for the outriders to finish eating. Vance abruptly ceased the tale of how he met Ted Morning Sky and, barely excusing himself, went to the main fire, leaving Karen alone to anxiously peer from behind her trunks. She could hear nothing beyond a muted hum of voices, could see little more than broad gestures and an occasional flash of a face as the men turned to look into the night. All very dramatic, she thought, giving up and lying back on the blanket, irritated at being left out of the discussion. *Men. They always whisper and carry on as if to lend weight to whatever they discuss. And then they decry women for using their wiles when it's the only way they have to find out what is happening.*

181

Despite the day spent dozing and daydreaming, the numbing fatigue of heat and hypnotic movement, fresh air and the smell of wood burning accompanied by the rhythmic pulsing of a million insects began to take their toll. And as she drifted off to sleep, Karen had the disquieting notion she knew what was wrong. Something about the men around the fire. What was it? Yes. Counting Vance there should have been eleven. But there were only ten. Only ten . . . ? Who? But she was asleep.

The night passed uneventfully. They breakfasted hastily on more of the beef and beans—the last she ever hoped to see, by that time—before light showed in the east. The men fell to their tasks with a minimum of talk and the usual efficiency. No one looked as if they had slept for more than a few hours. Even Vance's eyes looked puffy and red. Where they had made camp the Aransas flowed off to the west, and without the benefit of a nearby river the day's travel would be the worst yet. At least it was the last day, Karen rejoiced, thankful for any favor. She waited for Vance to come back to the buckboard before getting into her seat. Any minute she could remain on her feet she counted a blessing.

"You can relax some. We won't be heading out until Roscoe and Billy get back," Vance said, returning unexpectedly.

"But I thought we were to reach San Antonio today."

"Plan to. But we can't leave 'til Roscoe and Billy get back. We'll just have to push extra hard later," he said, turning back to the obviously nervous group of men.

Knowing further protest would be useless, Karen grumbled half-heartedly and walked away from the wagons, winding her way down to the creek bed. There among the scrub oak and ever present mesquite, she sat on a flat piece of stone, listened to the running water and contemplated the morning. *Peaceful . . . so peaceful . . .*

"Don't like waiting." The voice came from her right. Without thinking she shrank back into the foliage. Jersey Considine and another driver emerged from the brush a few yards upstream and crossed down to the water's edge to fill their canteens. They did not see her and made no attempt to lower their voices.

"Better than runnin' smack dab into trouble," the second man said. "Anyway, can't jes' run off an' leave Hoennig without at least tryin' to find him. Besides, havin' only two outriders don't leave us no one to scout the way we come. An' that Billy's mighty young to be ridin' point, no matter what he thinks or Bodine says."

"If Hoennig got himself in trouble it's best we leave well enough alone. Bodine can only bring it down on us. An' the lady."

"Was you Bodine, would you leave him?"

"Hoennig knew his job an' the chances he'd be takin'," Considine continued doggedly. "Can't tell me no German takes a job an' don't know his chances. If Jaco's or some other bunch come upon him, then Lord help him an' all the rest a' us.

"But dammit, Bodine's first responsibility is to get these wagons through. After we get to San Antone, let him come back an' take a look, if he's a mind to."

They finished filling the canteens and walked back up the bank. *So, I was right. There was one missing.* The vaguely disquieting suspicion of danger kept her hidden in the brush. Vance's warnings. . . . The concern with the barely visible plume of dust. . . . The shotgun Cathy carried. . . . No. She couldn't be so far wrong. The land was too empty. People needed each other. The dime novel stories were fine, as far as they went, but no one could ever imagine them real.

Roscoe and Billy returned to camp shortly after eight, their horses lathered from a hard ride. They rode in alone. The men gathered around the two outriders and Vance ordered Karen to stay by the buckboard. She bristled at his authoritative manner but, aware of the crisis, decided there was no point in complicating the issue by protesting. The conference lasted but a few moments and when Vance walked back and took up the reins, his face was grim. "We're leaving," he said shortly, offering her his hand.

"What about Mr. Hoennig?"

Vance was visibly surprised.

"Who told you?" he asked, his voice tinged with suspicion.

"No one. I merely listened. What of Mr. Hoennig?"

Karen in place, Vance hopped up beside her and guided the mules out and away from the river to take up their place at the head of the line. "Roscoe and Billy both

183

looked. There's no sign of him and we can't wait any longer."

"But what happened to him? People don't simply vanish."

Vance shook his head in disagreement. "Out here they do sometimes. He could have had an accident, but I don't think so. Roscoe says his tracks just played out. They scouted out and around but never did cut any more sign. Has to be he left on his own or someone found him and took him. Either way, we can't take the chance of running into trouble. Their job is to get these wagons to San Antonio. And my job is to get you . . . to a preacher."

Karen blushed and drew close, kissing him on the cheek. Vance's face reddened and he turned to look at the man in the wagon behind them. "Shouldn't do that where folks can see," he said awkwardly.

Bodine, riding a fresh horse, reined up at their wagon. "Run 'em an' walk 'em all the way. It'll kick up some dust but that don't matter now. Anybody see it, they gonna have to travel some to ketch us, an' we'll be ready for 'em. Ma'am, you better hold on tight. Trail gets a mite rough up ahead." Bodine touched his fingers to his hat, grinned broadly and spurred his horse into a gallop.

Vance urged the mules to a quicker gait. The buckboard jounced and bumped heavily at the greater speed. Karen kept a firm hold on Vance and the edge of the seat. "I can see why they call this a buckboard," she complained, yelling above the noise.

"What?"

"I can see why they call this a buckboard."

He grinned at her. "Do you good. Toughen you up."

The seat slammed into her bottom, jolting her fiercely. "What's getting toughened up doesn't want toughening."

Vance hollered at the mules, laughed at her. "Keep your girlish figure. How do you think western women keep so trim?"

Further conversation was nearly impossible. The wagon careened across the broad, sun-baked prairie, along the trail twisting in and around the mesquite. Vance kept the pace for half an hour then allowed the team to slow. "How you doing?"

Karen dabbed at the dust and perspiration on her face. "The ground looks flat, but my back tells me otherwise."

Vance nodded in agreement. He removed his hat and wiped his face, his eyes constantly scanning the depths of the mesquite ahead. "It can fool you. Don't ever count on anything out here being what it seems, what it looks like. Always take a second look. Always."

As if to reinforce the lesson, Billy appeared suddenly from their right, his proximity a complete surprise. He rode straight to the buckboard. "Stream down there. Checked it out. Ain't much water left, but she'll do. I reckon we better let 'em drink some."

Vance turned the team and, seconds later, guided them down a small but steep bank into a concealed arroyo. Behind them the other wagons stopped on the level and the men walked down and filled buckets which they carried back to the other mules. Karen was left alone. She walked back and forth slowly, shaking the kinks out of her back and legs. *Nothing is what it seems. Is that also true of the people? Of Vance?* In Washington she had been absolutely certain of him, thought she knew all she needed. He was strong, considerate, passionate, a man to love and be loved by. What more did she need to know? And yet his words, spoken so nonchalantly, tinged the dream with worry.

Somehow the day passed, and with dusky twilight a cool breeze sprung up. Under a fierce white moon, the ground rose more rapidly and the land became clearer where the mesquite had been burned off. They were passing buildings now, the first a solitary dwelling, an adobe hut left abandoned to the elements. A sign people had been there, it sat crumbling and empty, a sad and lonely ghost of the past. The mules, lathered and gaunt, strained at the harness and moved forward steadily despite the grueling effort of the day. Karen was numb. Her face felt hot and dry, burned by the wind no matter how many times she had patted it with a wet cloth. Her muscles were cramped from bracing against the jostling, pitching buckboard, and through her mind ran the single question, over and over again in a slow, steady, hypnotic rhythm. How does the rickety wagon stay in one piece? How does the rickety wagon stay in one piece. Sometime—was it dark?—a horse pulled up to the buckboard. She heard Vance speak to the rider and then slap the mules and drive them into a near trot. She didn't know how she hung on, knew only that the

185

pace had picked up recklessly, that every muscle was tired and ached.

It was through an exhausted haze she first saw San Antonio, the lights from the buildings looking like a cluster of winking stars scattered across the shadowed landscape. The roads improved and the buckboard rolled easier. The mules, smelling rest and food, settled into a rocking motion and Karen fell into a stupor, dozing and noting little of the town. Vague impressions of a raucous party echoed off to one side, followed by quiet, dimly broken by the wail of a child and the crooning voice of a mother. The scent of flowers . . . roses. . . . More voices sounded, masculine now. "Paxton!" one yelled. Vance's arm was around her and her eyes opened to stare dully at the glow of passing gaslights, diffused by the dust from a thousand feet. *Gaslights . . . here? Who would have thought it? One, two, three, four.* Accents foreign and unfamiliar formed a jumble of indistinguishable sounds. German, Spanish, Texan, French. Polish even, she thought, wondering at the cosmopolitan flavor of the voices.

Her head sagged against Vance's shoulder and she smiled as she felt the muscles flex under his shirt. *How could I ever have been angry with this man? I love him so much.* Off to her left a shot and a whoop. Her eyes jerked open again and she stiffened. Vance's arm tightened around her. "Easy. Just some of the boys starting the party a little early."

The wagon stopped. Drugged with sleep, Karen allowed herself to be helped down. Up two steps. . . . *What is this building? Where am I?* The light inside was bright and hurt her eyes. She squinted about, trying to wake up. *All these people. . . . I must look a sight.*

"This way, Mr. Paxton." Another voice. A new one. More steps, winding up forever. Behind her people stared, but she couldn't have cared less. Fourteen hours in a buckboard and under tension had leached all concern from her. *I could sleep for a year.* The halls were lit with quiet taste, the amber light suffused romantically and pleasantly dim. A door opened in front of her and she felt Vance half pick her up, half carrying her toward a vast white cloud. *A bed . . . !*

"May I get you anything?"

"No," she murmured, barely able to move her lips. "Sleep. Just sleep."

A woman spoke in melodious Spanish. Somehow she understood and raised her arms as the dust-covered dress was stripped from her, replaced immediately by a soft, cool nightgown. A second later she fell back onto the fragrant sheets and closed her eyes. The journey was over. The journey. . . . "Sleep, *señorita. Bueno sueño.*"

How lovely. BUENO SUENO . . . BUENO SUENO . . . asleep.

She awakened to thunder rolling in the streets and daylight streaming through her windows. How bright the flossy whiteness of the curtains, ruffled by a summer breeze. She wriggled her hips and scrunched down into the luxuriant sheets. A bed. A real bed and not a blanket on the hard ground. More thunder, sharp and hard. She leaned over and propped herself up on an elbow, tilted her head to glimpse a small rectangle of pale blue sky. Thunder?

She rose, puzzled by the nightgown before remembering the Mexican woman of the previous night. She crossed to the window and looked down on a broad avenue of low, single-floor adobe, wood and stone buildings. The streets were full of people, all heading in the same direction, west, toward what appeared to be the center of a riotous commotion. Shouting, music, gunfire. . . . The Fourth of July! Karen smiled to herself. Of course. The Fourth. It would be the same everywhere. In Washington she could look down from her window to the capital city, already alive with the sounds of celebration. A pre-dawn carriage ride through the festive streets was sure to meet with exploding firecrackers, banners, ornaments, streamers and later a parade.

The fabric of her dream unraveled beneath the very real warmth of a fierce summer sun. She was in San Antonio. Not as depressing as her first glimpse of Corpus Christi, she could see a bigger, sprawling city, boisterous and lusty but touched with squalor on the edges. Was there not one truly civilized city in Texas? A brightly painted carriage pulled by an elegant, high-stepping matched pair of blacks made its way through the swirling crowd. Perhaps there was more than met the eye. Turning, she looked at the room for the first time and realized it was elegantly appointed. The furniture was heavy and quietly ornate, the

187

facings exquisitely and extensively carved. The linens on her bed were spotless and worked with intricate patterns of lace. Wide floor planks gleamed, further shining evidence of Teutonic thoroughness. Her dressing gown was laid out to one side and her toilet articles had been meticulously arranged on a dressing table. A room this nice, this elegant, had to mean her first impression of the town could have been mistaken.

A knock sounded at the door. She slipped on her dressing gown and opened the door. A young Mexican girl, no more than fifteen years old at the most, curtsied as she entered. "*Señor* Paxton requests the honor of the *señorita*'s company for lunch. I am to help you dress. My name is Carmela."

Karen smiled at the girl. The child's voice was so soft and musical, polite yet supported with strength and pride. "Thank you, Carmela. I trust I am to be given time to bathe first."

"*Si, señorita.* It is but eleven. The *señor* suggested one o'clock?"

"Very well." Karen looked about. "My bath is . . . ?"

"The tub is in here, and recently filled." The girl opened the door to a smaller bathroom where a large metal tub stood brimful of steaming, scented water.

No sooner had the door closed behind her than she stripped and stepped into the tub, sighing ecstatically as she settled into the warm, relaxing watery depths. The river had been refreshing, but this was luxury. The heat soaked into her, soothing all the new muscles she'd found, so cruelly aching from the four days' ride.

By noon she was at the dressing table, methodically repairing the ravages of wind, dust and sun on her face while Carmela brushed her hair. From the Mexican girl Karen learned she was at the Menger Hotel, of which Vance had spoken several times. German in origin, the Menger typified all that was gracious and socially fashionable in Texas.

The gown she chose was a daring Parisian model of russet taffeta and umber silk trimmed with Belgian lace, with a startling décolletage certain to leave a lasting first impression on any stranger she might meet. And although Vance was the prime target of her beauty, the others would see at a glance what kind of woman he had chosen—a woman elegant enough to be a queen. She finished on the stroke of one, and with a hint of perfume bespeaking the magic and allure of some faraway land, Karen Hampton followed Carmela into the hallway.

Vance was seated in the lobby, involved in a heated discussion with a German friend of his father's passing through on his way to Fredericksburg. Glancing up he saw Karen descending the broad, rose-lined ornate stairway to the lower floor. The sight of her stopped him in midsentence, and as he rose, the man with whom he was speaking turned to see what Vance was looking at. "Good God, man, is *that* the future Mrs. Paxton? I'd have thought the north too cold for such a flower."

"It was. That's why I brought her back to Texas," Vance answered as he hastily excused himself and hurried to Karen's side.

All conversation stopped in the lobby. Men stared with unabashed envy at Vance's good fortune. Women barely disguised their jealousy with catty glances and caustic comments on the impropriety of the young lovely's fine garment. Secretly they wondered who she was and how she had come by such a gown, for none had seen the like outside of *Harper's*. One young girl, usually the center of attention, found herself ignored by the two men at her side, so occupied were they in appreciation of Karen's lush figure.

Vance took her arm and escorted her to the dining room, causing the same effect among the patrons there as in the lobby. Their table was waiting and as he seated her he smiled with pleasure, finally able to show her Texas wasn't as barbaric as she had evidently thought.

Karen looked about, impressed anew with the Menger's elegance. The dining room was of polished maple, ash and oak. Tables set a discreet distance apart were covered with white, delicately laced cloth, each painstakingly embroidered with satin silver thread, each unique and every one a work of art.

The specialty of the house was a turtle soup whose hearty flavor was enhanced by a faint touch of cognac. Karen elected to try only a small bowl as an appetizer and followed it with one of the wild game dinners but Vance suggested she allow him to order, for she'd be eating wild game enough in the next weeks. He whispered to the waiter who bowed and left, returning seconds later with a silver wine cooler and a schooner of beer. "A half hour, *señor*," the waiter said, pouring the wine for Karen.

Vance raised his beer to the light. "To us, and our new life."

Their eyes met in warm silence, the silence of a thousand unsaid words and more of love, a silence of shared intimacy, of the knowledge and acceptance of commitment. Of the miles behind them and the years stretching ahead they gave no thought. Only to the moment, sparkling as the wine, as full-bodied as the beer.

"This is the house beer," Vance commented, breaking the spell. "Made at the Menger Brewery. None better in the country. It's been a while and I've built up quite a thirst." The waiter brought another large mug of beer, the dark amber fluid crowned with a high ring of creamy foam. Karen sipped her wine, a local vintage from the German vineyards to the north, slightly sweet but with a fresh, open-aired tang. And before the young lovers had time to think twice, the half hour was gone and the waiter returned with a huge tray held above his head.

Karen gasped in delight when a huge bowl of boiled shrimp—brought all the way from Corpus Christi, unknown to her, in a wagon load of ice—was placed in the center of the table. The jumbo shrimp, no more than a half dozen to the pound, lay pink and tempting on a mound of slivered ice. Small jars of sauces, white and red, appeared, followed by bowls of steaming sweet peas laced with tiny new onions, minuscule carrots, steamed and as sweet as if they had been candied, and a bowl of rice covered with sweet white sauce seasoned with desert herbs Karen had never before tasted. Washington or New York couldn't have offered better, and after four days of beef and beans, they fell to with a will.

An hour later, appetites appeased and idling over coffee, they were interrupted by the waiter who bore an envelope on a small tray. Vance ripped open the seal and read quickly. "Rode in a hurry. This was sent only yesterday. Pa was figuring pretty close when we'd arrive," he said as he finished reading and folded the letter. Karen waited patiently. "It's business. I'm going to have to leave for an hour or so."

"Must you leave so soon? I thought we were going to the *fiesta*."

"We will. There'll be plenty of time. But I have to catch up with a cattle buyer before he leaves town." He finished the last of his beer and started to rise when the look on Karen's face stopped him. He reached across the table and took her hand. "It's important, believe me. Or I wouldn't leave you. I'm sorry. He's leaving for Austin. . . ."

"All the same, I think it very rude of you, sir." Karen remonstrated, only half in jest.

"I won't be long. Finish your meal, go upstairs and wait until I come for you. There'll be plenty of time. I'll be back around five and we'll wander around and see the sights. It will be cooler then, too. And later there'll be fireworks and probably some exhibitions. Any time there's a bunch of cowboys in town you can bet on a good show."

He kissed her hand and walked away from the table, quickly crossing the dining room with his lengthy strides. Karen watched him in the mirror as he left. She blushed, remembering his touch as they stood by the river. *My, how forward I've become. But I am a woman now, not a maid in spring. I've found a man to love. Headstrong, perhaps, but he'll learn.* A look of impish determination hardened her features. *Wait in my room? Hardly, sir. You must be taught, a Hampton waits for no man.* And confident of her ability to tame the man she loved, she dropped her napkin on her plate and rose from the table.

"May I get you something else, ma'am?"

"Yes. A parasol, if you please."

"At the desk, ma'am. The meal, did you . . . ?"

"The meal was wonderful, thank you," she said curtly, already walking out of the dining room.

She stepped out onto a board walkway and into San Antonio. San Antonio! A pretty name. Already the town was old. For over a hundred years white men had been living on the banks of the San Antonio River. She could feel the years weigh on her without moving from the front of the hotel. Across the street stood a ruined mission wedged against a warehouse of wood and limestone. *How sad it looks. Such a forlorn bit of rubble. Does no one care that a church lies in ruin?* She approached an old man who, with tobacco-stained moustache drooping down either side of his mouth, sat quietly in the shade. His face was wrinkled and sere, contoured by countless hours and days of wind and sun. "Excuse me, sir?" Karen asked.

191

The old man looked up slowly, then seeing Karen, rose awkwardly. "Yes'm," he answered, his voice ragged with the years.

"What is that poor dilapidated building? Is it one of the missions?"

The old man peered into the bright light, looked at the mission whose battered facade reflected his own timeworn face. "Ma'am, that there's the Alamo. Been like that since March the sixth, 1836. Not a hand'll be lifted to repair it. Other missions, mebbe, but not that'n. There's some who find a right special beauty in the old girl's scars. No, ma'am. Long as she stands, she stays as she is, an' I got a feeling," he added wearily, "she'll outstand us all." Without further comment the old man stood waiting for the young lady's pleasure.

The Alamo! So that's it. The old man was still standing, waiting for her to say or do something. "Thank you. Thank you very much," she managed quickly, embarrassed at her ignorance. She walked away down the street, allowing the old fellow to sink back in his chair and doze off, remembering the old days, dreaming of the empty plains, now filled with men and cattle.

She wandered, taking in the sights and sounds. A beautiful, dusky Mexican girl, her hair braided in a black rope down her back, walked with fluid grace, all too aware of the supple young body dressed in a white peasant-style blouse and full red and blue and white figured skirt. Obviously against her will, she was accompanied by a fiercely scowling old woman dressed totally in black, her eyes constantly roaming to pick out the young men who winked and postured for the benefit of her charge. There strode with honest gait a German farmer, carrying a shovel and rake, followed by his son, sober-faced and wearing a flat-brimmed black hat years too old for him. A strikingly handsome *caballero* rode slowly down the street on a huge white stallion. The rider held the reins loosely with his right hand, cocked the left nonchalantly on his hip. His black hat was trimmed with silver discs and filigree, and a white shirt and red tie blazed against an immaculate black suit, the jacket short and the trousers almost indecently tight, but with gashes at the ankles where red wedges stood out in splendor. Karen twirled the parasol and switched it to her left shoulder to get a better look at him, quickly covered her face with the edge of the fabric as the man's dark, piercing eyes gazed coldly, challengingly into hers.

And what manner of others, all characters whose history she couldn't tell. A young Indian lad, taken from the prairies and forced to live with unsympathetic white men, stared at her with eyes of dark fire, full of questions and confusion. An old man carried a scythe in the crook of his arm and moved with head bowed toward some unknown destination. A cowboy with one arm missing and a horrible scar across his face limped along at the side of a young Mexican lad missing both hands, the result of an Indian raid. An old Indian fighter, famous the country over, dressed in buckskins and reeking of rancid tallow, proudly displayed the grisly patches of scalp—his vouchers he called them—taken from Commanches and Apaches. And there on the bridge, a hauntingly-distinguished looking man, face sallow and drawn, gazed into the emerald green water in which the long grass flowed in undulating waves.

She was on Commerce Street, the main street. Shops were decorated with red, white and blue bunting. Flags flew, some of them very new, others left over from before the Civil War, and with only thirty-four and thirty-five stars. The multitude of horses and wagons and people broke the baked earth into chunks and ground the chunks into dust which hung in a soft, choking cloud over the street and shops, filling the lungs of animals and men alike. Barely able to breathe, she broke from the white dust and crossed the river via a small picturesque wooden bridge, following a course suggested by the hotel clerk. Crossing a second bridge she entered the second of the town's two dusty centers of activity, Military Plaza. Right then Karen decided San Antonio was a town of infinite variety—more so even than Washington. Small abode shops butted up against larger wooden structures which in turn sat in the shadows of limestone walls. Brightly painted white facades contrasted with the faded gray of unpainted, weathered wood. Down a little alley she saw a hut made of branches and wattle, the roof thatched with grass. In the plaza a vaudeville house crowed the laurels of the artistic performance to be seen inside and she remembered the two other similar houses she had seen. *Macbeth*, the sign said, and a craggy Gaelic face haloed with red hair glowered at her from a gilded frame. Her favorite Shakespearean play,

Karen had her doubts about the quality of the performance. A rustic production, more than likely. Still, she was intrigued and looked for the ticket office, only to find across another window was painted in block letters the message, "Open Every Night." Open air stalls on every side offered vegetables, peppers, pastries and tools for sale. Ahead of her near a post stood what appeared to be a tremendous mound of mesquite branches which had somehow managed to sprout two pair of legs. Drawing closer she noticed a short tail, and closer still, an ear tip covered with soft gray hair. As she rounded the load of wood the rest of the *burro* came into view, its long fuzzy face, sad eyes and sagging velvety ears the very picture of doleful resignation.

She passed shops with names reflecting the cultural hodge-podge of the town. Her throat was dry and felt clogged with grit. A sign said Bar Room, and from behind darkened windows she could hear the tinkling of glasses and a rumble of talk punctuated with bursts of raucous laughter. She paused, considering whether or not to enter. *But why not? It can't be any worse than the Crow's Nest.* The Piper and his friends had taken her there many times. Surely, this Bar Room would prove to be as innocuous as the Crow's Nest. Besides, the San Antonians she had seen had been more than friendly. As if to reinforce the feeling, two ranchers passed by, each tipping his hat and muttering a polite, "Howdy, ma'am." Her mind made up, she followed the sounds into the dimly-lit interior.

The double doors swung closed behind her and the chatter quieted immediately. Slowly her eyes adjusted to the dark. Around her were a number of tables, several covered with a scattering of playing cards and chips for gaming. Before her was a long counter with a brass rail near the bottom, not unlike the Crow's Nest. Half a dozen hard-looking men stared at her, glasses frozen part way to their lips. Two women dressed in cheap satin dresses, cut lower than hers and stained with sweat, stood among the men. The women's faces were smeared with rouge and their eyes and lips were heavily painted, an obvious sign of their profession.

Karen backed up hesitantly, then bridling at being upset by such as these, gathered all the Hampton *esprit* at her command and approached the counter, the men parting before her, one of the women turning and spitting on the floor before flouncing away to assume an angry, rebellious pose at a nearby table. And still the men stared, uncomfortable in her presence. An edge of fear caught at her but she stood her ground. *I will not back down. They will not drive me out.* Her defenses manifested themselves in the most gracious of smiles. "I would like some water, please."

The barkeeper, a man of immense girth, stared at her thunderstruck. "Uh . . . ma'am . . . this here's a *bar*. It . . . well, it ain't no proper . . . uh . . . that is, we ain't supposed to . . .uh . . . ain't supposed ta serve no . . ." he glanced uncomfortably at the painted women at the end of the bar, ". . . unescorted ladies, ma'am."

"But I am thirsty," Karen answered pleasantly, trying to put him at ease. "Surely a glass of water . . ."

"But ma'am, I already done tole' . . ."

"Give the lady some water."

Karen, startled by the familiarity of the new voice, spun around to discover Roscoe Bodine standing just behind her.

"Now look here, Bodine, you know rules is rules."

"She's with me. I'm escortin' her. Ain't that right, Miss Hampton?"

Karen chanced a tentative smile at the rugged outrider, sensing an opportunity to gain satisfaction for what she considered to be the bartender's rudeness.

"That takes care of your rules then, don't it, Miller," Bodine declared, a dangerous glint in his eyes.

"Uh . . . why, yes. I reckon so."

Bodine turned to Karen and ignored the bartender. "You want somethin' stronger, Miss Hampton?"

"No. Water will be fine, thank you."

Miller poured a glass of cool, sweet spring water from a pitcher and handed it to Bodine to carry as he guided her to a far corner table near the entrance to a narrow hallway from which exuded a dank, stale, musty odor, not at all pleasant. Bodine sat with his back to the wall. He had washed, shaved and bought some new clothes, giving him a dashing if rough look. The patch only added to his interesting face, a face not handsome nor ugly, but rather used and stern, reflecting the harshness of the land in which he lived and recalling the hardness seen in many of the men and women behind her at the bar.

Karen listened wide-eyed and with great intent as Bodine

spoke of places he'd seen, scrapes he'd encountered, battles he had won and lost. The whiskey bottle in front of him tipped from time to time to spill more of the disagreeable amber fluid—the label said, quite simply, "Whiskey," though a more evil-smelling potion she had never encountered—in his glass, and as he talked he drank, not quickly but steadily, his voice slurring at first imperceptively and then in a more pronounced manner. Karen wanted to leave but her confidence had been shaken and she wasn't quite sure of how to do so without creating a scene. Instead she smiled as she listened, laughing in all the right places at his humorous tales, never dreaming the man would construe her behavior as an invitation to further advances. A vague memory of Vance telling her flirtation could be dangerous tugged at her mind but she dismissed it, for she was on her own now and such was the way she was accustomed to win over men, to bend them to her will. Slowly, as she became used to the room, the sounds and smells, her confidence returned.

A woman at the bar laughed coarsely. She was standing close to one of the cowboys. Karen blushed and turned her eyes as the woman leaned against the man and whispered in his ear, her hand sliding below his belt. A second later the same two passed her table and headed down the hall. Again, she turned her head from them, focusing on Bodine in order to cover her embarrassment.

Bodine glanced sharply at the pair leaving the room, then looked back to Karen, a strange glow in his eye. "Rooms down there," he said huskily. "Want to go look?"

The question took her off guard and she glanced about nervously, a move he interpreted as an affirmative answer. He tossed off the rest of the glass of whiskey and reached across the table to grab her wrist. The move shocked her and she tried to draw away. "Mr. Bodine. . . ."

Weeks of loneliness and frustration transformed the outrider from a rough but well-meaning man into a lust-driven beast. His grip was like a vice and his voice rasped in her ears. "Honey, you been wantin' it ever since I first seen you. Maybe that boy you travelin' with don't know how, but I do. I got enough saved up to last you a long time. Warm that northe'n blood a' yours."

"Mr. Bodine, I am sorry, but you'll have to. . . ." She was frightened now. That which had seemed so harmless

196

only moments before had been blown out of all proportion.

"I don't have to do nothin', 'cept what I got a mind to. You been askin' an' puttin' on airs ever since we left Corpus. Hell, I can read sign on the trail an' I can read sign in a woman." He rose drunkenly from the table, hauling her out of her seat and pulling her to him, covering her mouth with a brutal kiss before she quite knew what was happening. Panic stricken, Karen fought to get free, only to feel a hard, demanding hand grope at her breast and savagely knead it.

"Bodine!" The name rang out clear in the sudden silence. "Leave her be!" As Roscoe lifted his head a fist shot by Karen and slammed into Bodine's face, knocking him back into his chair and spilling him to the floor. Karen leaped away, struggling to keep from screaming. Through tear-filled eyes she saw her benefactor, Billy, Bodine's partner and the other outrider.

"Are you all right, ma'am?" he asked solicitously. "Roscoe gets a mite mean when he drinks too much. It's a sorrowful way for a good man to behave."

Karen nodded. Suddenly from behind her Roscoe lunged from the floor, his fist describing a wide arc which connected with Billy's jaw and knocked him head over heels into a table. The boy moaned softly, then slumped unconscious. Bodine's momentum had carried him past Karen and he stopped, whirling to face her, his eye burning with lust and anger. She was trapped. He was between her and the front door. Barely thinking, she whirled and bolted down the narrow hall.

Behind her, several of the men made a move toward Bodine but he flipped a gun from its hiding place behind his waistband. They stopped suddenly, backing from the weapon. "Bodine . . . dammit, leave her be," the bartender shouted.

"Go to hell, Miller. I'll pay you for your damn room," he growled as he followed Karen into the hall.

Karen ran to the farthermost door.. Hoping it led to the outside she raised the latch and rushed through into a sour, musky, sweat-smelling alcove lit by a single sputtering coal oil lamp and then stopped, aghast at the sight before her. The prostitute who had left the room only moments before lay on her back on a dirty mattress, her legs naked and the red satin dress bunched up around her waist. The man on top of her had dropped his jeans and long johns to his knees and grunted wildly as he drove himself into the flaccid, unmoving and uncaring woman under him. The door closed with a loud click and the man looked over at Karen, as startled as she. The woman beneath him couldn't have cared less. "You lose somethin', honey?" she asked in a bored, matter-of-fact tone before turning her attention back to the cowboy. "Come on, Eddie. I ain't got all day."

Karen stood spellbound, near hysteria. Frantically she looked about for means of escape. The room had no windows, no manner of egress. Suddenly the door behind her flew open and Bodine stumbled into the room. The man on the bed clambered off the woman and hopped about grabbing at his trousers, trying to pull them up and still look angry. "What the hell is this?"

Bodine shoved Karen further into the room and in the same motion grabbed the half-naked man by his shirt and threw him into the hall. The prostitute disgustedly rolled off the bed with a curse. "Roscoe," she warned, "you're drunk again. You'd be better off with me, 'cause that there's a lady. And trouble to boot."

"Get the hell out, Lilly," Roscoe growled menacingly. "Get out before I throw you out, too."

Karen cringed at the sound of his voice. "Please, miss, get some. . . ."

"Honey, you gotta take care of your own problems," Lilly answered, patting down her skirt and heading out the door.

Bodine's eye was red and bleary. He kicked closed the door behind him and stared at the girl cowering against the wall. "Well . . . peel."

"Please, Mr. Bodine. . . ."

"We're alone. That's what you wanted, wasn't it? Hell, ain't no one gonna see you. It's what you come here for."

"No. No, you're wrong."

"You smiled an' smiled at me, cast me longin' glances. I could tell you was fancyin' me." He stepped closer, his hand reaching out to touch her face, somehow more gently than she had imagined he would. A confused look came into his eye and he hesitated. "Why you cryin'? Never understan' women. Lonesome where I been, with nothin' to talk to but the tumbleweeds an' the sky."

He staggered backward, stooped over a moment to hold

198

his head. *"Hijo!"* he exclaimed in Spanish. "My head. That goddam rotgut whiskey. Ought to make him drink his . . . hey!" He reached out as Karen bolted past him, his hand tearing at her dress and tripping her. Karen tumbled to one side and fell on the bed. The man lurched closer to her and stopped. "I don't understan' you, miss," he said, his speech becoming more and more slurred as the whiskey tightened its hold on him. He reached out to touch her again.

"Bodine!"

The outrider's one good eye went wide with recognition. Vance Paxton stood outlined in the doorway, the bartender's gun stuck in his belt. Karen started to speak but Bodine cut her off, screaming, "Get out of here, Paxton!" He grabbed at the gun in his belt.

"Don't, Roscoe!" Vance shouted, even as his own hand dropped and, on reflex alone, scooped out the heavy army Colt. Karen stared horrified. The sound of Vance's gun was deafening in the small room. Karen tried to scream for them to stop, knowing the unspeakable climax had already been reached. The report from Roscoe's pistol was just as loud as, slammed back against the dresser, he fired his own weapon, sending the bullet into the soiled mattress and barely missing Karen.

In the sudden silence, time stopped. Roscoe slowly raised his pistol, the chore almost too much for him. He looked puzzled at the gun in his hand, at the man in the doorway, at the girl on the floor. Vance did not shoot again, though he kept his revolver aimed at the outrider. "Roscoe, for Christ's sake . . . enough. Don't make me shoot again."

Bodine shook his head. "You won't need to. That one's done it," he said, his voice small and far away. His eye seemed to clear and his arm lowered, the pistol slipping from his grip and falling with a thud to the floor. He stepped away from the dresser, his face a puzzled frown as he stared at Karen. "You . . . you fancied me. I could tell. All the way . . . up from . . . Corpus. . . ."

Karen covered her mouth with a pale and bloodless hand to keep from screaming. There was a hole in front of Bodine's shirt, a dark smear spreading around it. Behind him a gleaming white chip from the limestone wall where the bullet had struck glowed in the dim light. Slowly, she rose and stepped aside as the man stumbled and fell forward onto the mattress. The springs creaked as he bounced and lay still. On his back, a larger hole streamed blood and gore.

Vance stepped to him quickly, rolled him over and swung his long legs onto the bed. Pink froth bubbled from the front of his shirt as he breathed, sucked back in with each inhalation. Vance sat by him, ripped off the shirt and exposed the wound. Working quickly he tore the shirt into strips, plugged the wounds and bound them. Bodine seemed lucid and watched calmly as the man who had shot him tired to save him. When he spoke the whiskey slur was gone. "Sorry, Paxton. Shouldn't a' tried you. Knowed better, if I'd thought about it." A wave of pain caught him and he winced, his teeth gritting with effort. When the pain subsided he chuckled grimly, the sound garbled with the blood welling in his throat. "Damn it, Paxton, you done gone an' . . . ruined my . . . new shirt. An' it cost me . . . cost . . ." He stopped, his face contorting with a new wave of pain. As it ebbed he swung his head to look at Karen. "She fancied . . . she . . ." But the effort was too much. His eye glazed over, not with drunkenness, but death.

Silence lay heavily on the room. Slowly, Vance stood, laying the dead man's head back on the bed and closing his eye. He turned and faced Karen, his face hard and set, eyes slit and cold. Three steps and he stood in front of her. Neither said a word as his hands, red and wet with fresh blood, rose to hover in front of her face, the bloody fingers clawed in talons before her eyes. "You just got a good man killed," he said quietly, almost whispering.

Karen shrank back from the hands, the terrible blood-covered hands. "I . . . I didn't . . ."

He reached and grabbed her arms, the fresh blood smearing on her sleeves. "I said," he interrupted fiercely, "you just got a good man killed."

Someone coughed nervously outside the room. Vance stared hard at the offender before grabbing Karen's wrist and heading for the door, hauling her behind him. The men in the hall parted silently and let them through, the narrow pathway closing behind them as the whispers started. The saloon was empty save for Billy, who sat at one of the tables, holding his head in his hands. He looked up and as she passed, Karen saw the side of his face was puffed out and blood still streamed from his mouth.

Vance paid no attention, merely continued dragging her

across the empty floor and out the door where a knot of people stood, drawn by the story of a killing. A single look from him opened an avenue for them and he hauled her to a fancy buckboard and unceremoniously dumped her in. Leaping to the seat beside her he grabbed the reins and whip and lashed the horse into a startled run.

The buckboard left a chorus of shouted protests in its dusty wake as people leaped aside to avoid being run down. Vance slashed the whip across the horse's rump, urging it to greater speed. He had not spoken a word to Karen, who sat glumly next to him, holding the torn fragments of her dress together while trying not to fall from the wildly careening buggy. They pulled up to the rear entrance of the Menger and came to a shuddering halt. "Get out," Vance said shortly.

"This is the servants' entrance," Karen answered, attempting to sound braver than she felt. "I shall go in by the front door."

Vance jumped out and pulled her after him, roughly led her through the back door, the kitchen, the laundry and up the servants' stairway to the hall leading to their rooms. Once in her room, Karen whirled around, her temper boiling, a flush on her cheeks. "How dare. . . ."

"Shut up."

Karen looked at the man she thought she knew, thought she loved. His hair was wild and unkempt from the ride. There was blood on his clothes, his hands, even his face. Blood from the man he had killed.

"I told you to stay here."

"I am not some trained underling to do as she is told. You had business more important than being with me on our first day here. I decided to . . ."

"Dammit, none of this would have happened if you'd done as I said."

"How could I know that?"

"By listening to what I've been telling you for the last four days. By not being so big-headed you thought you knew everything, thought your eastern ways worked out here. You could have gotten Billy killed. You did kill Bodine."

"I didn't shoot him, Mr. Paxton. You did. You and your gun."

Vance stood stock still, staring at her. "That's right. I

201

did, didn't I." He turned and walked to the window, held the curtain back and stared out. When he spoke his voice was low and troubled. "I killed Roscoe Bodine. He was a good man on the trail—a good man all around. Good enough to have saved my life twice during the war and once on a trail drive. And I repayed the debt by putting a bullet through his chest!" He slammed his hand on the wall and turned violently back to her, his voice shaking with rage. "I warned you on the trail, but you were too bull-headed to listen. Your flirting brought a man to his death, shot down in a damned filthy bar for no good reason. This is not Washington."

"It most certainly is not. Civilized men do not attack women. Civilized men do not carry guns and kill people."

"What would a 'civilized' man do had he left his wife, whom he takes to be a lady, at their hotel, only to find her in some saloon back room, half naked and behaving like a painted slut?"

Karen slapped him across the face. "You forget yourself," she said, panting with emotion.

Vance grabbed her by the shoulders, his bloodstained fingers bruising her flesh. "Don't you ever do that again."

She lashed out at him, her anger overriding the shock of the afternoon's experience. Her fists pummeled his face and chest. Like a tigress she fought, sobbing and crying bitterly. Vance shoved her back, tripped on her gown and fell against her, sending both of them tumbling onto the bed. She struggled furiously to free her arms as he pinned them to either side of her head. Her bodice was already torn and as the struggle intensified the fabric ripped open the rest of the way, exposing both breasts, the nipples erect with the excitation of the fight. Her hair was spread out on the bed cover, adding to her wild beauty.

Suddenly Vance sought her mouth with his. She struggled violently but found herself no match against the power of his arms and shoulders, imbued with even greater strength by the charged emotional state in which he found himself. He had been near death only moments before. He had taken a life. Now the very essence of life, the body his own had so fiercely desired, lay beneath him. He managed to free one hand and cup her breast.

His touch was fire. Awash with the anger of the moment, their uncontrollable hunger for each other so nearly released at Three Rivers once again took command. As her fists pounded his back her mouth sought his. Blindly, the tears springing from her eyes, she felt him rip the gown from her, then fumble with his belt. Her anger rekindled, she renewed her contention, but in vain. How, she never knew, but suddenly she lay naked and exposed, his muscular thighs forcing themselves between her own, bringing his virile organ inexorably closer to the gateway of his desire. Even as she fought him, Karen felt once again the betraying moisture from her loins. His manhood, swollen and hard, touched her in brief dalliance then pressed into the moist warmth. She could resist no longer. Her legs rose and clasped around his waist and she thrust herself upon his passion-swollen staff, moaning and crying out as he drove himself deep into her and parted the maiden's veil.

The pain subsided rapidly, forgotten in the feverish crescendo of desire, forgotten in the heat of motion and the excruciating sensation of him filling her as the swollen scepter of his love slid in and out, in and out, thrusting, thrusting, touching all of her. *Oh God! This is what it's like. This . . . this. . . .* Surprised, she felt herself swell against him, hold the swollen organ more and more tightly to slow the strokes which came with a driving, primitive rhythm.

And then ecstasy. Deep inside, the hard contractions started and built, surging through her as Vance's seed erupted and spilled into her, filling her, scalding her. She feebly tried to push him off but her loins betrayed her will with an insistent demand for more. Contracting again and again she could feel the pulsing organ press deep to touch the tip of her womb and lave it with life-giving fluids until the flame slowly subsided and her body relaxed. Sated, she felt her legs drop to the bed and she became aware of his weight on her. His mouth was close to her ear and he whispered over and over again, "Karen. I love you, Karen. I love you. . . ."

She knew then what it was to be a woman, the hard muscles of a man pressed against her, his manhood still swollen and warm, nestled moistly in her, still moving, but gently and tenderly. Tears of gratitude and fulfillment welled in her eyes and she turned her head so he wouldn't see.

My God . . . ! My God . . . ! His hand, still covered

with the bloody stains of another man's life, lay in front of her, inches from her eyes. *What has happened? What have I done?* It was all wrong. Wrong! She wanted to enjoy the happiness, to revel in the fullness of the moment. Wanted desperately. . . . .

She felt the dress bunched obscenely under her waist and the image of the man on the prostitute filled her vision, blurred by the tears of shame which coursed down her cheeks. A roar of rushing water filled her ears. Suddenly silence threatened, and in the silence, the voice of the prostitute. "You lose somethin', honey? You lose somethin', honey?"

CHAPTER V

Karen lay on her side and stared at the still form next to her. She had waked some hours earlier and remained utterly motionless in the darkness, longing for morning. Finally the first hint of day brightened the curtains and she felt the man stir, saw him, through slitted eyes feigning sleep, open his eyes. Wide awake at once, his gaze lingered on her a moment then scanned the room thoroughly before he rose without warning in one fluid, easy motion and moved quickly and silently from the bed to his clothes, strewn all over the floor. Once dressed, she thought he intended to wake her, for he stood by the side of the bed and laid a tentative hand on her naked shoulder before evidently thinking better, removing his hand and soundlessly slipping from the room. Karen heaved a faint sigh of relief.

Where was he going? More than likely to see to the preparations for the trip to the ranch. She rolled over on her back and pushed away the covers. Her blood had stained the sheets and left a dark smear on her inner thigh, a sign of his passage and her loss. Her loss? The driving weight of his body and his hardened manhood ramming her as if to pin her to the bed lingered in her mind and she blushed with shame at the tangible kinetic memory of the exquisite sensation to which she had responded with such lust and abandon. And then the fierce jetting of his seed driving her into paroxysms of furious contractions as her body betrayed its involuntary craving for the fluid of his fulfillment.

The bed creaked as she rose and crossed the room to peer through a slit between the curtains and see Vance stride purposefully away from the hotel. When he disappeared around the corner she sagged against the window sill, more alone than ever before in her twenty years. In front of her the sight of the rumpled sheets so like a battleground overrode the sensuous memories of the night before. All the emotions, the clashing currents of a tortured stream, surged and eddied in her mind until, shivering, she stumbled from the window and gripped the iron bedpost lest she fall. Their union had been far from an exquisite culmination of love's utter longing. More like a contest, or a battle of wills, they had used their bodies as carnal weapons to subjugate the other. Sex had been a tool, been employed, not shared as she had planned, not enjoyed as she had dreamed in Washington. The delight she had envisioned in the garden and during the final magic weeks of their courtship had been but a mirage. In vain she fought to control the tears that threatened to brim and flow down her cheeks.

Control shattered with full realization. Across the room a blurred vision in the mirror struck her, tore at the very fabric of her soul, the treacherous catalyst being the twin black-red smears on her shoulders. The blood of a dying man brought all the terrible events back with a rush. Sobbing wildly she ran to the basin, wet a cloth and scrubbed the telltale marks. Scrubbed and scrubbed the telltale marks as had Lady Macbeth. *What, will these hands ne'er be clean* . . . the helplessness, the filthy horrid room . . . *Here's the smell of blood still* . . . the ugly placidity of the harlot . . . Bodine, so pitiful, so dangerous, so frightening . . . Vance standing in the doorway . . . thunder in a dark room . . . acrid smell of gunpowder and violated flesh . . . *Who would have thought the old man had so much blood in him?* . . . a man dying . . . dying!

The girl in the mirror stiffened, a towel hugged to her, and stared at herself as the tears ran down her face. She had seen a man die, seen, felt, watched—close enough to touch—at the moment the precious spark of life left the parted lips and the single hurt and questioning eye rolled back, relieved of pain, the questions meaningless. And Vance's anger had been directed at her. He had raised his bloody hands to her face, hands metamorphosed into the talons of a beast. And he had blamed her!

Through the vision her own rage took form and grew. Angry at her? Blame her? Bodine had attacked her, would have raped her, yet Vance was furious with *her!* The woman in front of her changed, stared back at her with tight, angry eyes. *My fault Bodine was drunk and behaving like a*

*beast? No thank you, sir! My fault you chose to use a gun
to subdue my attacker? Not hardly, sir! My fault a man is
dead? No thank you, indeed!*

The Vance Paxton she loved in Washington had changed
and in his place she saw a stranger revealed whose inimi-
cal behavior was totally foreign to her heart. She did not
want, nor would she have, a man who wished to dominate
her and bend her to his will. *I am Karen Hampton, the
most sought-after young woman in Washington.* She
squared her shoulders, trying to convince the woman in the
mirror. *Who does he think he is?* The woman in the mirror
stared coldly back at her. "You are not in Washington, you
are in . . ." . . . *a brutal, terrible land where people you
thought loved you appease their carnal appetites by force,
where a man whose gentle openness won my heart killed a
man and blames me for the deed. He is capable of the vilest
insults. He is domineering, capricious, stubborn, ill-bred
and ill-tempered* . . . "He is the man you chose."

Karen reeled from the mirror and slumped onto the bed,
the tears flowing easily and the sleek lines of her body
shuddering with each racking sob. And like the most violent of storms, this too passed, all the more quickly for its
furious nature. She fought for control and won. Brushing
back the long meadow-gold tresses from her face she rose
from the bed and crossed the room, unsteadily at first, to
stand once more before the mirror. Coldly, she studied herself, cupping each breast then running smooth hands across
her stomach and down to her thighs where a faint ache
from his entry still lingered. The coldness was a calculating
chill she had never before known, out of which grew a renewed and resolute strength.

Washington was closed to her, at least for the while. She
had broken those ties and whatever rebuilding was needed
must be begun in Texas. She had made her choice and was
determined to hold her course. The Vance Paxton with
whom she had fallen in love would be the Vance Paxton
she married, and with whom she would find the happiness
which first filled her dreams. But dominate her? The
woman in the mirror straightened determinedly. *No, Mr.
Paxton, you shall never again make me weep.* And should
her resolve be tried? She smiled at the contours of her
body, the soft, full curves and angles of desire so capable of
arousing men and filling their heads with silly, never-to-

be-fulfilled notions. Only now she was free to use more than just enticing promises. She would use all her natural gifts, but hide from him until he acquiesced the one ingredient to make them complete . . . her love.

Vance pulled the buckboard around to the front of the hotel, climbed down and adjusted the harness, checked the trunks in back and generally attended to all the little things he'd already seen to. Anything to keep from returning to the hotel and Karen. When there was nothing more required he headed across the street to the tiny cafe and ordered coffee. Coffee to get his blood running again, to clear his head, for already he'd spent a difficult two hours. The obligatory talk with Sheriff Hodgdon had consumed most of the time, but in the end they'd cleared up the whole mess and parted friends, with Vance free to go as he pleased. It was from Hodgdon he learned all the details of the previous afternoon. Karen had been guilty of no more than bad judgment easily attributed to her recent arrival and consequent ignorance of what a Texas bar could be like. If she had only stayed in the hotel as he'd told her . . . the thought ran through his mind over and over again, irritated him beyond dismissal. If . . . if . . .

After the talk with the sheriff there had been supplies to see to, the renting of the buckboard and the mules, loading and so on. He'd kept busy in an attempt to keep the wild running thoughts from his mind. And during all the chores, no matter how badly they needed doing, one other thought lurked in the back of his mind: stay away from her as long as possible.

The door swung shut behind him and he found a place at a table. The coffee was in front of him. He dumped in the sugar, stirred. Find her in a place like Miller's bar room and with Bodine! If she hadn't flirted with the man in the first place. . . . Dammit, he'd warned her back on the trail and she hadn't listened. Now a good man was needlessly dead, killed by the combination of frustration, too much whiskey and the proximity of a beautiful, flirtatious woman. Why couldn't she have stayed where he told her? Doubts assailed the wisdom of his decision to bring her to Texas. The frontier was no place for a prima donna, nor was the Paxton ranch. He should have known something like this might happen. The fragrant romanticism of Washington nights had been burnt away by the fierce glare of the Texas sun. He thought again of their confrontation, how words of anger and spite had turned to heated passion and the breaking of his resolve. But she was so lovely. . . . No. It was more than that. Her hair unfixed, her dress torn and disheveled, the weeks of nearness, of touching and seeing without possessing, the tension and the explosive emotions elicited by Bodine's death and his own near brush with death, the raw sensuousness and elemental voluptuousness he had known all along lurked beneath the veneer of girlish civility and frivolity. . . . A torn gown had tripped him in more ways than one, and that tumble onto the bed followed by her frantic struggle underneath him had finally broken all bounds of restraint.

He had never before forced or taken a woman in anger. Damn! If she had only . . . if. If her gown hadn't been torn. If he hadn't tripped. If the writhing flesh underneath him. . . . He had not suspected such a tempest of hungry longing and indiscriminate rage waited in him. To master her with his own hard masculine strength was his initial objective, but the thought had fallen aside, lost in the emotion of their turbulent coition. Worst of all, he had tried to buy her off. He colored with shame to think he lay there whimpering his love for her. She had won after all. What flaw of passion was it whose aftermath left him a mewling infant on this woman's breast? And why only with Karen Hampton?

"Mr. Paxton, ol' Jess is saddled an' ready." Vance turned, startled from his reverie by the voice. Billy stood by the table. Vance cursed silently. The woman had gotten to him worse than he thought. He hadn't even heard the door open, hadn't heard Billy's footsteps. To be so off guard . . . The youngster's jaw was still swollen and ugly, marked with the color left by Roscoe Bodine's fist. For a second he stared at Billy, his mind so muddled he barely remembered having hired the young outrider to accompany them to the ranch, with the promise of a job when they arrived.

"Get yourself some coffee," he said. "I'll get Miss Hampton. Be a minute."

"How is she this morning?"

Vance started to answer, then caught himself. "Haven't seen her awake," he finally mumbled, rising from the table.

"Sure am sorry about yesterday, Mr. Paxton. Bodine

wasn't a bad man. Losin' them cattle up north an' not findin' anyone willin' to hire him on . . . well . . . Bodine, he took it hard an' let it eat at him. Leastways, that's how I figger it. But he weren't a bad man."

"I'm sorry, too, Billy. You and he were trail partners, I know."

"You done what you had to. Can't no man fault you for that."

Vance nodded, at a loss for a moment, then said with a sigh, "I'll see to Miss Hampton."

The hotel stirred with drowsy anticipation òf a new day. Vance entered the lobby and noticed the day clerk's eyes widen. The night man had made it obvious Vance might be happier at another hotel, said message coming from the management. The cattleman couldn't blame the old man, really. The Menger had undoubtedly heard about the difficulty in Miller's Bar and would be worried Bodine's former companions might attempt revenge for their fallen friend and bring violence to the hotel. "Don't worry. I'm headin' out this mornin'."

"Wasn't me, Mr. Paxton. I sure hope you don't think. . . ."

"Know it wasn't," Vance said, laying down a gold double eagle. "You can split the change with the night man."

"Yes sir," the boy said gratefully. "Marcus, he . . ."

"Know it's not him, too," Vance cut him off, turning to the empty lobby and stopping short.

Karen slowly descended the stairway. Carmela passed her going up, the Mexican girl burdened by an armload of folded linens almost above her eye level. She averted her gaze from the American *señorita* and only when she was several steps past her did she break down and giggle, trying desperately to muffle the sound in the stack of towels. But Karen heard her, heard and was not amused. Did everyone know of the incident in that horrible bar room? Or did the girl's laughter signify something more? Perhaps she had overheard Karen and Vance's argument in the room, or worse, the subsequent silence.

"Karen . . . I . . . "

"My bags are in my room," she said icily, picking up the hem of the pale blue-green skirt and proceeding out the front door, her shoulders squared haughtily.

Behind her she left a dumbfounded and utterly perplexed Vance.

"At least it's a different buckboard," Vance said in a conciliatory tone as he guided the team down the gradual incline to the crossing at San Pedro Springs. Karen didn't comment, though she was grateful for the appreciably greater comfort of the newer wagon. It was jostling and uncomfortable at best, but fell short of excruciating, a quality in which the first had managed quite easily to excel.

They stopped in the shade for five minutes to water the mules. The scene surrounding her was of unadorned bucolic simplicity upon which Karen gazed with that curious blend of wistfulness and superiority affected by the very wealthy. Along the banks of the San Pedro the Mexican women kneeled, kneading and scrubbing their clothes in the clear water, beating the soap and dirt from them on the rocks. The women chattered gaily in an increasing flow of rapid Spanish which blended with the chuckling, gurgling stream. *How easy and simple their lives.* . . . She did not see the swollen knees and wrinkled, split fingertips, nor would she have understood the stoical dismissal of aching backs when, later, the women carried the clean clothes back to the dismal *jacals,* those dreary huts of stakes and wattle, and hung them to dry in the dusty sun.

Once they crested the west bank of the stream the line of cottonwoods, cedars, pecans and oak began to thin and eventually they broke free of the wooded area entirely. Ahead lay empty land, stretching to the dim line between sky and earth. To their south was nothing. To the north, a low line of hills raised the horizon. The final tree to their rear, Billy pulled up alongside them. "Reckon I'll mosey up ahead a bit, Mr. Paxton."

"All right, Billy. First stop'll be Castroville. We'll get something to eat and then head out for Hondo."

Billy's face clouded. "I guess you oughta know."

"What?"

"Well, while I was in the cafe . . . ?" He glanced guardedly at Karen.

"Yes?" Vance asked.

"I heard the Rafter XO is ridin' to Hondo t'day," he blurted. "They said they. . . ."

The Rafter XO. Bodine's old outfit. He couldn't let

Karen. . . . "That'll be enough, Billy," he ordered, his face suddenly tight and grim. "Soon as we cross the Medina we'll cut north, noon in Broken Axle canyon. We'll keep near the foothills then. Not so close to be caught unawares, but close enough to make a run if we need to."

"People say Jaco's around. If he is," Billy said, gesturing to the hills to the north. He grimaced awkwardly. "Begin' your pardon, Miss. Don't mean to alarm you none. Chances are we won't. . . ."

"Billy!" Vance's voice was rough with command. "You can ride. We'll stop for the night at Cross Bear Creek."

"Them mules," he said, casting an appraising eye at the large black animals, "ought to make it some further, if you've a mind to."

"Cross Bear's a good camp. No point in pushing for the sake of an hour or two. We'll still get in tomorrow."

Billy nodded in agreement and nudged his heels into the steeldust's flanks. The gelding broke into a trot, then a slow, easy-paced gallop.

The sun, oblivious to the passions of men, the desires of women and the intertwining destinies of both, arched high overhead on its relentless path until the glowing orb hung swollen and crimson above the western edge of the world. With barely more than a dozen utilitarian words between them over the hours, Vance guided the wagon on an oblique path north to the line of foothills. Billy had already scouted a clear space among a grove of cedar, and finding it safe, called in the wagon to the far side of Cross Bear Creek. Karen jumped from the wagon alone and walked back and forth in an attempt to bring life back to her legs while Vance tethered the mules and Billy started a fire beneath the fanning branches of a huge old pecan.

It was quiet in the little glade. Vance had taken a rifle and gone off to scout around and Billy squatted in front of the fire, cutting strips of bacon into a skillet. A faint trail of smoke coiled from the fire and dissipated in the branches above. Karen, trying to remember some of the things Cathy might do, rummaged in the wagon for a sack of ground coffee and the coffee pot, took the pot to the creek and filled it, then carried both back to the fire and set the water to boil. Billy rose and started to take off his hat, but with a knife in one hand and a slab of bacon in the other, had to settle for an embarrassed grin and an awkward bow. Pay-

212

ing the young man as little attention as possible, she tossed a few pinches of coffee into the water.

Vance still hadn't returned. It was getting dark and the stillness, broken only by the slight sound of water in the creek and a faint crackling of the dry wood on the fire, began to oppress her, smothering the quiet peace in the glade. She had to talk. "Billy, who is this Jaco? Ever since coming to Texas I keep hearing his name."

"He's a powerful mean Mexican, Miss Hampton. Got a bad streak in him with no quit to it a'tall. Likes to kill. White folks mostly, but ever once in a while a' Indian or Negro. Mexes, too, should they cross him. Raids across the border into Texas. Not often. Three, four times since the war. Once over near Fort Davis, once even up on the Staked Plains. Maybe now, though nobody's seen him for sure. When the army or rangers, when we have 'em, make things a mite warm, well, he lights a shuck for New Mexico or back across the Rio Grande to home. Got him quite a following among the young *bravos* across the border, some of 'em ready for a revolution, they say, with Jaco as leader. Loco, they are."

Karen hugged her knees and shivered. "Would they . . . ?"

"Like I said. Don't you go to frettin'. Mostly I guess folks just talk. It's gettin' plumb civilized around here. Too many people an' too many men salty enough to whup him if it ever come down to it. Reckon he knows it too, 'cause he ain't tried nothin' with 'em, nor the PAX."

"The PAX?"

"That's Paxton's brand." He took a stick and drew the letters in the dirt around the fire. "I'm gonna be right proud to ride for that brand, too," he said, full of youthful enthusiasm.

"Ride for the brand?"

"Yes'm. You know . . . uh . . . workin' for 'em. Keepin' cattle on the range, roundin' up strays, brandin', whatever. Drivin' off rustlers if need be. I'm hopin' to run a herd up Kansas way."

"But you seem so young."

Billy set knife and bacon down abruptly and rose to his full five feet eight inches, his face set indignantly. "Ma'am, I happen to be sixteen years old." And with that he stalked

213

away to the wagon, rumaging through the supplies for a loaf of bread.

Later after Vance returned the three sat quietly, each brooding on the day and staring into the night. The fire guttered and collapsed in a pile of coals unable to warm the cool politeness lapping at its edge. Karen poured coffee and passed the cups around. Hers tasted fine. For once the brew wasn't too strong. But the two men took a single gulp, glanced at each other darkly and gingerly put their cups down as if they'd tasted poison. Karen finished the coffee, and feeling ill at ease, wondering what Cathy would have done next, found she couldn't remember. Upset and frustrated, she retired to the ground cloth and blankets Vance had set out near the wagon. More tired than expected, she was soon asleep, waking only once to see Vance putting a fresh pot of coffee on the coals.

Morning? No. It's much too dark. Karen snuggled down into the blanket, trying to recapture the dream. Visions of her bed in the Georgetown house. How soft and deliciously silky. A noise . . . breaking branches. Crackle of flames, tinny clatter of cups against a coffee pot. She opened her eyes again. The men were awake and preparing for the day. The smell of bacon hung on the morning air. Bacon . . . she had eaten more bacon in the past week than in her entire life. She rolled out of the blankets, washed and breakfasted while Vance and Billy hitched the mules and packed the bedrolls.

Billy rode out of the grove as Vance helped Karen into the buckboard. "We'll get there today. I. . . ."

Billy rode back into the clearing. "Looks good, Mr. Paxton."

"We'll move out, then." Vance rounded the wagon and took his place alongside Karen. The mules broke into motion at the graceful snap of the whip over their heads, pulled away from the pecan, out of the cedar brake and onto the trail west.

The day went quicker than any of the others she had spent traveling. Their path lay close to the hills, whose rolling swells were crowned with evergreen, skirted with oak and mesquite. They passed the mouths of narrow valleys, or canyons as Vance called them, dark and somberly mysterious, any one of which Karen was sure led to excitement and adventure. Who knew what lay between their walls?

They turned due north in the middle of the afternoon and headed for a solid line of trees between two hills where the mouth of a valley was choked with cedar. "This is the *Cañón de Uvalde*. Sabinal Canyon, we call it now, for the river. Gets its name from cypress, which is *sabinal* in Spanish. It cuts through the valley. We're home."

Home. How empty the word sounds. What is home when you are a stranger everywhere? A broad trail tunneled its way through the trees. The light dimmed to twilight as they entered and sudden panic seized her. What was she doing here? Who was this man beside her? The man she loved? He had changed and she did not know him. The man who had so captured her heart had become a dark and ominous figure at her side, transporting her through a nightmare cave to an unknown world in which romance had become plagued with remorse, adventure marred by ordeal.

And suddenly daylight. To their left a river, and on all sides lush green grass dotted with cattle which followed their passage with dull, senseless eyes. Like some impregnable gateway the mouth of the canyon fell to the rear and narrowed, finally closed. She was trapped. Cunningly, yet unwittingly, her own dreams had caught her. She had ridden into them even as they lay waiting, waiting, patient as are all traps.

Once past the cedar brake the valley widened to about eight miles, occasionally narrowing to three and then broadening again. The Sabinal, true to its name lined with cypress, theaded the length of the valley. A herd of antelope darted from nearby grove of trees. Startled, Karen gasped with surprise and delight as the sleek brown forms crossed their path and bounded toward the river. Flowers grew in rare profusion: daring spears of Indian paintbrush; bluebonnets demure and very proper; delicate lacy spider lilies quaking in the summer breeze; and dandelions, audacious butter-yellow dandelions, everywhere. Despite her grudging reluctance to admit it, the canyon was breathtakingly beautiful, grew more so the farther they ventured. *A trap? Perhaps I was hasty . . . harsh . . .*

The farther north they went the hills grew steeper, flanked with the ever present mesquite and covered at the sky line with jagged tips of cedar. The ground rose before them and as they crested one imposing swell Karen had her

215

first glimpse of the Paxton ranch. A cluster of sun bleached adobe and wood buildings shone brilliantly on the eastern slope just beyond the reaching afternoon shadows as the sun began to dip below the hills to the west. Buildings emptied as she watched and people ran about, mounting horses and raising a cloud of dust. Riding alongside the wagon, Billy took off his hat and waved it furiously. "They've seen us. Surprised we didn't run into anyone sooner."

Half a dozen men on horseback charged out from the ranch. Puffs of smoke followed by the sound of gunfire and faint shouts and whoops erupted from the riders and echoed through the valley. Vance laughed aloud and stood, cracking the whip and urging the mules into a fast run down a well-worn road leading to what Karen assumed to be the main house, only the red roof tiles of which showed behind a massive adobe wall. Clutching the seat with one hand and holding her hat with the other, she steeled herself to their arrival: whatever she felt would not show.

The riders bunched around the wagon, whooping and firing their guns. Vance shouted greetings to them and grinned broadly at the good-natured hazing of the men surrounding them. These were men he knew well, with whom he'd worked and fought, shared hardships and good times. They knew him not as True Paxton's son and heir to the Paxton holdings, but as one of their own. When there was work to be done, no matter how difficult or unpleasant, he pitched in and did his share or more.

The ride to the house was unsettling, a whirlwind of noise and dust, shouting and bouncing during which Karen found herself alternately fascinated and appalled by the coarse, uninhibited behavior of the ranch hands. The gates of the outer wall swung inward. Two men on the wall waved their sombreros and fired their rifles into the air as the party careened through and drew up in a spacious courtyard. The billowing dust drifted over them, obscuring Karen's view of the house, or hacienda as Vance called it.

The first detail she could make out was a man framed in a doorway, a man tall as Vance but thinner, as if the years had worn away the muscles of youth, leaving behind a tough shell of leather. He limped slightly, closer now and she could see a face lined and rough-looking from a lifetime of struggle against man and elements. His eyes were

216

dark in the shadow of his hat and tinged with hard impatience. He looked like Vance, only thirty years older, and with a shock of recognition she realized he could only be True Paxton. Vance stepped past her and dropped lightly to the ground in front of the old man. "Pa. . . ."

True shook his son's hand, looking past him to the girl sitting primly on the wagon seat. Vance turned and offered his hand to Karen, helping her down. She met True's hard, discerning stare, started to look away then forced herself to return his appraisal with a measuring look of her own. Somehow she thought she saw the corners of his mouth twitch in hidden amusement. "Pa, this is Karen Hampton. The one I wrote you about."

The older man's eyes narrowed. "Welcome to the PAX," he said gruffly. "You're as pretty as Vance said. Didn't know he meant to bring you back with him."

"It's very nice to meet you, Mr. Paxton," Karen answered, confused at his cool and abrupt manner. This wasn't the man Vance had described to her.

True grunted noncommittally and shifted his gaze back to Vance. "Expected you back a couple weeks ago. Reckon I can see what held you up so long." He nodded in Billy's direction. "Who's he?"

"Hired him in San Antonio. Looking for work and I thought he'd do. Rode with us as outrider from Corpus."

True scrutinized the young man. "What's your name, boy?"

"Billy Harmony, sir. I'm sixteen, been on my own since thirteen. I'll saddle and ride my own broncs, and know what's about," he answered, his voice full of confidence.

"We'll see soon enough," True returned, liking the kid's grit but not wanting to show it too soon. "Emilio, show What's About the bunkhouse and line him up some grub." One of the horsemen nodded and rode out the gate, Billy, complete with his new name, following.

They entered through a broad portal into a spacious front room running the width of the house. Overhead, huge ancient-looking timbers supported the ceiling and connected to native stone walls, each with a massive fireplace, at either end of the room. The opposite wall was of hewn cypress. In the center a hall led to the rear of the house and to the left an arch wide enough for three men abreast led to what was obviously a dining room. To the right a smaller arch opened into what she thought was a library, for though the room was dark she was certain a shelf of books lined one wall. A balcony ran the length of the opposite wall and upstairs Karen could make out doors leading to what were probably bedrooms. True had said something to her. "What? I'm sorry, I was . . ."

"I said, Texas will brown you up. You easterners are a pale lot. Spend too much time beneath a roof instead of the sky. A pale and weak lot."

"Mr. Paxton, it is obvious you have never been to New Hampshire or Vermont. Or Maine. There's many a hard-working farmer toiling beneath the same sun as here, and burned just as brown I warrant. As for weak, it was those same men, brown or pale, who counted among the Army of the Potomac that broke Lee's back at Gettysburg."

True bristled at the mention of the southern defeat, but before he could answer Vance entered and as if on cue a robust Mexican woman in peasant blouse and voluminous skirts rushed into the room from the rear of the house and embraced him. "My little *muchacho* . . . Marcelina! Marcelina! *Señor* Paxton has returned." She stepped back, hands on his shoulders, and gazed at him proudly. "*Dios mio,* you are all skin and bone. I think it is good you are back, before you starve, eh? You have been eating someone else's cooking, eh?"

Vance laughed, obviously delighted to see her again. "Only been gone a few months. Couldn't have done much starving. But I sure could use some of your cookin'." He disengaged the older woman's hands from his shoulders and stood with his arm around her waist. "Karen, this is Maruja. Without her we'd all starve and the place would dry up and blow away. Maruja, this is Karen Hampton, from Washington."

A questioning frown flashed across Maruja's ebullient face and was as quickly gone. She nodded in Karen's direction. "I hope the *señorita* will enjoy her visit here."

"Not visit, Maruja. Karen's come here to live. We're to be married."

Karen watched for the frown to reappear but was distracted by a fiery-eyed beauty who dashed from the rear hall, bolted across the room and leaped up to wrap her arms around Vance's neck. Vance flushed red and pried the girl

218

off him. Karen saw long black hair, deep brown eyes, the deliciously limber nubile figure of a girl barely fifteen or sixteen, whose affection for Vance was more than obvious. Karen's eyebrows arched at the suspiciously intimate welcome home. *That was certainly more than a friendly embrace. . . .*

"Marcelina," Vance said, recovering rapidly, "I want you to meet Karen Hampton."

The girl shot a wary glance in Karen's direction. Maruja said something to her in Spanish, the only words Karen recognized being *"Señora* Paxton." Marcelina scowled and with a swirl of her skirt muttered, "I will prepare a room."

"She can have mine, Marcelina," Vance said as she walked away. The girl stopped, back stiff, shoulders arched and her hair seeming to bristle. "I'll make a bed down here in the living room." Marcelina relaxed visibly and continued into the hallway and out of sight. Like a cat, Karen thought. A suspicious, angry threatened cat.

True stood to one side. With his hat off Karen could see his hair, white and plastered down with water. "Your mother'll be anxious to see you, son," he said, breaking the awkward silence.

Vance hesitated, hardly daring to ask. "She . . .?"

"She's upstairs. She's been waitin' for you."

Vance glanced up to the balcony, back to his father, sudden fear tightening his eyes. "C'mon," he said softly. "We'd better go on up."

The somber atmosphere left Karen ill at ease as she accompanied the men into the hall and up the stairs to the landing. True led them down the hall, paused at a door to his left than quietly opened it. "Elizabeth . . .?"

A voice from inside said, "Good heavens, True, you sound like I'm already gone. Now bring in that boy of mine."

Vance entered the room first, escorting Karen who hesitated, then forced a smile and strode in with an air of confidence. Elizabeth Paxton lay in a massive oak bed. She was propped up by several thick white pillows, down which fell a mass of silver hair streaked with traces of gold as bright as Karen's. A thousand tiny wrinkles creased her face and, as sometimes happens when two people are very close, gave a stranger the uncanny impression she and True were more than husband and wife, had passed that stage and become almost one person, so much alike did they look. She had, once, been not only beautiful but strikingly handsome as well, a forceful woman secure in her own strength and will. And though the frame had shrunk and the skin turned to near leather, the strength of will and the dominating power of life still shone in her eyes and filled the room with her presence.

Vance leaned over the bed and embraced her gently. When he stood, Elizabeth clung to his hand, unwilling to let go. "I'm glad you're here, son," she said, the first evidence of emotion in her voice.

Vance stepped back, still holding her hand. "Mother this is Karen Hampton. I've brought her here to be my wife."

The old lady's eyes took in every inch of Karen before she spoke. "Come closer, child. Let me see you." True stepped aside to let her by. "Always step forward. You have to push a little. Otherwise these men will stand in your way like a herd of old mules," she said, a twinkle in her eye.

Karen drew close to the woman. True, behind her, interjected, "She's from up north," as if it was some sort of malady.

Elizabeth laughed, surprising Karen with the youthful zest with which she dismissed True's statement. "So was I, or have you forgotten, True?" Vance's father managed a "Hhrumph" and left the room. "You mustn't pay attention to him, dear, at least not when he's in this mood. He's really a very nice man, but with Vance away so long and me sick it's been hard for him." The lines in her face deepened with worry. "When his hip's better and he can ride again. . . ." She paused, brightened. "Listen to me. We must have a long visit after you've freshened up. Vance, you show her to her room, now. Let her have yours. Tell the boys to get her gear up there on the double and make sure Marcelina fills the pitcher. I've made the trip from San Antonio often enough to know there's nothing more pleasant than sponging off and changing clothes."

"Thank you, Mrs. Paxton. It would be nice."

"Please call me Elizabeth, dear, and I shall call you Karen." She dropped her son's hand and reached for Karen, who jumped to take it. "Welcome to the PAX ranch, Karen. I'm glad Vance brought you to us." A tiny wave of pain showed in her eyes. "If you'll come back after supper. . . ? I'm tired now."

Vance took his mother's hand and laid it on the bed by her. "We'll be back in later, Mother." The old lady had closed her eyes and lay still, her store of energy already spent. Vance took Karen's arm and led her into the hall, closing the door behind him gently. For a moment he stood quietly, his face troubled. "She doesn't look good," he said, his voice far away.

"Nonsense, she looks. . . ."

He stopped her with a penetrating stare. "Don't say it, Karen. It's sooner than I expected, but we've known for a long time." A frown of concentration creased his forehead. "At least she isn't in too much pain. I hope." A strange smile replaced the frown. "Did I ever tell you about the time she. . . ."

Karen waited but the smile was gone as rapidly as it had appeared. She had known his mother was ill, but never thought she was so badly off. "Vance, I . . ."

"Come on," he gestured to one of the doors across the hall. "The next door down is the bathing room. There'll be hot water for you. This is my room." She followed docilely, wondering why he hadn't let her apologize.

The decor of his room was similar to Elizabeth's and the house in general. Sturdy utilitarian furniture with no-nonsense lines stood against the rough-hewn walls. The large comfortable-looking bed was long enough for two of her. A single window looked out onto the purple hills deep in the long afternoon shadows. Across the room a door leading to the balcony banged open and through it staggered two of the ranch hands, struggling with her final trunk which they had hauled up on a rope from the living room below. When Vance thanked them they tipped their hats to her and filed out, leaving only the sound of their boots on the plank flooring as they rounded the corner and went along the hall and down the stairs.

And then they were alone, the silence between them a clumsy barrier. Vance coughed, embarrassed. "Will you be all right? I'd best check with Pa and see how things have been. You can bathe and clean up and I'll see you at supper." He turned to go but halted in the doorway. "Karen, I . . . " He paused, searching for the words.

"Yes?"

"I . . . Elizabeth . . . Mother liked you. She's happy you're here."

Karen spun from him, her green eyes flashing as she stared out the window. "Even if no one else is?"

She could tell the words stung him and was immediately sorry. Yet she had given him an opportunity to refute her and patch the trouble-haunted fabric of their love. Instead the door closed behind her and she was left alone, a stranger in an empty silence.

CHAPTER VI

Dinner was a quiet affair on Karen's part. True held his son's attention with a recounting of ranch business and a thorough if complicated explanation of the current political atmosphere. This was a trying time for Texas, a time of rapid change, of plotting and political maneuvering. The corrupt Radical Republican reconstruction government, though fighting every inch of the way against the more traditional-minded Democrats, was crumbling and near dissolution. The state was in transition, with fortunes, reputations and destinies at stake. Governor Davis' hated State Police had been disbanded, but the men who had worn the badges gave them up grudgingly and, filled with rancor, could be counted on to resort to violence at the slightest provocation. Rights stripped from the men whose sympathies lay with the butternut and gray during the War Between the States were speedily being returned after a long, hard penance, but there was still far to go. The politicians were talking of a new Ranger outfit, but it had yet to be formed, and with the army in a state of disarray, Edward's Plateau—hill country as the Paxtons and their neighbors called it—and all points west lay open to the depredations of the Indians and Mexican renegades.

Karen understood only little of what she heard and soon excused herself from the table, having only dabbled at the strange and unpalatable food before her, an assortment of Mexican dishes prepared by Maruja and, as far as she was concerned, totally unworth the praise Vance had been so ready to reiterate at the drop of a hat. She ascended the stairs and was almost to her door when Elizabeth called to her.

"I recognized the sound of your footsteps on the stairs." The old woman smiled at her and patted the side of the bed, Gesturing for Karen to sit. "It's late and you're tired, I know," she continued, "but I won't keep you long."

"Nonsense, Mrs. Paxton . . . Elizabeth," Karen protested. "I would have come directly to your room had I not been afraid of disturbing you."

Elizabeth studied the girl's face, raised a frail hand to touch her cheek. "You are a lovely girl, Karen. Odd how these Paxton men choose women with golden har. Were you born in Washington?"

"No. New Hampshire. But Papa's business took him to New York so often we eventually moved there, and then to Washington when it became apparent he needed to be closer to the center of politics."

"Washington," Elizabeth sighed. "I've always wanted to see Washington. My father was from near Philadelphia in Pennsylvania. A strong, willful farmer defeated by the drought and blight, and forced to sell out. A lot of people were heading west, then, and Father, Mother, my sister Lottie, and I, joined them. Everything we couldn't take in one wagon was left behind. Everything.

"There was, we thought, land waiting for us. Virgin land, rich and fertile, wanting only strong and willing backs and shoulders to make it spring to life. Mother didn't want to go, neither did Lottie. Father was going because he needed to prove something to himself. I was the only one excited by the whole venture, I think.

"The trip started well enough. We went west to the Ohio and traveled on a flatboat to the Mississippi where Father had bought passage down to Natchez. And then tragedy struck when Father was killed in a fight and we were informed that no single women were wanted on the wagon train. They weren't going to let us go to Texas after all."

"But you did," Karen prompted, anxious to hear more.

"Yes." Elizabeth's frown changed to a soft and dreamy smile. "Because of True and his brothers, and one of the ugliest, most wonderful men I've ever known." She nodded, patted Karen's hand. "Hogjaw Leakey. I haven't the strength to tell you about him right now, but True will one day, if you ask him.

"We arrived in Texas in early winter. Day in and day out in that wagon, and Mother dying near where Austin is now. True tried to help and court me at the same time, but I was too stubborn to let him do either. My, but that trip was hard. Not

224

like now, with cities and towns and the land all full of ranches.''

Karen smiled. "Full of ranches? I've never seen anything so desolate in my life."

"You should have seen it then. Nevertheless, I finally came to my senses, and True and I were married in San Antonio. On the second day of January, 1835. I was just ten days shy of eighteen."

"Eighteen? Then that would make you . . . Excuse me," Karen stammered, embarrassed by her impropriety.

Elizabeth's laugh was soft and motherly. "Yes, I am fifty-six. 'But no!' you're thinking. 'She looks so old!' ''

Karen shook her head in protest. "No. I wasn't really . . ."

Elizabeth hushed her with a wave. "There was war in '36, and we were separated, fleeing for our lives from Santa Anna's army. True's youngest brother, Andrew, died at the Alamo. I thought True had been killed there, too, but we were reunited a few weeks before the battle that finished it all at San Jacinto.

"After the war, San Antonio was a town filled with men grown used to killing, so we moved on to this land Hogjaw had given us, and started all over. Those were the Indian years. Lottie and her husband, True's brother Joseph, moved to California, leaving us by ourselves. Not a day went by when there wasn't some awful crisis. Indians or weather, sickness among the stock . . ." Her face brightened and she laughed softly to herself. "Or babies to be born. Three sons! Three fine sons and a daughter. Vance was the youngest, born in '45."

"Vance never mentioned anyone else."

Elizabeth's eyes shut for a moment. When she opened them again they saw far beyond the room. "They're sleeping up on the hill. Sarah Ann was the first. She was born the second winter we were here. It was so cold and she was so pretty. So delicate. Her tiny fingers would wrap around my little finger and squeeze and squeeze . . . Four days of life she had. I didn't think spring would ever come, didn't think I wanted to see it come. But it did.

"Two years later Lee came. And then Maurice and Vance. Maurice was drowned, caught in a flash flood while trying to save a colt. Lee was killed in Tennessee, or so we believe. A friend of his was with him and saw him fall. The body was lost among all those innumerable battlefield dead. True made a place for him anyway, next to his brother and sister. That's the kind of man True is. We believe Lee's spirit rests there no matter where his body lies.''

She reached out and took Karen's hand. "There I go. Telling the sad things. There have been rich rewards too, child. Oh, not in anything I can count or hide away in a gold box. My life has been full enough.'' She paused, her eyes closed. When she spoke again her voice was distant, soft and dreamlike. "It's so difficult to explain. Thirty-eight years with one man! No woman I know could ask for more..''

She opened her eyes again and looked fondly at Karen. "These Paxtons . . . they run to men. A woman needs to be forceful . . . needs to make herself heard. . .'' Her eyes closed.

For a brief second Karen panicked until she heard the older woman's deep breathing and realized she was only asleep. Karen sighed in relief, turned the lantern down and quietly left the room, silently closing the door behind her. Lights were still burning downstairs and she could hear Vance and True talking. "I'll send a rider for the preacher come morning.''

"So soon?" Vance asked.

"Why not? That's what you brought her out here for, isn't it?''

"Yes, but. . . .''

"Then it's settled. Your Ma will be wantin' to see you wed, so we won't be waitin' any longer than we have to.''

Karen waited to hear no more. Exhaustion and confusion had dimmed her anger with Vance but she bridled anew at the way he and his father made plans for her behind her back. She had categorically repudiated exactly that sort of cavalier treatment at the hands of Barrett and Alfred, only to find herself? . . . *Married* . . . *? Married!?* She gritted her teeth to keep from crying out and ran silently to her room, driven by images of an old woman who wasn't really old and yet lay dying in the other room.

Only fifty-six! That isn't old. Not old enough to look so tired. I don't want to be a Paxton! Frightened, she inspected herself closely in the mirror, searching for non-existent lines and wrinkles. Thirty-five years? Would thirty-five years make so much difference in her—line her face, turn the sun-streaked luster of her hair to gray, callous her hands,

226

weary her and wear her down? Could she stand the death of her children, think of them as merely sleeping? *Sleeping!? My God, to buy three of your own flesh....I can't do it. I can't do it.*

Yet what else was there to do? Where was she to run? To whom ? She was here and that was that, with an interminable prairie between her and civilization, with a man who most certainly had a past she had never given much consideration. She brooded on Marcelina's distinctly amorous welcome, the way her body had thrust eagerly against his, as if an all too familiar receptacle returning to his hard form. They must have been . . . *No! I won't let myself* . . . She would simply have to accept the fact he had a past. *I'll manage that . . . somehow . . .* But accept everything? This life Elizabeth could not describe? Her appearance was a full, concise and telling description, told Karen all she needed to know graphically enough to curl her on the bed and bury her face in a pillow, hopelessly attempting to stifle her sobs.

True, on his way to bed and checking on Elizabeth before retiring, heard the soft sound of weeping. He paused at Karen's door then shook his head in despair. He had learned long ago there was just no understanding the whims and ways of northern women. A cantankerous lot, they were, and Vance had gone and brought one home with him. Elizabeth, now, wasn't one to carry on. She . . . he paused in his thought. She was right. He was so used to her he kept forgetting she was born a Yankee too. Well, perhaps the weeping girl would work out after all. She had been quick enough to stare back at him, salty enough to remind him of Gettysburg.

Morning slipped over the rolling line of hills to the east to the tune of bawling cattle, the crowing of three or four roosters and the sound of men and horses. With the new day off to a start and the house silent again, Karen rolled over and went back to sleep. Once Vance came by and knocked at her door, inquiring if she was awake then leaving when she did not reply. An hour later another knock, harder and more insistent, sounded at her door. Karen pulled herself from a deep sleep. "Yes?" she called.

The door opened and Marcelina stepped in, her deep brown eyes flashing with spirit and daring. "the *señorita* wishes a bath?"

Karen determinedly attempted to suppress her jealousy of the night before. "Why . . . why, that would be nice. Yes. I would."

Marcelina led her across the hall to the bathroom. An ornate iron tub, a replica of the one she'd had in Georgetown, stood in the center of the room, a cloud of steam rising from the water. "It was sweet of you to prepare this for me," Karen said, trying to be friendly.

Marcelina frowned. "*Señor* Vance told me to do this. I do anything he wish me to." The Mexican girl stepped past Karen and with a flip of her head sent her long black braids whipping scarcely an inch in front of Karen's face. Karen suppressed the urge to put the girl in her place, instead yawned unconcernedly and waited silently while Marcelina left. Once alone she shed her gown and stepped into the warm luxury of the bath, sinking into the homey comfort and letting the water ease the jangling tension generated by her arrival and the confusion of too many new faces, names and personalities.

Gradually she relaxed. The new and unknown world outside the walls of the bathroom came into perspective and her strength of mind and purpose slowly returned. The brooding apprehension of the future was replaced by a sense of curiosity and a willingness to be up and about. She would never admit it, but hers was the same ever-returning resilience which had made her father a determined, stubborn figure known for his uncanny business ability under the most difficult conditions. The character trait which had torn asunder the bonds of father and daughter would now be the source of Karen's strength and allow her to face an uncertain future with detached calculation. The Hamptons had ever refused to be mere victims of the whims of capricious fortune, had rather molded and resolved situations as they saw fit, shaped fate to suit them. Since coming to Texas everything had gone awry, but solutions would present themselves and Karen was determined to work things out to her own satisfaction. Though deep within her love had cooled, she could no longer blame Vance entirely for the incident at the Menger. He had not taken her totally by force, for her own tempestuous nature—more than a match for his ardor—had risen to the fore, shamelessly meeting the thrusting strength of his body against her, within her, filling and fiery. Her only reservation lay in the destruction

228

of the dream, the dream of heady romance, for her thoughts had not been of love, were not even now of love, but of animal fulfillment, the primeval urge, the exciting, abandoned ritual born of the mating act. Love . . . ? Their bodies' hunger couldn't have cared less. To hold one's heart away and yet succumb to the heady desires of the flesh. . . . Vance would sleep downstairs until they were wed. And then what? She didn't know. One part of her wanted him again, hungered, even demanded to repeat their turbulent consummation. Another shrank from the thought, counseled her to deny him until she could be more certain within her own heart how she felt about the newly-discovered facets to her husband-to-be.

She fastened the ribbons on her dressing gown and stepped across the hall into her room. The door was slightly ajar and when she entered Marcelina spun around in surprise at being caught rummaging through an open trunk. The Mexican girl made a vain attempt to regain her composure and walk with Latin arrogance past the eastern woman but Karen, indignant over such discourteous treatment, reached out and grabbed her by the arm. Marcelina whirled like a tigress, her fingernails claws and her breath a feline hiss. Karen stepped back, surprised by the girl's sudden ferociousness.

But even as Marcelina whirled and her hands lifted to strike, something fell from her waist where it had been tucked in the top of her skirt . . . a cameo pendant on a chain of gold. Both pair of eyes went to the heirloom on the floor. Caught in the act of thievery, Marcelina shrunk back, her momentary confusion giving Karen the time she needed to recover. "Pick that up," she quietly ordered with all the self-assurance at her command. Marcelina stared sullenly at the woman before her. "You were going through my things. You attempted to steal from me. I should imagine this household would be displeased by your conduct."

"They would not believe you."

"No?"

"No," Marceline hissed, confidence blazing anew in her eyes.

Karen smiled coldly, turned and walked to a large armchair in the corner of the room. "Pick up the pendant and hand it to me. It is a highly treasured keepsake. Now do as I say. At once." Karen's eyes were stern, her voice steady and compelling, shaped by years of practice handling servants.

Marcelina's gaze wavered and protests died in her eyes under the uncompromising gaze. Finally she could stare into the green eyes no longer. She knelt and picked up the cameo, thrust it toward Karen with a small, work-hardened hand. "I was looking through your clothes. Just looking. You have pretty clothes."

"Thank you," Karen said, relaxing her guard.

"They are pretty but they are not made for here. They will tear and wear away because this land is not for them. And you. You are not a woman for this land. You are not woman enough for *Señor* Vance. You are like your clothes. What happens to them will happen to you."

"And who is woman enough for *Señor* Vance?" Karen asked, somewhat bemused.

Marcelina thrust her small pointed breasts against the fabric of her blouse, the dark nipples brown beneath the white cotton. "I have fought Indians beside the men. I have no use for . . . *trunks.*" The young girl spun away and was through the door, leaving Karen at a loss, wondering just what else this Marcelina had done beside the men. And one man in particular. Slowly she raised her hands, looked at them; soft, white, dainty and unused to work. Sternly she quelled a tremor of apprehension as she remembered Marcelina's, which were work-worn, dark and hard. "I have fought Indians," she had said. With a toss of her head, Karen rose and headed for the trunks the girl so despised.

True was in the living room when she entered. He stared at her with obvious amazement, his eyes appraising her riding apparel. "I was gonna have Maruja send up some clothes for you," he said, trying to be polite.

"Thank you, Mr. Paxton. I have plenty to wear." Still he studied her and she colored. "This is for riding."

"Oh."

Maruja stepped out from the dining room. "The *señorita* is hungry?"

"No thank you. I thought I'd go for a ride."

True turned to Maruja. "You bring that food up to Elizabeth?"

230

"*Si*. But she says she is not hungry. So I take it back to the kitchen."

"I don't care if she's hungry or not. A body that thin ought to be eatin'. Now you step right around an' bring it back up to her. An' tell her I'll be along to see that she eats it, too."

Maruja threw up her hands in exasperation and headed back to the kitchen. True headed for the stairs, stopping only once to suggest Karen take one of the men to escort her if she wanted to ride. "An' make sure they give you a gentle horse," he added.

"I can ride perfectly well."

He looked back at her, his eyes sharp and uncannily piercing. "I 'spect you can. Northern horses. These are Texas mustangs, work horses, most of 'em barely broke to saddle. You'll find 'em notional and hard to handle an' I won't have you ridin' 'em. An' by the way. I sent a rider out for the preacher. Ought to be here tomorrow or the day after. If you got clothes in mind to get married in, you best set 'em out. Maruja'll help you get 'em ready." He watched to see what effect the information would have.

Karen forced her expression into one of total placidity. "Where is Vance? I thought I might ride with him."

"We got a ranch to run here. He's workin'," came the curt reply as he turned to follow Maruja up the stairs.

Karen waited for them to disappear, then changing her mind about her projected excursion for the moment, decided to explore the house. She walked down the hall to a door at the far end, slid back the bolt and stepped out into a vine-covered courtyard separating the kitchen on her left from Maruja and Marcelina's quarters on the right. The vines above offered a pleasant dappled shade in contrast to the glare of the sun on the dusty ground of the compound. The air was heavy with the scent of rose and the smell of water on dust. Morning glories, their delicate purple and blue fronts not yet closed to the morning sun, covered the kitchen wall to her left and a bed of brilliant magenta fan-shaped flowers covered the ground to her right. Bees buzzed industriously all about, content to search and dip for nectar and leave the more confusing tasks of living to the humans who had gone to all the trouble of planting the flowers. The door to Maruja's room opened and Marcelina

231

stepped onto the patio. Hesitating briefly when she saw Karen, she lifted her head high and stalked impudently past her rival with a flourish of skirts, leaving the patio for the nearby garden where Maruja kept colorful rows of spices, peppers and gourds. Karen followed a few steps then stopped, uncertain of what she should say, what overtures of friendliness she might extend. Beyond Marcelina was a larger garden where all the food for the house was grown. The girl picked a few peppers and moved on to the vegetables. Karen sighed to herself: what the girl felt for Vance was obvious and anything she said would be wrong.

Impulsively she strode back through the hacienda and across the compound where a ranch hand tipped his hat and opened the main gate for her. Karen headed for the bunkhouse and the solitary cowboy knotting strips of rawhide into a long, twisted quirt in the shade of the overhung roof. "Excuse me?"

The cowboy leaped to his feet, fumbling for his hat. "Yes'm?"

"I should like to go riding."

"Ma'am?" he asked, unable to keep his eyes from her riding habit.

"Would you prepare a horse for me?"

"Prepare . . . ?" He glanced nervously about, not quite understanding. Women on the Paxton spread always did for themselves. "Oh, saddle one up. Yes'm. Be glad to." He turned from the door and the corral, close to his left, and headed to the right for a long, low barn. Karen shot a perplexed look at the horses in the corral and followed him. The barn was cool, and when her eyes had adjusted to the darkness she could make out five stalls, each of which held a horse to match any of her father's. "We keep all the gear for ladies in here. Ain't been used much, what with Elizabeth bein' laid up."

"Doesn't Marcelina ride?"

"Yes, ma'am, but she rides the corral stock." He took the trappings from a wall and saddled a chestnut mare, then led it out the front of the barn and helped Karen mount.

"Thank you, Mr. . . ."

"Harley Guinn, ma'am."

"Thank you, Mr. Guinn." She touched a riding crop to the animal and rode out at a canter, not noticing the strange rider who pulled into view around the corral and stopped to talk to Harley.

She headed down the valley, keeping fairly near the line of cypress masking the course of the Sabinal. Before an hour had passed she could make out the cedar brake up ahead and guided her mare down to the river's edge, crossing in the shallows where the water ran clear and cool over a bar of white gravel. For a moment she paused, considering whether or not to ride through the tunnel, then decided not to, instead turned to the west and followed a broad path leading into the hills. She rode through clusters of mesquite gradually giving way to scrub cedar which in turn died out as taller varieties of juniper took over. The horse climbed steadily upward, following the path as if it had come this way a number of times and knew her destination.

The chestnut crested the hill and, a few paces later, stopped. Karen stared about her, eyes wide with wonder as she dismounted silently and tied the reins loosely to a post. The top of the hill was nearly flat, an acre or two in extent. Ahead of her two ancient, gnarled cedars twisted from years of wind and weather were the only trees in sight. She walked slowly toward them through the almost knee-high grass. Under the trees the grass was cut back in a small area bounded by a low, black wrought iron fence, inside of which stood three crosses, each no more than two feet high, made of the same twisted cedar, impervious to wind or rain. Around her was silence, utter and complete save for the sudden rush of wind which came from the south and whispered through the grass, bowing it in graceful sweeps across the slight crown of land.

It's beautiful. . . . it's beautiful. She stepped over the small fence and approached the graves reverently. The names were burned on the crosses, deep blackened letters standing out starkly on the weathered gray of lumber.

SARAH ANN PAXTON
Our daughter
February 18, 1837—February 22, 1837

Karen stared blindly at the dates. Four days. Four short days and no more, to see, to feel, to. . . .

Her eyes misted and her throat swelled, hot with the tears which she forced back as she made herself read the others.

MAURICE LEAKEY PAXTON
Our son
September 19, 1841—October 17, 1851
He died like a man.

Only ten years old, and died like a man? A boy's life to save a colt? The thought sickened her and a deep bitterness surged through her at the misplaced pride implied in the inscription. Like a man? No! *I will not accept that.*
The last one she could hardly bear to read.

LEE HOUSTON PAXTON
Our son
May 7, 1839—June 19, 1863
His spirit rests here in the Hills

Three of your own flesh and blood. . . . The windswept crown of the hill and the two cedars. Underneath them the lives and deaths, the hopes and loves. To the south lay the prairie, empty and rolling away as far as vision itself. The majestic expanse, across which the eyes of the dead could see infinity. There they could ride the wind, taste with bitterness or joy—who knew which?—the tang of life. To the north lay the mountains—high, rugged peaks, green and brown in the summer sun. Lower, a white dot of snowflake on summer-drenched land, were the buildings of the ranch. Home. Home nestled in the hills. Home of life contending against season and sorrow. Home of warmth. Home where hope and love lie collected in the heart.

Perhaps Elizabeth was right. Perhaps there was more here than she, Karen the outsider, could see or understand. If Vance were right, Elizabeth would soon be lying here with her children, collected in their hope and love. A shadow brushed the grass and Karen shivered and looked up. A buzzard, low to see more closely who stood alone, rose with the current in a great, circling, waiting arc. *Fifty-six. Only fity-six years* . . . *No!*

"You are Miss Hampton?"

Karen shrieked, startled by the sound of the voice of death calling her name. She spun to see a horseman dismount. He had ridden up the back of the hill and, his horse's hooves muffled by the deep grass, approached her silently as she stood lost in thought. the man was shorter than Vance but nevertheless exuded an almost tangible aura of purpose and strength. His skin was a reddish copper color, his eyes black and totally unrevealing of his inner thoughts. His hair hung long across his chest in two thick braids and he wore faded jeans and an equally faded blue work shirt. A huge knife was sheathed at his waist. *An Indian!* Karen felt panic as all the dime-novel stories of the depredations of the savages spun through her memory. But the Indian was smiling.

"I am Ted Morning Sky."

Karen blushed, suddenly feeling very foolish. "You . . . you're Vance's friend. He spoke of you."

"Sorry if I frightened you. I thought you heard me. Harley told me you were going riding and I didn't think you should go alone. He said Vance brought you all the way from Washington."

"Yes. We're to be . . . married."

The Indian nodded. "It is good. A man should take a woman to him." He glanced at the sky and the sun high overhead. "It is very hot. You are not used to the heat. The trail can be dangerous. Come." He paused, looking at her dress.

"What is it?" Karen asked defensively.

Ted Morning Sky pointed at her clothing. "That was not made for this country," he said. "It will never last."

She looked at herself. The fashionable riding dress was torn and full of burrs and thorns, the fabric ripped nearly to shreds almost to her knees. When she looked up again he had turned his horse and started down the trail. Suddenly frightened, she ran for her horse, his words echoing in her mind. "Will never last. Wasn't made for this country . . . will never last. . . ."

"Do you, Karen Olivia Hampton . . ." From the moment the Reverend Robert Straw appeared at the gates time had ceased its meaning for Karen. An unalterable tide of events began its course and though she could not quite bring herself to realize what was happening she went through the motions and functioned as if she did. The preacher's voice droned on, his words seeping through a distant wall of unreality and mingling sleepily with the buzzing of the diligent, ever-searching bees. Karen could see and feel the heat rising from the compound. That was

235

real enough. And the festive mixture of Mexican and Indian decorations was real. Wonderfully and exotically native, they lent a primitive magic to the ceremony celebrating a marriage . . . her marriage.

Her gown was of shimmering white material, a dazzling combination of silk and silver taffeta designed to affect an English heritage of grandeur and distinguished lineage. The bodice was cut virtuously high yet still managed to accentuate the wearer's full breasts and tiny waist. The skirt, covered with lace in the front and falling straight to her feet, puffed out in a moderate bustle behind, down which cascaded more lace and heavy bowed panels which caught and held telltale streaks of brown dust placed there by warm fingers of wind. A veil held in place by a circlet of flowers fell in celestial flowing folds beneath which her tightly-coiffed golden hair shimmered with a life all its own. The ensemble was a lovely and inspired product from Iantha Hampton's personal English seamstress, lovelier still in view of the contrast it offered to the simple wear of the other members of the wedding.

The garb of the men and women around Karen could hardly be called elegant. Mostly homemade, all had an air of simplicity, of practicality, of making do with what was available. The men wore dark suits, set off by pieces of brilliantly dyed cotton. The women managed a more festive air, but still without a gown or dress of note among them. Karen looked across at Vance, standing rigidly and obviously uncomfortable in black frock coat, string tie and coarse, stiff white shirt. True, his neck held stiffly away from a starched collar, was dressed similarly. Perhaps there was a proud tilt to his chin. *I still don't like him.* Karen looked over at Elizabeth who had demanded she be carried out to witness the ceremony. Wrapped in a comfortable blanket in spite of the heat and seated like a tiny doll left by a child in one of the massive chairs from the living room, her face assumed still greater age in the unflattering, harsh light of day. Her hair was braided and hung down to her waist, framing the parchment-dry face and, in contrast, still young, light blue eyes. Next to her stood Maruja in a white blouse and multicolored gypsyish looking skirt. Her hands bore the stains of cooking, for she had spent the night before and all the morning preparing an unbelievable amount of food for the *fiesta* to follow. Marcelina was conspicuously absent, though once Karen caught a glimpse of the girl peering furtively from between the half opened shutters of a living room window. *Poor Marcelina. So very young and terribly in love. My God, have I aged so? Could not those very words have been said of me but a week ago?*

"What?"

Reverend Straw cleared his throat and repeated himself. "It is customary for the bride to say at this point, 'I do.' You 'do,' don't you?"

Karen nodded her head. "Yes."

"Then you say, 'I do,'" the preacher repeated patiently.

"I do."

"Do you, Vance Paxton, take. . . ."

The ranch hands stood somberly in a half circle behind them, their hands awkward with nothing to do. To them, the ceremony they witnessed was sacred, and each and every one—all fourteen of them—had chosen to stand with their friend. Karen almost giggled at their solemnity: hard-looking men, they were in truth shy to the point of boyishness. But then, that's what she had thought of Bodine. A momentary sadness swept over her, its shadow darkening the day and occasion, but she fought to repress it. *Not now. Not now. . . .*

Ted Morning Sky stood next to Vance. Boots polished and in clean jeans and shirt, he stood alone and aloof, watching the ceremony with a detached air, an attitude which made him seem more formal and elegant than the others. Vance considered him a brother, he had said, and while Karen didn't understand why, she did have to admit a definite, different quality to the man, a mixture of the savage and civilized world she found altogether disquieting. He had guided her safely home from the hill that day, saying little more than the first words and offering no other conversation of his own, speaking only when spoken to. Gradually Karen had fallen silent and ridden without trying to make him talk. Only then did she notice he seemed to be always listening, listening. But to what? For what?

Near the Indian was a Mexican trapper and farmer, his wife and three daughters, the youngest thirteen or fourteen, the oldest Marcelina's age. *At least they'll have brides-maids . . . someone to give them away.* The trapper appeared to be True's age and, as was evident from their conversation earlier, the two men were old friends. The presence of his three pretty daughters helped account for the especially neat and orderly appearance of the cowboys, each of whom would later be particularly polite to the trapper and as eager to dance with his wife, lest either decide to leave early.

"I do."

Vance's voice brought her back. She looked at him, so tall and ruggedly handsome. And so different . . . changed? *I cannot change. It is not in me.* A bird circled high overhead. A hawk, perhaps. Or a vulture hunting carrion, searching for that which was dead. The symbolism of the carrion-eater angered her. *Go somewhere else. I am not dead!* The words screamed and echoed in her mind and the world whirled and tilted in a haze of heat and bright light.

"I pronounce you man and wife. You may kiss the bride." The veil lifted back, a slight touch of flesh, lips brushing lips. Man and wife.

One of the men played a guitar. Another an accordion, though he called it a squeezebox. A third was a virtuoso on the harmonica and not a one but didn't know how to stomp and clap. They moved to the back patio where tables were set up along the wall of the kitchen. By the time they got there, Maruja and the trapper's wife and daughters had filled every inch of table space with platters of *tamales* and steaming vats of peppery chili. The table groaned. Stacks of *tortillas* teetered against a kettle of *frijoles* that had been cooked, mashed and mixed with onions and peppers. Mounds of *rellenos*, large, mildly spicy peppers stuffed with cheese and meat then cooked in a delicious sauce were pounced upon and diminished rapidly. One table was coveded with an assortment of Mexican *pan dulce*, light, crusty, delicious breads baked in sugary twists and swirls. Outside in the compound a pit had been dug. Over one end two deer turned on spits, the meat crackling and smoking. A whole beef had been barbecued, some of the meat hanging in slabs over the fire, more which had been cooking underground for two days and, when the pit was jubilantly dug open, fell apart in the hand and melted in the mouth. To top everything off there were gallons of steaming black coffee and, a gift from the trapper, Cirilio Viega, a barrel of homemade whiskey.

As the afternoon shadows quickly lengthened and the

cool air of evening swept down from the hills, the party got underway. Everyone ate first, downing unbelievable quantities of the food and somehow going back for more. Maruja moved among them like an anxious hen, carrying trays of yet more food, exhorting those already stuffed to try a little bit more, just a little bit. By the time the lanterns were lit the dancing had started. Uninhibited and totally foreign to Karen's genteel, formalized idea of what a dance should be, the men leaped and kicked, swung their partners this way and that, the girls laughing, their bodies moving with simple, clean grace that became somehow erotic in the flickering light of the torches. Even the fourteen-year-old flirted seductively with her partners, lavishing much of her attention on Billy. A little shocked at the behavior of one so young, she had to force herself not to be angry when she recalled Vance's admonitions. *Why was it wrong when I flirted, and not wrong for this child?* When she asked Elizabeth, the older woman laughed at the pout in her voice. "Women grow up a lot quicker out here. So do the men. Most girls have husbands by the time they're fourteen. Even thirteen. Why, to them, someone your age is an old maid."

Karen straightened indignantly. *Old maid, indeed!* She wanted to ask more, but Shorty—she would later find out there was hardly a ranch in Texas that didn't have a hand nicknamed Shorty—was bowing in front of her and awkwardly asking if he could have his dance. A second later, followed by the twinkle in Elizabeth's eye, she was whirling about the dance floor in a pandemonium of skirts and petticoats, laughing in spite of herself at the good-natured antics and glee of the rest of the company. After Shorty, Brazos had his turn, and tired though she was, she was forced to admit there was something about the company of these men she enjoyed. Different than those she had known back east, they were direct, open and, if not childish, childlike in manner and candor. Ready to laugh and dance, they could be deadly serious and formal to a fault in exaggerated solicitude toward her. It was only Vance who seemed so cold, seemed to take her for granted. Vance and True . . .

The "orchestra" began a slow Spanish waltz and suddenly Vance was in front of her, his hand held out. Karen accepted, moving onto the dancing area. Her body knew this type of music and fell gracefully into the rhythm with smooth, elegant movements. The other dancers stepped awkwardly aside and soon the bride and groom were the only couple dancing, the others content to watch appreciatively. If Karen had looked she would have seen more than one eye mist and dampen, for not a one of the hands there but didn't want a woman for himself, hungered for the touch and nearness of a wife, a mate to ease the hard hours and harder work, to give them sons and daughters. Women in the hill country were rarely seen and most men became terribly sentimental and chivalrous whenever a woman was around, ready to fight to the death to protect her from whatever might threaten: for every thirty-dollar-a-month hand there, the grace and fluidity of this woman epitomized that which they held most dear and to them meant "a lady." True watched silently, his thoughts secret even to himself. And in her chair, Elizabeth hummed along with the music and watched the couple, her eyes soon closing and watching only she knew what. She was happy then. *Three of them . . . Sarah, Stewart and Lee. And only Vance left. He is enough, but oh, I wish the others were here. I wish I could wait to see her when she has learned. . . . I wish she knew she will be a good wife and he a good husband.*

The dance ended and Vance, embarrassed by their solo performance, quickly led Karen back to Elizabeth. There was a moment of quiet as the men looked at Karen in unabashed awe. Then the harmonica player struck up a lively tune, his fellow musicians joined in and the courtyard was once again crowded with dancers and men eagerly awaiting their turn.

Elizabeth grew tired and Vance and True carried her inside. True would have stopped the festivities had she not insisted they continue, saying it had been too long since music, dancing and laughter had brightened the ranch. She preferred to drift off to sleep to the noise and let it color her dreams. True smiled down at her, squeezed her hand and left the room. "You go on too, son. Karen will help me get ready for bed."

Vance nodded, held his mother's hand a moment, then left, leaving Karen alone with Elizabeth.

"Land sakes, child," Elizabeth said when Karen looked about, uncertain what to do to help the older woman get ready. "I've been ready for bed for the last two months.

Can't get any readier.'' She patted the edge of the bed. ''Sit with me a minute. I keep feeling there's something I want to say to you. Maybe it will come to me.''

The two sat without speaking, listening to the *fiesta* below, each sorting the emotions that beat at her, Karen could not decide what she thought, could not identify the feeling or the doubt. She had longed for this day with every fiber of her being and now it had come all was a disconnected numbness. ''What is it, child?''

Karen turned to look at the woman, the only person in the whole household with whom she felt comfortable. An old woman who shouldn't be old, shouldn't have given her life and youth to a ceaseless struggle against a formidable and uncaring land. Elizabeth put her arms around her daughter-in-law and held her while she wept. ''I had a daughter for four days. I wished for one to bring up, to be with. To see her grow and become a woman, so someone close to me would understand . . . how lovely it all is. Three sons I bore. But a daughter . . . to have . . . and now I have one.''

The shuddering, unexpected flow of tears gradually subsided, dissipating under the woman's gentle, calming tones. ''What is it, dear?''

Karen dried her eyes and attempted to recover her composure. ''It's everything. I shouldn't have come here.''

''Nonsense. Vance loves you. And you him.''

''Do I? How can you say that when I don't even know myself?''

''But you married him.''

''That's what. . . .'' She read the concern on Elizabeth's face and stopped dead, flushing with shame. What right had she to create such a scene? Elizabeth Paxton had but one desire: to see her son wed, to see him and his wife start building where she and True had left off. It wasn't much to ask for a lifetime of effort, of work and pain: to see one son happily married, to know what's begun won't die out; that a dream wouldn't be abandoned, left utterly, utterly empty save for wind and dust and the passing emptiness of years.

''Dear Karen, every girl feels like this after a wedding. Goodness knows, after marrying True there were many moments when I had my doubts. But they were the doubts of a bride and nothing more.''

This is different. These aren't just doubts. I know in my

heart what I cannot feel. The emptiness. . . . But these were thoughts Karen would not say out loud. Not to the woman who was so kind, so concerned. Why burden Elizabeth with worry and grief when she needed strength and the reassurance of a future of which Karen had lost sight? "I'm sorry," she said instead, a forced smile replacing the tears. "You're right. I'm being foolish. I was just . . . afraid for a moment. I'll be better now. Everything is still so new and strange. I know I'm being terribly silly."

"No, you're not. You're not at all. There's so much. . . . I wish I could help you, tell you . . . but there . . . aren't words enough. It's something . . . can't be talked about. It just has to be lived . . . lived . . ." She hid the signs of pain which ripped through her and threatened to tear the breath from her. "Now you run along and join Vance. I think I'll sleep some. I'm so tired."

Karen stood and looked down at her new mother-in-law. So tiny, so frail for one so strong. Impulsively she bent and gently hugged her. "Good night, Elizabeth."

"Good night, dear. I'm so very, very glad you're here."

Karen smiled at her, turned to leave, stopping at the door but not looking back when Elizabeth said, "He loves you, Karen. I know he loves you."

Karen closed the door quietly behind her. She was angry at herself for lying, yet knew it had been the right thing to do. As for the party, she was expected to return. She went to her room and glanced in the mirror. Already her gown was grimy from all the dancing and eating but she was determined to keep it on. Deciding an extra touch was needed she opened her trunk and took out her jewel box. The cameo pendant was gone!

In the courtyard, Marcelina had joined the festivities, dancing with first one then another of the ranch hands. Occasionally her eyes locked with Karen's but they remained cold and unrevealing. And Vance? Not dancing nor at the tables. Nor with his father. Then she saw him across the patio. He had changed clothes and was wearing exactly what he had worn the night of the party when they had looked into the depths of each other's heart and knew their love. He was walking toward her as he had then, through the dancers, through the clusters of amiable conversation, his eyes straight ahead, unswerving in his goal.

He is still the most handsome of them all. Close to her now, he stooped and picked her up, held her as if she weighed no more than a feather. The move surprised her and left her too shocked to struggle. The men cheered wildly and, to the sound of shouts and laughter and gunfire, she found herself half up the stairs before she realized she was not prepared, had not planned for the wedding night.

He shoved open the door to her room with his foot, closed it the same way. A coal oil lamp burned low, burnishing the walls with orange. Vance set her down and kissed her, but she broke free. "No . . . please, Vance."

"We are husband and wife now."

"That's not what I mean."

"If you're thinking of San Antonio, forget it. It is behind us now."

"Is it?"

"For me it is."

"Perhaps my memory is clearer than yours. Perhaps I cannot forget as easily as you. I can still see that poor man. What we did was wrong."

"What we did was right. Violence is only one aspect of life."

"I don't agree."

"Yes, you do. The violence before was always hidden from you. Done by other men far from your sight. Here we are more honest."

"Death is honesty?"

"No. Death is a change, to be accepted honestly."

Karen scowled. "Change, change, change. Everyone keeps saying *I* have to change, to accept."

Vance pulled her close, kissing her again, bruising her lips with his hunger.

"No. No, I don't want this."

"Yes, you do. We both do." He unbuttoned his shirt, kicked out of his boots. The rest of his clothes followed and he was naked. Karen averted her eyes. "This is our room, Karen. From now on."

"I shall sleep elsewhere." She started for the door but Vance stepped to her. This time his embrace was unbreakable, his tongue darting, provoking. The bed was beneath her now, the bed . . . how? She didn't remember being forced backward, only the kiss . . . the kiss. Suddenly the

243

hunger in her was unleashed. Her eyes glazed and closed as she watched the man and the woman; and the woman was her and she experienced . . . everything.

And when later she lay next to him in the night and felt the slowly cooling furnace of his body, she wondered how complete their passion had been, for there was still within her that which she could not give him. Their love had yet to be truly consummated. The dark closed around those thoughts, around the bed and the woman who would not change, who had locked her heart. And the man who pretended to be asleep, but knew he had lost the key.

Elizabeth dreamed of the hill, the twin cedars, gnarled and beckoning, whispering her name. Underneath the trees three restless forms shifted in their long wait. After all these years, did they too call? Or was it only the south wind, the wind of infinite whispers? Time. . . . Time. . . .

She awoke and reached out for True, then realized he was in the next room. *All for the best. Poor Karen . . . trying so hard to fool me when it is plain as day something is wrong between them. Love is never easy. Karen and Vance. They'll learn. They need time, is all. We did, too, didn't we, True. Two peas in a pod. Thirty-eight years, True. Thirty-eight lovely years. Vance! Three sons and a daughter . . . now a real daughter . . . I wish I could tell you. . . . I wish I could tell you. . . . True . . . ? True!*

"Did I ever tell you, True?" she asked aloud, grasping at an imaginary hand.

CHAPTER VII

The wind whispered eulogies of dust among the weathered crosses tightly clustered within the wrought iron fence under the gnarled cedars. The dust rose, swirled and settled, silent as memories. Her hair drifting out behind her like a cape of glittering flaxen gold, Karen kept her face to the breeze, savoring the faintest touch of fall in its northern breath. The oaks were changing from their deep green to brilliant yellow. Sumac there was on a far hill, purple now, tinged and ribboned with crimson and flaming orange. The mesquite would quietly slip to brown and shed their light summer coats, leaving naught but a puzzle of scraggly bare lines against the sky. The cedars would remain ever green. Enduring.

There were four crosses now. Four. . . . Karen placed a handful of tiny bright yellow button asters beneath the name of the only person she knew who might have understood her, led her to understand more clearly. It was the tenth of September. Elizabeth had been gone two months—how quickly time passed—and Karen still felt her loss deeply.

She had died the very night of Karen and Vance's wedding. True found her the next morning, lying peacefully, smiling, her face utterly calm with but a hint of an unanswered question in her blindly staring eyes. That same morning Harley Guinn shaped a crude coffin and lashed it between the two sure-footed mules which led the somber procession up the winding, broad path to the hill—to the waiting garden of crosses wrapped by the wrought iron fence and watched over by the wind—where Elizabeth was placed with her sons and infant daughter, at rest at last. A stranger ceremony Karen had never seen. The preacher, an overnight guest, read from the Bible. Then Ted Morning Sky stepped forth and chanted a Comanche prayer, having first built a little fire of fragrant cedar, the smoke of which he wafted to all four directions with a broad, fan-like eagle feather. The chant intrigued Karen. So lonely, a solitary, sing-song lament, sent to echo down the long corridors of wind and hide for all time among the wild, unvisited places. Yet not plaintive. Not pitiable. Rather a voice at one with its surroundings, a voice of peace, a voice of the ages gathered into repetitive syllables suggesting not so much an end but rather a continuation. The chant finished, True knelt, crumbled a handful of earth and sifted it onto the living flames until the fire was snuffed out and only a faint trail of smoke drifted up to dissipate in the sharp cedar needles above. True looked up at Vance, his eyes red-rimmed and old. "Over thirty-eight years, boy. It's hard. Goddamn, but it's hard." Vance nodded silently in answer, turning his face as the men set the cross. Like the others, the name had been burned into the wood.

ELIZABETH ANN PAXTON
Born January 12, 1817—Died July 10, 1873
A wife and mother. No man ever had better.

Karen read the inscription again. How little was left behind. A memory, a heart's pang, a name charred on a hand-hewn board. Was this all? And as if in answer the wind sprang up, washed around her with its airy tides. The cedars shimmered beneath the chilly caress and added their beauty, at one with the spirit of the woman gone but never truly absent as long as the evergreens pointed to the stars and the verdant yellow plains spent their grassy tides on the breakers of the hills.

This was not the first time Karen had come to visit Elizabeth. Hardly a week went by when she did not ask Harley to saddle the chestnut mare, by now her favorite. And always she came to this same sun-washed, lofty hill. There were other taller, bolder, greener hills to be sure, but it was here she came, where her one friend lay. She turned away, staring out across the plains. A blue jay squawled at her from the tree overhead, cocked an inquisitive and blaming eye, examining the woman who watched the tableland stretch into an infinity of shifting umber and cinnamon. "Elizabeth. . . . I'll be having Vance's child. I should have told you two weeks ago when I was here, but I was so

246

confused. Do you remember your first time? It's funny, in a way. I'm not frightened yet, even if I will be later. I still have trouble believing it. Vance and True. . . . Oh, the way news gets around, I'm certain the whole ranch knows. And everyone seems so different. So concerned. Even True, and he doesn't even think me a fit wife for a Paxton. But their attitudes toward me haven't changed, not underneath where it counts. They're being nice to me because I carry a Paxton, not because they've made any attempt to understand how I feel. I'm always being compared, Elizabeth, constantly compared to you and found lacking. Never quite measuring up nor meeting whatever standards they've decided I should meet. You are gone and nothing is ever going to bring you back, though I wish otherwise. If they'd only teach me, perhaps . . . no. No excuses. I am quite simply not you. Karen Olivia Hampton . . . Paxton . . . is not their Elizabeth."

It was early afternoon when she led her horse back up the valley, her mind still awash with thoughts she had not been able to reveal even to the dead Elizabeth. In spite of the haunting reminder of the dying woman's last words, she had come to believe the match between her and Vance had been ill-fated from the first. She didn't want to believe so, hesitated to admit she could have deluded herself so completely. And yet . . . what else could the last two months lead her to believe? Ruefully she had to admit she had adapted poorly to the new surroundings and way of life. Already teetering on the edge, Elizabeth's death had sent her plunging into a pit of despondency, bitterness and disillusionment, a state viewed by everyone else on the ranch as surly indolence and peevish, aristocratic incompetence. Consumed, exhausted and drained by the heat, the confusing business of running a ranch, of which she was totally ignorant, and the unexpected and unvoiced demands from all sides that she assume Elizabeth's varied and myriad roles, she could do little but reel about ineffectively from sunup to bedtime. At first she clung to Vance as she would a rock. She forced herself to rationalize and minimize the events in San Antonio and the irrational anger leading to and following their wedding night. The hazy confusion of the days was relieved by the incandescent fantasies filling the nights as she sought with her body the surety she could not find in her mind. And for a while the tactic worked. Vance disguised his growing fury at her ineptitude and inability and, driven by his own insatiable needs, reassured himself during the frantic nights: she would become the woman of whom he had dreamed.

But the deception could not last forever. One early morning Vance rose early as usual, silently so as not to waken her. He dressed in the dark and headed for the door, tripping on a small box Karen had inadvertently left lying in the middle of the floor. Karen wakened in time to hear him curse under his breath and add, his voice low and venomous as he stalked out of the room, "Jesus Christ! Can't you do *anything* right?"

The words froze her, curled her stomach in a knot. His true feelings, stripped of their disguise, shocked her into a stupor from which she could emerge only slowly and with great difficulty. The day that followed was a nightmare. She noticed little things theretofore passing beyond her recognition. Maruja's patience as she tried to teach her for the tenth time how to make *tortillas* was followed by a secret, despairing shake of the head. And worst of all, she picked out the tiny, subtle differences in Vance at supper and afterward when they sat around the living room. He seldom looked directly at her, and when he did his eyes slid quickly back to his book. He seldom spoke, and when he did the tone was faintly conciliatory, the dissatisfaction but barely hidden. That night when they went to bed, Karen turned her back to him and ignored his probing, teasing fingers. Real love denied her, she would deny them both the false balm of flesh.

The next two weeks were a hollow charade in which she turned every bit of Hampton energy in her to the problem at hand, forcing herself to listen and learn, to become, at the very least, coldly efficient in spite of the emptiness in her heart. Her plan was simple. When she knew all she needed to know, she would leave, somehow return to San Antonio and from there eventually to Washington or New York. Not back to her father, certainly, for that was denied her. Yet there were friends she could count on in either city. Somehow she would function.

The simple plan was thwarted the day she suspected another life grew within her. Assuming the first missed period the result of the arduous journey, she hadn't worried, but when the time came again and nothing happened, the thought of a child crept in unbidden. A thought that would not be shaken. Four days later she knew as surely as if the best doctors in Washington had issued a proclamation and that night, as they were preparing for bed, she told Vance.

The world changed. Vance warmed to her, watched her carefully lest she do too much. The tension in True's eyes eased suddenly and he could be seen looking at her with what might even have been called tenderness. Maruja was more patient, more explicit, could be seen at odd hours with a sewing basket filled with blue yarn. At first Karen enjoyed the change, but joy switched rapidly to bitterness as the realization grew that no one cared about her, cared only for the new baby—the new Paxton—burgeoning inside her. Then even the bitterness waned: for whatever the reason, she was grateful for any respite from the theretofore unnaturally formal atmosphere in which the house was so thoroughly steeped. She remained wary, though, and still resisted Vance's nightly suggestions, guarded though they were. In spite of the enforced celibacy she imposed so completely, the new warmth persisted until that morning when she awakened to scalding tears and the shattering knowledge she was even more intricately, inextricably caught by the swiftly growing, unseen baby. With a logic as sharp as crystal she realized all earlier traps were but artifices of the mind compared to this one. Vance, no matter what his real or hidden opinion of her, would not be denied his own child. There would be no escape, and there was no one to tell but Elizabeth. But when the time came to speak, even to the empty wind, she had not been able to say the words.

The ranch was fairly bustling with activity when she arrived. Ted, with half the ranchhands, was off up the valley rounding up a herd of horses which had grazed half-wild during the summer months. Now they would be needed to fill out the remuda for the fall roundup, and would have to be caught and once again conditioned to the feel of men on their backs. Those already brought in from the range were in the back corral, waiting their turn to be topped off, as the hands put it. She paid no attention to the line of men strung out on the top rail of the front corral, but rode on around the bunkhouse and out of sight, reining up near the small corral in back of the shed where the women's horses were kept and dismounting on the large wooden block Vance had installed when he'd learned she was pregnant.

Billy Harmony, now called What's About by everyone but her, sauntered over to help her unsaddle. "Good afternoon, Billy."

"Howdy, ma'am. Can I he'p you with that?"

"Yes, thank you." The youngster quickly unsaddled the mare, rubbed her down and gave her some corn, finally setting her loose with the others in the corral. Karen watched them a moment. They were beautiful beasts, those proud steeds. Two sorrels, a blue roan, the chestnut mare and a small pinto. Hermann would have loved this place and these horses—even the tiny pinto. He would be at home here. She tried to picture his reaction to the half-wild mustangs or broncos the men rode and smiled at the thought of his long, dour face dropping even further at the sight of the scraggly, unkempt appearance of the wiry animals.

"Uh, ma'am . . ." Billy coughed, rubbed his forearm across his brow.

"Yes, Billy?"

"I was wonderin' if I might not borrow them two sorrels an' the good buckboard, come Saturday. Them tamer horses are a sight lot easier to use as a wagon team."

"Why do you ask me?"

"Mr. Paxton told me to. He said it was your say so 'cause they was your horses now."

"Vance said that?"

"No, ma'am. Mr. Paxton . . . uh . . . Vance's pa."

True had told him to ask . . . they were hers?

"Is it all right with you? Ya' see, I'm headin' over to *Señor* Viega's place." He puffed up proudly, as if daring her to refute him or, as the hands had, tease him until he fled the bunkhouse, his face flushing with embarrassment. "Gonna call on Amaranta, his daughter, an' I'd like to be able to take her to a church social they're havin' down in Uvalde. She'll spend the night at her uncle's an' he'll bring her back later in the week so's I'll be able to get on in here early Monday. I'd sure be beholden to you, ma'am."

"Why, of course. You take the horses you need, Billy. And stop by the *hacienda* before you leave. I'll see if I can't find something you can give her for a present. Perhaps a comb or a locket."

Billy reddened. "Thank you, Miz Paxton. That's mighty kind of you. It purely is." The young ranch hand headed back toward the main corral. Karen watched him leave then started for the main gate into the *hacienda* compound. The men on the rail suddenly whooped and jeered, laughing raucously over the frenzied whinny of a half-wild horse and the assorted answering calls from his companions, from whom he'd been separated. The rowdy clamor swelled then ebbed, filling the valley with more noise than Karen had heard since her wedding night. The main gate was open yet she paused in the shadow of the compound wall, listening to the activity, held by the promise of excitement. What was waiting for her in the house? The library? She was sick of reading. What else? Maruja? The woman had warmed to Karen, it was true, yet she would be busy cooking or working in the garden. Anything else? Only Marcelina's stony glances and bitter innuendos. Of course, there was always Elizabeth's work room. In it were stored a spinning wheel, bolts of hardy denim and canvas fabric, even a small loom. More mysterious was a box full of tiny polished beads, strips of rawhide and a bundle of porcupine quills.

Deciding suddenly, she walked away from the gate and in the direction of the corral. Her riding dress snagged on some brush and she heard a telltale rip. And this was the last one, the only one without a tear. Now there were none. Well, at least she could sew on patches. That was something she could do, had practiced amply over the past two months, for not one of the dresses she had worn outside the compound walls had not returned without some manner of disfigurement. A horse rounded the wall and Karen stepped back in surprise, catching her skirt on another thorn and momentarily losing her balance. Marcelina, wearing a blouse and men's jeans, reared the animal back, its hooves pawing the air, then let it go, sending the pony plunging forward and bolting down the path to the south. Karen stood and patted the dust from her skirt, staring off at Marcelina's dusty passage down the valley. The girl had been straddling the horse on a man's saddle. *I am not going to wear men's clothes even if every article I wear is covered with patches.* But something else bothered her. Marcelina . . . She tried to picture the Mexican girl once again, the horse rearing back on its hind legs, the rider facing into the sun . . . Marcelina's bare brown shoulders . . . her neck . . . That was it. Had she been wearing the cameo?

251

Karen's missing keepsake? She flushed angrily and promised herself to . . . No. It was not the missing jewelry that so roused her ire, but rather the way the Mexican girl behaved when Vance was around; subtly provocative and teasing . . . devices only another woman could or would see through. And Vance, Karen fumed inwardly, appeared to respond to the girl's conduct, even to the point of allowing her to accompany him, alone, up the valley when he went to deliver supplies to one of the line camps. Alone . . . Karen drove the disturbing notion from her mind, recognizing the very real dangers of such fantasizing.

Determinedly casual, she continued to the corral, quiet now as a cloud of dust slowly drifted away. A number of the hands were sitting along the split rail fence, talking quietly and watching and waiting for the activity to start again. A whoop went up from the men as Karen approached and she saw a mouse-colored stallion break away from the opposite fence and buck its way to the center of the corral. Shorty, the cowboy who had asked for the first dance at the fiesta following the wedding, was astride the animal. But not for long. One moment he was there, the next he was gone, arcing high in the air and then crashing with a loud thud to the ground. A few seconds later he was up and scrambling over the fence, only inches behind the general exodus which suddenly took place as the berserk mustang slammed into the railing, trying to get at the creatures who had captured him. Someone hidden in the dust finally roped the animal again and led it to the far side of the corral while Shorty endured the good-natured derision of his friends and slapped at the dust on his jeans and shirt with a floppy-brimmed hat. "Say what ya' will, I still don't see none a' you galoots ridin' anythin' but them rails. That's a heller, that one is. . . . Oh, pardon me, Miz Paxton." The short, bowlegged cowboy doffed his hat. The others, halfway up the fence again, did the same.

"Good afternoon, gentlemen," Karen said sweetly. "My heavens, but I hope you aren't hurt. That looked like a terrible fall."

"Aw, 'tweren't so bad, 'ceptin' he almost got a hoof into me. That grulla's a regular fighter. A real wild one. Never gives ya' time ta get settled, but takes off jumpin' an' a kickin' ever which way. Nigh busted Hogan's leg. It sure as shootin' bruised some bad. But if'n we ever get that critter back in shape, he'll be a right good cow pony. Be able ta turn on a quarter an' give ya' fifteen cents change."

Karen chuckled at the cowboy's remarks, for here was one thing she definitely did like about the ranch—the colorful and highly colloquial descriptive language, most of which she'd never heard before. Another hand called down from the fence. "Yer husband's gonna take him on next, Miz Paxton."

The men cleared a space for her and Karen stepped onto the bottom rail and hooked her elbows over the top. The grulla, as Shorty had called the animal, was near the fence at the north end of the corral, a neckerchief tied over his eyes. Two cowboys were holding his head down while Vance slowly swung into the saddle. One of the men holding the horse was biting the animal's ear, his teeth dug firmly into the grulla's flesh. "Poor horse," Karen muttered.

Brazos snorted his disagreement. "Ma'am, that critter ain't got a worry in the world compared to the fella that's gonna try to ride him. I still got a sore arm from ropin' that salty ol' bronc."

Karen watched with growing interest as Vance settled himself firmly in the saddle. His long form was poised and ready, his blue work shirt open nearly to the waist, revealing a hard muscled chest thickly pelted with deep brown curls. He tugged at his hat, wound the reins around his gloved fist and dug his feet into the stirrups. For a fleeting second he looked up, unintentionally locking eyes with Karen then lowering his gaze immediately as he said something to one of the hands holding the horse's head. If he was surprised to see Karen at the corral fence no one watching would ever know. Karen heard his next command in the expectant hush settling over the corral. "Now!"

The cowboys sprang back, one ripping the blinder away, both diving for the fence, out of the way of the razor-sharp hooves. The mustang hesitated a fraction of a second and then exploded into the air like a coiled spring being released. All four hooves left the ground simultaneously and the animal twisted and wrenched in mid-air, came down with a bone-jarring crash then erupted into a spasmodic display of untamed fury. The cowboys on the fence whooped and hollered encouragement, surprised that

Vance had lasted the first awesome outburst, as indeed were both bronco and rider. For the space of two heartbeats the mustang stood still, wondering what the man was still doing on his back. With comprehension came a long, determined, cold-blooded effort to rid himself of the pesky weight. Karen felt her breath catch as Vance was whipped back and forth, leaned forward onto the horse's neck as the animal almost went over backwards and then far back on the animal's withers as the beast plunged to earth front feet first. The longer the rider remained on the frenzied mass of corkscrewing horseflesh, the more it seemed his back would surely snap from the punishment he was taking. Karen managed to conceal her own excitement, but her heart caught in her throat at the sight of the mustang's primitive fury and the elemental rugged strength of the man pitted in monumental struggle. Here was the contest of the ages—man against nature, intelligence against brute force. Without being fully aware of the fact, she was watching a greater adventure than even her dreams had pictured.

The horse charged the fence. Karen screamed and the men leaped to the ground, one of them hauling Karen roughly back from the bars. Just as it seemed horse and rider would collide with the railing, Vance yanked the animal aside. The horse's eyes were wide as the grulla screamed in rage and shot into the air once again. Through the swirling dust Karen could hardly make out anything at all. She heard someone shout, "Jump for it, Vance, he's gonna roll!" and splinters of wood flew past her face as the stallion's hind legs shattered the top rail. Then everyone was hurrying back to the fence, Karen included. The grulla landed on the run, circled the corral once then headed directly toward the watchers again, this time a few yards to Karen's left.

"Duck, ma'am! Shorty shouted, grabbing her and pulling her down.

"He's jumpin'!" another voice yelled. "That damned cayuse is gonna try to jump the fence."

Horse and rider hurtled at the fence as if to burst it asunder. Karen brought her hand to her mouth, stifling a silent shriek of fear and excitement. Then Vance leaned forward as the stallion leaped. The mustang's legs stretched long in front of him, and though it happened in the space of a second, the picture of animal and man in mid-air froze in an indelible image in her mind. The mouse-colored stallion, at the height of his leap, nostrils flared, eyes flaming in anger. And Vance, his hat long gone and trampled in the dust, his hair swept behind him like a horse's mane, his sinewy form outlined against an azure sky.

They were gone, horse and rider disappearing at a flat run toward the eastern hills. But that one frozen moment in time had nudged awake the primitive urgings Karen had forced herself to suppress. For a month she had kept her body from his, tortured herself with self-imposed abstinence, first in anger at him for his ill-concealed dissatisfaction, later upset at his solicitude when he learned she was pregnant. She neither wanted nor would have sex merely for the gratification of carnal desire nor as thanks for the biological condition of pregnancy. Sex should be an act of love, a mingling of two individuals to be cherished and held closely in the innermost soul, involving all of a human being and not one part this day, another the next. Why had she come to watch the scene which had so affected her? What imp had lured her to the corral where all she had hoped to avoid had come so vividly to life and left her limp with desire for the man who had ridden the horse and left her with a hunger she felt powerless to deny?

"Don't worry, ma'am. He'll be okay. That mustang's gonna have ta run for a while, but he won't be fightin' no more." Shorty had obviously mistaken Karen's withdrawn reflection for worry.

"Thank you. That . . . that was terribly exciting."

Shorty laughed. "Well, that's quite a feller you got there, Miz Paxton. Never thought he'd a stayed on that horse. Reckon Vance was a sight more notional than that wild ol' feller expected."

Karen nodded, though she hadn't been listening, hadn't heard a word he had said. For she was seeing Vance silhouetted against the cerulean infinity and hearing a call she could do little else but follow.

Vance stripped off his sweat-soaked shirt and plunged his head into the cold spring water, then ground picketed the lathered and still blowing stallion where he could both eat and drink. The animal had run far in its attempt to shake the rider clinging so tenaciously to its back, but Vance's angry frustration and dogged determination had matched

255

the mustang's fury. *Karen . . . what does she want from me?* A man needed a woman's comfort at night. And during the day he needed the comfort of knowing she was at his side, whether or not she physically stood there at any given moment.

But the woman he had brought from Washington stood by no one's side, much less his. She would not learn, would neither consent nor deign to let Maruja or Marcelina teach her what she needed to know in order to be useful in any sense of the word. Then, when for some still unfathomable reason she did start to listen—and despite the way she'd been acting he would not believe it had anything to do with the baby—she went about it in an unfeeling, clinical, calculated manner with no sense or pride or love of the work itself. Worst of all, she lay in bed at night with her back to him as if they were strangers, though she was carrying his child. Strangers? Seeing her there by the fence, watching him. . . . Damn, but he wanted her. The ride had punished him terribly, but in spite of the multitude of aches and pains his body screamed for the touch of her flesh. *She has kept herself from me. . . .* So he had taken out his frustrations on the bronc, goading the unsuspecting animal into even a greater frenzy than necessary, then racing him away, challenging him, meeting him on his own ground.

The exhausted mustang nibbled wearily in the shade of an oak. But Vance's own raging emotions had yet to subside, distracting him so completely he failed to see the grulla's ears flare back in warning, failed to note the presence of another horse until he heard the sound of a hoof striking a stone. The first thing he realized was he had no weapon. No Indian or outlaw would make so much noise, but a man could ill afford to take chances. Moving slowly and cautiously, he backed into a cove of cedar and oak behind the spring and stood concealed in the shadows, ready to right or run as the situation dictated.

Karen . . . ?! He stepped from the shadow as she dismounted, tethered the blue roan to a nearby root and stood before him, staring at him as if she'd never seen him before.

She had followed in a trance-like state. The men distracted at the corral, none paid any attention when she unobtrusively walked away from them to the barn, threw a

256

hackamore onto the roan and rode off bareback as she had as a child in New Hampshire so long ago. But she wasn't a child now. She was a woman with a woman's body and a woman's needs. She did not know any more what she felt in her heart, nor was she concerned. Her body demanded this man and by some undemonstrable rationale her mind accepted her body's knowledge: here was *some*thing, something tangible on which she could build. She was close to him now and his naked torso glistened with sweat. *He smells of sweat, of heat, of animal strength. Like a . . .* She searched for the word, then found it . . . *a stallion.*

She stood silently in front of him. Her hands moved languorously, undoing buttons and untying secret bows until the riding dress and her underclothing fell away, leaving her naked. Still he had not moved so she stepped close enough for her nipples to stroke the sweat from his chest, close enough to feel his heat, see the unasked question in his eyes. She took one of his hands, kissed each finger then placed his palm against her abdomen then lower still into the moist triangle of hair below as she slowly and shamelessly rolled her hips from side to side and let the hardened callouses provoke the tip of her femininity. Moaning with the heat of arousal she moved her hands quickly and his own staff was free and eagerly rising, tumescent as her fingers encircled him.

The grass hummock was soft beneath her buttocks as she lay back with her legs open in a gesture of invitation. Vance knelt before her, slipped his hands under her hips and pulled her up to him as she reached for his throbbing instrument of love, spread the clear, slippery fluid over the swollen head then guided it to the feverish gates of her own desire. Her neck arched and she watched him slide into her, slowly sheath himself inch by inch until his length completely filled her. For long seconds neither moved, but rather watched the union of their flesh, watched while their breaths held then quickened, watched until they could stand it no longer and the floodgate of seed was unleashed. Karen shut her eyes, in ecstasy, caught in the rhythm of the warm pulsing flow.

"How did you find me?"

"I watched . . . knew you would head back for water

257

for the horse. When I came over the hill I caught a glimpse of him at the water's edge." She looked down at the length of warm flesh, teasing it with her fingertips.

Vance lay on his back, chuckled softly. "I'm glad you followed."

"Shhhh. Don't talk. I've missed you. Let me . . ." She bent down to kiss away the single glistening white pearl on the tip of the drowsy flesh, then stayed to coax the soft spear back to rigidity.

The grulla stallion snorted and dipped its muzzle once again into the cool spring water, unable to quench a seemingly insatiable thirst. It had been a long, long ride.

CHAPTER VIII

"You can't do much with only two checkers. Not against my six."

True snorted indignantly in response as he stared first at the board and then at Karen. "Your move," he growled.

Karen smiled ingratiatingly. "I always used to beat my father at checkers, too." It was the truth, though her father hadn't played with her since she was twelve years old, and even at that time was too distracted by business affairs to pay more than cursory attention to either his daughter or the board.

True scowled. "I ain't your father, an' you ain't won yet, young lady. I see two red kings on that board."

"But I have six black."

"Don't make no difference. Ain't the number. It's the gumption involved. Now, you gonna move or not? 'Course if you want to toss in your hat I'll accept your surrender, same terms as at Appomattox," the senior Paxton chuckled. "Unconditional."

Karen only shrugged. "I think not. Now, let me see." Before she could move, Maruja entered from the outside allowing the cool night air to filter in. She hurried past the checker players and into the kitchen, reappearing almost immediately with an armful of clean rags.

"That mare foal yet?" True asked nervously, glancing up at the grandfather clock.

"Almost. It will be an easy birth, I think. *Señor* Vance says he needs no help. He requests the *señora* stay inside. He would not want her to catch a chill."

"Ha! There's the problem. Coddlin' her," he said, with a wink in Karen's direction. "That young What's About get back?"

"No, *señor*. I must hurry," she answered in a swirl of

skirts as a sudden gust tried to keep her from going out the door.

For a moment the only sound in the room was the steady tock tock of the grandfather clock. True rubbed his chin reflectively. "When'd you say he was supposed to get in?"

"Today. Vance told him not to leave until this morning. He should have been here by no later than three."

"Reckon there's no cause for worry. Can't travel any too fast in a buckboard anyhow. Not like bein' on horseback. 'Sides, young feller like What's About, just natural gonna take more time than he has to, you let him loose in a town." He paused, ineffectively trying to cover his worry. " 'Course, he coulda broke a wheel . . . horse picked up a stone in a shoe. . . . Well, if he ain't in by mornin' we'll send someone out to take a look." The old man returned his focus to the checker game, his fingers poised over first one piece then the other.

"It's still my move."

"You mean you ain't moved yet?" he asked in mock astonishment. "Why, I thought. . . ."

"It's my move."

"Humph. I never seen the like. Well, if you ain't gonna fold your hand then make your play."

Karen moved one of her kings, boxing him so effectively even True could see he'd lose the game in another move. Hope fled from his face and he stared glumly at the board, made the only move left to him. "Dadgummit! I never could win with red."

"Would you like black again?" Karen asked sweetly, jumping his two remaining pieces and lifting them from the board.

"No. Not after you beat me three times runnin' with 'em," he grumped, hands on knees and eyes staring dolefully at the six black pieces.

"I'm sorry, but those are the only colors."

"I know," he replied curtly. Then his face softened. "Elizabeth always used to beat me at checkers, too. Once when Vance was just a little 'un we were snowed in for a week. Couldn't move out the door. I must've lost fifty games of checkers. Never could play the dadburned game, an' never did learn to play nothin' else."

Karen remained silent, caught off guard by True's unexpected candor. He paused, piling the checkers and dropping them one by one from between his fingers. "She thought a lot of you. Told me so the night after you come. Right happy, she was, that Vance brought you here."

A branch popped in the fireplace, sending a shower of sparks onto the hearth and giving True the opportunity to escape the table and the situation into which he'd talked himself. He was a man given to hiding his emotions and sentimental talk always embarrassed him. His was the direct way, the way of action. Let others read his meaning, which, if they cared, was there for all to see. But this girl, pretty though she was, was different. Jumpy. On edge. Maybe she needed the words. Some people did. Elizabeth had been a good judge of character and True, although he'd been reluctant to give in, had finally convinced himself he owed his wife that much.

Karen was stunned by his words. She had sensed a gradual change in her father-in-law over the last month or so but assumed his new outlook stemmed from her condition. Now she must consider the possibility of a real change, an inner one reaching further than his concern for the continuation of the Paxton line and accepting her for herself, for her own worth as a human being. The man bent over the fire, coaxing the embers into life and sending a new shower of tiny glowing stars up into the chimney. Karen was glad his back was turned for she too, though grateful, was embarrassed by the necessity for words, for by a sudden insight she saw she had forced them by her intransigence, by her refusal to, as True would have said, "read the sign." She moved a checker across the board, sliding it from red square to black square, weaving a pattern around the five other black kings. First the strange, new, growing relationship with Vance and now . . . a gentling of what she had considered True's contempt for her and what she stood for.

The old man left the fire and returned to the table, his face flushed from the heat of the flames. "Mesquite makes good burnin' wood. Need it. Gettin' a mite chilly. That norther's stronger than I expected for this early."

"At least it isn't raining. In Washington it would be damp and wet as well."

"That's the trouble with them eastern states, they. . . ."

261

"Yes, Mr. Paxton?" Karen interrupted, ready to parry whatever verbal barb he might choose to hurl. A week— even a day or an hour ago—she would have bristled at the regional slur, but with her new appraisal of True's opinion of her, she realized that would she only permit it, the rivalry would take on the good-natured aspects of a game.

Instead of answering, True stiffened, grew suddenly serious and quiet. "What . . . ?" Karen began.

True motioned her to be quiet as he left the table and hurried to the door, throwing it open and staring into the dark. Only then did Karen hear the sounds of a commotion outside the protective walls. Tightening the shawl around her shoulders she joined True at the door as the main gate opened and Vance hurried through, followed by several of the ranch hands who immediately took up positions along the adobe walls. "What happened?"

Vance hurried into the house, brushing past them and crossing to the wall rack to take down a pair of rifles. He checked the loads and scooped a handful of shells into his pocket as he spoke. "What's About just came in riding one of the sorrels."

"The buckboard an' other horse?"

"Had to leave them. One of Jaco's bunch shot the animal. What's About managed to cut the live one free and slip past them."

True stiffened imperceptibly at the mention of the outlaw's name, steeled himself to show no further reaction. "How did he know it was Jaco?"

"Cirilio Viega told him before he died." Karen felt her blood turn frigid and she gave a sharp cry of horror. Vance looked up, noticing her for the first time. "He was on his way back from Uvalde when he saw the smoke. He headed the team around the back way and came in over Redstone Hill. Didn't see anything but the place in flames, so lit out to see if he could help. There was no one around when he got there. Drove around to the front of the house to find Viega, his wife and two daughters, all hit before they could get a shot off. It was lucky he'd taken Amaranta into town or she'd of been there too."

The door flew open behind them. Billy, his face drawn and one arm bloody and held tight to his stomach with a rope he'd looped around himself, staggered in supported by Harley. " 'Tweren't nothin' I could do, Vance," the boy babbled. "They was all dead, 'ceptin' the old man. I tried. I surely tried, but wasn't no use."

Karen walked quickly to the youth. "Billy . . ." Her voice was high with concern.

The boy shuddered, drew himself straight with an effort. A woman was in front of him and he had to make a good impression. He grinned weakly. "Ain't nothin' . . . Miz Paxton." His face turned white and he slumped in a dead faint.

"He taken one in the side, too," Harley announced. "Lost some blood. We better get him bedded down." He glanced at Karen. "You know anything about doctorin', ma'am?"

Karen blanched at the suggestion, forced herself to remain calm. "No. But I'll learn. Bring him upstairs. We'll put him in the back bedroom. Tell me what to do and I'll do it."

Vance stared after her as she and Harley half carried, half dragged the wounded youth past them and into the hall. "Well, I'll be damned," he said, looking over at True.

"You never can tell about a woman, boy," True said. "I reckon she just needed time." His manner changed. "How'd it happen?"

"Don't know. What's About says they must have caught them unawares. It looked to have been over pretty quick, 'cause Cirilio was hit hard and plenty of times—nine or ten bullets in him at least. He didn't get to say any more than that it was Jaco before he died, and then they hit What's About from a distance, killing the horse at the same time. He managed to fall near the wagon and cut the good horse loose, then ride out ahead of them. They holed him up awhile back in that cedar brake over by White Eagle Pass. He made a break for it and that's when they got him in the side. Says he thinks they weren't far behind him."

True walked to the window, looked out. "Damn," he muttered. "After all this time."

Vance headed for the door. "I'm bringing the men inside the gates."

"Maruja?"

"She and Marcelina are out back in the compound now, with the mare. Got them in first. All the commotion got the mare worked up. Nothin' we can do until morning but wait." He started out, stopped in the doorway. "You might

263

check and see how Karen's doing with What's About. I'll send in Maruja to make coffee." The door slammed behind him.

True stood unmoving at the window for a long moment, then opened it and reached for the shutters, pulling them closed. Five minutes later and all the others were shut and the house buttoned up against the night and what it might bring.

The night passed slowly for the men on the walls. Once the vague echo of distant gunfire rippled through the night but nothing followed and only silence ringed the adobe wall manned by PAX riders. For Karen the blurred hours passed without definition, counted by the ragged breaths of the youth in the bed, his face as white as the sheets and his legs twitching from time to time as in his dreams he ran and ran from the angrily humming, searching bullets. Somehow Karen hadn't passed out when Harley packed the hole in Billy's arm nor when he pulled the alcohol-soaked rag through the gaping wound in his side before stopping the rapidly oozing blood with a tightly-wrapped bandage. She stayed awake in the chair by the bed, dozing only fitfully as she watched. Three times during the night he waked. Each time he wanted to get up and help outside and each time she convinced him he should stay put and poured as much tea into him as he could take before falling back into ragged slumber. The news of the Viegas didn't fully register on her until near dawn when she woke, shaking, from a half-dozing dream in which she saw Roscoe Bodine's hapless figure, life ebbing from him with the bright red fluid, his rough-hewn form growing horribly limp and sagging lifelessly. She sat straight in the chair, the horror of the vision still fresh in her mind. Cirilio Viega, his wife Rosa and the two older daughters, Remedios and Juana Maria. They had done so little to deserve death. So little? Nothing, in fact. Hard workers all, they had lived alone in the hills with none to help them against the cruel riders and the angry chunks of mindless lead. Full of laughter, grace and life, they now lay in dark splotches of blood, laughter, grace and life snuffed out and covered by the swiftly settling dust in the trampled dooryard. How utterly sad, how inexpressibly cruel and unjust.

Morning. The ranch hands had spent the hours alternating between the wall and the living room, gulping a cup of coffee and a sandwich made of *tortillas* and beef, catching a quick nap and then heading back out to relieve the watch. The night was the first truly cold one of the year, on the heels of the season's first blue norther, a wall of cold air from the north which had swept down the valley and plunged the temperatures from the high seventies to barely above forty in no more than an hour. Maruja and Marcelina bustled about cooking and making sure the men kept warm and well fed until somewhere around five when the mare foaled, taking Maruja out of circulation for long enough to make sure both mother and baby were all right. At about the same time, with the first hint of light in the east, Vance and Ted rode down the valley to search for any telltale sign of the brigands who had perpetrated the terrible even at the Viegas' and were surely in the vicinity. By the time the sky was fully light Karen was dozing peacefully in the chair next to Billy, whose breath now came easier and whose face had taken on a little color. Downstairs, red-eyed men stumbled in from the wind-swept walls and stood in front of the fires, stretched their hands to the warm tongues of flame and gulped steaming mugs of black coffee.

Karen wakened sometime during the morning and, embarrassed at having slept, hurried downstairs after making sure Billy was all right. The living room was empty, the men having gone out to check on the stock and buildings. She paused in the hall door a moment then headed for the kitchen, arriving in time to see Marcelina struggle in the door with a huge armload of wood. Maruja sat next to the stove, exhausted, ready to collapse after more than twenty-eight hours on the run. Karen took the Mexican woman by the arm, shook her gently and helped her to her feet. "Go on to bed for awhile, Maruja," she said. "I slept some."

Maruja shook her head. "I will stay. The men will be back. They will need . . ."

"You've been taking better care of those men than they ever do themselves. Go on now. I'll make sure the coffee pot stays full and come wake you later." She led the indomitable woman out the door and across the courtyard to her room, saw her to bed and left again, a new look of determination on her face as she returned to the kitchen to face Marcelina. "How is the foal?"

"He is fine," she finally answered.

"You're tired too. Go up to the back bedroom and take a nap in the chair so you can listen in case Billy wakes up. I'll be busy down here."

Marcelina, tired as she was, shook her head defiantly. "I will stay," she said, turning to put some more wood on the fire.

"You will do as I tell you," Karen answered firmly, spinning the girl around. The two women glared at each other, each waiting for the other to relent. Karen suddenly relaxed, indicated the living room. "The men will be back soon. There is enough trouble for them outside. Now is not the time for women to fight in the kitchen. Go. He needs someone near him. I can pour coffee."

Marcelina started to speak, thought better, turned and stalked out of the room. Karen sighed and moved to the stove.

Vance and Ted returned late in the afternoon. The bandits had evidently left the area and headed west, probably trying for the border before the norther dumped snow on them. They brought word a cavalry detachment had made camp at the mouth of the valley. With the easing of tension the hands filed out of the living room and returned to the bunkhouse, save for Billy who was kept upstairs. Karen managed another brief nap and when she came downstairs for dinner Vance and True were at the dining room table, involved in a lengthy discussion. She heard her name mentioned before she entered the room, which fell silent as soon as the men saw her.

Vance rose and took her by the arm. "Karen. . . ."

"Making decisions for me again?"

"I'm afraid decisions like this were made for us," True interjected.

"A detachment of the Frontier Battalion is returning to San Antonio with their wounded," Vance explained as he seated her. "I'm sending you with them."

"But why?" Karen asked, amazed at her own dismay.

"The ones who stay are going after Jaco and they want Ted and me and some of the other PAX boys to go with them. It will be a long scout and safer for you in San Antonio."

"But you said the bandits had ridden off. Surely. . . ."

"The place will be short-handed. They rode off all right,

266

but we can't see any further than the tracks before our eyes. With the cold they might turn and come back. Any one of a dozen Comanches I can think of might decide it would be a good time to pick up some free horses and extra grub for the winter, not to speak of a woman. I can't take the chance."

"But my place is here," Karen argued, for the first time almost believing herself.

"There's more to think about than ourselves. We have a child to consider and I can't count on the ranch being protected, not with the place so short-handed. We'll leave barely enough to handle the work as it is."

"What about Maruja and Marcelina?" she asked, trying hard to put no emphasis on the latter.

"They're frontier women. They're used to it," Vance explained matter-of-factly.

Karen colored at the implication of her own ineptitude. "I am perfectly capable, Mr. Paxton, of taking care of myself. However, since you wish to be rid of me I will return to San Antonio, and perhaps even farther, should I find the way." And with a flounce of her skirt she rose from the table and stalked angrily from the room.

Vance stared after her. "What did I say?" he asked innocently.

True shook his head in reply. "The wrong thing, son," he growled. "You said the wrong thing."

Karen sat primly next to the driver, the ranch hand named Brazos. The last twelve hours had been more exhausting than she cared to think. The immediate anger at Vance had diminished slowly as she paced her room, and by the time most of her good clothes were packed she had made herself think things out. Perhaps the trip was best. There was a lot she didn't know, more perhaps than she cared to admit. Elizabeth had lived through incredible and hair-raising adventures by the time she was Karen's age, but then Elizabeth was better prepared, expected danger and knew its varied aspects. Later when Vance came to the room they talked for almost two hours and then made love, tenderly, quietly. When Karen waked in the middle of the night and lay watching the man sleep beside her, the core of anger still remaining shriveled with his every breath. It was true he was concerned about the child, but for the first time she felt he was truly concerned about her, too. Falling back to sleep she let herself dream of how nice it would be to visit the city, if only for a week or two.

Vance, Ted and six of the other PAX riders escorted the wagon to the cedar brake where a ragtag party of men met them. Karen couldn't believe such a motley group masqueraded under the prestigious sounding name of a Frontier Battalion. Sixteen strong—an unlikely number for a battalion—they were dressed in ragged riding clothes without a hint of a uniform among them. Ten of the riders split away from the main body and drew off to the west. Most of them bandaged and all armed to the teeth, Karen couldn't imagine any group of bandits looking more fierce. The group assigned to accompany her to San Antonio numbered six, two of whom were too badly wounded to sit a horse so would ride in the wagon with Karen and Brazos. The other four were wounded too, but capable of riding. The PAX riders went to join the ten men of the battalion as Vance guided his horse to Karen's side. "You take good care of her, Brazos."

The cowboy nodded. "Don't you worry none, Vance. This here'll be a stroll compared to what you boys is liable to run inta."

Karen shot a worried look toward her husband. Lost in the frenzy of repacking and the seesawing emotions of the last few hours, she had forgotten the very possible danger waiting for him to the west. What if he . . . ? Vance leaned over and took her hand, kissing it as Brazos and the soldiers looked away discreetly. "You have the note for Jared Green?"

"Yes. Vance, I . . ."

"They'll be delighted to have you as a house guest." He grinned. "And if they're not, you tell me. He owes me."

"Vance, please be careful. This all sounds so dangerous."

"You do what Brazos tells you. I'll be all right. And I'll come get you in a couple of weeks." He smiled, doffed his hat in a gallant gesture and wheeled his horse away, galloping off toward the receding line of men disappearing to the west.

The trip was nerve-wracking but uneventful. Brazos and the men on horseback treated her as if she was the precious charge of each individual and Karen reciprocated by tending, as best she could, the two badly wounded men lying in

268

back, neither of whom complained in spite of the horrible pain. When they neared San Antonio Brazos gave up his place on the buckboard to one of the others, took the frontierman's horse and rode ahead to deliver the note Vance had given him for Jared Green in order to give the banker's household at least a few hours' notice of Karen's arrival. He rejoined the party as they were coming into town, resuming his place on the wagon.

They rumbled into the heart of the city. Brazos swung the team north and they crossed the San Antonio again, following St. Mary's Road out of the town proper.

"Where are we going?"

Brazos indicated the limestone bluffs overlooking the main sprawl of the city, rising north east of the river. "Travis Park," he said as they drove along the western edge of a broad open field dotted with scraggly bare cottonwoods and leafless mesquite, from which still hung dried seed pods imitating the sound of waterfalls as the October wind gusted through them. After the vastness of the empty prairie the park seemed forlorn, despondent and yearning to join with the great expanse of earth surrounding the city, to be free of fences and roads and houses and people.

The homes around them changed in character. Clean and tidy, built with fitted limestone blocks and cedar, many were painted white with blue trim in contrast to the dingy earth-colored excuses for shelter in the southern sections of town. Even the smallest and most unpretentious betrayed the effect of hours of loving labor and maintenance. "Germans," Brazos explained. "Mostly from up around Fredericksburg. Moved on down this way for the business, I reckon. Most of them are pretty good folks, though a mite standoffish for my taste."

Karen shaded her eyes and looked at the homes on the bluffs. They reminded her of Georgetown and her father's manor, but though they were undoubtedly grand structures for the likes of San Antonio and the frontier, they were smaller in every way compared to the ones she had known back east.

They pulled up at a gate of wrought iron and filligree on which hung a freshly painted, elaborately bordered sign. "Green Hill," it read, rather more ostentatiously than had Karen commissioned the work. The wagon turned and went up the drive to a two-story manor of limestone and cedar from which, to Karen's surprise, a butler emerged to greet her and inform her Jared and Bertha Green were absent for the afternoon but would return shortly, that she was welcome, her luggage would be taken care of and would she please be so kind as to enter.

The house was pleasantly warm. A front hall led to a large living room to the right and a dining room to the left, both of which were appointed, as far as Karen could see at a glance, simply but pleasantly with a combination of English, German and purely western pieces. The floor was of strikingly huge planks, rubbed smooth and waxed to a dark, warm sheen, contrasting to the white walls and pale green draperies. Cozy, she thought. Cozy fits perfectly. The butler explained the bustle of activity she felt rather than saw around her as he showed her up the front stairs and to a small but comfortable room with its own fireplace. "A festive gathering, madam. Mr. Green is one of the foremost citizens of San Antonio. Whenever a dignitary visits the city Mr. and Mrs. Green entertain, welcoming him to the state and San Antonio."

"Dignitary?"

"Yes, ma'am. Here we are. Mr. Green sincerely hopes you will enjoy your stay. Dinner will be at 7:00 sharp. If you care to rest I will have Cecilia wake you at six."

"Thank you. When is the party?"

"Tomorrow evening. A most important occasion. For the Under-Secretary of the Interior."

"The Under-Secretary of the Interior? Here?"

"Yes, madam. Something to do with the railroad. Mr. Green is terribly keen on making a good impression on the gentleman. Is there anything else madam wishes?"

"You're English. How on earth did you come to be here?"

The butler reddened at the directness of the question, sighed despairingly as if reliving in a moment a lifetime of bad luck. "The war, madam. Our favors at home were with the Confederacy. I was swept along by the notion of southern gallantry." He paused, embarrassed. "If you've no further needs I shall see to the downstairs," he said, stepping aside stiffly as Brazos and a handyman struggled through the door behind him, carrying her large trunk and giving the nameless butler a chance to escape.

"The rest of your gear'll be up in a minute, ma'am."

Brazos looked around the room, grinned broadly in appreciation. "I reckon you'll be all right here, so I'll be ridin'. Get a head start on tomorrow."

"Thank you, Brazos. You've been very kind."

"Yes'm. Well. . . ." He stepped back as two more servants carried in her carpetbags and another small trunk, set them down and left again.

"Brazos . . .?"

"Yes'm?"

"Nothing. Good-bye. Be careful."

"My ma didn't raise no careless boys, ma'am." He doffed his hat and left, obviously in a hurry to start back to the ranch. Once again Karen was left alone in a strange room, in a strange house, surrounded by people she didn't know.

She bathed quickly and sat at the small make-up table with her bag of toiletries while Cecilia, the servant girl, brushed her hair until it hung in smooth waves down her back, glowing with the vigor of the outdoors and healthy living. She chose for her first night a plain gown, very English and undecorative, of white muslin trimmed with cream lace, a gown which, through its very simplicity, displayed her form in natural beauty.

Bertha Green entered without knocking just as the last hook was fastened. The massive, austere woman looked im personally at Karen, her eyes raking the guest from head to foot in a single withering glance. Karen stiffened, surprised at the hostility she met in that first moment. She had expected warmth and, if not friendship, at least friendliness. "Good evening, Mrs. Paxton," the older woman said, her voice heavy and endowed with masculine power. "I thought I would personally bring you down to dinner. I am sorry Mr. Green and I couldn't be here when you arrived, but we simply had far more important business to which we had to attend." She smiled coldly, emphasizing her self-imposed superiority. "When one assumes the place of leadership in a community one finds it increasingly difficult to fulfill all the social obligations required of one."

Obligations. And I shall be made to pay for them. Very well . . .

The older woman's voice put to shame the autumn breeze rattling the leaves outside. "We're having a few friends for dinner. Mrs. Carstairs and Mrs. Britt, Olin Britt's widow." Mrs. Green was plainly and painfully con-

271

scious of her own position in San Antonio and, bent on putting her guest at a disadvantage immediately, displayed her social credentials as a weak general did his medals. Karen had seen both types before. Her mother for one, but of course Iantha was so much more subtle and poised than this ponderous San Antonian.

"I'm flattered you should take me in like this, Mrs. Green. You're very kind," she said sweetly, giving no indication the innuendoes affected her, nor of the seething anger welling in her breast.

"Well," Bertha smiled, her initial appraisal modified by the unassuming demeanor of the untutored ranch girl who, obviously docile and malleable, would bend easily to her will. "If you'll come with me, please." She led the way, steering Karen out of the room and downstairs.

Snatches of conversation hung in the air as the two women approached the open double doors of the dining room. Karen stifled a quick rush of anger as she realized the words were meant to be heard, for no one could have missed the sound of Bertha Green's footsteps on the polished hardwood stairs. "Of course she's the one. Back there like a common trollop arm-in-arm with a drunken cowboy."

"Really, Constance. I think . . ." a man's voice replied.

"It's true, Jared, and you know it," a deeper feminine voice interrupted. "The story was all over the city. Got that man killed, she did. That rowdy young Paxton found her half na . . . half-clothed in the room with a drunken cowhand and went berserk with jealousy. Poor Bertha, having to. . . ."

Bertha suddenly and quite loudly said, "Right this way, dear."

But Karen had heard more than enough. So they thought her a trollop, did they? No wonder Bertha hated her at first glance. Iantha would have too. The old lessons learned so easily, so naturally, flooded back. Three months on the PAX had convinced her the west was different, but the sad truth was San Antonio differed not a jot from Washington, was a den of malicious chatter and back-biting gossip. Head erect and registering all the Hampton spirit she could muster, she strode into the dining room.

"Ah, Mrs. Paxton." Jared Green, a still handsome, frock-coated man, rose and walked across the room to her, giving her his arm and showing her to a seat opposite the two women who so blithely had been discussing her. "Delighted to have you with us. Sit down, my dear. You must be famished. Let me introduce you. Constance Britt . . . " the shrill-voiced woman nodded stiffly, ". . . and Alice Carstairs. Mrs. Paxton. Her father-in-law and I are old friends."

"How do you do," Mrs. Carstairs began, her deep voice tinged with an unusual rasp.

"We've heard so much about you," Olin Britt's widow added, her voice neutral, waiting for Karen's first words.

Karen smiled graciously. "It's good of you to allow me to impose on your hospitality. Vance spoke very highly of you. I feel almost as if I know you, Jared." She caught herself, lowered her head, embarrassed. "I'm sorry. That was rude of me. But it was Jared this and Jared that . . ." She sent a dazzling smile at her host. "I do hope you'll forgive me." Out of the corner of her eye she watched Bertha's shoulders straighten stiffly at the familiarity with which Karen addressed her husband.

Jared Green positively beamed. "Not at all. Not at all. Please. You are perfectly free to call me Jared as you wish. Too much formality around here as it is. Vance is a good boy. Good boy, and we're more than delighted to have you, aren't we, Bertha?"

"Of course." Her matronly beam hid a dark warning confirming her first appraisal and dismissing her second.

Mrs. Britt gave a what-did-I-tell-you glance toward Mrs. Carstairs, who nodded in silent agreement.

"We were surprised to see you back in San Antonio so soon after . . . after . . . " Mrs. Carstairs stumbled over the words.

". . . after leaving for your new ranch," Mrs. Britt picked up smoothly. "It's rare that ranch people come to the city more than once or twice a year. To shop, usually. I'm afraid culture and civilization get to be a little too overwhelming for them after the simple rigors of the frontier."

"Sometimes I think I can understand why," Bertha sighed dolefully, ringing a little bell to summon the servants from the kitchen. "We who live on the Heights try to foster an atmosphere amenable to the outsiders who visit us, but what an uphill struggle it is, with all the goings on and rowdyism running rampant in *some* parts of town."

Karen ignored the disguised barb and smiled innocently at the three women who searched her face for a reaction. "It must be difficult," she sympathized before turning her attention back to Jared. "Vance tells me you've tried to get him into politics." She noted how her host's eyes, caught resting on her breasts when she unexpectedly turned to him, jerked upward guiltily. Daringly, she thrust herself forward against the fabric of her gown and had the satisfaction of seeing the older man, unable to stop himself, glance down at the ripe form. To the side she could see Constance Britt and Alice Carstairs redden and turn suddenly to the plates being placed in front of them. A sharp clank of a fork on a plate told her Bertha's reaction had been similar.

Jared, aware he'd been caught, rushed the words. "Vance Paxton is a fine young man with a great deal of promise. I've been trying to lure him to Austin, but he shuns the very notion of entering the political arena. Like his father. He'd rather stay in the hills on that ranch of theirs. Do him good to get out."

The idea was intriguing, Karen thought. Perhaps when the Jaco business was settled she'd be able to influence him. First state politics then national; a logical progression all the way to the east coast, and back to real civilization. She'd love to see the faces of all those who had sneered and laughed behind her back during that last week or two in Washington.

Dinner was a strange affair during which Karen was filled with conflicting emotions. Conversation, all designed to impress Karen, centered on the coming party at which Marvin Rutledge, the Under-Secretary of the Interior, was to be the guest of honor but Karen, much to the women's chagrin, remained singularly unimpressed with their chatter and paid only peripheral attention, concerned as she was with the confusion of her own thoughts. Was she getting more used to the simple ways of the PAX than she had thought? Had her own values been subverted, suborned by those of the men who moved so guilelessly around the ranch? Was Vance completely right after all? The glittering crystal and shining silver place settings convinced her anew he wasn't. There *were* finer things in life than eating dust and cooking in the west Texas hills. *And yet . . . and yet . . .*

The repast ended wtih coffee and a modest liqueur, obviously a rarity here, a refreshing mint cordial shipped from New Orleans. Karen let the three women who held her in such low esteem do all the talking, listened with a polite and attentive air as Bertha, Constance and Alice lulled themselves into a sense of complacency over their easy victory. Finally the two guests tired and indicated a need to be off. The entire assemblage left the room. "We certainly hope you enjoy your stay in San Antonio, Karen dear. Perhaps we'll see each other again before you leave," Constance Britt remarked.

"Oh yes. Tomorrow night, no doubt," Karen answered.

"Tomorrow?" Alice queried archly, amused by the very idea.

"Of course. At the party for Mr. Rut. . . . Oh, dear." Karen lowered her gaze modestly, looked up at Bertha with innocent eyes. "How terribly *gauche* of me. I *do* hope I'm invited, though."

"My dear. . . ." Bertha was cornered and knew it, unfortunately couldn't decide if Karen's *gaffe* had been purposeful or truly naive. There was no way out. "But of course, dear. We wouldn't think. . . ."

"I guess I just got carried away with it all," Karen continued, eyes wide and the words gushing from her in a torrent. "I'm just so impressed with San Antonio. Especially after living on the ranch all these long months. I had no idea such a city could exist out west. Such pretty, pleasant little houses . . . almost like cottages in a fairy tale. And everyone managing so stoically, trying so gallantly to bring a glimmer of civilization to the raw frontier. I guess I just expected everything and everybody to be so far behind, and here I find such a charming, rustic elegance much, much farther along than I had ever hoped. We simply must sit down and have a talk and let me fill you in. I'll have lots of time, and . . . well, I just think you've managed so very well for being so terribly provincial . . ." She stopped, put her hand to her mouth in a gesture of embarrassed self-chastisement. "Listen to me prattling on, and you must have very many important things to do. Perhaps I'd better. . . ." She looked around, caught Jared's eye. "Would you mind terribly seeing me upstairs, Jared? I'm sure Bertha has some last-minute plans to make." She took the unsuspecting man's arm and steered him away from the group. "Good night to you all."

The three women watched, daggers in their eyes, as the bustle swept away from them, out of range of protest or retort. Karen half-heartedly scolded herself. *It's awful to take advantage of them, but they asked for it.* Rounding the stairs she noticed all three women bunched in the front doorway, heatedly exchanging words in sanctimonious reassurance of their own incomparable worth and desperate rationalization of the defeat they refused to recognize. And still they didn't know they'd never had a chance. *Wait until tomorrow night, ladies. Just wait.*

Jared decided the bank could run itself for one day. His duty was to show Karen the sights on her first day in San Antonio. After all, she'd had a bad experience her first time in town and he, as any civic leader should, didn't care to see an important cattleman's wife disappointed with the city in which he had so much at stake. Of course, he decided all this only after Bertha Green left to attend a fund-raising breakfast at which Marvin Rutledge would speak and where everyone who qualified for the early morning affair in the illustrious private dining room of the Menger would be gathered. Jared, attired in immaculately tailored coat and trousers, knocked softly at Karen's door.

"Yes?" a voice responded sleepily.

"It's Mr. Gr . . . Jared Green, Mrs. Paxton."

The door opened and the banker's face flushed deep crimson. Karen's tousled hair hung down past her shoulders, swelling in twin glittering mounds where it spilled over the voluptuous swell of her scantily clad breasts. Hair like the rarest of silks, thought Jared. He stuttered, swallowed, coughed twice and began again. "My dear Mrs. Paxton, I feel personally responsible for not being here to welcome you yesterday. If you would allow me, I should like to make some small semblance of amends today by showing you the sights of San Antonio."

"That would be wonderful, Jared. But I'm afraid I shall need some time to dress. Will a half hour be too long?"

Jared, pleased and flattered, protested as gallantly as possible. "No. No. I assure you. The wait will be a pleasure.

Jared Green's walk down the hall and stairs gave no indication of the state of his mind, roiled and seething with tantalizing after-images of the young woman framed in the doorway. Green eyes like emeralds, hair to play over a man's body, breasts to be . . . He caught himself mentally, forced himself to back off from the heady temptation. "Fascinating woman," he muttered, "fascinating," lowering his voice as he passed beneath the large portrait of Bertha's domineering countenance, glaring down at him from over the stairs.

The sun was high overhead when Jared pulled up the carriage on the shady banks of the San Pedro, upstream from the spot where Karen had first passed and seen the Mexican women kneeling on the stones and washing their families' clothes. Here the pristine waters narrowed and ran quickly over the smooth stones. Willows and cottonwoods grew down to the rocky shores and under them the grass was still green and sweet. Karen walked to the water's edge, marveling at the beauty of the place so much like Rock Creek. Yet older somehow, stretching uninterrupted from the past, unimpressed, somehow untouched by the tread of peoples long since returned to dust, uncompromised by later generations. Jared watched as the wind sighed among the trees, ruffling Karen's skirt, pressing the fabric against her legs and outlining the shapely limbs against the reflected light from the stream. "A beauty," he reflected. "A woman worth marrying for more than prestige and advancement." The scene in front of him glistened like some Frenchman's painting, a picture of a girl as pure and virginal as the water and the air, yet ready to explode with the suppressed sensuality of total womanhood. A drop of perspiration trickled down his temple and he pulled a handkerchief from his pocket and dabbed at the moisture, caught himself in the gesture, saw himself for the first time in years. Forty-three years old . . . balding . . . an important citizen in the community . . . banker . . . money . . . one of the finest houses in the southwest. Without looking he knew his stomach protruded too far, knew his legs had gone to flab. His wind was a faint memory. How long had it been since he was young and lean and hard, a feisty, wolfish man hungry for all the things he'd never had and always wanted? So he married Bertha and got them, and looking at himself felt a deep sorrow for another time and another place and another girl who stood with her back to him by a stream. *Twenty-one years. Twenty-one years, and I'll never get them back.*

The day passed quickly, moments lost in the silent limestone ruins of quiet missions, time squandered happily among the squabbling vendors in the Mexican section. They refreshed themselves with coffee and pastries in a snug little shop whose German proprietor delighted in Karen's ability to recall a few German phrases and by the time they were ready to go back, Karen had grown to like Jared Green far more than she had that morning when she had fed her contempt for him behind closed doors. She sensed a sadness in the man in spite of the very real financial power he so obviously wielded. Quietly, he grew on her as a friend, one to be trusted and defended if necessary, and of whom she should never take advantage.

By the time they arrived at Green Hill, afternoon was well on the way to evening. Bertha was a veritable tornado of nervous energy with barely enough time to spare in the midst of a multitude of last-minute crises to chastise Jared and send him packing to his room to get dressed in time to meet the first guests, due in less than an hour. Karen stood to one side during the short harangue, watching the woman quietly, feeling sorry for the man she had come to like. Her mind made up, she moved timidly, as if afraid of the woman. "It's my fault, Mrs. Green. I'm sorry. The afternoon simply slipped away. If you'll pardon me, I'll go on to my room. I think I need to lie down. Something in the pastry I ate, no doubt." A doleful expression capped the act and she sealed it by turning as she started up the stairs. "I doubt if I'll be down. I feel so miserable . . ." she whispered, then fled out of sight. Behind her she could feel Bertha's hostility and following sense of relief.

Two hours later the party was in full swing. All of San Antonio's best had gathered to drink champagne, mingle and show they were close and cherished friends of the Under-Secretary of the Interior and blessed by the socially prominent Greens. The house was bright with the light of many lanterns and candles, sparkling with laughter and conversation spiced with the knowledge that all present were the unquestioned elite. Gowns never before seen in San Antonio graced elaborately coiffed ladies. Men

278

gathered in tight clusters and spoke of cattle and lumber and land and the railroad and what it would do for San Antonio and their respective fortunes. And in the dining room Marvin Rutledge laughed and listened, kissed the ladies' hands and shook the gentlemen's.

In the hall, a distraction. One head turned, then another. A new face . . . someone coming down the stairs . . . gold hair glowing like the sun, a gown from Paris, deeply cut and leaving very little to the imagination, a chorus of aquamarine and blue and green, of taffeta and swirling lace, of tiny slippered feet peeping from under the leading edge. The hush broke into a dozen whispered questions which spread out in jealous ripples flattened by the walls, caromed back to the bottom of the stairs and headed for the dining room. Karen smiled at all of them, secure in herself, secure in certain victory.

Her entrance into the reception room caused much the same reaction as in the hall only on a grander scale. Heads turned, tinkling goblets and jeweled champagne glasses halted halfway to lips, conversation ceased in mid-sentence and left behind a stunned silence. The festive crowd parted unobtrusively, not a one there knowing who the woman was, not a one but curious, envious or in awe.

Marvin Rutledge, the center of attraction, held court in the center of the room, attended and jealously guarded by Bertha Green, Constance Britt and Alice Carstairs. All three, senses finely tuned to the slightest variation in the tone of the crowd around them, turned to stare in the direction of the hush. Bertha's face went white when she saw Karen striding toward her. The girl was supposed to be sick. And whoever would have guessed she was so . . . But before she could utter a sound, Marvin Rutledge, Under-Secretary of the Interior of the United States Government, respected businessman accepted in New York and Washington's finest circles, guest of honor at the most prestigious party in more than a year in San Antonio, broke from the combined grasps of three determined women and, to their horrified astonishment, hurried toward Karen, his arms outstretched. "My God, it's Karen. Karen Olivia Hampton!" the Under-Secretary exclaimed as he wrapped his arms around the girl. "I never thought I'd see you *here!*"

Constance Britt's mouth froze in a perfectly framed "O."

Alice Carstair's eyes narrowed with unabashed hatred. Bertha Green's face drained bloodless with shame and fury, and everyone in the room stood stunned.

"Hello, Uncle Rutty," Karen said . . . oh, so sweetly.

CHAPTER IX

Sunday, the 5th of December, was a bright, cold Texas day with a sky tinted the ice blue of frozen pond water. The air, so still and silent the slightest sound was magnified, bit to the bone with its invigorating breath. Vance had been gone six weeks, not two, and there was little to show for his absence save a face strained and haggard from long hours on the trail. Beneath his fleece-lined buckskin coat and flannel workshirt a jagged line of new white scar tissue contrasted with the still summer-bronzed flesh of his shoulder, a new scar added to the roster streaking his torso. The bandits had split as they were chased, the main body heading northwest for New Mexico and the remainder crossing the border into Mexico. Captain Alexander left Vance and the men from the PAX patrolling a hundred miles of border while the battalion itself continued in pursuit of the larger force. And little Vance could say in the way of protest, there being simply no one else to handle the job. For three weeks eight men working in pairs rode the hard, cold miles and searched for sign indicating their quarry had crossed back over the Rio Grande.

The tedium was broken only by the brief incident in which Vance received his wound. He and Shorty all but blundered like tenderfeet into a small war party of Apaches, five braves bent on stealing horses and causing as much havoc as possible among the sparsely-settled inhabitants of Val Verde and Maverick Counties before returning to their *rancherias* in Coahuila for the winter. The fight lasted but seconds and ended with Vance on the ground and losing blood while the braves scattered for the river, carrying their two dead with them. Shorty trail-patched Vance's wound with strips from a torn shirt and a poultice of tobacco. Surprisingly enough, the wound healed with no trouble.

By the time Captain Alexander returned, half of November was gone and the men had had it. Jaco's bandits were obviously holed up in a warm place across the river while the men of the PAX were freezing themselves and their horses on a wild goose chase. They rode for home. Vance returned to find the ranch in good shape and with no evidence of neglect in spite of being short-handed. What's About was up and working. True was in good health, back riding again in spite of the hip which still stiffened if he tried to do too much. Vance rested the night and started out for San Antonio before dawn, breakfasting on beans, *tortillas* and coffee. He chose a dun for himself and Karen's sorel gelding for her, and though both were alternately lazy and feisty from long activity they quickly settled down for the long trip. On horseback and not having to stick to wagon trails he made good time and a little before noon of the following day he crossed the San Pedro, skirted the heart of the city, picked up the San Antonio south of the bluffs and made his way to the Heights and the nobler homes of San Antonio.

Green Hill appeared deserted save for wisps of smoke curling from the chimneys. Jared was probably at the bank and Bertha undoubtedly off to one of her infernal ladies' committees designed, ostensibly, to better the community but in reality to relieve the boredom of those with nothing better to do, and to establish and maintain a pecking order so necessary to the social structure of the city. There were, Vance opined, better ways to spend one's time. Worse, too. At least they hadn't tried to reform the wilder parts of town. Yet. The front door stood ajar and the house was quiet save for a woman's voice softly humming "Green Grow the Lilacs." Karen's voice. He let himself in and followed the sound down the hall and into Jared's study. Karen was standing, her profile to him, busily perusing the wall of books before her. Her stomach clearly betrayed indications of the miraculous burden within and, while she was not yet ungainly, her condition was obvious. *A boy. Let the first one be a boy. A boy to teach. A boy to carry on. A boy to become a man, a Paxton.* For a second he stood silently, unmoving, struck by the hope and awe of life.

Karen was reaching for a well-worn volume of Shakespeare when her hand suddenly halted in mid-air and began to tremble. Knowing without seeing, she stifled a cry, turned toward the door and rushed to meet him, throwing herself into his arms and searching wildly for his lips. She broke the embrace and stepped back, frowning playfully. "I really should be quite put out. There is a serious difference between two weeks, Mr. Paxton, and six weeks."

"True sent word. . . ."

"Yes," and her eyes clouded, thinking back to True's letter delivered two weeks earlier, explaining Vance's absence and mentioning how well things were going at the ranch. For a whole day after receiving the scrawled note she moped about the house in a depressed state, sure she had read the implication "now that you've gone everything is fine and back to normal" in True's words. But the letter had come at an inopportune time. She had not been feeling well to begin with. The pregnancy, while not bothering her physically, exerted more pressure than anticipated, filling her days with fear and her lonely nights with nagging, apprehensive dreams. The child was growing rapidly and only the morning before she had broken into inexplicable tears after awakening from yet another nightmare and seeing the unquestioned bulge in her lower abdomen. Alone and abandoned, she was wanted nowhere and by no one. The feeling lasted until the next night when an overheard conversation at a party cheered her immeasurably. "I don't care. If I were carrying Vance Paxton's baby I'd want the whole world to know."

The remark jolted Karen back to reality and the next day she began the work of altering her dresses so they would be more comfortable and, indeed, proclaim her condition to all the world. She *was* proud to be carrying Vance's child and the longer they were separated the more she realized how much he meant to her. The blue mood fled and True's note took perspective. Smiling as she sewed, she decided Karen Paxton could be a very, very silly girl indeed.

"I came as soon as I could. Rode into the ranch night before last and out again yesterday morning before dawn." He took her shoulders, held her from him for a better look. "Let me see how he looks."

Karen arched out her stomach in exaggeration. "What happens, sir, if he turns out to be a she?"

"Wouldn't dare," Vance said, grinning. "The Paxtons breed boys. Let the others get girls."

"Vance Paxton!" Karen twirled from him, putting Jared's desk between them. "That's terrible. That's a terrible thing to say."

"Truth. Come here."

"I will not. Any . . ."

"Come here." Grinning, he darted around the desk for her, barely missing a handful of skirt as she skipped playfully behind a chair.

"You are conceited, vain, egotistical, arrogant . . ." Vance hooked a foot under the chair and slid it aside, leaving Karen nowhere to run. Suddenly his arms were around her again, his mouth seeking hers ". . . and I love you, Vance. I love you so much."

"Oh! I *do* beg your pardon." Vance released Karen abruptly, startled by the voice. The butler stood in the doorway, glancing down the hall to see how Vance had gained entry. "Mr. Paxton. I didn't hear you come in."

"Sheehan, would you have some lunch brought for Mr. Paxton, please? He's had a long, tiring ride."

The butler nodded, smiling. "Of course, madam. In ten minutes, if you please." He disappeared as silently as he had arrived.

"Looks like you've become part of the family," Vance chuckled.

"I'm in my element."

They sat together in the sun parlor. While Vance ate Karen recounted her adventures of the past six weeks, beginning with the party for Marvin Rutledge. The Under-Secretary had brought disturbing news from Washington. Barrett Hampton's business was sorely affected by the depression. He had been forced to cut back drastically, ended up losing the house in Washington and had to move back to New York where he could exercise close personal control of the trembling remnants of the Hampton fortune. With the house went any further immediate chances for political speculation, and while they were by no means destitute, neither would Iantha be able to indulge her extravagant nature.

Washington society had been shocked to the very foundation by the brutal murder of Angie Leighton followed by

Earnest Leighton's incriminating disappearance. The scandal had undoubtedly provided ample fodder for more tea party gossip sessions than the city had seen for some time, and while many an indignant matron decried the foul deed, as many more muttered "Good riddance," beneath her breath.

In short, Karen chattered on about parties and being pregnant, about Bertha and Jared and, slyly, the banker's hopes for Vance's political career. Vance said little and concentrated on the food, the first really good meal he'd had since before leaving on the extended scout for Jaco. Most of the information Karen thought so interesting didn't concern Vance in the slightest and though he nodded and appeared to be listening he was really thinking of what a fool he'd been to bring a saddle horse for a woman in her present condition. The meal finished, he broached the subject but Karen only laughed, insisting that riding horseback would be no more traumatic nor uncomfortable than a jostling, bumpy trip in a buckboard.

Bertha, whose attitude toward Karen had changed abruptly since the night of the party, was the first to arrive. She made a wonderful show of greeting Vance and wishing he and Karen could stay longer. Uncle Rutty, Karen had called the Under-Secretary. Almost like family. And the girl was staying at Bertha Green's house. My, how burdens turn to blessings in disguise, the banker's wife reflected, smugly considering how her social position in the community had been elevated beyond that of her envious friends. Karen Olivia Hampton—Paxton too, of course—of Washington was her house guest.

Jared arrived just before dinner and visited with Vance over the evening meal. Anxious to be alone with her husband, Karen picked nervously at the meal. Finally the conversation lagged and Vance excused himself. Karen self-consciously accompanied him upstairs, trying hard to ignore Bertha's knowing smirk. A tub of hot water was waiting for Vance and as Karen watched he stripped and plunged into the water with a groan of relief. "Six weeks on the trail. You don't know how good this feels."

Karen knelt by the tub and began to scrub him with a sponge, reacting sharply when she noted the new scar, still red around the edges. "How did you . . . ?"

"Apache. It's all right now."

"But you could have . . ." Her face was white. ". . . you could have . . ."

"I didn't." He noted the tears in her eyes, drew her face close to his. "Hey, no call for that. I'm all right."

Suddenly her arms were around his neck and their lips met, crushed by the six long weeks of loneliness and longing. Karen stood abruptly and her eyes shone with voracious hunger as she stripped the gown from her body and stood naked before him. "Just sit back . . . relax. Let me wash you." The sponge became a tortuous, erotic tool playing over his chest, abdomen, groin, thighs and calves. The soft caress of her hands was a direct contradiction to the six celibate weeks, and tired though Vance was he responded as she hoped, followed where she led. Then she was in the water with him and he was soaping her breasts and the insides of her thighs, touching the body eagerly waiting for him as softly as possible with work-roughened hands. He could stand it no longer. Rising, the water cascaded from him as she cupped the twin spheres and caressed the rigid staff until Vance shuddered and grasped her hands.

"No more. Not yet. Not yet." Quickly he pulled her from the water, tenderly dried her with a warm towel and carried her to the bed. Seconds later he was rock hard again in response to the quick fingers which played over him. "My God! I forgot!"

A look of alarm crossed Karen's face. "What?"

"I . . . I mean we . . . well, we *can't*, can we?"

Karen giggled, suddenly became serious. "If we don't, I'll never forgive you."

"You sure it's all right?"

"I'm very, very sure."

Tenderly he rose over her and, their eyes locked in unity of purpose, eased into the warmth and moistness. Karen's eyes widened and she gasped, caught her breath. "Easy."

"Mmmm." The slow rhythm built in long, lazy strokes, culminating in a sweeping release that held them both frozen in attitudes of ecstasy for long, long seconds.

Vance pulled back the covers, opened the warm sleeping gown and stroked the swell of her belly where his son was growing. *My son . . . my son.*

"I must look like a cow to you."

286

"You look like a beautiful woman." He put his ear to her stomach, listened. "Can you feel anything yet?"

"Yes." When he started to lift his head she held him there, enjoying the warmth and pressure. "Vance?"

"Mmm?"

"I was talking to Jared." Vance stiffened, certain of what was to follow. "San Antonio is so festive. Not like Washington of course, but in its own way bright and cheerful. And with all the nationalities, almost a smaller version of New York plopped down out here in Texas."

"I can assure you San Antonio wasn't just 'plopped'."

"Jared tells me you're very highly thought of here . . . and in Austin."

"I have some friends. From the war. When the reconstruction government dissolves they'll more than likely be elected to take the places of the carpetbaggers and scalawags."

"You could be one of them."

"Oh, Karen."

"It's true. Jared said you could go far."

Vance sat up, cross-legged, facing her and unconsciously tugging on his moustache as he collected his thoughts. "I don't want to go far."

"Think of it. Austin . . . living in the capital."

"Karen. . . ."

"A few years in the state government and then who knows. Certainly a seat in the House."

"Karen. . . ."

"Think of it, Vance. Back to Washington. And not just as an individual pleading a cause, but with real power behind you. And you wouldn't have to be out on horseback for six weeks at a time, or carry a gun."

Vance uncoiled, leaned over and languorously kissed her, brushing the hair back from her face with his fingers, his hands sliding down to cup her breasts and his head lowering to kiss her again and again in a sweeping arc.

"Vance!" Karen paused to catch her breath. "Vance . . . no. This is important."

"I know."

"No!" she ordered, pushing him away. "You know what I mean. Do you want to be stuck out on that ranch all your life?"

Vance sat up. "Do you want to be Bertha Green? Or Iantha·Hampton?" Karen shrank back with the inherent truth of the question as Vance turned from her and fumbled in his vest until he found the makings, shook the tobacco into the paper and rolled a cigarette. A match flared, illuminated a face creased in thought, then winked out with a flick of the wrist. He crossed to the window. Outside the moon shed its pale light over the sleeping town and eerily brightened the corner of the room, silhouetting his stark frame against the night sky. The bed was in darkness behind him but Vance could hear Karen's even breathing. The end of the cigarette glowed fiercely as he inhaled. "I am not stuck . . . on the ranch. It's where I want to be. It's home."

"But not to me."

"Because you won't let it. Elizabeth was happy there."

"I am not Elizabeth," she answered softly, punctuating each word.

"I know." He paused. "I like the feeling of walking out into a clear morning so still you can almost hear the shadows fall from the hills as the sun rises . . . the smell of a cedar fire . . . the rush of a hawk as it sweeps low overhead . . . the startled look in a deer's eyes . . . and the sound of the river, fresh and clean and sparkling. They are things I cannot give up."

"And what of me? And our child? Will you give us up?"

He turned instantly from the window, his eyes glowing in the dark. When he spoke his voice was low and ominous, a voice she'd never heard before and didn't recognize. "What's that supposed to mean?"

"I don't know, Vance." And frightened, she didn't. "Only . . . I . . . I don't think I'm strong enough."

"Of course you are," he said curtly, turning back to the window. His face hardened, unseen in the night, at the implication of her words. "Give *us* up," she had said. The boy was his son too, if it came to . . . But that was no answer. He stood in the moonlight feeling the chill bite deep into him, seeing the land beyond the night, feeling the gulf of silence between him and the woman he loved, warm in the bed, and wondered what life would mean without her.

They left two days later. The morning broke brisk and chilly but the rising sun soon bathed them with faint

288

warmth and made their way not unpleasant. Karen rode the sorrel gelding and Vance led the way on his dun. The trunk full of fancy gowns had been left behind to be stored at Green Hill and the remainder of Karen's luggage divided into two large carpetbags and packed, along with other assorted purchases, on the back of a sturdy mule Vance borrowed from a Mexican friend. No more was said of the disquieting discussion, nor was the subject brought up again during the next weeks though the indelible mark of their conversation traced a jagged line across both their minds.

Noon of the second day found them cresting the last rise leading to the ranch. Most of the hands were out working but Harley Guinn hallooed them from the wall as the gate swung open. Karen looked up, waved a greeting in return to the older cowboy outlined against the rim of the hills and the ever green line of cedars. *I'd almost forgotten how beautiful they are. Like being surrounded by Christmas trees.* Her breath formed a cloud in the chill air. *Christmas . . . only seventeen more days.*

Billy Harmony came out the front door, his face breaking into a wide grin upon seeing them. "Howdy, Miz Paxton. Sure is nice to see you. It purely is. The boys was talkin' just the other night how it don't seem quite right aroun' here without you lookin' pretty an' all."

"Thank you, Billy," Karen said, touched by the sentiment. "I hope your arm and side are well."

"Yes'm. Good as new." He swung one of the heavy packs from the mule to demonstrate his strength. "Everything's fine, Vance. Got a wagonload a' gear out by the corral. Ted's up the valley at the Split Tree water hole, movin' around some stock the boys missed while you was gone. Said he could use some help."

"Saddle up that grulla for me," Vance ordered. "I'll be along soon as I get this in."

Karen sighed in exasperation. *Not back for a whole minute and he's already off to more important matters.* Stiffly she stalked to the front door and entered. The spacious front room was warm from the heat of both fireplaces, and from the hidden depths of an armchair in front of the east wall came a tremendous sneeze followed by a deafening bellow as True blew his nose. Maruja came in from the kitchen, a steaming mug in her hand. "Aieee, such a sound.

Loud enough to call *el oso* from his den. *Señora!*" She ran across the room and embraced Karen, holding the mug high so as not to spill its contents. True's face appeared around the side of the chair, his look of surprise immediately contorted by another sneeze. "It is good you are back with us. We are lonely here since you are gone. No one to talk to but men. And Marcelina. Ah, but that one. All she can talk of is men."

"Been quiet for a change," True grumbled as he approached them. Stepping back from Karen, Maruja handed him the cup without comment. "What the hell is this?"

"Look at her! Aieee, *Señora*. He will be a big son. A true Paxton!" Her face clouded. "*Señora!* You are all right? Such a long ride."

"I'm fine, Maruja. I feel fine. It's good to be back."

"I said, what the hell is this?" True barked, staring into the mug.

"Soup," Maruja answered defiantly.

"I told you to rustle me up some of that chili."

"A sick man needs soup, so I kill a chicken and make soup." True glanced at the mug, up to Maruja's unwavering expression, back to the mug. Maruja sighed, shrugged her shoulders. "You have sixty-two years. I tell you don't go out without your coat in the sleet, but you go. Now you drink soup."

"Waste of a good goddam chicken," he muttered, defeated, and shuffled back to the chair before the fire, sipping the broth as he went.

"Oh, *Señora*. You must be tired and we must take care of *el machito*. I have Marcelina heat water for your bath," Maruja said, leading Karen toward the rear of the house.

"That would be nice, Maruja. Thank you."

Vance came in the front door as Karen started down the hall. "I'm going to ride on up the valley with What's About," he said. "Be back around supper time."

"Might not be a bad idea," True answered from the chair. "You'd best check on Willow Creek too. Had us a gully-washer while you was off playin' border guard. Might of made some rough goin' up that way an' trapped some cattle in the bend." True sneezed again.

Vance grinned. "You take care of yourself, now."

"Don't need to," True grumbled. "That Mex woman is doin' it for me. Soup!"

The front door opened again and a gust of cool air blew through the hall to billow Karen's skirt. "Oh, son?"

"Yes, Pa?"

" 'Bout time you brung her back home."

Karen paused on the stairs, astonished by what she'd just heard. "Why didn't you tell her that yourself?" Vance asked.

" 'Cause she's too damn good at checkers, is why," came the answering growl, broken off by a sneeze and fit of coughing. The door slammed and the house was quiet.

Snow. For the first time in years there would be a white Christmas at the PAX unless the wind shifted capriciously and melted the thin cover during the night. The possibility seemed remote. Karen thrust another stick of cinnamon into the cider bubbling cheerfully in the iron pot hung over the flames. The ranch hands were drifting out of the sunset into the hacienda to strip off their heavy fleece-lined coats, stack them in a corner and head for the steaming pot and a cup of the cheerful Christmas brew. Ted Morning Sky had ridden in that morning with half a dozen wild turkeys hung across the pommel of his saddle. Now the birds were dressed and basted, all crispy orange-brown from the flames. Maruja had been cooking all day long and the house was filled with a mouthwatering variety of odors, each sufficient to rouse a stomach-grumbling hunger from the men of the PAX who, in spite of threat, cajolery or flattery, would have to wait until Maruja the implacable took pity and rang the bell calling them to the dining room.

Two hours later the table was nearly bare and the men retired to the living room with full stomachs and glazed eyes. Karen slipped away to the kitchen where, after struggling to remember Retta's recipe from long ago, she had managed to prepare and hide two heaping platters of hot doughnuts. Full, warm and relaxed, the hands had fallen into a near stupor by the time Karen and Maruja carried the platters into the front room. Harley Guinn saw them first. Sitting by the door, he rose slowly and stared at the incredible sight. "By God!" he exclaimed. "Bear sign!" Fourteen pair of eyes focused as one and a groan of disbelief rose from the men. Doughnuts—bear sign to them—and not a hand in the room who wouldn't ride a full fifty miles to get some, as full as they were. Karen was the instant hit of the evening. She passed among the crowd and not a man, from youngest to oldest, from talkative to taciturn, but failed to rise and fill a fist then sit back and dream as he slowly munched away, careful not to drop so much as a crumb.

By ten o'clock it was time for the tree. Billy had cut and carried in a fresh evergreen a week earlier and Karen, determined to have as merry a Christmas as the PAX had ever seen, lavished special attention on the young sapling, transforming it into a sparkling, festive creation. She made the men close their eyes while she and Billy carried the baby cedar into the room and set it in a corner. Feeling sheepish and more than a little silly, the men obeyed, obdurately grumbling over all the fuss on their behalf. Moments later Karen told them they could open their eyes, and rough, tough, hard-bitten crew though they were, not a one but didn't have to blink back the quick watering, swallow the sudden nostalgic lump in the throat.

Karen had bought a number of little gifts for the men during her stay in San Antonio. Things a man might enjoy: tobacco and paper, a pair of warm socks for each, bandannas and a stack of books and magazines—they would be read and re-read a hundred times before spring came—to be placed in the bunkhouse. One handsomely wrapped package sported TRUE spelled out in bits of bark on the silver wrapping. Inside, much to the amusement of all, was a playing board and box of checkers, the playing pieces painted blue and yellow. "Now you have two *new* colors," Karen told True, as seriously as possible.

True glared in mock sternness at his daughter-in-law. Successful for about ten seconds, his face finally gave up and split into a smile. He looked at the grinning faces around him. "I'll win with 'em, too," he exclaimed defensively. Later, he brought his face closer to Karen's and whispered, "Woman, you sure got a lot of salt."

The festivities continued into the night. The ever present squeezebox and harmonica were brought to the fore and a raucous semblance of yuletide carols filled the room. Karen brought Vance a cup of steaming cider. Their eyes locked for a moment, each trying to plumb the unfathomable depths of the other but to no avail. Aware of the distance between them even as she leaned up to him, she whispered

"Merry Christmas" and kissed him on the cheek, handed him a long, narrow package.

Vance glanced at the box, secretly touched her swollen stomach. "This was the only present I needed. My son."

"Open it."

He undid the red ribbon, carefully rolled it up and handed it back before opening the box and discovering a new bowie knife, the blade reflecting his face back to him. Lifting the gleaming weapon out, he checked the balance. "Feels good."

The door from the outside flew open and Ted Morning Sky entered, shaking new flakes of snow from his hair. He carried something bulky and covered with a piece of canvas, handed it to Vance who placed it on the back of a chair. "Open it," he commanded. Karen looked at him inquisitively. "Go on. It's yours."

Her fingers tugged at the knot but couldn't get it open. Vance used his new knife to slit the leather thong and the canvas fell aside to reveal a new side saddle, the leather a deep brunt orange immaculately and intricately inlaid with a seat of tapestry cloth woven with a design of flowers in gold and green and light blue. "Oh, Vance, it's lovely."

"Figured you been riding Elizabeth's long enough. Time you should have one of your own." Impulsively, Karen reached up and threw her arms around his neck and held him close, much to the delight of the rest of the company. But over Vance's shoulder, Karen noticed Marcelina staring vehemently at her from the dining room.

Vance, grinning self-consciously, pried her from him. "I have a request. The boys got together earlier and asked me to ask you to sing a song for them."

Karen blushed. "Me? I can't. . . ." She looked around in the silence. Each man in the room stared at her with the unspoken request. "I'll try."

"Sing 'Silent Night,'" Hogan said from his place in front of the crowd. Karen had never heard him speak before and his voice was a deep and rumbling bass, belying a skin-and-bones frame.

"All right."

The squeezebox and harmonica combined behind her with the haunting melody and the room stilled to the words. "Silent night . . ." Listening to the words and going far beyond them into the past, the men retreated from themselves and the world. Memories of hard men at home in a harsh, unrelenting environment which tested them daily, each of whom had been at one time a child . . . a boy. Each remembered a home far away and a time—however short— when there was softness. Mothers, sisters, fathers paraded along the dim trails of memory as each reconstructed the moments somehow flown, somehow lost. Life on the PAX was good but it was hard. Hours in the saddle, hours in the sun, hours in the rain and cold. Bad trail food cooked by themselves, many times no food for two or three days at a time. Danger, pain, always the unknown facing them around the next bend in the trail. And what beyond? A woman and family of their own? The odds were against it. A life at thirty dollars a month until a man was thirty or thirty-five and too old to keep it up, too old and too crippled to take the hard work? That was the future most of them faced, yet such was the life they freely chose to live. No man would hear a one of them complain, for none of them would trade for any other way of life. Cider swirled in mugs, gazed on by eyes narrowed by resolute yesterdays and uncertain tomorrows. "Silent night, holy night . . ."

The tune lingered in the chinks between the stones, caught in the small blue flames and spiraled upward into the night to spread over the sleeping land. No one spoke. Hogan set the squeezebox down with a single sighing note, a final punctuation of nostalgic relief.

True coughed. "Boys," he looked around the room, waited until they were all out of their past and with him again. "This here's the first Christmas since 1836 that Elizabeth ain't been here. The house feels empty." He paused, a slow smile creasing his worn face. "Did I ever tell you about the time me and her was . . ."

Vance slipped outside to escape the painful memory. The night was near day-bright with a full moon that peered through a rent in the clouds and shone on crystalline snow, its rays bounding from hill to hill and gathering in the valley below. He crossed the courtyard as new flakes of snow fluttered and choked the stillness. Once outside the gate he hunched his soulders and crossed to the barn, the iced mud crunching beneath his boots and causing him to grit his teeth from the sound. Inside the barn it was warm, snug against the wintry evening. The gentle animals chomped the grain in feed troughs or slept, waking as the man walked in to disturb their rest. All the gear was in place and the leather, having been newly-oiled against the stiffening cold, added its aroma to the earthy smell of animals, grain and hay and weathered walls. He stooped to grasp a strand of yellow straw and placed the stalk in his mouth, savoring the faint sweet taste of summer. Why had he run from the warmth of the house? What thoughts darkened what should have been a happy occasion? *Karen . . . Karen.* He wanted her, but enough to wear the brand of a politician? What kind of life was that for a man? He couldn't envision himself trapped inside a frock coat and listening to the ceaseless boring reiterations of self-important men.

The door opened behind him and he spun about, caught off guard. Marcelina walked softly toward him, a coal oil lamp turned low to illuminate her way. She hung the lamp on a nearby hook and stood before him, proud and terribly pretty, her eyes flashing with elemental promise and desire. "I see you leave. And follow." She dropped the shawl from her shoulders, thrusting proud young breasts against the light cotton blouse. Vance felt his blood quicken and the first faint stirring of desire in his loins. "Why you not send her away?"

"She is my wife."

"That is no excuse," she spat.

"Then, I want her to stay," Vance replied, trying to keep his voice as free of emotion as possible. "How's that?"

"Why?" Marcelina asked. "A woman knows things. A woman can see there is little between you and her. She is not fit to be your woman."

"She carries my child."

"Bah!" Marcelina gave a haughty flip to her head, sent her long dark hair spilling across her shoulders. "Any woman can do that. The woman of *Señor* Vance should do more. Send her away."

"Are you so old and wise to talk of what a woman should and shouldn't do?" Vance asked, partly amused, partly afraid to be serious.

"I am sixteen, and I would show you how much woman

295

I am. We . . . you kiss me before. Then I was your woman. But you leave and go to this Washington and forget Marcelina."

"I kissed you once. *Only* once. You were never my woman, Marcelina. You were and still are a sweet, pretty girl. And one I kissed. But only that and nothing more. I suppose I shouldn't have, but I was doing the work of three men and out every day. Seeing you like you were—like I was—I needed the softness of you and the pretty thought of you."

"Let me be your woman again."

The haunting melody of a guitar drifted out of the house and to the barn. A haunting Spanish melody only Emilio could play. Marcelina began to sway and gently match the notes with rhythmic, evocative movements of her own. She danced in the stillness of the stable, her feet on the scattered straw. She danced and the graceful motions of her lithe body conjured heady notions of lust and made the very air thick with an aura of passion. *"Mi caballo,"* she purred, her voice ripe with passion. *"Mi caballo,"* this time more of an entreaty. Skirts swirled and slender coppery thighs gleamed in the lamplight. *"Mi caballo,"* an incessant chant, a challenge. She shrugged brown shoulders free of the blouse and thrust barely covered swollen nipples against the fabric. Her movements wantonly provoking, she clutched the full skirt, raising it as she danced, revealing perfect calves, knees, thighs. *"Mi caballo, mi caballo, mi caba. . . ."*

Vance grabbed her by the shoulders. Her lips parted to receive his feverish kiss as she arched her body to him. Suddenly he shoved her back into an empty stall. Marcelina lost her footing and fell backward into the cushioning hay. Vance quietly, firmly, and not without effort, said, "No."

She rose, furious and shaking with rage, but he was already gone. *"Mi caballo!"* she taunted, the words acid and dripping with venom. *"Mi cholo!"* She spat at the closing door and grabbed her shawl. "Go then," she whispered scornfully, her voice choking with malice and humiliation. "Return to your *gringa*. I offer myself and you refuse. You have shamed Marcelina and she will not forget. Never will she forget." The girl slowly rose to her feet, the love within

296

her like a candle extinguished. "I hate you both. From this moment, I hate you both."

Save for the markings on the calender, Karen could not tell when one year ended and the next began. January the first came and went as any other day and Karen found herself settled into the routine of a winter's existence. Mornings she spent with Maruja, learning to prepare the various ranch fare. The kindly Mexican woman taught Karen to work with skins and furs, to weave, to plan for spring, which seeds would be planted first, what crop should go where. In the midst of the days, Karen came to think more and more of Maruja as the mother she wished she'd had.

If the afternoons were clear and bright, Ted Morning Sky or Billy would accompany her into the hills to instruct her as to which plants were edible, which held medicinal value, where to look for water and how to read the calligraphy of the trail, identifying the tracks of animals and man. Every day, rain or shine, she longed for more time with Vance, but he spent most of his days out on the PAX range keeping tarck of the stock through the heavy winter months, driving them to better feed and delivering supplies to the line cabins on the boundaries of PAX range. At first she begrudged his absence, but as she slowly assimilated herself into the workings of the ranch she began to understand the necessity of his being gone and concentrated on the business of taking care of herself and learning the thousand details involved in running a ranch house on the frontier.

Her girth increased as the child within her developed and grew. To fill the increasingly lonely hours she and Maruja altered some of Elizabeth's dresses, plain though they were. She promised herself the provincial apparel would serve only until she regained her normal figure, but after wearing the new clothes for three days, had to admit they were more comfortable than anything she had brought with her. The first time True saw her in one of his wife's dresses his eyes narrowed. That night, as unobtrusively as possible, she let him win at checkers. With the blue.

It seldom snowed. Worse, the winter manifested itself in bright, crystal cold days contrasting with gloomy periods of freezing sleet and rain. It was on one such rainy afternoon she amused herself in Elizabeth's old workroom. Sick of sewing, she dusted off a canvas and started on a painting she planned to keep secret from everyone. And during especially inclement times she would bake several batches of doughnuts, filling the entire *hacienda* with their delicious aroma. Bundled up in a heavy coat she traversed the icy distance to the bunkhouse and left heaping platters full for the men when they came in, an action that ingratiated her to the PAX riders more than anything she could have done.

February brought more of the same, days of bright clear cold sunshine, days of ferocious rain and gloom when wind and thunder threatened the security of the adobe walls, when driving sleet took the measure of horse and rider and made a body yearn for the stifling heat of a summer day. It was on a bright morning in early February that Marcelina saddled a half-wild Appaloosa and, bearing an assortment of food, magazines and a book or two for the line shack at the northwest edge of PAX range, rode west on the trail leading to Sleeping Giant Mountain. How she hated the Paxtons. All of them! And so she volunteered to ride to the line shack simply for an excuse to be out of the house and away from the *Señora* who mocked her with incessant, pretended attempts at friendship, and from Vance, the only man to whom she had ever offered her body, the man who scorned her.

The Appaloosa fought her lead but she was an expert horsewoman and brought the animal under control, heading him up the northwest fork in the trail. The weather had been clear for several days, but February in hill country was a time of rapid changes and Marcelina was wise enough not to trust the pleasantness of the moment. She looked warily to the north where even now the sky was awash with a scattering of high cumulus clouds. Gibson, the PAX line rider, would probably be anxious for a visitor, especially before the new storm hit. It was early afternoon by the time she drew near the cabin nestled on the chest of the Sleeping Giant, having taken a roundabout path merely as an excuse to prolong her journey and the time spent away from the ranch. She reined up the Appaloosa in front of the house and, not getting an answer to her halloo, tethered the horse near a patch of grass growing a few yards from the door, slid out the Winchester from her saddle scabbard and strode up to the shack. "Hey, Gibby!" There was no response. More than a little pleased she wouldn't have to fend off the cowboy's awkward advances, she decided to leave the supplies inside and be on her way. She went back to the Appaloosa, slung the burlap sack over her shoulder, crossed to the shack and stepped inside where without warning the carbine was torn from her grasp and she was spun into the center of the room. Her fingernails slashed the air but the man only laughed and stepped back out of range.

To her surprise he was not Gibson. Against the closed door and holding her rifle stood a lean hard wolf of a man, a cruelly handsome half-breed with a scar, a vivid trail against deep brown skin, marring his high cheekbone. Long black hair hung down to his narrow shoulders and a mandarin moustache ranged along his lip. His eyes glittering with singular malice, he wore the clothes of a *vaquero*, tight black trousers flared at the boots, a short coat of faded buckskin and a sombrero hanging down his back, held by a rawhide thong across his throat. He had the look of one who was a predator among men, and despite her initial fear, Marcelina felt her face flush and her blood quicken beneath his unwavering, sensual stare. His grin revealed even white teeth, sharp like a rodent's, and there was an aura of power about him, a look she had seen in only one other man, Vance Paxton. "Who are you?" Marcelina asked, her voice trembling.

"The man who was here. He is out back where I kill him," the man said.

"What are you doing here?"

The man leaned the rifle against the door, stepped closer to the girl. His hands reached up, curled the fabric of her blouse and tore it to the waist. "This," he said. His hands caressed the girlish breasts. "And this."

Her head tilted up to receive the crushing, hungry kiss and she fell back on the cot as his hands ripped her jeans from her and his own weapon of flesh, brutally large, was exposed. Only then, suddenly panic-stricken, did she recover enough to struggle, but her hands were held to the side and he was over her and into her, inside, tearing her with seething strokes of fire. "And this," he laughed, ". . . and this . . ." in rhythm with the fierce strokes.

With his sudden release she lost consciousness. His words were a final fearful echo reverberating hollowly down the long final plummet. "And this. . . ."

It was late afternoon. The sun drifted lazily on its way, dipping below the crown of the Sleeping Giant, bathing the cabin in shadow. Without those rays of warmth, feeble though they were, the cabin soon grew unbearably chilly. Riders, many of them, approached and the man unsheathed himself from her and, catlike, strode to the door and grabbed the carbine as the weapon tilted and began to fall. A man with only one ear, the right one being but a knob of flesh, waited outside. He tried to look over the naked wolf's shoulder even as he gave his report. "The men return, Jaco. There will be a storm soon."

Marcelina sat up in the cot at the mention of the man's name. Jaco! *But what of it. He is a man.* Her eyes narrowed. *A man to keep. A real man.*

"What of the rangers?" Jaco asked.

"José believes we have lost them."

"José is a fool. What do you say?"

"We have lost them. But not for long, I think."

"Tonight, then, Jaco said, his voice heavy and foreboding. "Tonight we burn the ranch."

The one-eared man hesitated in the doorway. "What is it, Arcadio?" Jaco growled.

"The men . . . Marquez wishes to know if the girl is for all the men."

Jaco glanced over his shoulder, a grin splitting his face, then back to Arcadio. "She is mine. For a special reason."

"Marquez will. . . ." Jaco spat on the floor and Arcadio stopped talking. The message was explicit. He nodded and closed the door.

Marcelina, her feet on the cot and her back against the wall, sat wrapped in a blanket, knees bent and against her breasts. She studied the bandit's naked form as he stirred the embers in the iron stove, tossing in a few pieces of kindling and grunting with satisfaction as they burst into flame. Jaco. Jaco the bandit, Jaco the feared. He placed the carbine on the table and neared the girl. Marcelina's small pert breasts were bruised from his rough caresses, yet the dark brown crowns tightened as he walked toward the bed. He sat near her, his hands touching her knees, separating them then traveling down across young thighs chafed from his demands. She shuddered as the strong hand with skin as brown as the dead leaves sought the tender flesh and teased it, oddly gentle, until the moisture of desire flowed to warm the calloused fingers. "You bled well," he said. The first and second time she had fought him, but now, beneath those feral eyes glittering with power and primeval hunger, Marcelina felt the flood gates of her own frustrated passions unleashed, sweeping her along to what tomorrow she did not care, as long as this man, this Jaco, was with her.

He ripped the blanket from her to reveal the exquisite form and his hand sought her again even as hers entreated his massive staff. Together they matched coaxing provocations until his free left hand clasped around the back of her head, forcing her over and down to taste the searing, surging brew she had so wilfully instigated. A wind soughed mornfully through the chinked walls and his laughter echoed the crackling of the spitting fire.

The two of them rode together, the remainder of the bandits keeping their distance to the rear lest a party from the ranch come upon them, for there was the possibility someone might have felt her absence peculiar and gone looking for her along the trail. The full weight of the pact between them had not yet made itself fully known to her. Pulling the coat tighter around her torn clothes, Marcelina was glad for the darkness bathing her, for the swelling clouds, the towering airy battlements carried on the north wind. "You will not harm the older woman," Marcelina reminded the man at her side.

The wind howling down the canyon whipped his serape open yet Jaco seemed immune to the icy breath that caused the shivering girl to burrow deeper into her fleece-lined coat. "I will treat her," Jaco laughed cruelly, "like she was my mother. This I promise you. I come for the old man and his son. They are what matter to me. Arcadio, Marquez, José and the others care only for plunder—what they can carry away to buy women and whiskey. Maybe guns or horses. Nothing else matters. They kill only because there are those who try to keep them from what they want."

"And you?"

Jaco's sentiments were made all the more horrible because he smiled. "I will kill True Paxton. I will kill his whelp."

"And the woman?"

"Maybe I keep her." Marcelina's brows knotted angrily. Jaco laughed, oblivious to the Mexican girl's concern. "Or maybe I give her to the men."

"She is with child," Marcelina said.

"Then it is all the better, *mi chula*. Maybe I even keep her man alive long enough to watch." Jaco's vehemence surpassed even Marcelina's anger and made her curious, but as she started to speak he held up his hand in warning and blended back into the darkness of an overhang. Someone was ahead, coming up the trail. Marcelina nudged the Appaloosa into a trot to increase the distance from the bandit's hiding place. She reined up as Ted Morning Sky rounded an outcropping, rifle across the pommel of his saddle.

"You are late, little one. The trail is dangerous at night."

"I . . . Gibby was not there so I wait for him. When he return I visit with him because he is lonely. But I did not want to stay with him the night." She guided her mount past the Indian and continued down the trail. "I am glad for the company," she said.

Ted peered into the hills. His keen ears searched for the sounds of the night, inexplicably stilled. He sniffed the air but the north wind would tell him of nothing to the west. Still . . . the elertness of a Comanche entailed more than just the rudimentary senses. Something there was, an instinctive warning. He backed behind the protection of a boulder, then wheeled his horse deftly and followed Marcelina down to the valley floor toward the *hacienda*.

CHAPTER X

The fire crackled, twigs split open from the heat. A cluster of gleaming comets shot up the flue as a large oak log settled into the bed of glowing coals. Karen stirred the chili bubbling in the huge iron pot hung but a few inches over the flames. For the first time she had prepared the meal from scratch, without any help from Maruja or the tardy Marcelina and, though she had imitated the older woman's cooking step by step, the meal was hers and hers alone.

The patio door swung open and Marcelina entered, frowning at the pale rival who had usurped her duties. "I am here now," she announced, expecting Karen to relinquish her place.

"We were worried about you."

"You leave now."

Karen shook her head. "Perhaps Maruja could use some help."

"This is my place." Marcelina reached for the wooden ladle but Karen held it away.

"No," she said firmly.

What could have escalated into a major confrontation died aborning as Maruja entered with Vance and True close behind. Karen, anxious for praise from her husband, turned to offer him a bowl of the chili. "No time for that now," he said brusquely, and her smile turned to a worried frown at the sight of the forbidding armament he and True carried. Maruja spoke not a word but fell to clearing the heavy oaken table, shoving vegetables, spice and canisters of sugar, salt and flour aside. Vance and True laid the rifles and pistols on the table.

"I'll bring in the cartridges," True said, turning to leave.

Karen felt her heart quicken with heavy pulsing beats.

"Vance. . . ." Her voice, thick with worry, faltered as she spoke.

He reached out to grip her arms. "If anything happens, stay here with Maruja and do what she tells you."

"What's happening?"

"Don't know yet. Maybe nothing. Ted has a feeling." Vance looked at Marcelina, who struggled to keep her face free of guilt. "You saw nothing on the trail?" he asked.

Marcelina shrugged noncommittally. "The night sometimes plays tricks," she answered. "But I saw nothing, heard nothing I have not seen or heard before."

Across the room True shrugged on a warm coat, buttoned it to the chin and tied a scarf around his ears. "There's a wind up," Vance remarked.

"So?"

"So your leg will stiffen if you get out there too much."

"So?" came the cantankerous reply.

"You'd best stay inside."

"Like hell!" The old man's eyes blazed "You just try and keep me here."

"But your leg. . . ." Vance protested.

"If there's trouble I'm gonna be shootin', not runnin'. Over thirty-seven years here—which is more than you are old—says so. So hesh up an' tell your wife the meal she cooked up by herself an' that you ain't gonna get to eat at least smells mighty good." The old man peered keenly at Marcelina. "You may be havin' to run to the walls. You up to it girl?"

"Yes," Marcelina muttered, shivering with fright and secret knowledge.

Maruja opened a box of cartridges. Checking the action of the first rifle, she began to load the dozen or so lying on the table. True stepped up behind her, gently touched her on the arm. "You keep 'em loaded an' dry?"

Maruja's brown eyes turned soft and she paused, gazing closely at the old man. "I always have, *Señor*," she said in a voice traced with memory.

"Yes," True answered. "You have." His face was a reflection of hers. Then he was gone from the room.

Karen followed Vance to the front door. He smiled and started to kiss her cheek but she threw her arms about him and held him close. "What is it?" he asked.

"Be careful," was all she allowed herself to say. Her eyes

lingered on his earthy handsomeness, examined the fabric of the man she loved and never completely knew, grew moist despite every effort to avoid such a display. *His face is made for smiling, for bearing the easy burden of the smile.* And she had seen him smile so seldom. Close now, his lean rangy frame kindled desire in her flesh, a passion that, strangely heightened by the aura of impending disaster, refused to fade even in this, her eighth month.

He reached out to touch her abdomen, his hand resting lightly on the swell of life within life, the fruit of love. "In a month, Mrs. Paxton, we shall have a son."

Karen smiled despite a premonition lurking beyond the closed door, brought by the north wind. "Yes. A son." She paused, searching his eyes. "Are you so sure?"

"I know," Vance said, "because a wise old Indian told me." He opened the door and the wind forcibly gusted into the house, knifing through Karen and filling the house with the sharp odor of night and cold and. . . .

"Coffee strong enough to float a horseshoe," she called cheerfully, choking back as yet unknown fears. He waved back to her and, ducking his head into the wind, headed toward the wall.

The main gate was open and men were bringing the horses through, tethering them to a line strung along the base of the wall. The animals reared and tugged at the ropes pulling them, whinnying with fright, calling to each other. The palpable fear they exuded stretched through the dark and the wind to the door itself and the girl standing there. Quickly she shut the door against the milling pandemonium, leaned back against the planks and faced the empty room. The wind outside increased, beat at the door behind her. Darkness . . . the lamps had been extinguished to lessen the risk of fire. Only the flames in the fireplace kept the dark dread brought by the storm from engulfing the entire room. Shadows, serpentine as the uneasiness choking her thoughts, danced and flitted along the walls. She hurried to escape them, anxious for the usually cheerful warmth of the kitchen. But even there the dark threat had entered.

"Shall I help?" Karen asked, anxious for any task to wrench her from the labyrinth of fear in which she found herself.

"You had best help me with these, *Señora*," Maruja instructed.

"But I . . . I don't know how."

Maruja held out a Winchester rifle. "I will show you. It is time for you to learn." Karen numbly accepted the heavy weapon and, under Maruja's tutelage, checked the action and began to feed it a leaden meal of death.

Marcelina stepped outside, her mother's voice still faintly audible through the thick walls. She hesitated, reluctant to leave the shelter of the patio. What would Maruja say when she learned her daughter was a traitor? What would she think? *Mama . . . No . . . !* Shuddering, she wrapped herself tightly against the cutting edge of wind. The storm had come sooner than expected, growing in violence even as she walked across the open courtyard. Supposing he did not come, she thought. No, that was foolish. He would come. His hatred burned deep, keeping him safe from the fierce kiss of the north wind. *But not from my kisses.* . . . She laughed to herself. She no longer cared about this family of *gringos* for whom she and her mother had sweated and worked so many hours, and for nothing more than food and a bed. *Señor* Vance had scorned her, forsaken her for an undeserving, haughty pale bride. Ha! She drew the warm *serape* close about her shoulders and braced herself against the chill, remembering the warmth of Jaco's caresses, still lingering on her breasts and between her thighs, and the bandit's smouldering form enwrapped in hers, lost to the inexorable rites of love. She was a woman, no longer a child, a subservient daughter to be ignored or ordered about like a common servant. Maruja would understand, and if she did not, that was just too bad. She shoved away from the woodpile and headed toward the rear escape door, well concealed in the hidden northeast corner of the wall, each step carrying her closer and closer to a future to be born in blood.

Brazos watched the last of the horses disappear into the protected courtyard from the corral. He grinned as Vance and Ted approached. "This Injun sure takes the fun out of a night. Nigh worked myself to death bringin' them durned steers up from the creek, an' now I gotta roust these here broncs in the middle of a norther."

Ted, concealing his good nature behind a stolid Indian

306

countenance, replied sternly. "Brazos, you never 'nigh worked yourself to death' in your life." Brazos, visibly stung by the words, feigned indignation and strode away from them toward the corral, grumbling about unappreciative bosses and smart aleck Comanches who saw visions in the wind.

Vance smiled as the cowhand left, but his smile faded as he noted the worry creeping back into the Comanche's features. Ted was staring into the darkness down the valley. Without warning the rain began, thick, icy droplets, born as a plague from the north. The two friends—more like brothers—stood side by side in the face of the storm's opening salvo. "How many?" Vance asked.

"More than we are, I think," Ted answered.

Vance hunched his shoulders against the cold, tugged his moustache. "It is the wrong time of year. I ask myself, 'who?' and 'why?'."

"It does not matter. They come."

"I hope you are wrong, my friend."

Ted nodded in agreement. "The storm . . ." his face rose to the sky and the driving rain. ". . . will bring more than snow or rain. Listen to the voice of the wind. Once long ago, among my people, there was such a storm. That night many people die. Some go mad, kill their families and even themselves. When the morning came my father gathered the people together and we leave that valley. To this day no red man sets foot there. Vance Paxton, my friend, this night the coyote wind howls down from the hills as it did long ago."

"There is a difference," Vance replied firmly. "In the morning we shall still be here. I will not be driven from this valley, neither by men nor spirits." He studied the bunkhouse for a moment then started toward it, thinking to place three of his men in the structure along with Hogan, already stationed on the roof. He glanced upward, barely able to make out the ranch hand atop the building, called for him to come down and get inside, then shouted for Brazos to bring two more and join him.

The wind increased to a baleful roar, whipped Ted Morning Sky's coat about his legs and blew away his hat. His long hair, unbraided, streamed past his cheeks as he faced the south. A smooth hand reached up to touch his cheek and the Indian half of him becried the lack of paint.

A brave should go into battle wearing paint, for it made the enemy fearful and satisfied the Great Spirit. No longer listening, no longer searching the now screaming darkness, he stood like a statue before the storm, a man carved from virgin rock, motionless, enduring, at one. . . .

And then he knew. A cry cut through the raging elements: the warrior cry of the Comanche. He whirled and fired at the man who rose to stand on the roof of the bunkhouse. The man who was not Hogan. In the kitchen Maruja paused. Karen started sharply at the sound. "It has begun," the Mexican woman said calmly. Karen stared with unseeing eyes at a hanging gourd, clenched her bloodless hands together to keep them from trembling.

Ted swerved his rifle and fired at the gathered patch of darkness lodged against the bunkhouse wall, darkness that was not a cluster of trapped tumbleweed. Caught in the open, Vance instinctively drew his gun and leaped the few remaining yards to the bunkhouse wall. A bullet whistled through the empty air where he had stood by a second earlier. The man on the roof tumbled to the ground, his bandit's face staring into the rain. Gunfire sounded at the corral and flames darted from the corner of the bunkhouse as the surprised Mexican renegades recovered from the unforeseen onslaught and returned the Comanche's fire. Bullets chewed the mud brick wall, spattering Vance with jagged fragments. Crouching low, he ran the few steps to the front door and bolted through the opening. A flash of movement to his left sent him diving to the floor as four rapid shots thundered in the confines of the room. Slugs thudded into the bunk he heaved over on its side for protection. The wind ripped the open rear door back on its hinges, slamming it against the adobe. A figure lunged to his right. Vance fired, rose firing again. Someone screamed. Muzzles belched fire and lead, the roaring explosions followed by the careening whine of ricocheting bullets clanging against the stove, shattering wood and glancing off stone and leather. A dimly-lit coal oil lantern dropped from its hook, burst into flames and starkly illuminated the men in the bunkhouse. Vance shoved cartridges into his revolver, rolled onto his stomach and fired from beneath the shattered frame of a bunk bed at two bandits rushing him. One of them spun and fell back against a table on which another lantern rested. Table and renegade collapsed to the floor where a tongue of coal oil spread to the flames and burst into life of its own, swiftly carrying the flames back to the broken table and wounded bandit. The second outlaw's gun snapped. Empty. He threw it at Vance and leaped back through the flames. A gun fired. A man screamed and fell. There was a muffled curse of surprise. The greedy flames began to devour the wood furnishings, to grope for the plank roof with fiery fingers. Obscured by the crimson and orange curtain, Vance grabbed a third lantern. It was useless to try to save the place. Cursing, he hurled it at the far end of the room, heard with satisfaction the sound of exploding glass and roaring flames and one drawn-out wail of pain and terror before he covered his face and leaped a rapidly diminishing clear space near the wall, fell through the open door and into the freezing night.

The storm lashed the valley with incredible abandon, rivaling the unleashed struggle of men with a violence of its own. Ted Morning Sky and Brazos were backing away from the corral, firing steadily as they withdrew. Beneath the fury of the wind Vance could hear the drumming of hoofbeats. The barn was ablaze and, outlined against the flames, a half dozen riders swept down on them. He grabbed a rifle from the ground, checked the action as he ran to Brazos and Ted. "Get to the compound!" he shouted hoarsely, gesturing to the riders.

Figures darted toward them from the corral, catching the three in a crossfire. Ted fired twice then grabbed Brazos by the shoulder. "Let's go!" he screamed, striving to be heard above the fury of the storm.

Brazos started to follow, then stopped in his tracks. "Damn!" he exclaimed. He toppled forward, a neatly-rounded hole between his now sightless eyes.

A rider charged. Vance and Ted fired simultaneously. Vance grabbed the bridle, hauled down the plunging, panic-stricken animal, leaped into the empty saddle and grabbed Ted's arm as the horse bolted forward again. Ted jumped up behind Vance and the pair headed for the main gate. Bullets whirred angrily about them as they ran a corridor of screeching death, a gauntlet of gunfire from the bandits to their rear and the men on the compound walls. Thirty feet from safety the horse crumpled, its skull shattered, sending the two men tumbling onto the frozen earth. The bandits charging down on them met a withering fusillade from the men on the walls who ripped the darkness with searching shots. José, the burly brigand, Jaco's lieutenant, appeared out of nowhere, looming out of the dark. He held two revolvers and fired them as one at Vance. The Comanche ran between them just as the outlaw loosed his shots. Ripped by the slugs, he stiffened and fell before Vance could catch and support him. Vance rushed back to his friend, dropping to the ground by him as José fired again and missed, then staggered back as if kicked, hit by a bullet from the wall. Vance, enraged, emptied his revolver at the bandit who twisted away from the terrible punishment and was lost in the swirling, driving sleet. Vance hauled Ted to his feet, slung him over his shoulder and ran crablegged toward the gate, the icy air searing his lungs with terrible cold. The open maw in the wall was too far away . . . the sleet blinded him . . . pain in his leg—had he been shot—but he must run . . . the cacophony of screaming horses and men, gunfire, the shrieking of the coyote wind.

"*Señora*."

Karen didn't answer, stared instead into the hearth, drugged by the unbelievable, horrifying conflict outside so tellingly announced by the sullen, continual roar of gunfire. "You've been protected. . . ." Vance had said, and now she couldn't tear herself from the waking nightmare. Graceful fingers trained to etiquette now gripped the heavy wooden handle of a revolver, unconsciously clasped its weight as one might cling to a branch in the middle of a raging current.

"*Señora*." Maruja's incessant voice, so terribly calm, brought her back from the flames, from the hearth, from the corridor of her inward escape, back to the situation at hand.

"*Señora!*"

"What is it?" she snapped, immediately sorry for the tone of her voice. She stared wide-eyed at the Mexican woman. "I'm sorry. It's just . . . I . . ." On the brink of collapse, her voice trembled. She put the gun on a back table and embraced Maruja, seeking to share the woman's strength. "I'm so frightened. Vance . . . what if he . . . the noise . . . why don't they stop?"

"It's all right, *Señora*. I understand. I am afraid too. All of us are. But we . . . see to our duties. I must take these rifles to the walls and help the wounded to the house. You will stay here. I will need your help when I get back. Put another pot of water on. You stay here."

"Yes," Karen replied weakly, standing alone now.

"*Señora*. Many times we fight. We are still here." She gathered an armful of rifles, started out the door, then turned momentarily. "I am glad you come here. It was hard to understand your ways, but we have learned. And you have learned." Maruja turned again and disappeared into the dining room.

A moment later a gust of wind blew through the kitchen from the opened front door. The fire popped and sputtered and Karen flinched at the sound. The wind stole around the side of the house and rattled the door leading to the patio, trying to enter, striving to extinguish the warmth of the kitchen. Only it wasn't the wind. The door latch turned and Karen's eyes widened with apprehension. Suddenly she thought of Marcelina. Of course! But how long had she been gone? The door opened. It was not Marcelina! A man . . . a strange man. . . . !

The wind rushed in with him, billowing his *serape* like wings of a giant bird of prey, adding to the terrible apparition that was Jaco. "You are the whelp's woman. You are indeed beautiful, as hungry men have said." His face formed a cruel semblance of a smile.

Karen shuddered beneath his stare. "Go . . . go away," she managed.

Jaco laughed. "No, *Señora*. I think perhaps I stay. Maybe I put something else in your belly besides what you got there now."

Karen glimpsed the handle of the revolver she had placed on the rear table near the door to the root cellar and began edging toward it. A smattering of gunfire sounded from, she thought, within the walls. The noise diverted Jaco's attention and Karen grabbed for the gun and brought it to bear.

Jaco's face remained singularly calm when he looked back to her. His laughter was brutally mocking. "Your hand trembles, *Señora*. I do not think you have the strength to pull the trigger." Slowly, confidently, he walked toward her.

The sounds of gunfire and storm faded to dull confusion

before the onrushing panic loosed within her mind, screamed for her to shoot yet clouded her vision with tumbling images of Bodine, face taut, puzzled as the blood spewed from his chest. The face of the man before her shifted, wavered. Who was he? Why did he look so familiar? "Shoot him! Shoot him!" the voice within her screamed over and over. "Shoot him!"

"Like a dance, *Señora*, you back away as I draw near. Our movements match in this our dance of death. But I think you do not kill Jaco, eh?"

Jaco! No! "No . . . no! Stay away from me!"

He laughed again, white teeth shining in the firelight as he reached for her, toying with her, knowing she would not fire. A sharp explosion sounded behind him. Jaco winced under the impact of a bullet, whirled about, drawing and firing in the same motion. Karen froze as she saw Maruja slammed against for door jamb, a look of incredulity and horrified understanding sculpted on her face. "Look what you have done, Marcelina, my evil daughter," she moaned, then crumbled to the floor, dead.

Karen dropped the pistol, screaming. She lunged for the door to the root cellar with Jaco, roaring like a mortally wounded beast, behind her. Gunshots and a man's voice calling drove her deeper into the dark maw. The cellar was icy cold. Its depths blotted her vision and she lost her footing. Darkness reached for her and steps rushed up to meet her, jutting stone bruised her face and slammed into her abdomen. She clawed at the air and toppled into searing pain and merciful unconsciousness.

Her child was a boy. And the boy was dead. Lying in the soft comfort of her bed the thought came to her unbidden out of the terrible quiet. How did she come to be in bed? In her room? She remembered. The laughing face, unknown but familiar . . . Maruja's pitiful collapse . . . hands reaching for her and her panicked descent into the cellar . . . falling . . . pain . . . quiet . . . emptiness. Her swollen abdomen was dramatically decreased now, but no child suckled at her breast. *Another grave, Elizabeth, to be added to the hill* . . . graves . . . quiet. . . . It was quiet now.

The door opened. Karen tensed as the light from the hall fanned across the bed. "Vance?" Her voice trembled.

He took a few steps into the room, his face, only faintly discernible in the lamp's soft glare, weary and old. He stood at the edge of the bed, a lantern held high. "My son is dead," he said hoarsely, his voice a mixture of grief and accusation.

She had known for hours but no tears would come, not even now before the man who so grieved. Her sorrow defied release, hid itself in a hollow place in her heart, beyond the touch of tears.

"I know what happened. For three nights and days I've been here fighting your fever with cold cloths and listening to you repeat the story over and over again. You had a gun. You could have stopped him." He placed the lantern on the table, leaned over and gripped her by the shoulders, his fingers bruising the flesh of her arms, his voice quaking. "Karen. He killed Maruja. *You* let him. *You* ran. *You* . . . killed our son."

He held her there in silence, his eyes burning with the fever of unspeakable agony. Suddenly he sagged and his arms went slack. He backed away from the bed, his face lost in the shadows of anguish.

"Vance!" His name was a plea for absolution, raised from the vast lake of despair threatening to drown her.

He paused in the doorway, his back to her. "*You* killed our son," he repeated, his voice a hollow whisper.

Like the rush of raven's wings against an interminable night, his words reverberated in her mind, punishing . . . punishing . . . long after the door closed and his footsteps faded from the house.

PART III

CHAPTER I

The charred remnants of the bunkhouse and the black patch of ground once a barn and stable were ugly scars on the valley's pristine wintry floor. The snow stayed for four days, during which time ragged lines of soot-darkened footprints radiated from the dark circles like spokes of a broken wheel. Little moved during those first days, for a numbness had settled over the ranch. Upstairs in her room, Karen gradually regained her strength. Downstairs, the front room took on the aspects of an infirmary where the wounded ranch hands were treated by True, for only he and two others had escaped unscathed and the two were busy outside. After two weeks had passed the men, with the exception of Ted, had healed and the front room became the new bunkhouse. The same two weeks saw five PAX riders buried. Brazos, the good-natured jester, and Hogan, the quiet one whose squeezebox was destroyed in the fire in the bunkhouse, died quickly on the night of the raid. Of the three others, Emilio lingered the longest, finally succumbing despite heroic efforts to the body-searing complications of pneumonia. His death was a sad blow. Never again would his talented fingers coax a sad or lilting melody of Spain from his guitar. Of Vance there was no word. He left the night her fever broke, the night he uttered his brutal malediction, and had been ten days away from the ranch, away from Karen.

Only when she was up and about did Karen learn of what happened on the night of the coyote wind. Marcelina had betrayed them, or at least such was the distasteful presumption, for someone within the walls had shot Emilio in the back at close range and then opened the hidden rear gate. Proof there was none, for Emilio never regained consciousness, but no one could believe he would ever allow anyone other than a trusted friend to walk up behind him

317

in the dark. Supposition of her guilt was compounded by her continued absence, during which no one had seen nor heard of her. The gate opened, Jaco with three confederates entered. The plan, evidently, was to hit the wall from behind in conjunction with the heavily mounted frontal attack. The men of the PAX boxed and fighting for their lives, Jaco would force entry to the house and wipe out opposition there, hopefully killing the old man in the process. The plan could well have worked had it not been for a series of flukes, the first of which was the unexpected absence and return of Maruja and the bullet she put in Jaco. Worse, Billy, intending to check on Emilio and report back to True, came face to face with the three renegades in the east courtyard. He reacted rapidly, killing one and holding the others at bay until Shorty came up and helped dispatch the remaining two. At the same time, Harley carried Ted into the house and Jaco, wounded and bleeding, was forced to withdraw. He luckily managed to pin down the older man in the dining room and make his escape through the patio, barely evading Shorty and Billy, hurrying to secure the back gate. Five minutes later the fight was over. The remaining renegades withdrew into the howling wind and driving rain, leaving the men of the PAX binding their wounds and waiting out a restless night.

The next morning dawned clear and bright, so cold everything was covered with a thin, glistening sheet of ice. Sun sparkled like diamonds from trees and stones and the awkward, huddled shapes of the dead. Twelve lifeless outlaws lay in and around the compound, and by the end of the day, six more were located in the immediate vicinity, some at the base of the nearby hills, others as far away as the banks of the Sabinal. One poor soul was in full view, sitting upright on the ground and, with sightless eyes, staring into the heart of the remnant of the coyote wind, the spirit wind. All was quiet and he glistened with the sheen of ice in a sparkling vigil of death.

Karen had been up and about for three days, during which, enclosed in the curtain of shock, she kept to her room save for occasional trips downstairs to eat whatever was available, careful at all times to go down only when the men were out and at work for she could not have borne the looks in their eyes. Once, on the stairs, Karen thought she heard Maruja humming as she prepared the evening meal. She hurried down the last steps, across the hall and plunged into the kitchen. The room was empty, chilled and devoid of life.

Two weeks to the day after the attack and on the fourth morning of her recovery, wan and drawn yet restless in spite of the desultory mood which gripped her, she ventured outside and climbed the ladder to the walkway, stood peering over the wall and into the distance. The snow was gone and the landscape a bleak brown, relieved only slightly by the dark green of cedar above her on the hills. Below her lay mute testimony of the fight—pocked, chipped and ragged adobe, a legacy of the many bullets that had spent their fury against the sturdy battlement. She straightened when a wisp of movement caught her eye and a rider to the south came into view and stopped, outlined on the crest of a knoll. *Vance?* Horse and rider stood unmoving.

"Mighty chilly, ma'am." Harley Guinn stood below her, climbed up the ladder. Of all the men left, only Harley seemed to bear no blame, hold no grudge against her. The others, she knew, shared Vance's estimation of her value, but, and for this she was thankful, to a lesser degree. But then, they had never expected as much from her. *What did I expect of myself?*

"The sun will warm us some," she remarked, eyes lifted to the cloudless sky. "Who is that?" Harley followed her gaze toward the retreating figure.

"That would be True. Saddled up an' lit out. Never seen him quite like the way he is, an' I been with True Paxton nigh on to twenty year. He's hit hard, ma'am. He's hit almighty hard."

The decision to ride after him came quickly, from where she did not know. "Harley, saddle up my sorrel for me, will you please?"

"What . . . ? Oh, yes ma'am. But. . . ." He paused, embarrassed.

"Yes?"

"We ain't got no saddles. That is, all we got is reg'lar saddles. Yours . . . all the sidesaddles got burnt in the fire."

"A 'reg'lar' saddle will be fine, Harley," Karen said, smiling. "I'll be back in a minute." She hurried down the steps and into the house, to Elizabeth's workroom where

319

she dug into an old trunk, made up a small bundle and carried it to her room. Standing in front of the window, she faltered. *Am I strong enough? Will he want to see me, talk to me? What will he say when he sees me in . . . ?* But the time was for action, not questions. Quickly she stripped and donned a washed-out pair of jeans and warm flannel shirt of faded red plaid, earlier Elizabeth's. The unfamiliar clothing felt strangely uncomfortable, but just as strangely exciting. She had wanted adventure and now she would seek adventure. A Hampton was not one to let tragedy stand in her way. Tragedy, rather, should lead to renewal of life, reassertion of strength. She squared her shoulders, confronted the new image in the mirror and smiled at the reflection. "I shall never wear men's clothing," she had said, such a long—or was it short—time ago. The statement was an earlier, empty, mistaken piece of society-bred silliness. If men's clothes were what it would take, she would wear them with a will. Determined, she pulled the silver pins from her hair and tossed them negligently to the table. "Let them lie there. They've done me no good," she told herself sternly. Shaking the curls down around her shoulders, she stepped out of the room and headed downstairs, without a look back at the gown crumpled in the corner.

The house was quiet, the men gone, riding north to locate the remnants of the herd and drive the scattered beeves back down into the valley, for the storm had played havoc with them. Ted was in the rear patio, grudgingly handling the cooking chores, for the wounds he had received prevented him from working with the others. Seeing him, Karen felt guilty. The hearth in the kitchen had remained cold and unproductive, for she had not been able to bring herself to enter what had been so obviously Maruja's domain. She stopped, looking at Ted's back. *The truth is I was being silly. I was afraid of the memory of Jaco and my own. . . .* Ted, sensing her presence, turned and stared at her, looked back immediately to the campfire to stir the kettle of beans. Sharing Vance's estimation of her more than the others, he found it difficult to look at her and not let the anger show. In addition—and almost as much as the men who had to eat his fare—he resented her for not doing the cooking. Because she wouldn't, he was stuck with a woman's work. The Comanche and white in him agreed.

The task was onerous. He stayed only through loyalty to True and the absent Vance.

She walked to him, stood by his side and looked into the pot. "Let the fire die down, Ted. I'll be back in a while and get supper ready in the kitchen," she said, smiling at him before heading for the front gate. Ted stared after her in amazement. There was simply no way to figure out white women. Men's clothes, now. He didn't know what was happening, but if she was going to cook it was fine with him. He dropped the ladle and strode away from the fire.

The sorrel was waiting, saddled with a regular saddle, a man's saddle. Harley, already shocked by the idea of a real lady riding astride a horse, was blatantly surprised at Karen's apparel, for always before she had deigned to wear nothing but finery. Without a word he helped her into the saddle and watched her ride off. A moment later Ted Morning Sky was at his side, watching with him. "That woman," Harley said in a strangled voice, "has to be full of more surprises than any other three I ever seen."

Well away from the ranch proper, Karen noticed a definite change come over her. For the first time since the attack she was away from the confinement of her room and the *hacienda* where, infected by Vance's punishing recriminations and her own overwhelming sense of guilt, she had fallen into a moody, dreamlike rhythm of listless malaise. Life had gone on, but without direction. The PAX existed, as did she, but little more. Vance was gone, where, no one knew. But one could punish oneself for only so long. One could accept punishment for only so long. Sooner or later a person of strength must either succumb or accept the crime, accept the punishment and climb out from under both. Clear-headed, able to think and attack problems, she sat straight in the saddle, let the terrible burdens slough off her and drop behind with the dead grass. She breathed deeply and the air was fresher than ever she remembered. She looked up and the sky was bright and clean, an infinite sea of blue. She looked around, and through the brown grass she could see hints of green, fresh and sweet, the sure promise of a spring to come, of the annual resurgence of life.

Past the third hill she stopped and glanced down, following unconsciously the route True had taken. Some yards farther along the trail she reined in suddenly. Looking back, then down, she realized with proud amazement she had been following the tracks, reading, with no more thought than a book, the sign left by True's horse. Ted and Billy's training had indeed taken effect, and by his tracks she could plainly see he was heading for the family cemetery where now lay three generations. She knew a shorter way. Urging the sorrel into a gallop, she rode hard, exulting in her newfound sense of ability, of responsibility, of capability.

She followed the all too familiar trail up one hill and down into the draw which lay like a moat around the hill of the graves. The sorrel lunged up the final slope and stopped by True's ground-tethered roan gelding. True himself was standing just inside the wrought iron fence, a thin, bowed, weary figure among the graves. Karen tied the sorrel to the post and walked quietly across the grassy field as the gate creaked shut on rusty hinges. The north wind, a zephyr, she thought, rolling the sound of the word through her mind, was chillier than expected and she buttoned the flannel shirt high up her neck before stepping over the fence and to True's side.

He glanced around as she drew close, peered at her garments as if seeing them for the first time. "It's still winter. Should have worn a coat."

"I thought the shirt would be enough."

He was standing before the two freshly dug mounds of earth. Two? Of course there would be two. Maruja's and . . . her pulse throbbed heavily as she read the words burned so recently into the cross thrust into the ground at the head of the pitifully small mound of earth.

ETHAN PAXTON
A son
Born February 8, 1874—Died February 8, 1874.
In Darkness and Fire

Her son . . . and her husband's. *Ethan.* It was a good name. He would have been a bright, happy child. The attack came on a Tuesday. *Tuesday's child is full of grace . . . Ethan . . . Ethan . . .* a ragged sob welled in her throat and she tried unsuccessfully to stifle it. True laid a tentative hand on her shoulder and, almost on reflex, she turned and buried her face against the old man's chest.

"There, there. . . ." True said uncomfortably, patting her shoulder. "It's all right, daughter. . . . It's all right." *Daughter* . . . he wondered at the word he'd so long avoided. Looking over her shoulder, he read the faded words. SARAH ANN PAXTON . . . *Well, why shouldn't I? A man needs a daughter, same as he needs a son.*

The racking sobs finally ceased and True led her to a granite outcropping that formed a perfect view of the vast, distance-devouring plains stretching forever to the south. "Did you see him, True?"

"Delivered him," came the brusque reply.

Karen looked at him sharply inquisitive. "You mean, you. . . ." She blushed deeply.

"Shouldn't let it fret you. I done four a' my own, plus how many calves an' foals I can't remember. It ain't somethin' a man dwells on." He paused, the memory still strong in him. "Nor forgets, once he's done it."

"What did he look like? I mean . . . ." she faltered, groping for words. ". . . was he . . . all right?"

True's face was rock hard, all emotion held carefully in check. "He looked fine," he said at last.

"Was he . . . ?"

"He's dead, Karen. You can ask an' ask, but he'll still be dead, an' all the askin'll bring you is more pain." He gestured with tired eloquence toward the row of simple graves. "I know."

The tension eased slowly, soaked by the beauty and quietude of the unbroken vista before them. When Karen spoke again, her voice was stronger, matter-of-fact. "Where has he gone, True?"

"Vance?"

"Yes."

The old man's eyes squinted in thought. "Hard to tell. The boy's ridin' the devil. Got a hurt eatin' away at him. Hard to tell where he'll end up, but when he gets there I only hope he's got the sense to realize he can't ever escape, 'cause what he's runnin' from is inside. The only way to face that sort of trouble is to come back to where it all begun an' face it down."

"Will he come back?"

"You want him to? Knowin' the way he feels about . . . about what happened back there?"

"Yes."

True smiled into the distance and nodded. "I knew you had grit. From that first day you come here. I could tell."

The wind sighed down the long hills. Karen glanced back at the graves. "Perhaps he's right, you know. Perhaps it is . . . was . . . my fault."

"Nonsense," True grumbled. "We start handin' out guilt, ain't one of us but is gonna get his share. If anyone is to blame, it's me." Karen waited, puzzled by his remark. True tossed a chip of granite, watched the white speck tumble and careen down the long slope, disappear from sight. He rose and walked back to the graves. Karen sensed his need to talk, followed a few paces behind him. They stood together for several silent moments, letting the drifting hawk overhead the shadows playing across the far valleys seal the new covenant between father and daughter. "Jaco is my son."

No pronouncement could have stunned her more. "Jaco . . . !"

"It happened during the war of '36. One of those things you don't mean to happen. I'd been at the Alamo, but had rode out for help." True's voice faded and a faraway look came into his eyes as he recalled that wild ride and the impossible odds he'd faced. "Should've been killed that night, I reckon, but Firetail—the best damned horse I ever owned or rode—saved my life."

Karen remembered the painting of the hammerheaded roan stallion that hung in a place of honor over the mantel in the living room. "He must have been some horse."

"Yup," True agreed. "At any rate, Elizabeth was gone, for all I knew dead, like lots of others was. Weren't a day went by when a man couldn't a got hisself killed, an' that afore noon.

"Anyway, I hooked up with a bunch of folks lookin' for Sam Houston's army after the Alamo fell, an' among 'em was a little Mex beauty with black hair an' eyes like fire. Danced for us, one night, she did, an' made us forget the Mex army breathin' down our backs an' that, chances were, none of us would live long enough to put down roots. Me an' her . . . I followed her from the campfire 'cause I could see she had her eye on me. There was no family, no tomorrow. Only me an' her an' the wind in the cedars an' the moon overhead.

"Well, two days later, we found Sam Houston, an' durned if the next day Elizabeth an' the folks she was with didn't show up in time to help us whip the Mexes once an' for all at San Jacinto. Found Elizabeth again after peace was declared an' we took up where we left off, tryin' to build a life.

"It was twenty years later I run across Maruja again." Karen gasped in surprise but True ignored her reaction and went on. "I was on a scout to look for some horses been stolen from me an' run across a band of Comanches attackin' a sheep herder's spread. I helped run off the war party, an' then found out the people I rescued was her an' her family. Ever'thing they had was wiped out by the Comanches an' Maruja was married an' pregnant again so I brought 'em back to the PAX an' took 'em on, with neither of us lettin' on we'd ever seen each other before. Three months later Marcelina was born, an' two month after that Alfredo, her daddy, taken off. Disappeared one day an' never was seen since. Injuns, probably. Maruja stayed. She would have left, but Elizabeth insisted." He paused, glancing down at his wife's grave. "To this day I think Elizabeth knew about what happened long ago. Knew . . . an' must of understood, for she never said a word.

"It wasn't until after news of the renegade, Jaco, first come to us I found out he was my son. Maruja had born him that winter after we'd first met, an' when he was eighteen, told him he was my son. Poor all his life an' already hatin' whites, the boy was furious. Took to walkin' around in a state, fussin' an' fillin' hisself with more an' more hate. The name Paxton was pretty wide known in this part of the country an' it didn't take too much ta set him afire. Figured he shoulda had his share in the PAX, an' knowin' he wouldn't, swore he'd find time someday to kill me. Wasn't long before he'd killed a man, lit a shuck for Old Mexico an' hit the renegade trail. Within a year he had hisself the name of a bad man an' started raidin' for real. I tried to get word to him, but the messenger I sent never returned. Instead, we found his boots an' . . . ." he hesitated briefly, ". . . part of him . . . nailed to a cedar down at the brake. I knew the boy had a hate in him, but to kill his own mother. . . ." He looked at Karen, his eyes moist with emotion.

"So you see, I am the cause of this Jaco. I am responsible for Maruja's death. And for your Ethan's, the Lord rest his little soul. We answer for our actions, daughter. Oh, how we answer for them. No man escapes."

How tired he looks, thought Karen. I have never seen him

this way. A strong man, yet frail as well.

True knelt beside Maruja's grave. *"Vaya con Dios, amiga. Vaya con Dios."* He straightened, turned to face Karen, his face set sternly. "Vance knows none of this, about Jaco." He paused meaningfully. "Or Maruja."

"Nor will he ever," Karen assured him. "Unless you wish it so."

"A lot can happen in a lifetime. I'll leave it to your judgement," True said. Without looking back, he walked stiffly toward the horse. "We best head on back. It ain't gonna get any warmer, an' you with nothin' more'n that shirt." He started to take off his coat but Karen wouldn't let him. .

"I don't need it, True. I feel warmer than I have in a long time."

He glanced at her speculatively. "I don't need it neither, you know."

"I know," she agreed gently.

They kept their horses to a walk, following a northern trail Karen had never seen before, crossing the backbone of the hills on the western edge of the valley until they topped the crown of the hill directly opposite the ranch. Karen started to guide the sorrel into the descent but True restrained her, his hand on her arm. "Karen. I been thinkin' on it an' figure there's no way to get around it."

"What are you talking about?"

"I'm gonna have Harley take you back to San Antone."

Karen flushed, her heart quickening its pace. He wanted to send her away again. "Why . . . ?"

True pulled off his hat and brushed his fingers through his silver-gray hair. "Short-handed as we are, Harley tells me some of the boys are quittin'. Come tomorrow, there'll be only me an' Ted, neither of us fit to scare a steer out of a barn, much less the brush, Harley, What's About an' Shorty. Can't blame the others for leavin'. We've had a bad year and' don't no way does it look like things are gonna get better. Why, look down there." He gestured to the panorama spreading below them. "The place looks like when I come upon it thirty-eight years ago. Burnt ground, ruined buildings . . . an empty house. The spirit's gone from the place. Maybe they're doin' the smart thing. Anyway, this here's no

326

place for a woman.''

"You brought Elizabeth here. You packed up and traveled to a spot miles from home and hearth, neighbors and kin, surrounded by hostile Indians, to a ruined ranch much worse than what I see now. You brought her and expected her to stay and do her fair share. You did not send her back to San Antonio. She stayed and helped build.''

"Yes,'' True mused. "But that's different. Different times, different woman, different. . . .''

"No sir, it is not,'' Karen said boldly. Erect in the saddle, resolve grew in her, for at that moment she knew what needed to be done, what she would do. Unseen by True, the strength of the Hamptons combined with the dramatic circumstances of the past months. Karen Olivia Hampton, the silly, prideful girl of society, was a creature of the past, beyond her now forever. The mysterious alchemy of the soul, the mix of unknown elements reacting in the presence of the catalyst of tragedy, worked the miracle of transformation. Aware of the change and at peace with herself at last, Karen Paxton surely and deftly spurred the sorrel down the hill toward the waiting remnants of the PAX.

True kept the roan from following, held the animal back. He chuckled to himself, smiled for the first time in two weeks. "No sir, it is not,'' he repeated, echoing her words. "Come on, horse. Let's go see what that young 'un's up to.''

The riders had yet to return and Ted was nowhere to be seen. She stripped the saddle from the sorrel, fed him and let him loose with the other horses gathered in the compound before entering the house, its interior gloomy and shuttered. The door closed behind her and she stood alone in the silence. *Elizabeth, I love you. And you too, Maruja. But you'll have to step aside now. There'll be no more time for mourning.* Her face set, she moved purposefully about the room, opening windows and shutters, lighting lamps and setting a fire in the east hearth, waiting only until a cheerful blaze danced crisply, sending out heat to the cold room.

Satisfied, she strode determinedly to the kitchen, into the musty, haunted air of the very spot she had so assiduously avoided. The hearth was cold, the air dank. She gathered wood from out back, bringing in a huge armload, laying and lighting a fire before returning twice more in order to

327

fill the woodbox to overflowing. Soon a roaring blaze combated the chill and the smell of woodsmoke drove the spirits from the room. She found a broom inside the cellar door, and glancing down into the darkness, was stricken with panic and pain as she remembered the terrible fall and its aftermath. Her resolve faltered, weakened. . . . "No. I'm not ready for that yet," she muttered as she took the broom and closed the door firmly. There would be time enough for such a confrontation later. Briskly, she attacked the dust gathered on the floor, forcing herself to ignore the long, brown-red smear on the wall and floor near the dining room doorway. There would be time enough for that, too. The floor swept and the attack on the dishes and work surfaces well under way, she didn't hear the latch raise nor the rear door open, didn't see Ted enter and stop short, gaping in surprise at the burst of activity.

"I saw smoke from the chimney. For a moment I thought . . ." He stared inquisitively at her.

Karen whirled, startled and about to scream, at the sound of the voice behind her. *Jaco . . . !* Relieved, she smiled grimly. "I'm cleaning out the ghosts."

Ted nodded in taciturn agreement. "It is good." He glanced over his shoulder, checking the patio. "I will carry in the pot."

"No. That is woman's work. Go now. Dinner will be ready at the usual time."

Dark was descending on the valley when the ranch hands rode in from the northern range. Five of the eight riders intended to draw their wages and leave on the following morning despite the protestations of Harley and Billy. All reined up shy of the hacienda when Shorty pointed out the tendril of smoke drifting from the back chimney. "I tol' you," one of the riders exclaimed. "The durn place is ha'nted. Y'all better pack your warbags an' come with us. Ain't no call to hang aroun' where ha'nts is waitin' for you."

What's About sniffed the air. "Well, sir, if that is a ghost, she surely cooks a mighty fine smellin' pot a' chili."

Harley inhaled deeply. "That ain't all, neither. I smell bear sign. Ghost it may be, but if it makes bear sign, I'm ready an' willin' to take my chances." He spurred his horse into a gallop, the others close behind.

A half hour later, their animals stripped, rubbed down

and fed, they gathered by the well, washing faces and hands, wetting and slicking back hair despite the brisk evening air. When they filed in through the front door they found True and Ted sitting in front of the fire, surrounded by the fragrant odor of hot chili, *tortillas* and *frijoles* and the unmistakable scent of freshly-baked doughnuts. True had to know what was going on but, as the riders crowded around the fire to warm up, only grinned in response to the unasked questions. Someone coughed nervously. Another rolled a smoke. A third inspected first the ceiling and then the floor, both with great care. All waited, none daring to speak.

When Karen appeared in the dining room arch, the men stared in awe, hardly able to believe she was the same woman they had last seen two weeks earlier. "Dinner's on, boys. Come and get it," she said, as natural as if she'd said it every day for the past ten years. She wore a Mexican blouse whose thick cotton lacing merely accentuated her voluptuous form and a thickly-woven gypsy skirt, a print of red, white and black, which swirled almost to her ankles. Hair the color of straw beneath a midsummer sun hung unbound, flowing in gentle waves over pale creamy shoulders. Around her was an aura of daring and almost forbidden beauty, and her smile was a warmth to contend with the glowing fireplace. She stood confidently in the arch and the tired but fully alert riders were compelled to pass her as they filed into the dining room, each hesitating as he walked by her, then moving awkwardly toward the table, the smell of food forgotten for the moment.

Dinner ended when the men, groaning, pushed themselves away from the first good meal in two weeks. Karen excused herself and asked them to remain seated. She reappeared moments later with a small iron box in her hands and stationed herself at the head of the table. All eyes stared, mesmerized, as she opened the box and withdrew a packet of currency and a leather pouch of gold, placing them on the table next to the money box. "There are some of you who have spoken of leaving in the morning. I would be sorry to see any man here go, but I can understand why some might, and will hold nothing against anyone who does. You will want to draw your wages, of course, and True and I are prepared to settle all accounts now as you will probably be anxious to leave early. You go with our prayers and our thanks. You have been faithful to the brand and we could ask nothing more. I've fixed starter dough, sandwiches and bear sign enough for each man who wants to leave. Should any man here come back through this valley, there'll always be a place for him at the Paxton table." She paused, leaned slightly toward them to emphasize her words. "We *will* be here, gentlemen. This is Paxton range. This is our home. We will be here."

The men at the table sat in uneasy silence, furtively looking at each other and the gold, then to Karen and beyond her to the dream that had brought True and Elizabeth to the valley, the dream Karen had assumed and which now shone brightly on her face, filled the room with her presence and the quitters with shame. The leader of those who had been about to leave coughed nervously. "Excuse me, ma'am."

"Yes, Broadus," she said.

"Ma'am . . . uh . . . I reckon I'd best turn in. I got to check the north range again tomorrow an' round up them strays we missed today."

Someone started to laugh. Broadus looked about uncomfortably, then grinned sheepishly and joined the laughter which spread infectiously around the table. Not a man asked for wages. Karen took a smaller sack of coins and tossed it to Harley.

The old-timer's face registered shocked surprise and the laughter faded abruptly. "Not me, Miz Paxton. I don't want to quit. Never did."

"Harley, you and What's About . . ." Billy grinned wanly, ". . . ride down to Uvalde tomorrow. We need half a dozen men. Use your own judgement. Just remember, only the best are good enough to ride with the men of the PAX." She looked at each of the hard faces around her, staring at her with mute appreciation, each one obviously moved by her words.

Shorty broke the silence, slid back his chair and stood. "I don't know about the rest of you, but I got work to see to tomorrow. I'll take the north range with you, Broadus."

"Okay."

Another voice spoke up. "The rest of us'll start on Silver Canyon. Must be two hundred head stuck up in there somewheres." Grunts of approval followed as everyone pushed back their chairs, stood and bade Karen goodnight.

Their Karen, she was, for in a way, and through a curious chemistry, she did belong to each one of them as they, in turn, did to her. True, who had remained silent through the meal, was the last to leave the room. Following the men into the front room for a final smoke before heading upstairs to sleep, he paused in the door to look back at the woman his son had brought to the ranch. That society Yankee, he playfully reminded himself. She met his eyes . . . and when he winked at her, by golly if she didn't boldly wink right back.

CHAPTER II

Karen found herself serving in a capacity other than purely cosmetic for the first time in her life. The discovery there was more to living than a turn of a phrase, a beautiful coiffure or an elegant pose designed to show off a pretty profile filled her with awe. She was useful! Men depended on her! The very idea that work was not slavery came as a profound and delightful shock. Here was knowledge her mother would never possess, never comprehend. More exciting was the feeling she had wakened from a deep and befuddled sleep to her true role in life, and she accepted the multiple challenges of that role with a relish, reveled in the pride of a thousand daily accomplishments, large and small. She was up at the cold crack of dawn. First light saw the men fed and on their way. Alone in the house she started the daily chores. She prepared bread for later in the day, sewed, cleaned, went over Maruja's instructions for the spring garden and, finding the seeds in neatly arranged packages in the dead woman's quarters, laid out the garden and planted. She made time to accompany Ted, still on the mend, to the sun-warmed hills where he continued her lessons in the lore of the land. An avid and rapid learner, she soaked up information and stored it away for certain use. Karen's metamorphosis was complete, and with the silent but evident approbation of True, she took over more and more of the responsibilities of running the ranch, putting to good use Maruja's earlier, unheeded lessons and her own keen, native intelligence.

The unspoken gloom of early February melted as the men set to work. The severe winter had scattered the herd widely, mostly because there had been no one to handle the cattle during the critical time of the ice storm, and until the complicated and wearing task of searching each distant, secluded valley and canyon was completed, no one could rest. It soon became evident the herd had been decimated, for every day the tally of carcasses found by the hands rose grimly. When a rider from the north told them a small ranch had been wiped out, they listened carefully. Over two hundred head of mixed stock were wandering loose and could be had for little more than the effort of rounding them up. True, feeling his oats with the coming of the warm days, took four men to buy the herd and drive them back, an unusual trip for the middle of March, but more than worth it at the price asked.

Karen was left nominally in charge, with Harley acting as foreman while Ted continued to regain his strength, carried on with Karen's lessons and scouted the far reaches of the PAX range, keeping an eye out for trouble and spotting strays which he hazed back to Sabinal Canyon where the other riders could pick them up more easily. As important as was the work of rounding up the herd, Karen instigated and pushed the men to begin the work of re-building the ranch. Every day at least two men were split from the ten available and set to work at the less rewarding labors of cutting trees and snaking them back to the building site. Harley had chosen well on his trip to Uvalde and the men he brought back were workers, not shirkers, and though they grumbled incessantly, complained they were hired as cowboys and not lumberjacks, they fell into the spirit of the work, coaxed on with liberal doses of bear sign served with an irresistible smile. The adobe skeleton of the bunkhouse had survived serious damage from the fire and soon the first logs were notched to size and ready to become the roof. The last Saturday in March, the day True rode in with the new stock, Karen declared the next day, Sunday, a *fiesta* and had one of the men kill a yearling steer. Together the men put the roof timbers in place, laid the roof itself and then sat down to a huge dinner of beans and barbecue, followed by an enormous platter of *pan dulce*, the sweet Mexican bread Maruja had often pre-pared, the recipe for which Karen had found in the kitchen. After the meal there was a general exodus as the men prepared to move their gear to the new bunkhouse, but Karen insisted they wait a few days until the building, freshened by the spring rains, should dry out. At the same time, she decided the hands would continue to take their evening meals in the *hacienda* until the bunkhouse could be equipped with more hospitable furnishings—bunk beds, tables, chairs and a new stove, for the old one had broken when a beam fell on it and cracked the firebox.

Karen worked harder than ever before, but the multitude of responsibilities and tasks, rather than wearing her down, left her pleasantly exhausted and satisfied. She could not help, however, missing Vance, for underlying her state of exultation of a job well done was an ever-present and growing concern for his whereabouts. Where the whims of grief had led him she could only venture to guess. No one had seen or heard of him, not even the drifters who passed through from time to time. True assured her he would return, but the confidence with which he spoke, while comforting, also left her more than a little fearful. What would happen when he did come back? Would the emotional chasm between them become an insurmountable obstacle? Would he stay? Leave again? Could they take up again where they'd left off, or was there nothing left on which to build? There was little time for such thoughts until the day was done. But then, in the solitude of the evening, in the quiet of the night, her thoughts turned on themselves in a confusing mix. She felt wronged, for though she shared his profound sorrow, still he had deserted her, his accusations tempered by neither love nor forgiveness. At these times she could stand the constriction of her room no longer and walked out to pass a lonely vigil on the walls of the compound, afraid of what Vance might have become, yet wishing desperately for his return and the touch of his hands. Below her in the shadows, Ted, unseen and unheard, kept watch over his friend's wife, wondering at her thoughts as she stared out into the silent vastness of the hills and sky which kept her company.

March brought visitors to the ranch. Drifters, men of shady pasts and uncertain futures, men riding "the grub-line," as they called it, looking for a meal and a place to spend the night. Karen, hesitating at first, opened her table to such men only because such was expected of her. But after the first few, she accepted the custom as commonplace. No longer afraid, she lay aside her misgivings and opened the door willingly to one and all of good intentions, taking added comfort in the fact that either Ted or Billy always managed to be near on such occasions. Gradually, she learned to read the character behind the rough and oft-times fearsome countenances, learned a man could not be judged by the state of his clothes or the condition of his beard. The eyes were the real clue to a man's character, for in them he could hide nothing. Two such men, looking for work, were hired on at Karen's request and with Harley's approval. Karen's judgement proved sound for they were reliable, and the one who claimed to be a carpenter when he wasn't chasing cows, proved his word. Within no more than three days, work was well under way on the barn. Soon the walls were halfway up and the ranch was rapidly taking on the look of prosperity it had enjoyed before the raid.

The day after the *fiesta*, True and Karen sat down together and went through the PAX bookkeeping. Never one long on figures, and uncomfortable with the reckoning required, True was happy to let Karen do most of the work while he spun yarns that stretched back to the Paxton's first years in America. Later, it was decided the spring trip to San Antonio would have to be moved forward. Supplies were short as a result of the raid and arrangements would have to be made to cover their extra expenses incurred in the purchase of the cattle. Karen would make the trip in True's stead, for the drive had taken more out of him than he'd expected and he was in no shape, as he was reluctantly forced to admit, to take four more grueling days in the saddle. Harley balked at going all the way to San Antonio when Uvalde would have served amply, but the necessity of visiting the bank and arranging a delay in paying off the note made the difference. "If you're goin'," he grumbled, "you might as well pick up some lumbered wood for beds in the bunkhouse, an' you'd better go on an' get a new wagon too, seein' as the big 'un burned. Lord knows we don't need no more mules."

The next morning they left on horseback, Karen, Ted, Morning Sky and two of the new men, a long-legged sharp-eyed rider named Huller and a hard-bitten cowman who called himself W. Bell. What the "W" stood for, Karen never knew. Leading four mules to haul back the wagon they would purchase, they took the back trails, the same she had ridden once before with Vance. The mildly pleasant weather made the going easy and Karen, remembering her earlier experiences on the trail when she had been all helpless and useless, took great pleasure in refining and showing off her newfound abilities as a cook. Huller, trail-wise as any man, taught her how to make trail dessert, hardtack covered with brown sugar and fried in bacon drippings. Though not exactly what Karen would have called *haute cuisine*, she had to admit, after the first tentative bite, the concoction was tasty and a perfect complement to a trail-cooked meal. When, the second morning out, she woke before dawn and had the coffee going before the men woke up, she realized with some surprise and pride she was becoming what the dime novels so badly described as a "western woman." Two hours later, Ted watched out of the corner of his eye as Karen broke into silent laughter. He didn't know, but she'd just realized she'd drunk two cups of coffee that morning, two of the blackest, strongest cups of coffee a man could want, and enjoyed them.

Heads turned as they crossed the San Pedro and entered the outskirts of San Antonio. Who was the tawny-limbed, golden-haired beauty who dressed in coarsely-woven blouse and flowery print skirt as the women kneeling at the creek? Who was the *señorita* dressed as *los Indios* yet with the manner and bearing of a *princesa*, one of noble birth, whose retinue was a half-breed Comanche and a pair of down-at-the-heel, dangerous-looking *gringos*? When the riders were close enough for the brand on their horses to be read, the women buzzed with excitement. A fine, eastern-dressed lady had ridden west to the PAX. If the *señora* was the same woman, she had changed indeed. The subject filled their day and, later that night, was discussed around the fires in a hundred *jacals* and *jacalitos*.

Once in town, Karen handed the list of supplies and money to Ted. If spent well it would barely cover their needs, but Karen felt confident of Ted's ability to dicker for the best possible price for, as True had told her, "No one drives a harder bargain than an Injun."

"Would you not like one of us to ride with you?" the Comanche asked, upset at leaving Karen on her own. "Bell can go with you an' Huller can scout for the wagon."

Karen laughed. Admittedly, San Antonio could be rough at night, for despite the law's vigilance, there was no way Hodgdon's deputies could watch over every trouble spot. But her six weeks' stay had taught her more than a few things. The city was safe enough by day if one took care to stay away from the worst bars and *cantinas* where, on the slightest pretext, violence could bloom at any moment. "I learned my lesson the last time, Ted. I can find the bank easily enough. You go on. We'll meet at five in front of San Fernando Cathedral."

Before the men could protest further, she confidently wheeled the sorrel and trotted the animal down a narrow side street. W. Bell looked at Ted. "Maybe I better follow her anyways."

The Comanche considered briefly. Karen was his friend's woman, and while his friend was gone he felt responsible for her safety. Someone should watch the blonde one he had grown to respect and like. White women were strange creatures, this one more so than any other he had known. A man got a good feeling just looking at her. He scowled to himself. His friend was a fool to leave such a woman. "Keep out of sight. She learns fast, but does not know as much as she would like to believe." His mind made up, he pointed Huller toward the wagon shops and turned his steeldust toward the stores where he would spend the afternoon.

Karen rode through the streets as if she owned them, unaware of the man who watched over her, who trailed her like a shadow. Six weeks in San Antonio had taught her much and she took great pleasure in her knowledge of the town, reveling in newfound strength and independence. The side streets wound among haphazardly laid-out *jacalitos*, crude houses built of sunbleached brick and bound thatch, tenanted in the main by the Mexican element of the city. Three children bolted from a side alley, laughing, shouting their enthusiasm, a barrel hoop rolling ahead of them. Each time the hoop wandered off course, one of the youths struck it with a stick and sent the makeshift toy careening forward. Karen reined in the sorrel as the children ran past in front of her. Suddenly they noticed her and stopped. Two boys and a little girl, their faces besmudged with the dirt of the street, stared with bright and innocent eyes at the vision before them. Here was a strange sight for the *barrio*—a *señora* dressed as one of their own but with hair shining like *el sol*, with skin like a *castellano*. The *barrio* was no place for such a woman.

"*Buenos dias,*" Karen said, remembering one of the few phrases learned from Maruja. The hoop, with no one to guide it, rattled off to the side and interrupted a flock of feeding hens who squawked their dismay and scattered in all directions. The commotion shattered the spell Karen's presence had woven around the children and they scampered back from the horse toward the safety of a nearby door, calling in shrill voices for their mothers to come and see the *señora blanca*. The way clear, Karen urged the sorrel down the passageway, emerging into Military Plaza and the early afternoon crowds choking the marketplace, not yet cleared for *siesta* time.

The Plaza hummed with strident cries of vendors and buyers alike, haggling over the slightest purchase as if their very lives depended on the gain or loss of a *centavo* or two. The air hung heavy with a thousand odors—peppers, *frijoles*, beef, the heavy smell of frying grease. Above all she was assailed by the sweet smell of eggs frying. Eggs! The PAX hadn't seen an egg since she and Vance had returned from San Antonio in November. Dismounting, she walked the sorrel in the direction of the smell, arriving at a tiny stand where an old woman, wrinkled and sere, sat behind a small brazier on which lay a slab of cast iron. To the woman's left was a wicker basket filled with eggs which, for a *peseta* apiece, would be fried to the *señora's* directions and rolled in a hot *tortilla*, freshly made. Karen's mouth watered at the very idea and, without thinking twice, she reached in a pocket and pulled out a half dollar, not stopping to haggle as well she knew she should. The *vieja* scowled and glanced sideways at her, no doubt wishing she had asked for double the price, then quickly patted out a *tortilla* and dropped the flat dough on one side of the grill. Seconds later a dab of grease sputtered on the other side. Staring as if she'd never before seen the progress, Karen watched the old woman break open the shell and drop the egg onto the sizzling plate of iron, sniffed appreciatively as the aroma flooded the air. Soon the sandwich, hot and greasy, was handed to her and she took the first succulent bites, laughing with the old woman as the yolk broke and ran onto her hand before she could lick it away.

Famished from the long ride since their early breakfast, she finished off the first egg in short order. The edge off her hunger, she led the sorrel away from the stand as she slowly ate the second, taking time to savor every bite. Across the way the bright sound of birds calling rose above the noise of the crowd and she ambled in that direction, discovered a series of stalls selling cardinals, mockingbirds and canaries in homemade wicker cages. She hadn't seen a canary since Washington. Only a little homesick, she stood and gazed fondly at the tiny yellow fluffs, lost in the gentle songs of the imprisoned birds.

The sound of bells rolled over the plaza. Twice the big, low bell rung. Two o'clock. There was little time left to get to the bank. Promising herself to return to the stalls and buy a pair of canaries for the kitchen at the ranch, she hurried away north, crossing the plaza and skirting the false front shops, stores, *casinos*, saloons and music halls which doubled as theaters. *Macbeth* was gone, replaced by the single word *Othello*. Evidently the same troupe was in residence, for the face of Othello was the same as the late Macbeth, save for darker skin and a new wig. Amused but with no time to look, she mounted and rode down the street past a woman who stepped out of Miller's Bar. For a moment the two women's eyes met. Karen turned in the saddle and stared hard. The prostitute was the same woman Bodine had known, the one he had driven from the carnal bed in which he planned. . . . The scene ran quickly through her head and she shuddered briefly. *Could that have been I, cowering in that horrible room filled with gunsmoke and fear so long ago? Long? No. Not even a year*. . . . It was hard to believe the changes that had taken place. She had been frightened since then, had plummeted to the depths of panic but two months past. She now saw the fear as the price she had to pay, for rather than breaking her spirit, the claws of despair stripped away the social trappings, tore away the last vestiges of the "belle of Washington" she now despised, and revealed in her place the resolute woman who, she marveled, had rallied to partake of the joy of life, and even now assisted in the management of one of the more important ranches in their part of the country.

Confident, she urged the horse onward, unaware of Bell who, hungry himself, stopped briefly to buy a *burrito*, hot beans wrapped in a *tortilla*. Ahead of her an unruly commotion among a group of teamsters effectively blocked access to Commerce Street. Unconcerned and in a hurry, she turned off the main road and took a side alley out of the plaza. When Bell looked up from paying for his food, she

340

was gone. Cursing, he rode hurriedly down the street, forcing his way through the teamsters. Still he could not see her. He headed his horse for Commerce street where he would be sure to pick her up again.

Traveling but a dozen yards down the alley, Karen noted the course she had chosen would take her past the door of a secluded *cantina* fronting the lane. An unimposing structure, she paid little attention until the sound of coarse laughter, the tinkling of shattered glass and a shouted curse issued from the *jacalito*. She could afford to pass Miller's Bar without flinching, but here was an unknown place, away from the main road and help. She guided the sorrel to the opposite side of the street and kept a wary eye on the door, ready to break into a gallop at the slightest hint of trouble. So intent was she on the *cantina* she failed to see a brutish figure lurch drunkenly from one of the hovels to her left. The sorrel, made skittish by the sudden appearance of the man, danced back nervously, almost losing his rider. Regaining her balance, Karen tried to still the horse, to send him down the street away from the half-hidden shape in front of her, but a massive hairy fist caught the bridle, restraining all progress. Karen forced a note of calm into her voice. "Sir, I would suggest you release your hold."

The rowdy leered up at her. Karen jerked on the reins but the man held tight, pulling the frightened animal's head down and reaching up for the coarse cotton blouse. "Talks nice," he muttered drunkenly. "Let's see how she feels." Karen slipped a booted foot from the stirrup and drove the pointed toe into the man's face, catching him low in the cheekbone and knocking him backward into a puddle of slop, refuse tossed from a nearby window. The sorrel, free, reared back as the cursing bully staggered to his feet, his hand swiping across the top of his boot and drawing a cruel-looking dagger from a hidden sheath.

"Brownrig," a voice called from the front of the *cantina*. Both Karen and the drunk turned toward the new participant. He was a man of medium height, dressed in a frock coat and gray vest over a white lace shirt, hatless with a shock of blond hair newly cropped. Thick wire-rimmed glasses made his eyes appear slightly smaller than they actually were and gave him the mild-mannered appearance of a middle-aged clerk. The glasses keyed Karen's memory.

Such a man had come to the PAX two weeks earlier riding the grubline. Dressed in a ragged shirt, torn jeans, and down at the heel boots, the trail showed heavily on him. At first glance an innocuous youth, his scruffy, studious appearance was given a dangerous cast by the gun he wore tied down on his thigh. He sat at the table with the rest of the crew, and seldom speaking or being spoken to, was gone before morning, disappearing before anyone else rose. Later she heard one of the ranch hands refer to him as Kid Kania, allowing the Kid was one from whom a smart man would steer clear.

"Killed a man up Mobeetie way," one ranch hand had said. "Weren't no tenderfoot, neither. A regular shootist."

"Shot his way out of a scrap up in the Indian Territory," echoed another.

Now here he was again, shaved, barbered, immaculately tailored. He pulled back his coat. The gun was still there, tied down and deadly. Brownrig blinked and stumbled a few steps back. "Law says you ain't supposed to be packin' a gun, Kania," he slurred.

"The law stops at Military Plaza. You know that," came the soft reply. The gunman's voice was totally unemotional, as if issuing from a metallic throat.

The knife wavered in Brownrig's hand. "This *puta* ain't your concern, Kid, " he shouted, the statement almost a plea. "I ain't got a gun." He was rapidly sobering up. People stared from doors and windows on all sides, their anxious faces glittering with nervous anticipation, drawn to the confrontation like moths to a tragic flame. Brownrig was a bully and wouldn't be missed. His death would be a small price to pay for the chance to see Kid Kania in action.

"The *lady* is Mrs. Paxton. Vance Paxton's woman," the gunman said in a voice as quiet and foreboding as the rustle of dead flowers. Brownrig was completely sober now, his mouth open in horror at the mention of her name and the trouble he had brought himself, if not from the Kid, then surely from Paxton and every rider the PAX could muster. He backed further away from Karen as if trying to disassociate himself from any contact whatsoever with her, real or implied. "Further, Brownrig, she opened her table to me of her own free will two weeks back. Set out the finest meal I've had in a year. Now, you doff your hat, apologize to the lady an' then give that Arkansas toothpick of yours its best toss, because I'm gonna put a bullet through you."

"I ain't got no argument with you, Kid. I ain't gonna go up against a gun with no knife."

"Yes you will, Brownrig. You'll apologize first, an' then you'll make your try."

Brownrig backed further away, bumped into a wall and stopped. His voice shook in obvious contrast to the flat, even tones from the Kid. "I ain't gonna. . . ."

"You yellow, Brownrig? We're standin' close enough. Ain't ever heard you to miss at this distance."

"Ain't no fair, Kid. I got nothin' more than a knife, an'. . ."

"Heard a lot of talk about that knife. May be it was all lies. I guess you are just yellow."

Brownrig stiffened and, his eyes narrowing, he took a step away from the wall. Karen, the sorrel now under control, spurred the gelding between the two men. "Mr. Kania . . ." she said. The gunman and Brownrig froze in amazement at her action. No one ever stepped between two men involved in a difficulty. ". . . I do appreciate your concern and assistance. But I have seen drunken men before and would hate to think of a life being taken over a momentary indiscretion. I should not have ridden this path. However, I do thank you and would consider it a favor if you went no further."

Kania's hand fell to his side. "Madam," he said, his voice more personable, "I defer to your merciful judgement. From what I hear, there are a good many men hereabouts to whom you have offered food and a place by your hearth. I would deign to say you are one person who could travel in safety, wherever you please. I am proud, ma'am, to have been of service. Now, if you'll excuse me," he said, bowing graciously, most unlike Karen's image of a gunfighter, "I'm drawing to an inside straight." He touched his forehead in deference to her and returned to the *cantina* without another word. Karen found herself alone in the alley, the faces already gone, lost behind the shuttered windows and closed doors. A glance told her Brownrig was also gone, evidently taking the opportunity to make a hurried escape during her final exchange with Kania. His knife, the blade already tarnished, lay half buried where he'd dropped it in a puddle. Still shaken, Karen prodded the gelding on his way and rode from the alley to Commerce Street, forcing herself to think no longer on the incident, totally unaware of the indelible image she had left behind in the minds of the audience and the participants. To her left, Bell shrunk back into another alley. She'd been out of his sight for more than two minutes, but luckily nothing had happened, for which he could be more than thankful. The half-breed Comanche took great stock in her, and had anything happened.... Bell was afraid of no man, but he wasn't fool enough to go looking for a fight with Morning Sky. Quietly, he nudged his horse forward, keeping her in sight and letting nothing more distract him.

"Karen Paxton! If this isn't a surprise!" Jared exclaimed, coming from behind the polished rail. "Please . . . please come into my office." He turned, spoke to one of the tellers. "Swenson, if Mr. Lanier comes in, tell him to come into the office. I have someone here I'd like him to meet."

"Yes, sir," Swenson nodded, silently reeling off numbers to himself as he counted a stack of bills.

"Come in, come in. I hope you can stay. Lanier is *the* Sidney Lanier, the poet. Here for the consumption. They say the climate is conducive to a cure. I'm not certain it is, but I'd never say so publicly. A good man. Different, but good. You'll like him." Jared's office was small, neat and well cared for. The furnishings consisted of a massive oak desk, behind and in front of which sat a matching pair of black leather chairs. Another chair, constructed entirely of horns from cattle, the seat and backing of tanned cowhide, had been placed in front of the one window. Jared noticed her attention and smiled. "How do you like my barbaric throne? I sometimes sit in it when no one is looking."

"It doesn't look very comfortable," Karen replied.

"Oh, but it is, it is." Jared protested, leading her to the chair and seating her. "I do freely admit, however, I haven't quite figured out where one puts one's arms," he added with a boyish grin, totally out of context with his position as one of San Antonio's leading bankers.

"I should think high over your head," Karen laughed, happy to see her friend.

Jared chuckled, moved the other chair out and indicated

she should sit across from him. Seating himself behind the imposing desk, his eyes roved over the wondrous swelling of the Mexican blouse cloaking the riches of her figure in provocatively concealing fabric while allowing her form an unrestrictive, lush freedom. She had changed, he noticed, and radically. Her flesh was no longer pale, but a firm, deep healthy cream. Her hair, unbound, was the essence of a golden spring day. Her eyes, less a piercing green, shone more assertively, alive with the hidden mysteries of a rare gem. Karen blushed beneath his gaze and Jared reddened in embarrassment. "Excuse me, my dear. I'm too forward for an old married man. But it seems as if you've been away a year or more. You look so . . . different."

"It's the clothes," Karen answered. "These used to be Elizabeth's. They're sturdier, more honest. Made for living on a ranch."

"No, it's more. *You* have changed." He glanced down unconsciously at her abdomen, flattened and trim from her active days. "Oh. Forgive me. We heard about the . . . the attack on the ranch. About your. . . ." He faltered.

"It was a boy, Jared, and he would have been a fine son. But. . . ." She took a deep breath and stepped away from the chasm of sorrow within her. "I did not come to talk of grief, Jared."

"Of course. Forgive me. Of business, then?"

"Yes." She placed a saddlebag on the desk, withdrew from an oilskin wrapping an assortment of papers illustrating the financial situation of the PAX, not only at the present but of the past and projected future. "We've been having problems. . . ." She went on, displaying an adroitness and facility for such matters inherited from her father. Jared listened and was impressed in spite of the moments when his mind wandered and he lost himself in the daring eyes, her challenging beauty. In the midst of a cold, hard financial analysis of the PAX, he heard again the distant magical trumpets of his youth while the shadows of time past danced in his imagination, until the chattering voices outside the door brought him unwillingly back to the present. The door was flung open and Bertha and Constance Britt entered, giggling and carrying on like a pair of clucking hens.

"Jared, you must hear this. The story is all over town.

345

Our little hussy, the Pax. . . ." Bertha's words died in her throat. Constance's face took on the expression of a distraught fish. Bertha stared unbelievingly at Karen's attire, at the woman who looked so shockingly different. "Good heavens, you poor dear. It is *you*, isn't it?" she asked, her concern reflected in an anguished sigh from her companion.

Karen flinched beneath their scrutiny, realized with dim consternation she was at a loss for words. She covered the momentary panic by shuffling the spread papers into a neat pile, wrapping them again in the oilcloth. *I no longer wish to be an adept at the cutting phrase, the paring nuance. Games, they are, and I have no inclination to play. No thank you, ladies. I have a life to live and haven't time for charades.* "Good afternoon, Bertha, Constance. I'm sure you'll want some time with Jared. Jared, I'll wait outside for your decision."

"No need to wait, Karen," Jared answered as Bertha's countenance turned predatory. "Your credit . . . uh . . . Paxton credit will always be good with us. You have your men by what you need and the bank will cover it. I'll have the papers drawn up before you leave town."

"Thank you. Ladies, if you'll excuse me." Her eye caught the piece of jewelry worn by Bertha and the panic of a moment before was replaced by anger and then amusement. *I can't help it,* she thought impishly, the words and intonation already planned. "Why, Bertha," she exclaimed innocently, "that's my brooch, isn't it? It looks simply lovely on you. I hate to think of all those beautiful pieces stored at Green Hill, going to waste and not being worn. I have a locket that would look stunning on you, Constance. You'll find it in the jewelry box in my other trunk." Her smile was dazzling. "But surely, Bertha can show you where it's hidden." Bertha's cheeks tinged with red and she glanced guiltily at Jared and averted her eyes from Constance. Karen turned from them to the desk, took up the package of papers. "Thank you again, Jared. If ever you find occasion to come west, you are welcome at our table."

The banker mumbled a return, glancing helplessly at the piled receipts and notations, at Karen's back as she strode out the door, at anything, only hoping to avoid what was surely to follow. To no avail. The moment the door closed, Bertha whirled on him. "How dare you. . . ."

"Now, Bertha," Jared broke in, trying to calm her. "She is a friend of the family."

"Not after today. Such unmitigated gall. The story is all over town, and here you sit lending her money."

"I don't know what you're talking about."

"The same old story. The same as the last time."

"What?" Jared reiterated.

"That . . . that trollop," Bertha exclaimed. "Dressed like some wanton from the *Villita*, only this time riding the back alleys—astride—off the plaza, visiting *cantinas* and consorting with desperadoes and assassins. Why, she almost got another man killed. Makes one wonder just why she left Washington. It wouldn't surprise *me* if her conduct drove her from the city in disgrace."

"The hussy," Constance concluded.

Jared slammed his hand down on the desk and the sharp report echoed in the confined room, making the sound even louder. Both women stepped back in surprise.

"That woman. . . ." Jared began sternly, anger barely in check. He drew a deep breath, plunged on. "It is primarily because of Karen Paxton that Under-Secretary Rutledge, her Uncle Rutty, *if* you remember, is smoothing the way for the railroad to come through San Antonio. His influence has eased our task considerably, taken a great burden off our minds and purses. A railroad through San Antonio will increase our wealth, attract business and make San Antonio a true city, not some sprawling pioneer town. San Antonio will be important and, dear ladies, *we* will be important. You, my dear," he dug viciously, "will have access to jewelry of your own instead of rifling through an 'unconscionable hussy's' possessions."

Bertha stared at him, a red flush creeping up her neck. Constance backed toward the door, mouth agape. Jared paused. He felt good. For the first time in years he'd talked back to his wife and, the barrier once down, found himself unwilling to stop. He drew himself to his full height. "And furthermore, Karen Hampton left Washington and came to Texas for only one reason. Love. And that, my dear wife, my dear Constance, is something neither you nor, sadly, I, will ever be given to understand." He turned his back to them and stared out the window, seeing not the street nor the drab faces, but a waterfall and a woods alive with song and the scent of flowers, a forest of love where a sun-kissed girl forever ran toward him, where he was young and sturdy as the boughs. The girl could well have been Karen, or so he wistfully imagined.

Several hundred miles to the west and a little south, across the Rio Grande in the little village of Rio Lobos, Jaco watched the night accept the surrender of the sun. He pulled his *serape* about him, wincing only slightly as the heavy cloth tugged at the newly-healed wound. From the doorway of his *jacalito* he could see the entire village. The two main buildings, a *cantina* with three rooms out back for the *putas,* when Rio Lobos was lucky enough to have them around, and a general store, the *tienda* with bare walls where, in better times, goods were stacked, faced each other across the tiny plaza. Three other sod huts and a common corral made up the remainder of the town. Rio Lobos was ideally situated in the hills, close to the Rio Grande and the rich prizes to be taken in the United States from the *gringos.* Only once had the *federales* moved against the bandit village, and then only because they had been pressured into the attack by their Anglo neighbors to the north. The bandits, led by Jaco, easily trapped the soldiers in a nearby canyon. Jaco was not so unwise as to kill the soldiers, for then the generals would have sent more. Instead, he trapped them and stripped them of horses and guns and food, leaving them afoot to wander back as best they could, giving them plenty of time to make up a good story about how hard the bandits had fought before they were wiped out to the last man. At the same time the young lieutenant was explaining to the *capitán,* the renegade citizens of Rio Lobos were hard at work celebrating the wisdom of their leader, their great victory and the acquisition of much booty.

The night in question was little different from any other night in any other bandit or outlaw town scattered across thousands of miles of mostly empty territory. The *cantina* was the center of activity. Lights streaming through the shuttered windows formed a pattern of vivid welts on the dark earth. Around the tiny speck of life the hills were dark and quiet, a bastion against the outside world. Few cared about the beauty of the sky overhead. Jaco stood motionless, his mind seething with the shifting image of a beautiful *gringa.* In the darkness behind him Marcelina came through the open door to stand at his side. She wore a man's shirt and nothing else, pressed her naked lower torso against his unresponsive frame. His hips tightened beneath the pressure of her thighs. "Your wound still pains you?"

"No."

"It is cold."

"It is night, it is cold. Why do you bother me with this?"

Marcelina pouted, hurt by his indifference. She did not know how he had received his wound, knew only the attack had failed and, fearing the wrath of her mother and the others, had fled with the bandit leader. "I love you."

Jaco gripped her hair and brought his mouth savagely down on hers, the strange laugh welling in his throat. She reached for his belt but he pushed her hands away. "Wait for me, *chica*." And he was gone into the night. The wind sprang up and Marcelina shivered, hurried back to their bed and what warmth was left there.

Jaco strolled across the plaza. He had suffered more than a wound. The failure of the attack weakened his position as a leader and his own estimation of himself, for the failure was his first. No one openly questioned him or flouted his word, but he had seen the hesitation in their eyes, had heard wisps of conversations when none thought he was around to hear. The blame lay with the Paxtons, the cursed Paxtons, the old man and his son, with their wealth, their fine *hacienda*, cattle. And a beautiful *señora* who troubled his dreams, he reminded himself. He relished the memory of her face and pictured her on the ground underneath him, her legs spread and her eyes wide as he entered her and brought her much pleasure. Such a woman would be a pleasure to take—many times. His eyes hardened. She was a *gringa*. Paxton's woman. Such a one deserved no pleasure. He would take *his* pleasure, and roughly, then turn her over to the men to do with as they pleased. But perhaps she would love him, prefer him and his strength, for would he not be a grand general? A woman of her beauty would bring him much luck, bring him many. . . .

"Jaco."

The bandit dropped his hand to the butt of his revolver as Arcadio, the knob-eared one, approached. "What is it, *amigo?*"

"I have said nothing, but you must know. The men talk."

"As men of little courage will. What do these *gallinas* talk of when *el gallo* is not in front of them?"

"Marquez."

Jaco's eyes narrowed and Arcadio stepped back, fearful he might become the object of his leader's wrath. Jaco listened to the raucous clamor, the squeal of feminine laughter bought for a few coins. He heard men boasting and braying of their feats of bravery, found in the vanquished depths of an empty bottle of tequila or rum. The cackling of hens, of *gallinas*. Nothing more.

"Marquez!" Jaco shouted, the word ringing in the clear night air, bounding back to him in multiples from the mountains. The *cantina* grew silent, all the more ominously for its abruptness. Everyone knew what must now happen. A figure stepped from the doorway, a slight, thin whip of a man, but *muy hombre*.

"*Si?*" he answered laconically, accepting the challenge.

"*Mañana*. We ride together. The two of us. Alone."

Silence. In the face of the unexpected there was always silence. A different kind of challenge. Marquez and Jaco, alone. They would watch each other very closely. "Where do we ride?"

"Back, *amigo*," Jaco said, the bold idea gleaming brightly in his brain. "Back."

CHAPTER III

Karen, Ted, Huller and W. Bell arrived back at the PAX five days later, bringing with them the four mules hauling a new wagon full of lumber, a stove, two dozen blankets, four hundred pounds of flour, two hundred of sugar, fifty of salt, a hundred of Arbuckle's coffee, five of mustard for plasters and four for eating, four kegs of nails of as many sizes, eight bolts of cloth, a box full of harness metal, four brand-new fifteen-shot Winchester '73's and eighteen boxes of assorted cartridges, six dozen eggs and a pair of canaries.

"The hell with all that," True exploded. "What about the note? Did he extend it?"

"Of course."

"Well, why didn't you say so first?"

"I didn't think there'd be any doubt in your mind," Karen answered with a laugh, heading for the kitchen to install the canaries in their new home.

True followed, pleased she was back but still contentious, for he'd been eating his own cooking for the last eight days, which always put him out of sorts. "Hmmmph. Suppose not. Dressed up like a pretty *señorita*, you would turn a banker's head."

"Where do you think they should go?"

"Who?"

"The canaries."

"Canaries?"

"Canaries."

"Why in tarnation did you buy canaries?"

"Where do you think they should go?"

"Outside where they belong. With all the other birds. All this ranch needs is a pair of canaries to help with the cookin'." Turning on his heel, he stalked from the kitchen, leaving the decision to Karen.

"Don't listen to him," she told the frightened birds as she

351

hung their cage in the corner near the window looking onto the patio. "Once you get to know him, you'll like him. He's really glad we're back. Just hurts him too much to say so." She paused, looking at the kitchen and the pile of dishes. "Well, seeing as I'm back, I guess I'd better get to work."

She settled quickly into the life of the ranch again, happy for the break and the chance to go to San Antonio, happier yet to be back. The ranch was in good shape, the barn almost completed. That night, sitting with True before the fire in the front room, she gave a complete report on the trip, and when she was finished, asked the question most important to her. "Have you heard anything of Vance?"

True shook his head soberly. "Not a word. Nobody seen him, nobody heard of him."

"True . . . ?"

"Don't even ask it. He'll be back. I didn't bring him up to be a complete fool. He'll be back."

Karen acquiesced, stared moodily into the fire. A few minutes later, exhausted from the trip, she stumbled upstairs and into bed. She dreamed of a silent, troubled man who somewhere roamed the empty land.

A few nights later, True, checker game in hand, prowled the house searching for his favorite opponent. Unable to locate her indoors, he threw on a light coat and went outside. Karen was on the walkway, silhouetted from the shoulders up as she paused in the middle of the western wall and stared into the hills. Beyond her, the moon, full and bright, threw the cedar-crested ridges into stark relief against the starlit firmament. She wasn't wearing a coat, True noted to himself. "Dang fool girl," he grumbled. "Catch a sickness if she don't take care of herself. Just 'cause it's spring don't mean the night's gonna be like summer." A nearby movement drew his attention. A match flared in the dark shadow of the house, briefly illuminated Ted's face. "I must be gettin' old, not to see you when I first come up." Ted remained silent as the older man joined him, rolled a cigarette of his own and gestured to the wall. "You keepin' an eye on the girl?"

Ted shrugged. "This one . . . she has her own mind, own ways. Once she needed much help. Now she needs nothing but one man. It is always the way with the Comanche. The women wait for the warriors to return, and count with fearful hearts the riderless horses. It is much the same with her, I think. She has done all a woman can, and shown her strength. Now she waits for the man to show his."

"Where the hell is he, Ted? You an' him was close as brothers. Where's my son? There's no sign you can't read."

"I followed him for a time. Heading west. Always west. I was needed here so I came back. It is a time of drifting men, riding the grubline. The man who was at our table last night came through west Texas on his way here. This morning, before he rode off, we traded tales over a coffee pot in Silver Canyon. His name was Clayton. He told me there was some trouble while he was in El Paso. A couple of rough hombres, Jory and Will Tern, jumped a stranger in a saloon. The stranger was a big, wide-shouldered man, full of a meanness waiting to bust out, like he'd been turning on himself for too long and was waiting to let loose on someone. Anyway, he whipped them with his fists. They went for their guns and he put the nails in their coffins without half trying. Clayton figured he'd better do his drinking in a healthier place. Said there was too much lead in the air to suit him. On his way out he paid some attention to the stranger's horse. It was a grulla stallion wearing the PAX brand."

"Damn!" True muttered. "Crazy fool's gonna get hisself killed."

"Maybe. Maybe not. Sometimes a man needs something like that to bring him back."

"Killin' two men?"

"They threw down on him."

"You know what I mean."

"Would you rather. . . ."

"No," True interrupted. He took an irritated drag on the cigarette, pinched out the live tip and shredded the remainder. "Reckon there's no point in tellin' her to come in," he growled. "You keep an eye on her. She may carry on like she can handle herself, but won't hurt nothin' to have somebody around just in case."

"That's what I was doing." Ted threw the glowing stub of his cigarette to the earth and crushed it with a boot, stepped back and blended into the shadows again, out of sight.

True returned to the house. The hearth in the front room

blazed cheerfully and he was glad for the warmth . Suddenly he felt the age in his bones, experienced the weary penalties of a lifetime of debilitating work. "Get on back here, son. Safe an' whole. There's been too much buryin' this year. I don't want to lay another of my blood into the ground." He sank back into the chair with a sigh. A buryin' year. "Buried too many, son," and tiredness overtook him.

Ted Morning Sky guided the Appaloosa beneath an empty, bright blue morning sky, along a winding, treacherously eroded trail laid among the boulders and ravines like a twisted ribbon. The Appaloosa had grown up in the wild, and a more sure-footed steed couldn't be found. Over and over again the gelding avoided patches of loose shale or nimbly picked a way along a slick watercourse without missing a step. Why the Indian was going to the line shack he could not say, for the land there lay on its side, tossed and tumbled by ancient forces. The terrain was much too dangerous for both men and cattle and the PAX had taken to keeping its stock away from the boulder-littered canyon mouth which led to that section of the hills. Consequently, the cabin had been abandoned and the surrounding area left alone except during a major roundup or, when game was scarce, someone rode in to hunt for deer for the table.

Ted was here for neither reason. Rather he was following a thought, a fragile suspicion his Comanche sense told him to pursue. By noon he was far from the ranch. The hills thrust savagely upward all about him and a corridor of wind, already hot and dry though the year was young, whooshed among the ravines with implacable ferocity. The hot air carried a heavy fragrance of sprouting cedar, of fresh water from a mountain spring, of heated granite and more...which his nostrils quickly identified. Woodsmoke. Someone was at the line cabin, and Ted was positive he knew who it was.

The grulla stallion, gaunted from many hard miles, stood with head up and ears pricked, snorting nervously at the intruder. Ted paused, rode into plain sight and stopped again, waiting a prudent moment before riding toward the cabin. Vance, no more than many and much less than most, didn't like being stalked. The Indian rode slowly wanting no chance of misinterpretation on Vance's part.

When he was close to the grulla he dismounted, loosed the cinch on his own gelding and tethered the animal. "Hello the cabin," he called softly.

"What do you want?"

Ted was as adept at reading the sign in a man's voice as he was the markings on a trail. This one sounded surly and dangerous, yet tired as well. Vance Paxton stepped out of the cabin and watched as the half-breed approached. Ted studied his friend's appearance, for he had indeed changed. His haunted eyes and scruffily-bearded face gave mute testimony of the past two and a half months, the raging incriminations and grief that had waged war within him and turned his very being into a battlefield.

"Well?" Vance asked.

Ted stopped a few feet from him. "I smelled the beans. Figured my friend Vance Paxton would not refuse his red brother a meal."

Vance's features lost none of their sternness, yet he stepped aside. Ted walked past him and filled a tin plate with beans, poured himself a cup of coffee and quickly glanced around before rejoining Vance outside.

"Didn't plan on anybody riding up this way."

"They won't be," Ted assured him. "I just followed a hunch. Woke up early and knew you were up here." He squatted down and began to eat, grimacing at the first bite, then looking up at Vance with a wry grin. "*Amigo*, you cook worse than me."

"No one's asking you to stay and eat."

"You and your pa are sure alike. Even to the point of saying one thing and meaning something else." He put down the plate of beans and sipped the coffee.

"Don't ride me, Morning Sky," Vance said with a threatening note.

"All right." He drank silently, feeling the calm in the clearing, liking the sound of the wind soughing in the cedars. "If you won't ask, I'll tell you. Your Pa's fine and Karen is still there."

"I know," Vance retorted curtly. "Word has a way of traveling."

"She's changed, Vance."

"Sure, if you mean keeping company up in the hills with a goddam Injun."

Ted set down the tin cup. "I was teaching her," he said carefully. "Teaching her sign. Same as before, when you were there."

"I'll bet she's picked up a lot from you—and all the rest of those drifters they tell me she's taken in."

Ted's face clouded with anger of his own. "Everyone feeds drifters. You know that. I don't know who you've talked to, but an echo never rings as true as the voice that spoke it, never repeats the whole message. You're believing only what you want to hear."

"Why shouldn't I?" Vance countered, his voice filled with bitter vehemence. "She got Maruja killed. She killed my son. She ran when a real woman would have stood and shot back. So why not believe the rest? Word is she's taken up with any drifter who finds the door, and when there's none of them around to suit her, she runs with Vance Paxton's Injun friend. Who knows? Maybe she'll be having a little red whelp before lo. . . ."

Ted launched himself from the ground, his hard shoulders ploughing deep into the larger man's abdomen. Vance grunted and went over backward as Ted rolled with the momentum, ending up on his feet. A second later Vance sprang up and Ted leaped again, both moccasined feet striking Vance squarely in the chest, slamming him back against the cabin with enough force to knock gear from the wall inside and send it crashing to the floor. The entire shack shuddered as if dealt a mortal blow.

Vance staggered forward, trying to clear the cobwebs from his brain and Ted, realizing the danger of ever letting the larger man catch his breath, waded in, delivering three brutal punches that Vance managed to shake off before returning one of his own. Ted reeled away from the blow but Vance pursued him furiously, digging hard, short blows into the stomach, ribs and wind, finally landing one that hurled the stocky Indian to the ground. Ted rolled over on his back as Vance charged again. Using an Indian fighting trick, he thrust one leg between Vance's ankles and with the other flipped him over to one side and into a woodpile. Vance cursed as he slammed into the split logs and cordwood avalanched down about his shoulders and head. Both men staggered to their feet, Vance inadvertently clutching a solid length of cedar in his fist. Ted straightened indignantly. "Hey, no clubs!" he shouted.

Vance glanced around and noticed the piece of wood for the first time. Caught by surprise, he dropped the log. "Oh, sorry. . . ." A rush of air, then something hard exploded against his head.

He came to, groaning. His lips felt puffy and his head throbbed wildly. Ted sat near him, wetting a bandana which he placed on Vance's scalp. "Wha . . . you . . . hit me . . . with?" Vance managed, his voice thick and muffled.

"Tree limb," Ted said matter-of-factly. "Never trust a goddam Injun."

Vance sat upright, wincing with the effort. "You don't have to grin like that, you know. Isn't funny." He leaned back groggily against the shack as Ted sat up and disappeared inside, came back out with a cup of coffee. "You carry me over here?"

Ted shook his head "no." "Drug you," he said, handing Vance the steaming cup. "Too damn heavy to carry."

Vance clutched the cup, almost dropped it. "Feels like you drug me across every rock, stone and root you could find."

"Serves you right for carrying on that way."

Vance noted the bluish bruise coloring the Indian's jawline. "Looks like I landed one, anyway." He took a sip from the cup, grimacing as the hot, bitter liquid stung his lips. Ted walked over to his Appaloosa and led the animal to a nearby spring seeping from the rocks and forming a shallow pool, a tank of water not more than three feet in diameter and a few inches deep. Vance drained the contents of his cup and rested his head back, gathering his strength then rising shakily to his feet. He took the bandana from his head and tremulously stepped away from the shack. Moving carefully, he tested each muscle and bone, checking for damage. Nothing major seemed to be wrong. He felt stiff and sore . . . and better than he had in days. For he had borne not only the anguish of his own grief but also a heavy load of self-recrimination for the fell accusations with which he'd lashed out at Karen. The words were cruelly unjust and he knew it even as they spilled from his mouth. A frightened girl confronted with a killer: what else could he have expected? Karen's protected upbringing had never prepared her for such a situation and he should have known it— did, in fact, recognize the fact when he brought her west. He had wronged her and was too stubborn to admit his error, compounded by listening to idle rumors and vicious slander propounded by lesser men; poisonous spewings he knew in his heart to be false. *I was wrong. Too damn proud to accept the fact. I've missed her since I rode off, and was just too bull-headed to admit it. You're a fool, Paxton. Loved her, still do and always will. What are you doing here in the hills, riding the high lonesome and knowing in your heart, all along, where you should be?* He remembered the moment, how long ago, when he stood at the edge of a meadow and watched the sun pick out Karen's retreating figure as she fled from the heady passion each had discovered. *Fled. . . . I did the same thing. I ran . . . when I should have stood and stayed.*

"*Amigo,* do you travel with me?"

Vance dipped the bandana into the clear cold water and pressed it to the back of his head. "No. Not yet." Ted's eyes narrowed. "Soon," he added. "I need a little time to figure out the words."

Ted shook his head in dismay. "The white man. He must have words for everything. Not so the Comanche. I choose my woman. I bring my horses to her father's camp. Aieee. I steal her away at night, braving the wrath of her father and brothers. All to prove what I feel. What good are words? What can they tell her that my courage, my horses, my wedding lodge, all I have dared and done cannot say?"

"All you have spoken is true, my friend. But the Comanche way is not our way. I have no wickiup, no lodge but the one in which she waits. And I have wronged her, and myself. I killed two men in El Paso, Ted. They'd been drinking and came looking for trouble, but I was itching for them to try, hoping they'd go for those guns, just so I could. . . ." He paused, pensive and brooding, going over the fight in his mind, smelling again the acrid smell of gunsmoke and seeing the men sink to the ground, hearing the final, ringing shot as the one called Jory fired into the floor, the trigger pulled by a dead man's finger. "The law didn't say so, but I was guilty as hell. I didn't have to push them. So there are a couple of things need sorting out, words within me that need saying. I know this is so. And I must find them."

"Shall I tell her you are here?"

"Tell Karen . . . tell her I will start down before sunrise."

"It is good." Ted rose, untied his horse and led him to the edge of the clearing. Vance followed, held the animal, stroking the Appaloosa's nose as the Indian mounted.

"Ted?"

"Yes?"

"I didn't ask. How is she?"

Ted smiled warmly, the gesture softening his enigmatic facade. "You might not know her, my friend. She has changed in many ways. She has become . . . a woman to ride the river with."

Ted Morning Sky paused at the foot of the ravine, gingerly fingered his discolored jaw. The club trick had been a lucky break. Otherwise, things might have gone differently. "Won't ever work again," he sighed, guiding the Appaloosa out of the draw and along the arid shoulder of a broad hill. For well over an hour he picked his way across the loose shale, skirting precarious boulders, crossing treacherous gullies carved through solid rock by countless flash floods. The land was as harsh as any he'd seen and he hoped to achieve easier going before sunset. Once on the valley floor he could easily make his way back to the ranch, following the familiar trail by moonlight. Another hour saw him over the difficult part of the terrain. Twice he saw deer, but the *hacienda's* larder was well stocked and he passed up both opportunities, easy shots though they were. Near one outcropping, the Appaloosa's ears twitched erect. Ted slipped his rifle from the scabbard and cautiously edged around a huge boulder obstructing his view of the trail ahead. "Karen . . . !" Clad in jeans and work shirt, she sat forlornly in the saddle as her sorrel drank from a seep in the rocks. Her face brightened on recognizing Ted. The Indian could not have been more surprised. "What are you doing here?"

"Following you," she said ruefully. "And not doing a very good job of it, I'm afraid. I couldn't sleep and saw you leave early in the morning. I . . . I had a feeling, so I dressed and followed. I've never been this way and lost your trail." She nudged the sorrel closer to him and her voice tightened with urgency. "Ted, you found him, didn't you? I just know you did. Take me to him. Please?"

"No."

"But why?" she asked, panic tinging her voice. She looked at him closely. "Your face is bruised."

"It is nothing. You should see *him*." The half-breed grimaced. "There's nothing to look so frightened about. He is fine. Better, I think, than he has been in a long time."

"Then why . . . ?"

"He needs this night alone, and we must not disturb him. He is finding his way back home, on a path he must discover by himself. Come. We have little light left and we need to reach the valley."

"But . . ."

"Come. Your man will be with you soon. He rides for the ranch before sunrise."

Ted led the way out of the draw and Karen gave a last look in the direction from which he had come. Vance was up there somewhere and tomorrow he would be with her. "Hurry, darling," she whispered to the wind. "Hurry."

She had been thoroughly lost. The thought was frightening, for only by the sheerest luck had she been anywhere near the trail. "I would have found a way back," she told herself in an attempt to bolster her confidence. Exhausted, she let herself drop into the rhythm of the horses' walk, lost again, but now in happy anticipation of the next day.

Karen was yanked abruptly back to reality by the whisper of metal on leather. They had stopped. Ahead of her, Ted sat erect in the saddle, listening intently, his rifle drawn and ready for action. Everything was still, and what had been peaceful now became pregnant with menace, the very silence an enemy. Karen's horse moved up beside the Appaloosa as Ted's eyes searched the slope to either side of the parched creek below. For the first time, Karen became aware of the temperature. The season had been so gentle, and in the valley of the Sabinal the air was cool and fresh over the rich grass. Here the pink granite walls reflected the spring sun, trapped the heat and returned tremulous, shimmering waves to the sky. Opposite them on the far bank of the empty watercourse, a cluster of freshly greened mesquite provided the only source of shade or cover. Ted, after a long searching look, started to cross the creekbed when a low-flying hawk dipped down to light on a branch, just as abruptly swooped upward to the sky. The Indian held his horse back, studied with apparent interest the southern bend of the creek while appearing to ignore the mesquite. He leaned close to Karen and spoke in a hushed and guarded voice. "Can you find your way back to the draw where I found you?"

"I think so."

"From there, follow the trail as I have taught you. The way is dangerous, but you should be able to handle it, with care. The trail will take you to a line shack, and to Vance. Ride in suddenly. Do not sneak up on him. Call his name."

Suddenly she was frightened. "Ted, what is it?

"I do not know. In my hurry to see you to the *hacienda* I have not been as watchful as I should. But I did not think. . . ." He paused as a hint of movement caught his eye. "Go now. I will stay here a few moments longer."

"I can't just leave. . . ."

"Go," Ted commanded emphatically, slapping the sorrel's rump as Karen turned the animal. The slap resounded between the walls of the draw and the gelding leaped forward sharply, scrambled for footing then bounded up the trail, Karen clinging expertly in the saddle until she rounded a hillock. A figure on horseback lunged from behind a boulder, slamming into the sorrel. Off balance and starting to fall, she tried to catch herself and failed as a dirty clawlike hand pushed her out of the saddle. Her single sharp, brief scream was broken as she fell onto the trail and her head slammed into the jagged stones. Darkness shrouded her senses. Three rapidly-fired gunshots sounded in quick succession from far away, and then a man was standing over her, his serape fluttering in the wind, outlined against the receding glare of the sky like some terrible and all too familiar . . . bird . . . of . . . prey.

True to his word, Vance left before the sun glimmered over the horizon. The ravines were still black with shadow and he picked his way with care, holding the grulla to a walk. Now he had finally straightened out the confusing array of emotions beating at him for the last months, he had no intention of breaking his neck in an accident. He was going back to Karen, back to the woman he had tried so hard to deny, returning to the truth his heart had hidden.

Two hours deep into the morning and making good time beneath the bright, clear mid-April sky, he guided the grulla out of an abrupt draw and onto a rounded knoll from whose vantage point the steep hills and granite out-cropping fell away dramatically. A flicker of movement in the dry creek below caught his eye, repeated itself. And then again. Vultures .. . . . carrion feeders. Nothing unusu-al about their presence; the country was harsh and death was never far from hand. Some animal, perhaps, or. . . . A shape lay sprawled on the fringe of Dry Wash Creek. Too big to be a man. . . . He searched in his saddle bag and pulled out a pair of binoculars brought back from the war. The shape swam into focus through shimmering heat waves. A dead horse, body swollen and bloated . . . Ted's Appaloosa!

Thirty minutes later he'd maneuvered himself to within fifty feet of the carcass. There was no doubt about it. The animal had been there since the evening before. Shot. He studied the surrounding area with care but could see no trace of Ted. The suggestion of tracks beneath puzzled him. Cautiously, he followed them around a hillock to read the story on the ground. A rider had waited here. Another horse came galloping up from the creek and the hidden rider intercepted the running animal, struck the rider to the ground. Later, the galloping horse had been led off behind the hidden rider's horse. Vance dropped to the earth, stud-ied the tracks. The realization struck him like a slap and turned his blood icy despite the sweat which ran down his neck and back. The galloping horse had been Karen's sor-rel! He was sure of it. Karen . . . ! But was she riding? He studied the tracks closely and found a small footprint, a woman's. She had been there, was taken by. . . .

Where was Ted? A faint sound, to which he had been listening for some moments without realizing what he heard, broke into his conscious mind. He was hearing a Comanche chant, a death chant lingering on the south wind thrumming up the canyon. Slowly, rifle in hand and leading his horse, he picked his way through the rocks along the hill sloping upward from the creek. Buzzards, startled from the Appaloosa's carcass, flapped into the air and settled on the branches of the mesquite cluster across the dry wash, waiting patiently for the man thing to leave so they might return to their feast.

Ted Morning Sky lay propped among the rocks, his back to a sandstone outcropping, legs splayed before him, rifle

362

across his lap. There was blood on the Winchester's action and wooden stock, more between the reclining Indian's thighs and a sickeningly dark red tinge to the ground around him. Shot twice through the back, the bullets had torn a frightful exit from his stomach. So devastated was the fragile flesh, Vance found it incredible any man should sustain such a wound and still be alive after so many hours. His eyes clouded with pain and weakness, Ted looked up at Vance with fatal resignation. He ceased his chant. ". . . knew . . . in the mesquite . . . Karen screamed . . . I turn . . ."

Vance knelt by his friend. Knowing full well the meaning of those awful wounds, he made no effort to touch the red man. "Who, Ted?"

Ted shut his eyes and spoke as if each word had been planned over and over during the long hours of the night, planned to tell the story precisely and with the least amount of energy possible. "Karen . . . look . . . for you. Followed . . . me. I find . . . bring back . . . to valley. Jaco . . . Jaco."

Jaco! No name could have. . . . Grimly he scanned the hills where the threat lay. Jaco had stolen his woman. Jaco had Karen.

"My brother . . . it is . . . fault . . . my fault . . . I . . . call on Great . . . Spirit . . . to keep me . . . alive. Tell you Jaco . . . and one other . . ." The dying man's head fell back, his mouth taut with a silent scream. He looked around wildly, no longer seeing Vance. "Buffalo Woman," he called in Comanche, only some of which Vance could understand. "Buffalo Woman," the Indian's voice mellowed, ". . . bring water . . . fill my lodge with warmth, with laughing . . . many moons . . . she was . . . so young to travel . . . dark trail . . . Buffalo Woman . . . I burn my lodge . . . and follow . . ."

The inexplicable hand of pain released its clutch and the torn vision faded. Clear and bright, his eyes locked with Vance's. "Help me . . . to stand . . . White Brother."

Vance lifted the frail form. The movement must have caused unimaginable pain, but Ted's face remained calm, betraying not a hint of his dreadful wounds. Using the Winchester as a crutch, he thrust Vance away with surprising strength.

And stood alone.

A breeze sprang up, a river of air binding the hills with a timeless flow and chant all its own. The Comanche stared into the heart of the south wind. His voice was firm but gentle.

"Here . . . I am here. . . ."

Vance found Jaco's trail winding off among the rocks. Every effort had been made to blot out the tracks, but a stone bearing the fresh scuff mark of a horse's hoof and a broken mesquite branch where there should have been no broken branch served to show the way. Only once did he look back to the hill where Ted lay. There had been no time for a proper burying so Vance had carried the bullet-torn, empty shell of his friend the rest of the way up the hill and laid him to rest on its solid, bare granite crown, a crest upon which nothing grew. On the second trip he carried Ted's Winchester and blanket roll. A few minutes later and the blood- and sweat-caked clothes were off and the corpse, weapon in hand, wrapped in the blanket. At one with the weathered rock, Ted Morning Sky lay facing the horizon of his namesake. A fitting final resting place for a Comanche warrior, Vance thought, the words sounding silently within his heavy heart. "Flesh to nourish the animals and birds, bones eroded by rain and wind, a spirit to feed the stars. Farewell, my friend."

He turned and studied the way ahead. Jaco had Karen. Calming the rage welling in him, he nudged the grulla forward and the hill fell behind, lost from sight. The trail took him beneath a high serrated ridge, gouged in places by dry watercourses. The spring rains had been light so far this year and the going was thirsty but safe. At least the sky was clear: during a storm the path he and his quarry now traveled would be suicidal. The grulla snorted his displeasure and picked a careful trail among the rocks, leaving behind his time of rest as his rider forced his mind to a coldly analytical bent and settled into the work at hand.

The decisions necessary were few but complicated and important, all to be considered in light of one single overriding fact—Jaco had Karen—and the equally overriding conclusion—Vance intended to get her back. Briefly, he considered riding to the ranch and gathering the men, quickly decided against it. Every man jack on the PAX would want to mount up and ride, leaving a deserted ranch vulnerable to attack by anyone who came along, Indian or white, outlaw or renegade. And who knew? If Jaco had taken Karen, the rest of his men—however many there were left—might be around. Precious hours would be lost on the trip. As it was, he was little more than a day behind them, and traveling alone would be able to make fair time, depending on how much they did to throw him off the trail. The country in which he would be traveling would be relatively arid. A large body of men would find the more heavily traveled routes to the border mandatory, for such routes were governed by the frequency and plentitude of water. Alone, one could travel the broken hills, the arid backbone of the country, existing on small pockets and seeps holding enough for himself and his horse. Finally, had he not caught them by the time he reached the Rio Grande, it would be far safer for one man to risk the forbidden crossing into Mexico.

There were other factors to be considered. Karen was sure to be missed—had undoubtedly been missed already. The men would be searching for her. Sooner or later they would find the dead horse and Ted's body, signs of the struggle. Grimly, he decided they must be turned back. Jaco, whatever else he might be, was no fool. Ten men added to the pursuit would be nothing less than disastrous. If cornered, the bandit would execute Karen without a second thought. Any note Vance left might very well be interpreted as a ploy by Jaco and hence ignored, for no one knew Vance was anywhere in the area. Even so, he would try. Stopping, he scratched the message on a boulder where they would have to see it. "Am on their trail. Go back. Vance." Still not trusting they'd believe him, for the grulla's shoes had been changed and his sign would look different to those who had known him three months ago, he tore up the saddle blanket he'd taken from Ted's Appaloosa and wrapped the stallion's hooves to insure against any telltale marks on the stone.

The only consideration left was food. No one knew where Jaco hid out, but surely somewhere south of the border. There was little or nothing between where he was and where he was going. Mentally, he tabulated his supplies. A little more than a pound of coffee, a half dozen hardtack biscuits, a can of milk, a pound or so of beans, two or three strips of jerky and a pinch of salt. Not much of a larder for at least four days' travel, he'd have to make it last. Luck was with him, though, for later in the day a small deer, surprised by the silent downwind approach of the horse, bounded from the rocks ahead and fell with a single bullet from Vance's rifle. A day behind, the chance he took was reasonable, but it would be the last such he took. Quickly field dressing the small carcass, he buried the remains in the hot sand, covered all evidence of his presence and rode on.

He came upon the remnants of a camp late in the afternoon. Jaco . . . the sign was easily read. Karen was most certainly with him. She had been bound to a nearby mesquite, for the trunk was chafed where she tried to wear through the rope. So far there was no indication she had been harmed. After a quick meal he rode on until the failing light called a stop to the day. His horse cared for, he lay down with a small clump of cedar at his back and slept soundly, the grulla watching over him.

The morning after their first camp, Karen lay exhausted against the mesquite trunk, her wrists and ankles sore, rubbed raw by the rope which so cruelly bound her. Her captors were up before first light and, after quick cups of coffee all around, they broke camp and headed away from the rising sun. The emotional shock of her kidnapping had worn off and Karen, in the cool morning air, appraised her situation. Vance would not be far behind. She had to believe he would follow—or give herself up to utter despair. All she could do was keep her wits and wait, eat and rest whenever she might and be prepared for whatever happened.

But there was no chance for food and rest. She had to pay the price of obdurance—she would accept no food the night before—and unnecessary tension—she had not slept as she should have. Fatigue, physical and spiritual, in spite of the best intentions, struck with the first rays of the sun, bored into her inexorably until she almost fell from the horse, for fear and hunger had robbed her of all energy. She had ridden a great deal since her arrival at the PAX, but never for two solid days, and as the sun rose higher and higher each step of the horse became a torture until the struggle not to cry out filled her dulled senses and consumed every leaden minute. Thirsty, hungry and tired beyond her wildest nightmares, she doggedly held her seat in the saddle, shifting weight often in an attempt to alleviate the shooting pains running up and down her legs, buttocks and back. Grimly determined not to break, cry or fail agan, she anaesthetized herself with a rhythmic, mesmerizing repetition of the name of the one man upon whom her life depended, upon whom rested all hope of rescue and sustenance: *Vance . . . Vance . . . Vance.*

Neither bandit found time to speak to her during the day. Always their eyes searched the way behind, searched for ways to throw off any possible pursuers, for they too knew she would be missed and men would seek her. Periodically, Jaco rode away to the north and east and Karen was left alone with the other outlaw. Marquez, as Jaco called him, was a slight, spare individual with skin like rawhide stretched over a bony frame. His nose was hooked beak-like under a pair of close-set, challenging eyes and when he grinned she saw his teeth were bad—yellow and rotting. Huge and heavy in contrast to his spare physique, two guns hung at his thighs. When Jaco disappeared, wiry fingers hovered near the low-slung guns. Marquez, nervous already, was more concerned with the problem of his unseen companion than the unknown pursuers, whoever they might be.

She was not tied the second night. Karen looked into the darkness surrounding their tiny camp, realized she was just as effectively bound by the measures taken by her captors. They had taken her boots. If she tried to escape she would not go far over the arid, hostile land capable of shredding the flesh of her lightly-stockinged feet. Her bedroll lay between Jaco and Marquez and she would have to step over them to reach her horse. Once to the horse, her problems would only begin, for the sorrel was staked between the bandits' mounts and there was no way she could lead him off without the other two waking the men. Marquez reached out and added a piece of mesquite root to the tiny blaze, glanced over at Karen and grinned, his face lurid and evil in the flickering orange light. Karen shuddered and looked away: his intentions were only too clear. And who, she wondered, would stop him? Who was there to help her? Vance, possibly, but despite the earlier, forced optimism, she had to admit he might not be. Ted? She could guess his fate with certainty. The shots heard before losing consciousness, followed by the exuberant half-phrases heard when she came to, indicated he was dead. She had allowed herself no time to mourn, had suppressed the tears before they started. Jaco and Marquez watched too closely and she was determined to keep any display of emotion from them. Coldly, she vowed they would derive no satisfaction from her in any way. Instead, some way or other, Karen Paxton would see they paid for her friend's death.

Jaco finished with the horses and re-entered the camp, exchanging a silent glance with Marquez. The tension between the two men was almost palpable, even to Karen's eyes. Jaco laughed softly and contemptuously turned his back on the other man, yet Karen noticed the alertness in his face. His face . . . his very appearance was unsettling. The Mexican heritage was evident in his dark skin, coal-black hair and moustache, but his features were uncannily similar to Vance's. The knowledge of their common origin notwithstanding, she found herself staring at him in horrid fascination. The Mexican nudged her foot with his boot. "We are hungry."

Karen looked defiantly at him and did not move, did not speak lest her loathing and fear show.

"You have changed much since last we meet. Not so much the *gringa*. I like that. A *gringa señorita* you have become." He laughed, the sound an unnerving rumble deep in his chest. "The *señorita* is not happy to see me? But did you not fear I might be hurt, that I might have died out there in the snow and ice?"

"No. I wished for it," Karen answered in a murderous undertone.

"What were you doing so far from the *hacienda* with that Indian? I think you are very naughty, maybe. And hungry, eh? A woman travels in the hills alone with a man other than her husband for only one reason, *verdad*? But now you are with Jaco, and Jaco is very good for the hungry *señoritas*. He fills them with pleasure."

Karen glared at him, contempt written broadly in her eyes, her head raised defiantly. "I am no *señorita*. I am a *señora*, the woman of Vance Paxton. I will have no other man, for there is no other man."

The smile on Jaco's face disappeared. Slowly, his booted foot moved, slid between her ankles and forced them apart.

"Marquez likes you, *señorita*. All the men of my village will like you. Maybe there will be other men. Maybe I give you to them, after I take you myself."

Across the way, Marquez' face darkened with a malevolent frown. Karen slid away from Jaco until her back pressed against a rock and she could move no farther. Jaco merely stepped closer, slid his foot between her knees, then along her thighs.

"I'll cook," Karen blurted out, rising to her feet.

Jaco did not move, so she stepped around him and hurried to the fire. For long seconds he continued to stare at the empty surface of the rock, stare at the tiny marks left by time and weather, then turned and leaned against the boulder, braced on his elbows. His eyes were dark and serious as he watched her go about the task of preparing a meal. She was much woman, this one. There was much spirit in her—a real woman's spirit. Not like the temperamental Marcelina. The little one knew how to please a man, knew instinctively and exquisitely where and how to touch him, how to move. But such a girl was for a moment and no longer. There were many more like her. The woman at the fire was one of strength, of character as strong as the hills and rocks themselves. A man who was blessed with the love of such a *señorita* would need no other woman except occasionally, for the sake of diversion. He contemplated her, considered her closely. The jeans clung tightly to the sensuous curve of her hips and buttocks and the workshirt strained at the swell of her breasts, outlined against the light of the fire as she moved about. His blood stirred and he felt his loins stiffen as he became aware of the throbbing member between his legs. He would fill her until she cried out for more, until his soul exploded like a bursting star. If only he were alone with her.

Karen moved as quickly as possible. She hadn't eaten since the morning before and the smell of food drove her nearly to distraction. A movement across the fire caught her eye and she glanced up to see Marquez grinning at her, undressing her with his eyes. Food forgotten, she worked mechanically, keeping him in the corner of her eye as he picked at his teeth with a dirty fingernail, then reached down to scratch the crotch of his elaborately stitched trousers, humming at the same time a child's tune . . .

Esta es la viudita de Santa Isabel
Que quiere casar y no halla con quién.

The song was the same Karen had heard the children sing
in the streets of San Antonio, the words repeated over and
over in a rhythmic chant. Huller, a man who had been
about and spoke Spanish as it was pronounced on the border, had translated for her. A song of terror, coming as it
did from the tight-lipped, steely-eyed man across the fire.

This is the little widow of Saint Isabel
She wishes to marry, with whom she can't tell.

How macabre the words sounded, coming from the outlaw
who watched her, his eyes lit with insane hunger.

Jaco noticed as well, considered the man closely. The
putas of Rio Lobos would have nothing to do with him. He
was too cruel, took pleasure only in giving pain. Jaco could
not understand such a man. Ruthless as the bandit leader
was, his cruelty stemmed from hatred, from revenge against
an unjust father and undeserving half-brother. Against
these and other *gringos* like them he vented his spleen. A
woman was different, with the possible exception of Maruja, who had played into the hands of the men he hated.
Even her . . . he was sorry he had killed her. No man in
his right senses killed a woman lightly. But she was trying
to kill him, was shooting at him—he forced the thought
from his mind. With other women—the ones he bedded—
he would never be cruel. Hard and demanding, perhaps,
but women needed to know they had a real man. Never
would he make love in order to inflict pain, never seek the
twisted gratification Marquez so loved.

Marquez. Jaco scowled. The thin one posed a threat to
Jaco's leadership and would have to be dealt with sooner or
later. The road they traveled would be the test, and the
more Marquez watched the *gringa*, the less he concentrated
on Jaco. Lust made him careless, broke his concentration,
filled his head with useless thoughts, drove him to tortured
fantasies. In any confrontation, the calm, relaxed man had
the advantage. Still, the wait wasn't easy, for a woman like
the Paxton *gringa* did things to a man. He could feel him-

self drawn to her, worked hard to control his own fantasies. The confrontation with Marquez had to come soon.

The next night passed much the same as the night before. The day had been long, filled with danger, with hiding their trail from those who would certainly follow. Within moments after eating, Karen fell soundly asleep, waking abruptly from time to time with the feeling of roughened hands tearing at her. Each time the hands were only a dream, the movement of air or the rush of a bat across the darkened sky. Each time she waked to hear only the rapid beating of her heart, the stillness from without broken only by the popping of a twig in the fire, the rustle of unseen insects and the soft suspiration of one or the other of the bandits as they slept. Or did they? Once she found Marquez watching her, the fire reflected in his eyes. And Jaco . . . breathing evenly, deep in slumber, or listening? She dared not let her mind dwell on what they had in store for her. The only reason she could guess that nothing had happened yet was neither man wanted to turn his back on the other. She studied Jaco's Latin features, so achingly similar in the dim light to Vance's. Vance . . . ! had to follow the same trail she and Ted had traveled. There couldn't be that many ways of coming out of those hills. If he left that morning . . . there was a chance he was following this very minute, might be close enough to see her. Perhaps he was waiting for the right chance.

Speculation raised her spirits, dropped them as quickly. What would happen if he did catch up with these men? They had killed Ted, a man of whom True had said, "He's a smart man to steer clear of in a ruckus, unless he's on your side." Could they kill Vance as easily? *No! Vance, be careful! Vance . . . !* She was glad she hadn't told them he was in the line cabin. As it was, they could only assume they would be followed by an unknown number of men at some undetermined time. If they knew how close Vance might be, they would be doubly cautious, might lie in ambush for him. *Vance! Hold me, Vance.*

The boots dropped against her leg and she woke with a start, supposition and dream mixed in her mind. Still dark, a vague suggestion of light tinted the horizon, barely dimmed the low-lying stars. Shivering, she stepped out of the blanket and, after tapping the boots against a rock to drive out any unwanted stinging inhabitants left over from the night before, slipped into the sturdy footwear. Jaco was busy with the horses while Marquez poured himself a cup of coffee. "The *señorita* dresses like a *vaquero*. But she is much woman, I think." Karen ignored him, gathered up her bedroll and started past him to the fire. A grimy hand reached out and gripped her thigh. "The nights are cold. Perhaps the blanket is not enough warm." She pulled her leg free of his grasp and walked to the sorrel.

Jaco watched as she threw the saddle on the gelding's back and tightened the cinch. "The *señorita* has indeed changed," he chuckled. "But her beauty is still the same as when I see her first."

"You have not changed," Karen countered. "You are still the animal who killed his own mother."

Jaco struck with the speed of a snake, catching her across the mouth with the back of his hand. Karen spun around, slamming against the saddled gelding, then stumbling and falling to her knees. Blood welled from her bruised lips. Marquez tossed his coffee aside, waiting to see what would happen next. Karen fought back the tears, let the stinging pain serve to feed her growing anger and drive inward and hidden the screaming fear. "You do not ever say that again, *chica*. You understand this thing I tell to you? You understand?"

Karen's face flushed crimson when she looked up at him, but she nodded silently, at the same time noting how his eyes widened with appreciation at the glimpse of her partially-revealed breasts, rising with each rapid breath. The top buttons had been torn away when she hit the saddle and there was nothing she could do but pull the fabric tightly about her, an action only serving to reveal the fruits of her beauty in other ways. Slowly, she got to her feet, finished with the horse and headed back to the fire, where she forced herself to eat.

They struck open country, heading southwest. Jaco and Marquez kept constant vigilance, their eyes ever scouring the dry distances around them, a rolling sea of barren arroyos, sandy gullies and thirsty creeks. A hot, arid land fit for growing catclaw and wait-a-bit, sparse grass, cactus and mesquite. Every half hour or so one of the outlaws would cautiously skyline himself on the crest of the highest ground available and study their back trail as well as the way ahead. They took their noon break around a small muddy seep, digging out the moist earth so the depression in the ground could fill with water which the horses drank dry within minutes, forcing Karen and her two kidnappers to endure their unslaked thirst until the cavity refilled. Jaco handed her a strip of jerked meat and Karen accepted greedily, tearing hungrily at the dried beef and relishing the salty nourishment. A half hour after arriving, Marquez kicked sand and mud back into the seep and they were on their way again.

By the passage of the sun, Karen noticed they had altered their direction and turned south. Near sunset they came to a series of deeply eroded bluffs and followed a winding passage which dropped to the banks of a broad river, swollen with rain that had fallen to the west. Marquez rode down to them from where he had been stationed high on the bluffs, keeping an eye on the trail behind them. "I thought you said we cross at the usual place."

"*Si*. It is what I said."

"This is not the usual place," Marquez protested. "It is a full fifty *varras* across. Our horses are too tired."

"It is deep only in spots, and there are many sandbars where we will find footing. If they do not find where we broke the trail, they will not suspect this place."

"The current is too strong," Marquez insisted.

"*Si*. It is the rains. What do you expect of a river? Come . . . before there is no more light," Jaco said, spurring his horse into the water.

Karen, never having crossed such a river before, was about to protest when the sorrel leaped forward of his own accord. The animal lunged, found footing and started after Jaco's mount until the sandbar ended abruptly and he stepped into deep water. Karen gasped with surprise. Startled and off balance, the racing current plucked her from the saddle. Somehow she grabbed and clung to the pommel while the gelding swam the remaining yards. The shock of the cold water numbed her hands, and just as she felt herself falling free, the animal scrambled onto the opposite bank and Karen dropped to solid ground. Marquez followed close behind, his mustang surging out of the river. The bandit cursed, slapping his soaked *sombrero* against his leg. "A hat is made for the head, Marquez, not to catch fish with," Jaco remarked, laughing. Marquez' eyes blazed furiously and he spurred his horse past Jaco's, plunging deeper into the boulder-strewn bush lining the Mexican bank. Jaco waited for Karen to remount, then led her in the direction Marquez had taken.

They made camp a mile from the crossing by the last light of day. Jaco tossed Karen a sack of food. "Cook," he said, then led the horses into the rapidly deepening shadows. Marquez made a fire while Karen went about her assigned tasks, all too aware how the wet fabric of her shirt clung provocatively to her breasts, revealing even the nipples in stark outline for Marquez' leering eyes. She glanced anxiously into the shadows, hoping for Jaco's return, feeling safer with both outlaws present, each keeping the other in check. The shirt was taking its own damnable time to dry, but the alternative was no shirt at all as she had nothing else to wear. Gritting her teeth and determining to make the best of a bad situation, she went about her business as nonchalantly as possible, scooping coffee into the pot and setting it near the fire. On a slab of stone she shaped *tortillas*. The beans had been soaking in a leather pouch and she dumped them in another pot, searched in the sack, found some dried peppers, crumbled them in the palm of her hand and leaned over to throw them in the pot.

Marquez sprang. Before Karen knew what was happening she had been knocked off balance and onto the ground. Scrambling, she felt an iron-hard hand grab her arm and flip her onto her back, then the cold bite of a knife blade against her throat. "Do not scream, *señorita*," Marquez said, his voice choked, his body trembling with pent-up desire, unreleased now for too long. Brutal fingers dug into her breast, kneading the firm flesh with punishing, inhuman caresses. His mouth sought her shoulder and tore her shirt, his horrid lips lowering again to pull, to bite in a vile semblance of a kiss.

His head was gone! Karen jerked her eyes open. Jaco had grabbed Marquez by the hair and yanked his head from her, pulling him almost to his feet. From behind her a foot flashed over her face and buried itself in Marquez' stomach. The outlaw rolled over and off Karen, clutching his midriff and gasping for breath as he rose to his feet. The two renegades faced each other, twin slivers of steel gleaming evilly in their hands. Marquez' free hand fluttered near the gun in his belt. "There are Apache in these hills, Marquez. They would like to know where we are. Little good the *gringa* would do you with your skull roasting over a slow fire."

Marquez cursed softly in Mexican but his hand fell from the gun, as quickly raised to parry Jaco's first thrust. Karen rolled from between them, pulled her torn shirt about her and crawled away from the fire. "The *puta* is mine," growled Marquez. "I killed the Indian. She is mine."

"Of what use is a woman to a dead man? You think because you are fast with the *pistolas*, you can kill Jaco? You are a fool. I bring you here for one reason only. Not to take the woman, but to die. The woman has been mine since I first see her. Do you think I would need a *gallina* to help me take her? Come, *amigo, gallina*. I hold your death. Let it embrace you. Come, little sparrow that would fly with the hawks."

The soft whispers of death in the air behind her, Karen sneaked out of the camp. *They are animals . . . animals.* Stumbling and cutting herself on the thorns, she plunged in headlong flight, unheard by the single-minded combatants in the clearing by the fire. The horses were . . . where? There, by the boulder . . . "Shhhh . . . shhhh . . . it's me . . . only me . . ."

The horses reared, shied from her. She caught the sorrel's bridle and stroked his nose a moment, shushing and calming him. Jaco had unsaddled him and she lacked the confidence to cross the Rio Grande bareback. Quickly, her breath rasping in her throat, she swung the saddle onto the sorrel, tightened the cinch. The knot where the reins were tied to a tree was tight and she lost precious seconds. . . . *Don't let one of them win. Not yet . . . not yet . . . Vance! Help me . . . help me . . . !* Sobbing with bitter frustration by the time the knot finally loosened, she pulled the sorrel free. Gripping the pommel, she swung over into the saddle, but something caught her right leg as she cleared the cantle and her momentum, aided by a solid tug, pulled her over and off into Jaco's arms. His mouth covered hers with a bruising kiss, his powerful arms subdued her struggles. "The little *chica* would leave me. I don't think so. Not now. Not ever."

Half fainting, she felt him carry her through the tangled

brush back to the camp, drop her on the ground near the fire. There was something. . . . his hand clamped brutally over her mouth and stopped the scream. "Better this than the Apaches, *querida*. Remember that, always. You have not seen how Apaches treat *gringas*. I think you do not want to see. Remember." Slowly, he took his hand from her mouth and she lay quietly, staring at Marquez' grotesquely twisted, blood-splattered corpse, throat slit from ear to ear. She tried to turn her head from the ghastly sight but Jaco wound his fingers in her hair and forced her to stare through terror-, tear-filled eyes at the dead bandit.

"Look at him," he said, his voice curt and demanding. "See what I save you from. Now you are mine. I spill the blood of my *compadre* for you. This moment I could take you by force, plunder the ripe, rich gifts of your body. But I would have them given freely. You will learn to love Jaco, for there will be no other to help or protect you, save me. You will learn to love me, *querida*. I can wait. . . ." He released his hold and she curled up into a ball, sobbing. Jaco squatted near Marquez and filled a plate with beans. The fight had made him hungry. He ate with gusto, a man happy to be alive. The food tasted good, and much pleasure awaited him. "I can wait, *querida*. But not for long. . . ."

The next day they came to Rio Lobos.

CHAPTER IV

The floor was of dirt, the walls of dried mud. The tiny room in which Karen was incarcerated was her new world. A fireplace, a cot, a simple table and single chair. A bucket of water. A lantern. Exhausted, she slumped to the chair and stared out the door to the afternoon-orange plaza. Alone for the first time since Ted's death and the fall from the horse, the full import of her predicament descended and she succumbed to despair. There was no hope, no chance. Jaco had her, Jaco would keep her. For a full five minutes she allowed herself the luxury of wallowing in self-pity, of morbid fantasies of degradation and death. Then from somewhere, some hidden recess, she recalled Uncle Rutty's story of her father's reaction to the news his empire had crumpled about his feet. "Damn them, then," he had said. "Damn them all!" She gathered strength from the dim, ravaged corners of her mind. There were a great many ways in which she despised her father, yet one thing she had to admit: he would never give up. And she was his daughter. There was nothing yet irrevocable about her situation, and she was damned if she'd hand herself to Jaco and his men without a struggle.

Alone in a squalid town, surrounded by alien, unfriendly faces, Karen dispassionately confronted her position in its entirety. She was a prisoner in Jaco's stronghold, his lair. Very well. As such, she had a simple choice to make: give in or resist. The decision came of its own accord. Never would she give in. She would resist with every power at her command.

What assets had she? Vance? He was out there somewhere, she felt sure, but there was little he could do in the face of such odds. Indeed, she prayed he not attempt any action lest it lead to his death. She had to depend on herself. She was in Mexico, beyond the legal jurisdiction of any and all American authority, even the free-riding rangers under Captain Alexander. The border lay somewhere to the north, and the path there led through the mountains, rugged, dry, cold and, for all she knew, teeming with unfriendly Apaches every bit as dangerous as Jaco's bandits. Somehow, though, she would have to try to escape and hopefully meet up with Vance before he tried to enter the town where she was kept.

"Damn them, then," she repeated aloud. "Damn them all!" Her lips set, she rose to her feet and walked to the door, pausing inside the wooden jamb. Outside, the late afternoon sun lingered alone above the jagged hills. Across the plaza was another building, function unknown. The only person in sight was a young bandit standing guard outside her prison. Jaco had called him Manuel, and of him she remembered nothing but his eyes, deep-set and angry except when he looked at *el jefe,* his leader. That Manuel worshiped Jaco was obvious, and not in the least remarkable. Karen imagined the bandit's reputation made him a hero among the dissatisfied youth of the sparsely-populated and poverty-stricken mountain area. Squatting against the building, Manuel glanced back at her, his expression indecipherable in the dusk, save for an impenetrable aura of contempt which sent her backing away from the door, her new-found resolve in jeopardy. Jaco had rightly placed the guard so close, Karen admitted sourly; she would have bolted immediately to the barren mountains rather than submit to the otherwise ignominious alternative—to be Jaco's subservient partner, to let him rut and sport in the ardent heat of her body, the warmth she had saved for Vance.

Footsteps sounded. Someone was approaching and a rapid flow of Spanish, of which Karen could distinguish only an occasional word, followed from outside the door. Manuel and a woman. . . . But who? The voice sounded familiar. She heard a short exclamation of delight, then a lithe figure bounded through the door. *Of course! I should have known. . . .*

"*Querido . . . ! Estaste . . . ?*" Marcelina halted abruptly, her eyes wide with surprise and recognition. The one woman in the world she despised . . . here, waiting for Jaco! Howling like a wounded beast, Marcelina launched herself at Karen. Now she would tear the golden hair, shred the *gringa's* soft white skin with her nails. Biting and clawing, the Mexican girl vented her fury on the captive woman, screaming in rage and unspeakable frustration. But in the dim room she did not notice the darker, firm tone of Karen's flesh, the fresh, clear, hearty beauty who had replaced the earlier, pampered easterner.

The initial shock of the attack jolted Karen out of her lethargic state and she fought back. For the first time in her life she was in a real fight with another woman, a fight not of innuendoes and cutting phrases, but of fists and nails and teeth, flesh against flesh. Strangely, the sensation was exhilarating; finally she could strike back, exact revenge for the way she had been treated during the last few days. Hands tore at hair, seeking a hold. Karen broke from Marcelina's grasp and, clenching her hand into a solid fist, delivered a staggering blow that sent Marcelina to the floor where she squirmed and rolled away, coming up hard against the wall. Surprised by what she had done, Karen looked at the battered girl on the floor. Trained to pour tea, to write delicate notes, to accept the homage of gentlemen, to always be a lady, she had actually struck back. Delighted with the thought, she started for Marcelina, only to shrink away as the girl slipped a knife from a sheath strapped to her thigh and, holding the blade before her, struggled slowly to her feet.

Face to face the antagonists stood, their shallow breaths the only sound in the room. Marcelina moved the blade back and forth in a short arc and Karen, eyes glued to the gleaming metal, glanced about for a weapon—any weapon. Suddenly the blade was slicing through the air and Karen leaped aside, backing away, searching for room to move, room to maneuver in the hopelessly small hut. Still backing, she felt the wall behind her, slid to her left toward the door, avoiding another slice of the deadly blade. Marcelina turned with her, now facing the door, the last rays of the sun lighting her face, contorted with a grotesque smile, a promise of death. "I kill you now, *gringa*. Now I kill you . . ."

A shadow darkened the room, moved quickly past Karen and tore the knife from Marcelina's hand as she stabbed. "I would not have you mark her, little one," Jaco chided, shoving the enraged girl against the table.

"You! You bring her back to this place . . . our place!" Marcelina spat at his feet.

Jaco watched unperturbed, his face impassive. "Wait outside, *chica*," he ordered flatly.

Marcelina's eyes flashed with fire. "*Putañero! Cerdo!* I hate you. . . ."

His hand, a blur only, flew to her throat and clamped there like a vice, cutting off her words. Marcelina's face grew taut with fear and she froze, afraid to move against the unbreakable grip which pulled her closer and closer. Gasping to catch her breath when he finally relaxed his hold, she slipped her arms around him and sought his lips while his hand lifted her dress and slid the flat of the blade along her inner thigh. Marcelina moaned deeply and thrust her hips and thighs forward into him, not even noticing when he slid the knife back into the empty sheath. "Wait for me outside," he commanded again, gently pushing her toward the door. Marcelina posed briefly for Karen's benefit, flung a final, searing glance at her, and left. Jaco laughed, leaned back on the table. "So. . . . Once again I save you from a knife, eh, *querida?*"

"I am not your *querida*. What do you want with me?" Karen gestured with her head. "She loves you."

Jaco shrugged matter-of-factly. "Many women love me. But you . . . you were Paxton's woman. I stole you. All my life he has what I want, now I have what he wants. *Señor* Paxton will now understand the empty years I have known. You will love me, *querida*."

Karen turned from the word. *Beloved.* . . . She looked out the door to the hills where her true beloved had to be. *Vance.*

Jaco's voice continued behind her, closer, softer, the bluster missing, betraying a hint of a child's dream. "Who knows. . . . The people wish me to lead them, to be their general. Someday I will become *el presidente*. Then I give to you a fine palace where you live like a real *princesa*. A woman like you does much for a man. You will have fine clothes." One hand stroked her hair and she whirled to face him, pressed her back against the wall and watched helplessly as his other hand touched the fringe of the shirt he had given her, traveled up.

"No. . . ." His fingertips sought her breast and she grabbed his wrist, tried to push away his hand, to no effect.

Slowly, he caressed, massaged, teased until she gave up, stood rigidly with back to wall, eyes staring blankly. Inwardly she quailed as her flesh rebelled in spite of herself, as her nipples tightened under his persuasive, practiced fingers. And then he was closer, holding her in his arms, pressing her to him. He was a handsome—cruelly handsome—man, quintessentially male with the fire of countless battles glowing in the depths of smouldering eyes. It had been so long since a man had touched her . . . so long since she had touched a man . . . so long, the emptiness unfilled. . . . A hand cupped her buttocks and drew her up to press against his demanding loins and swollen manhood. . . . "No! No!" she protested frantically, turning away her head.

Surprisingly, he stopped, let her go, and stepped back. "Not yet. You have not learned to love Jaco yet."

"You are an animal," she replied unevenly, shaken by her reaction to his touch. Never would she have believed.

Jaco's face registered mock hurt. "An animal? We are all animals, *querida*. Some of us are weak, some of us are strong. Here in Rio Lobos I am a strong animal. I do as I please. There is no one to help you." He paused, serious. "This morning, I could have taken you. I could take you now. Maybe even carry you to the *cantina* and straddle you for the men to enjoy my performance. But a general does not do these things. Even now I do not force you. Was any man ever so patient?" He stepped to the door, stood in thought a moment, then turned back to her. "Tomorrow, *señorita*. There, on the cot. You will wait for me, and I will come to give you much pleasure. If not, then. . . ." His countenance darkened with an unspoken threat all too clearly read. He waited only a moment, filling the doorway with his terrible size, then turned, and like a shadow before the moon, was quickly gone.

Karen slumped against the wall. *A day. . . . Only one day. . . . So little time in which to. . . .* Again she reconnoitered the room. Approximately ten feet by a little more, the *jacalito* was built strongly with thick walls pocked by gunports, far too small for a person to get through. Topped by a mud roof, the hut guaranteed adequate protection against most attacks, was a place of defense with but one entry and exit, the doorway. The sun had fallen below the rim of the mountains and the room

381

was darkening quickly. A lantern hung on one wall but she did not light it, preferring the privacy of shadow. Rummaging through the room, she covered every inch of floor and wall, searching for anything she might use as a weapon to assist in her escape. Moonlight was streaming through the doorless entryway when she caught a glint of metal beneath the cot. She reached under and grasped a crudely-wrapped wooden hilt. A knife . . . broken, but with an inch of jagged blade protruding from the grip. It was better than nothing, and properly used. . . . She had to move rapidly. Quickly, she fumbled on the cot, wrapped one blanket in a roll and tied it with a piece of rag found hanging on the wall. With luck, she could wrap the second blanket about her and, in the heavy shadows outside, slip past Manuel. . . . Voices again! She had heard no one approach. . . . Frantic, she flung herself on the cot, wrapped herself in the blanket. If they thought her asleep. . . .

"*Buenas noches*, Arcadio. What is it?"

"Jaco sent me to take your place."

"*Gracias, amigo.* Do the riders search?"

"For what?"

"Marquez. He has not returned."

"Nor will he. You are young, *amigo,* and have not ridden with us but a short while. Now hear me when I tell you. Do not ever speak that name again, if you wish to keep your tongue."

"But. . . ."

"The man with that name wished to lead. Two men rode north. He who is fit to lead returned. The other is food for *las hormigas*. It is our way."

Manuel lapsed into silence. To be eaten by the ants was not a pleasant thought. Better to be a contented soldier in *el jefe's* army and ask no question. "*Gracias.* I will speak no more."

Karen heard the clink of a spur. Immediately alert, she clutched the short knife, waiting tensely. A squat, portly figure appeared in the doorway. His back lit by the moon, she could not see his face, could see only he was missing one ear.

"The *señorita* is asleep?" Not receiving an answer, the figure entered the room. "The *señorita* sleeps?" Arcadio repeated softly, stepping closer.

"No," Karen replied, suddenly afraid.

"I am sorry. Perhaps the *señorita* is lonely. Arcadio can be good company for a lonely *señorita*. So they say."

"Pay them and they will say anything," Karen hissed. "Get out of here. Leave me alone . . . " Arcadio stepped nearer. ". . . or I shall scream for Jaco. What he would do to you, if he found you here, would not be nice."

Arcadio stopped, scowled, and muttering an oath in Spanish, retreated through the door. Karen loosened her grip on the knife. *So. Jaco's name will keep me safe from the bandits. Small comfort. Now, what will keep me safe from Jaco? I must escape. Another hour and he will think I'm asleep. Then, if I can just . . .*

Marcelina watched as Jaco and five others, who were to be stationed as guards, rode from Rio Lobos toward the North Pass, far up in the weather-battered reaches of the mountains. She had passed the night with her lover, finger-nails raking his back as she matched his violent thrusts with equally tempestuous sexual frenzy until both lay limp and exhausted, released from the tensions generated by their week-long fast. Her body felt good, this morning. Soft, sated, warm and relaxed. She waved once as her man, her lover, rode past, so handsome, strong and arrogant. Within little more than a moment he was out of sight and, as if his very presence was enough to keep her bouyant, she experienced a sinking sensation of dissatisfaction. What were his plans for the Paxton *gringa?* Why had he brought her to Rio Lobos? For revenge on *Señor* Vance? Or something more? If only he weren't so *tacito*, if only he'd tell her more. . . .

A girl not much older than herself stepped from the *cantina* and, checking the load in a revolver, headed toward the *jacalito* where Karen was kept. "Ursula, where do you go?"

The girl turned as Marcelina neared. "I am to take the *señora* Paxton to the river."

"I will do it."

"But I was told . . . "

Marcelina took the pistol from the girl and thrust it into the waistband of her skirt. "I will do it." The emphasis in her voice curtailed any further protest from Ursula, who shrugged indifferently and returned to the *cantina*. Tossing her head, Marcelina walked across the plaza and stopped at the prison hut. *"Señora."* There was no answer. *"Señora!* Wake up!"

Karen woke, a dream of Vance and. . . . *My God* . . . It was light, daytime. *No. . . . No . . . I couldn't have.* . . . Wildly, she looked about. Nothing had changed except the night. She had slept, her chance was lost. A figure stood in the doorway. As inconspicuously as possible, she ripped open a slit in the straw ticking, shoved in the knife. *Control . . . have to control myself.*

Marcelina stepped to the bed, ripped the cover from Karen. "Wake up, *Señora* Paxton," she said with a sarcastic laugh. "Time for your bath."

Karen sat up groggily, playing for time to think. "I don't want. . . ."

"I am to take you to the river. You will bathe."

"I better go too," grumbled Arcadio quickly from the door. "She might try to escape."

Marcelina pulled the revolver from her waistband. "She will not escape. You only wish to watch. Come, *señora.* We go now." Brandishing the pistol, she stepped to one side, jabbed the weapon into Karen's ribs as the hated *gringa* passed. Karen, startled, jumped through the door, squinted in the strong morning light. "Is the beautiful *señora* frightened?" Marcelina asked.

Karen's eyes flashed indignantly and she straightened her shoulders. "Certainly not," she said flatly, and strode past the guard without a backward glance. *How could I have slept so long? How* . . . ? The answer was obvious. Four days of terror and tension had exhausted her. The shadow of the revolver in Marcelina's hand preceded her down the path.

Rio Lobos, from which the settlement took its name, was little more than a creek whose waters, fed by an underground spring, were piercingly cold in contrast to the sunbaked rocks around them. Safely concealed behind a curtain of mesquite and upthrust boulders, Karen stripped and stepped tentatively into the creek, shivering violently as the chilly current bit at her feet and ankles, enveloped thighs and waist. She was forced to squat in order to completely submerge herself, and after the first breathtaking immersion, found the waters refreshing. Marcelina stood by silently, regarding Karen's body with no small degree of astonishment. The *gringa* was different. No longer pallid, her skin glowed with health. Flesh firm from riding and hours of work, face, arms and shoulders tanned lightly, Karen was as lithe and trim as any ranch girl. Marcelina scowled angrily. The Mexican girl had expected a weak, pampered physique, not the hardy, capable yet utterly feminine loveliness that made her feel sour and unkempt, cheap and faintly tawdry.

Karen stepped from the creek, dried herself and dressed, beating the dust from her jeans before putting them on again. She felt better for the bath, refreshed in spite of the dangers with which she was surrounded. Sleep and the frigid, crystal clear waters had soothed some of the worry of her spirit, imbued her with a reckless sense of buoyancy. It still wasn't too late. Alone with Marcelina, she could . . . the metallic click of a revolver being cocked brought her back to reality. "Now, *señora*, you will run," Marcelina said from behind her.

Karen pivoted slowly to face the Mexican girl, cast an experienced, calculating eye up and down the one obstacle between herself and the hills. The wind ruffled Marcelina's skirt. Her brown, tawny bare shoulders were marked and scored from Jaco's intense love-making. The peasant blouse, low-cut, was pressed tightly against small proud breasts, the nipples dark and erect with the thrilling prospect of danger, of the deed she must commit. One other thing Karen noticed during the silent, searching interval. Marcelina wore the cameo locket about her throat. Karen had dismissed its loss as unimportant, but seeing the carved profile brought back the past months with a rush, and in the briefest of seconds the chronicle of her metamorphosis flashed through her mind in a pastiche of a myriad moments, monumental and insignificant, spanning the months from her arrival in Texas to that very second when she stood alone and faced a gun pointed at her heart. The broken knife was back in the *jacalito*, but the lack of a weapon didn't bother her. She doubted if she would have used it, either on Marcelina or, had the time come, on Jaco. But if she lacked the courage or inclination to take a life, Karen was not afraid to lose hers. Not that she would give up without a fight. . . . She looked at the revolver with abject scorn. "Is that the gun you used to kill Emilio?"

Marcelina blanched. "No!" She had not expected such news. "I . . . I did not. . . . I mean . . . he is dead?

385

The gun. . . ." She drew herself up, refusing to grovel in front of the *gringa*. "I was only going to wound him, but the gun went off before I expected."

"You killed him. He died horribly, after nearly two weeks of pain. One of the few words he muttered before he died was your name."

"Stop it."

"I remember how he would play for you and watch you dance. He loved you, I think. His death is on your soul."

"Stop! I did not mean to. I don't think he is dead."

"You know what I say is true."

"Shut up. Jaco is my lover. He would tell me. . . ."

The key! My God, why didn't I think of it. . . . Karen forced herself to relax, to think clearly. "Jaco is too much man for you," she said scornfully.

"I am his woman! When he is *el presidente*, I will be his *señora*. But you come. First you come to the ranch with *señor* Vance and then here, only things are different. See? I have your jewelry. I take it a long time ago. First, the jewelry, now your life."

"If Jaco loves you, why worry about me?" Karen asked.

"I am his woman. He loves me," Marcelina repeated insistently, more to convince herself than Karen.

"Then why are you afraid?"

"You . . . you have magic."

"Nonsense."

"You have ways of . . . twisting a man's thoughts. No more talk. Run. Now!"

"No."

Marcelina aimed the revolver directly at Karen's chest, only inches away. "Run!" she screamed, her voice echoing from the hills.

"No. If you are going to kill me, then you will have to shoot me like this, in the front, and explain to Jaco why you did it."

Marcelina's face darkened with fury and frustration, yet her gaze faltered. She could not meet Karen's piercing, accusatory stare. "You . . . are evil!" she hissed, but the gun wavered, lowered.

Her life at stake, Karen pressed home the attack with the verbal weapons that never had failed her. "Evil? I? Am I the one who opened the gates, who betrayed her friends? Am I the one responsible for all those who died? Emilio . . . Brazos . . . the others. I am not she who betrayed her loved ones to a man like Jaco, the man who murdered your mother."

Marcelina stepped back, eyes widening. "Do not say that," she whimpered, aghast at the revelation, struck to the quick by the news of her mother's death.

"It's true. Look at me and you will know what I say is true. She lies on the hill with Elizabeth and the children. And he never told you. The man who killed your mother never told you. I was there. I lost my baby. He was born dead during the attack. I saw him shoot her. Maruja is dead." Marcelina was reeling now. Her lips trembled, the gun dangled from her fingers, useless. Karen sensed victory and would not be dneied. "Maruja is dead," she repeated. "Murdered by her own son."

A blade of grass dropped in the water would have sounded like a rifle shot in a small room in the silence that followed. Marcelina's face turned bloodless. Her voice was a hoarse whisper. "What . . . ? What . . . ?"

"Murdered by Jaco, her own son. True was his father. He told me. Jaco is Vance's brother; he is your brother. Look at him closely. You will know, as he has all this time."

Marcelina staggered drunkenly. The gun dropped to the sand. Sobbing, she put her hands to her mouth to force back the bitter acid taste. Jaco killed her mother. Jaco was her lover. Jaco was her brother . . . her own brother . . . and she had . . . Moaning in anguish, despairing in the enormity of her sin, she spun about and ran down the creek bed, disappearing around the clump of mesquite.

Karen sagged, spent with the emotion of the scene. Marcelina . . . poor Marcelina. The shock had staggered her to the core and now, in the aftermath, Karen was suddenly embarrassed by the viciousness of her attack, ashamed for the way she had so totally destroyed the girl. The destructive power of words was as deadly as a gun, for did not Marcelina and Bodine have much in common? Karen shook her head sadly. No matter what Marcelina had done, she now deserved pity, for only . . . the gun! It lay on the sand within easy reach, forgotten when Marcelina flew down the path. *Now . . . Now. . . .* A quick glance showed no one was watching and Karen ran to the weapon. Stooping to pick it up, she recoiled with sudden fright as the revolver exploded and jumped away from her. Arcadio stepped from behind the clump of mesquite, his rifle ready for another shot. "The *muchacha* is very careless, *si?*" Karen's spirits sank in the face of the smoking rifle. "I ask myself, why does she do this thing?"

"You will never know."

Arcadio laughed, picked up the pistol and shoved it in his belt. "Come. The story will amuse Jaco. I shall. . . ."

"You will mention nothing of this," Karen interrupted. "If you do, I will tell Jaco you forced me."

Hesitant, Arcadio looked about furtively. "He will not believe you," he said, nervously wetting his lips.

It was Karen's turn to smile. "Won't he?" Turning away, she stalked down the path, ignoring the troubled outlaw.

Arcadio stared glumly. If only he could figure out what had happened. The *gringa* . . . of her he was afraid. A glimmer of an idea formed in the back of his mind. He was not afraid of Marcelina, and she did not know the *gringa* had forbidden him to speak. The next time Jaco rode, he would find a way to stay behind. He and Marcelina could discuss the matter in great detail, for certainly she would not want Jaco to know what she had done. Grinning in anticipation, he hurried along to catch the *señora* and escort her back to the *jacalito*.

Shadows crept down from the hills, swept irresistibly across the rocky slopes and brought the chill cloak of evening to wrap the baking earth. Manuel, pretending he was a soldier already, shifted his rifle from one arm to the other then resumed his stance, leaning against the mud brick wall. Karen studied him from inside the door, praying for him to doze off before Jaco came. A moment of indiscretion, of untimely relaxation, was her only hope, but even that faded as a solitary rider made his way into town. Jaco was returning. From across the plaza she could hear singing and shouts of laughter filtering from behind the closed bat-wing doors of the *cantina*. The rider halted, listening to the festivities within, then dismounted and entered, disappearing into the glare of the lanterns. Time was running out. First he would drink with his men, then come for her. She shrank back into the darkness until the back of her legs touched the edge of the cot and she sat down, staring at the moonlit door and waiting.

How long she remained there, motionless, she could not say. Seconds? An eternity? She had no more plans. There would be no escape. Tomorrow she would be . . . what? And Jaco, with or without her, would ride off to a self-proclaimed generalcy and as easily attained glory. Suddenly she was no longer alone. Her heart leaped, caught in her throat. Jaco stood in the doorway, filling the frame, cutting out the light. As casually as if arriving home after a day's work, he lifted the *serape* over his head, dropped it to the floor. Gunbelt and hat followed. "Your clothes, *señorita*," he said softly.

The knife . . . ! Where had she placed the knife? On the cot, the table? *The mattress. It's in the mattress . . . don't panic . . . whatever you do, don't panic . . .*

"Never mind. I shall remove them myself. You would like that? Many do." He drew close to her, his hand touching, tilting her chin. "But first, the kiss."

Karen's silent acquiescence lulled him, made him overly confident. He failed to see her hand, only heard the whisper of motion as the jagged metal arced through the air and carved a crimson furrow through his cheek. Jaco howled with pain and rage, stumbled backward and crashed into the table. The bloody knife blade clenched tightly in her fist, Karen ran for the door. Jaco lunged from the floor, one outstretched arm tripping her and sending her reeling against the wall, the weapon skittering from her hand. A second later his weight fell on her and he was kissing her, brutally, cruelly. Karen twisted her head away. *"Ramera! Mujer perdida!"* he cursed.

"The bleeding general! Pahh!" She spat in his face. "Braggart! Butcher of your mother! Do you think I would give myself to you? I would rather die first."

Jaco slapped her, the palm of his hand drawing blood from her mouth. Lurching to his feet, he dragged her upright by the hair and hauled her from the *jacalito*. "So . . . you would rather die first. Before my men are finished, you will wish you had, *señorita*. You will beg me for forgiveness, beg me to shoot you, to put you out of your misery." He touched the bloody streaks along his cheekbone and cursed her again. She had carved him, marked him for life. No woman had ever done such a thing to Jaco. Wherever men gathered the story would be told, and men would laugh.

Karen fought, tried to strike, kick or claw him, all to no avail. He was simply too powerful. She could not stop him, could only clench her teeth in desperation as he kicked open the *cantina* door. Smoke stung her eyes. A cacophony of coarse laughter and obscene mirth assaulted her ears. The stench of sweating, unwashed bodies, the aftermath of debauchery, of stale tobacco and hard liquor, was nearly unbearable.

A shot rang out and the men's voices fell. Jaco spoke in the silence, his voice tight and forced through his seething fury. "Tonight many of you leave to visit your homes and your villages, to say good-bye to your families before you become *soldados*. My loyal *compadres*, tomorrow I will be your *general*. Tonight, to celebrate, I bring you this gift so you will remember your good friend, Jaco." He looked about the room, reading the faces as they stared at the *gringa*, the untouchable woman for such as they. A murmur of startled realization grew as the men whispered to themselves and each other. Jaco waited until the tension could be touched, until the men became a single beast, then thrust Karen into their midst, shouting, "Enjoy her as you will!"

A ragged cheer rose, filling the room. Several bandits fired revolvers into the ceiling, adding the roar of gunfire to the overwhelming clamor. Leering faces formed a circle around her, closed in. There was no time to think. Time, life, blurred in a haze of unrelieved animal terror. Karen lashed out wildly as groping hands caught at her, touched her hair, breasts, shoulders, buttocks, thighs, grabbed and caught between her legs, spun her about dizzily. Lights and smoke swirled about her in a purgatorial conspiracy. Derisive shouts swelled and faded, swelled again and diminished, unheard in the hallucinatory sea of hands and grinning faces. Her shirt tore and she clutched at the shredded strands, no longer aware, only acting on instinct. Hair flying, she was sent careening to the other side of the circle, then back across to more eager, monstrous hands. Above the din, the women of the *cantina* urged on the men with shrill cries.

An outthrust ankle sent her tumbling forward. More hands caught her, set her upright. Hands clawed at the top of her jeans, tore loose the buttons then spun her away again. Hands tugged violently on a trouser leg. Karen grabbed at her waist, but as she did the shirt was torn away. The sight of her breasts roused the bandits to new frenzy, and an undifferentiated roar of lust went up as a sea of hands caught her arms, lifted her bodily into the air and laid her down on a table. One of the bandits leaned over and covered her breasts with a series of repulsive, slobbering kisses. As he straightened, Karen freed one leg and drove her foot into his groin. The outlaw paled. Through the roar of laughter at his plight, a bottle crashed over his head and he dropped to the floor. Arcadio stepped to the table. "I am first," he roared. The crotch of his filthy trousers was unbuttoned and Karen averted her terror-filled eyes from the swollen flesh standing in full view. Her leg was caught firmly this time and Arcadio leaned over and slowly, more for the effect on his compatriots, slowly slid Karen's jeans down. . . .

"Hold!" Jaco shouted, pushing his way through to the table. Men backed away from him, still trying to keep in sight the prize they had been promised.

Arcadio glanced up, his eyes red-rimmed with dissolution and lust. "The hell I will. . . ." Jaco's revolver slapped across Arcadio's skull and the outlaw collapsed wordlessly on top of Karen, covering her nearly naked figure with his unconscious weight.

Jaco was not alone. Gonzales was with him, and Gonzales was supposed to be at the North Pass. "A *gringo* is at bay in the hills," Jaco shouted. "Medrano is dead, killed by the *gringo*. But the *Americano's* horse is dead. He is afoot and trapped in the rocks." He paused while the news sank in then went on, his voice silky with anticipation. "The *gringo* belongs to this one. We will save her until we have him, and then . . ." The men glanced about, muttering their discontent. Jaco fired his pistol in the air. "Quiet! I say we will save her until we have him. You will still have your chance with her. Manual, take the *señora* back to my *jacalito*. Watch her well." He reached over and shoved the unconscious Arcadio to the floor, hauled Karen to her feet and shoved her toward Manuel. "Do not let any harm come to her. *Vámonos, amigos!*"

The thought of a second prisoner, of an *americano* so close to town, was sobering at best. If there was one, might there not be more? The bandits hurriedly strapped on their cartridge belts, gathered their rifles and rushed from the *cantina*. Karen, dazed but somehow still on her feet, pulled her jeans about her waist and stared numbly at the outlaw leader. Jaco gazed with appreciation at her naked breasts. Streaks of dried blood caked his cheek. "So, *gringa*. An *hombre* in the pass, and we both know who it is, no? If you were my woman, if they stole you from me, I would ride after you myself. *Si*, even if it was to my death." He grinned widely. "You have seen how much my men like you. I will bring your man here. He, too, shall witness the enjoyment of my *soldados*. Tell me, *gringa*, which of you should I watch? You? Or him?"

Manuel licked his lips nervously and led her outside, back to the mud hut that was her prison. The sight of her naked torso filled him with delightfully stirring images, all of which were evident in the hungry set of his features. But Karen no longer paid heed to the threat of the present or the promise of her predicament on the morrow. Vance was near. Nothing else counted. Vance was near. Numbly, she plodded away from the nightmare *cantina* filled with hands and shrieking demons, oblivious to the sound of gunfire in the hills.

CHAPTER V

Karen collapsed on the cot, exhausted and drained of all resistance and emotion. The horrible ordeal at the *cantina* had taken a fearful toll. Never in her wildest imaginings could she have conceived the depths of depravity to which she had been subjected. Cowering in the comparative safety of the *jacalito,* she shrunk from the imaginary hands still clutching at her, the leering faces still smiling as they retreated, leaving behind ringing echoes of demonic laughter in her mind. "Tomorrow . . . tomorrow . . . tomorow . . ." they said until she could bear the refrain no longer and clapped her hands over her ears to shut out the clamor. *Tomorrow . . . tomorrow . . . tomorrow . . .* Sobs wracked her body. What horrors did the morrow hold in store? More of the same? Worse? What could be worse? *No! Don't think it . . . !* Compelled to appease the brutal appetites of men, of beasts, to endure the living nightmare until . . . new fears, hellish fiends of the night rose to engulf her being until the echoing thunder in the hills broke through her trance-like state to shatter concern for her own safety.

She sat up, listening. They were hunting Vance. He was here! But what chance did he have, on foot and alone against Jaco and the rest? More gunfire rippled across the dark valley, a smattering of volleys, and then silence. Was it over? How long would she have to wait? The quiet grew to ominous proportions and a mantle of silence settled over the *jacalito,* ghostly gray in the brittle pale light of the moon. *Is it over? Is it over?*

She woke in the half light of dawn, stiff from the cot, uncertain as to her surroundings. A moment later and the full recognition of her predicament once again consumed her thoughts, left her huddled and shivering against the

393

wall, broken in spirit. A figure in the doorway roused her. Manuel entered, lit the single lantern. "I bring you fresh water, *señora*," he said in halting English.

The solicitous gesture warmed her. Looking back, she was sure Manuel had not been among those in the *cantina*. *Perhaps he.* . . . The young man stiffened purposefully as she moved toward him. *No.* . . . The fire of revolution burned too deeply in his eyes. "Thank you, Manuel," she called as he retreated through the door.

The water refreshed her, lifted her from the deadly malaise. A wink of light on metal showed her Manuel had overlooked the broken knife blade in the excitement of the night before. Quickly, she retrieved it and sawed a hole in the blanket, fashioning a crude *serape* to provide cover for her nakedness. The length of rag previously used to roll the second blanket served as a belt for her jeans, and with the moccasins given to her on her arrival, completed her wardrobe. Returning to the bucket, she drank again and rinsed her face and hands. The cool water bolstered her resolve to face with equanimity whatever the day would bring. Waved back from the door by a now gruff and taciturn Manuel, her resolve faded as quickly as it had been born. Reduced to nothing more than waiting, she paced the empty room, keeping a lonely vigil in a circle around the broken table.

The sun was high in the sky and the morning heat had parched the dew from the few blades of grass in the plaza when the shambling wreck that was Arcadio came to relieve Manuel. The older bandit, unconscious on the whiskey-stained floor of the *cantina*, had been left behind in Rio Lobos when Jaco and the others rode out. Now, the unexpected blow on his head having dramatically cooled his ardor, he stared sullenly at the woman inside the hut. Karen, the image of his obscene form looming over her, the horrid, rigid staff and his hands pulling at her jeans, shuddered violently. She could not meet his eyes, could not. . . . A movement against the pale brown backdrop of hills caught her attention. Her imagination . . . ? But again, at the corner of a huge boulder. . . . Men on horseback! They had to be the bandits. Jaco was returning. Ten minutes later he came into full view, weary from a sleepless night and the chase, but straightening as he approached the little town. A rope led from the pommel of his saddle to the bound wrists of a man some ten feet behind the gelding. Half obscured by the dust, the man was forced to keep to a lope in order not to fall behind and be dragged. Vance! Her final chance for escape, captured and bound like an animal behind his enemy's horse.

Karen did not know whether to rejoice or despair. Jaco's hatred ran to such extremes, Vance might have been better off had he met a quick, merciful death rather than endure whatever diabolical scheme his captor might concoct. Yet amidst her sinking spirits there was a secret joy. He *had* come to her, and for better or worse they would be together again, if only for a short time. No matter what happened afterward, she would be able to tell him she loved him more than anyone, anything, more than life itself.

The outlaws looked worn and haggard. Three sported crudely bound wounds. Two others were draped over their saddles, lifeless arms swinging in funereal cadence with the horses' movements. Jaco, in the lead, rode nonchalantly, one hand on hip and a wry smile of victory on his face, once goading the horse to a brief canter. Behind him, Vance stumbled into a run, somehow managing to remain on his feet. The tiny procession halted across the wind-swept plaza and Jaco stared at the prison hut where Karen waited, barely visible inside the doorway. The scab on his cheek itched. His eyes burned with fatigue. "Tonight," he reminded himself, then drove his spurs into the flanks of the animal beneath him. The gelding leaped forward and Vance was jerked off his feet and dragged skidding along the dry ground, barely missed by the flashing hooves of the other bandits' horses.

Karen screamed involuntarily and tried to rush to stop Jaco, but Arcadio moved quickly to grab her arm and hold her back. "No! Let me go!" she begged, beating ineffectively at the bandit's arm and head. "Let me go!"

Jaco reined up in a choking cloud of dust billowing high in the air to obscure the riders. As the dust settled, vague shadows took form, materialized. Jaco spat to one side, swatted the sand from his clothes and bowed grandiosely, indicating Karen should approach his mount. "*Buenos dias, señora* Paxton. I have good hunting and bring you a gift—" he grinned broadly, "—the illustrious *señor* Paxton."

Karen started toward the prostrate figure behind the horse but Arcadio, at a signal from Jaco, grabbed and restrained her again. Jaco kicked the taut rope, cruelly jerking on Vance's outstretched arms. "Rise, *señor* Paxton," he commanded with a mocking voice. "I have brought you to your woman. Do you not go to her?"

Vance stirred in the dust and rose slowly to hands and knees, then painfully to his feet. Pausing but a moment to get his balance, he stepped shakily around to Jaco's side, held up his bound hands. "The least you could have done," he croaked through bleeding lips, "was drag me through the creek. I'm a mite thirsty."

Jaco scowled. The long run down from the hills and the drag across the plain should have left a broken man, Wracked with pain and cringing in fear. Instead, the hated one confronted his captor with brave words, paid no heed to his wounds and thrust bound, misshapenly swollen hands steadily in front of him. To see such a one squirm, crawl and die would be a great pleasure. The outlaw grinned and his hand slapped at his side, came away with a broadbladed knife whose keen edge glinted in the air, hovered above the dusty, bleeding *gringo*. Karen gasped, misreading his intentions, so he held back to savor her fear for extra seconds, then slashed downward with the blade, laughing at her cry of relief as Vance's bonds fell away. "Do not worry, little *gringa*. I would not harm him—yet. You may have him while we rest."

Vance turned slowly and looked directly at Karen for the first time, hiding his surprise. The last time he'd seen her she was pale and wan, a shrunken figure lying in a sickbed. Before him now stood another Karen, vibrant in health, darker, tawny-skinned. Clad like a bandit princess, her sunburst hair tumbled flowing over her shoulders and back. She straightened proudly to meet his gaze as he soaked up the sight of her, for which he was more thirsty than water by far, then crossed the few yards to her without stumbling. Karen shot a final contemptuous glance toward Jaco, who signaled to Arcadio in defeat. Then she was free and in his arms, heedless of all save his touch, his embrace, the indestructible reality of his love and her own soaring joy.

Jaco, his face darkening with anger, watched them disappear into the hut. What did he care for a *gringa*? Why should it bother him the way she opened her arms to the Paxton whelp? The resemblance between Vance and himself was galling, as if he were an alter ego, a young Jaco who had everything; wealth, power, a magnificent *hacienda* and a beautiful woman. *While I have nothing . . . am nothing but a half-breed. . . .* The frustrating truth rang in his head, pounded in the feverish pit of his soul and fed his hatred. *Every time I reach for them, they disappear. I cannot touch them. He should be dead. She should be mine. The ranch should be mine. . . .* He forced himself to sit straight on the horse. "No," he muttered fiercely. "I am wrong. I have them." He laughed aloud but the sound failed to convince him.

"Did you say something, *jefe?*" Arcadio asked.

"I said," Jaco replied grimly as he turned his horse away from the hut, "I have *them.*"

Vance slept, his cheeks hollow beneath a ragged growth of beard, his skin worn and leathery to the touch. A deep gash ran along his scalp, several open abrasions on his legs, arms, chest and face oozed blood and a gunshot wound gaped in his left forearm. Luckily enough, the bullet had not lodged in the muscle or hit a bone. Not certain of the proper treatment, Karen knew no wound couldn't stand cleaning, so set to work. There was water left in the bucket and firewood in the hearth. Soon she had a small blaze going and water heating. Tearing a strip from the blanket, she boiled it then laved the abrasions, gently working out the sand and dirt ground into his flesh while being dragged across the plaza. There was nothing with which to treat the bullet wound save more strips of blanket. Carefully, she made compresses, bound them tightly in place. As she bathed his chest, one of his hands rose and cupped the back of her head. He was awake. She looked into his face, into the lines creasing his forehead, lines etched by worry and fatigue as well as sun and wind. "I was a damn fool, Karen."

"Don't," she said. "There's no time for that now."

"This may be the only time. It's got to be said now."

"But you don't have to say anything. Not for me."

"I do. For you, and for me." He paused, collecting energy, trying to recall the words so laboriously chosen during the final long, introspective night at the line cabin. "I wronged you, Karen. I knew it even as I was saying the words. I was really blaming myself, but was too damn proud to admit I'd done anything wrong. Too weak to take the responsibility."

"But I . . . I did run," Karen stammered.

"I shouldn't have left you alone. You had no way of knowing what the west would be like. Nothing had ever prepared you, a fact I failed to understand all the way along. From the moment we landed in Corpus, I was putting you up against problems you had never encountered, with which you had no way of dealing, and then judging your performance. If you made a mistake, I compounded it by blaming you, not giving you a chance to learn. I pressured you to assume a way of life utterly foreign to you." He leaned back wearily. "I was wrong."

Karen pressed her face against his chest, not desiring he should note the tears moistening her eyes. His hand stroked her hair. "Didn't do such a good job of getting you back, did I?"

"You came," Karen whispered, lifting her head to gaze into his eyes. "You came. More than anything anyone has ever done for me, you came. That's what counts." Gently, inside the gossamer tent of her tumbled hair, her lips met his in a slow, languid kiss of sweet contentment, interrupted when Vance winced involuntarily. She drew back, stroked the hair from his forehead. "I missed you."

"I missed you too. All the time." He grunted, pulled her down to his side where she nestled in the crook of his arm, careful not to brush against his wounds. For a long moment, neither spoke, only lay silently in the brief, fragile security of the afternoon. "Ted told me about you," Vance said finally.

"What did he tell . . . ?" The memory of the gunshots broke her thought. "Ted? Is he . . . ?"

"He was telling me about what you'd been doing at the ranch. Spent a few hours at the line shack with me, just before they found you." He paused, went on, deciding there was no point in holding back anything. "He's dead. He lived long enough to tell me about the ambush. How he held on so long, I don't know. I watched him die." His voice lowered, strangely choked. "Funny how you think you know a person. I rode with Ted Morning Sky for almost fifteen years, from the time we were kids. Even during the war. We were like brothers . . . and I didn't know him at all."

"The one who shot him is dead," Karen replied.

"The man I found on the trail? Just this side of the Rio Grande?"

"His name was Marquez. He and Jaco didn't trust each other, and when he attacked me, Jaco pulled him off. There was a terrible fight. I tried to escape, but Jaco caught me and took me back to camp."

"I know. I could tell. By that time he wasn't trying to hide his tracks. I've heard of Marquez. You were lucky." He glanced down at her, noted her bruised cheek. "Karen . . ." he hesitated, continued with a rush. "Has he . . . harmed you?"

"No. He tried, but I cut him with a knife."

Vance chuckled mirthlessly. "I wondered who did that. Good girl."

"Vance, he hates us so. There's nothing he won't do. . . ." She grew quiet, ashamed at her display of weakness, reluctant to tell him of the promise Jaco had made, of his plans for them. There would be time enough later for such knowledge. Now, Vance's presence instilled in her the desire to depend on his strength, to lie protected in his arms. No matter what Jaco did later, they had this little time together, this little time of love to share. Trembling, her fingers ran lightly over his chest, gently caressing the skin of her one love until she realized his eyes had closed and he had drifted off to sleep again, exhausted from the days on the trail and the final desperate night in the hills. *Vance . . . I love you, Vance. . . .* She kissed his hand and lay quietly at his side, keeping watch over his sleep. *I'll not let you down, my love. Not this time . . . you'll see.* The room grew warm and close and the long day eddied into afternoon.

"This is very touching." Jaco's voice jolted her awake. How long had she slept? Karen blinked her eyes and tried to focus on the shadowed figure blocking out the late afternoon sun filtering through the doorway. The bandit tilted a bottle to his lips and took two long swallows. Beside her, she felt Vance nudge her gently and knew he was awake. His hand clenched to a fist, but she covered it with her own, then stood and glared defiantly at the outlaw chieftain as he strode into the room, followed by the light.

Jaco placed the bottle on the broken table, his arm moving across and down as if exploring each position with agonizing slowness. He wore a short coat of brushed buckskin and a pair of high-waisted trousers, elaborately stitched and showing little sign of wear. Save for the scarred face and bitter, hardened eyes, he was a dashing figure fit to fill the pages of a dime novel. His right arm suddenly swept out to encircle Karen, bringing her body next to his. Vance leaped from the couch only to stop abruptly as Jaco's left hand darted from under his coat, a revolver in his fist.

"Vance . . . no!" Karen exclaimed. The barrel was pressed against Vance's sternum.

' The *señora* does not wish her lover to become a dead *campeon*. It is wise. Dead heroes make terrible lovers, so it is said."

"Put away the gun, *chacal*," Vance said, oblivious to the cold touch of death at his chest, "and we'll see how much of a dead hero I am."

"*Si, campeón.* I take the gun away," Jaco chuckled. The pistol lifted until the barrel was placed to Karen's breast. Karen stiffened at the pressure of the metal through the blanket, forced herself to remain calm. Jaco's face neared hers and, his eyes on Vance, he kissed her on the lips, again and again, each kiss more lasciviously antagonizing than the preceding. But this time, Karen did not struggle, for to resist now meant certain death, not only for her, but her beloved as well.

Knuckles white, fingers dug like claws into the wood, Vance gripped the edge of the cot. Self-restraint was nearly impossible, but the position of Jaco's revolver made fruitless any display of the grating emotions building within him. Forced to watch, not dreaming of what intolerable extensions of this same scene he would later be forced to watch, he saw his most hated enemy taste the lips of the woman he loved. Jaco finally released her and stepped back against the table. Transferring the gun to his right hand, he took the whiskey bottle in his left. Karen backed away toward Vance while the outlaw studied her. "The *señora* is much woman. Her lips are sweet. I understand why the *gringo* is fool enough to come to Jaco and Rio Lobos."

"You harm her and I'll kill you, Jaco. I don't care how many men and guns, you won't have enough to stop me."

Jaco lifted the bottle in salute. "*Muy bueno, señor.* Spoken like a *genuino* Paxton, *verdad?*" He spoke the name

400

with contempt. "But that is the way with you Paxtons, is it not? The magnificent *hacienda*, many cattle and riders, the best women and big words. Very big . . . words."

Vance's face darkened. When he continued his voice was solemn and thick with malice. "I don't make empty threats, *amigo*."

Amigo?" Jaco laughed awkwardly. "No, *señor*. I have news for you. You should say, *'hermano'! Si. Medio hermano.* Half brother. Would that not be more interesting?" He paused, ready to be amused at Vance's disbelief. Instead, Vance only stared noncommittally. "You think much of your father! Ha! There is much you should learn."

"No," Karen protested, realizing what he was about to say.

"Be quiet," Jaco ordered. "*Medio hermano*, we are brothers by the same father. *Señor* True Paxton rutted with my mother, took his pleasure and left her. I am his son as much as you, yet when we hungered, he did not come to feed us, when the north wind howled in winter song, when we shivered beneath its breath, he did not offer us shelter in his magnificent *hacienda*.

"My mother, she always gave reasons. 'Paxton has forgotten us.' 'The past is better left dead.' 'He does not know of us or where we are.' Pah! I spit on her reasons. As a boy, I wondered why I have no father as the other boys. As a young man, the wonder grows to hate, fed by hunger and the scorn of the *norteamericanos*. I ask myself, what does a few *pesos* mean to a man like that? If he truly wished, he would find me, bring me to him.

"And then one day I hear more. I hear of the great Paxton ranch, the fine sons who live like the *dons*, like men of title, and I can abide no longer. I leave my mother, taking only the clothes on my back, a gun and my hatred. Later, I find out my mother is taken in by the kind and gracious True Paxton to be a maid and servant to the *gringos* at whose table she should sit, not like a humble dog, but resplendent, the head of a magnificent household. When I learn this, I curse the very gods. My mother permits this injustice, and I grow to hate her as much as the old man— the *putañero* to whom you listen with such respect. A man of character? Pah! I spit on his character!"

Karen looked worriedly at the features of the man she loved, found it difficult to believe he remained so utterly calm. *"Putañero?"* Vance began. "No. A man like any other. True met Maruja once during the war. They had one night together and were separated. He didn't see her, know where she was or about you until the day he rescued her from the Comanches. Maruja was a fine, gentle woman, a woman of patience and warmth. It never surprised me he loved her once, or that he still loved her, in a quiet way.

"My own mother knew this. She told me . . . and understood. In war, many things happen that might not otherwise occur. It is a sad truth, which does not demean the people affected. I believe my father often wondered about Maruja, but in the early years he never had the time or money to find out what had become of her. He was trying to build a ranch and he had children of his own. He had no way of knowing you even existed, but your hatred and jealousy made you believe otherwise.

"I have known of you for years, *mi medio hermano*, and it was from Elizabeth Paxton, my mother, I heard the tale. She first heard the story in San Antonio and then, much later, from Maruja herself, who was afraid of what you had become, of your insane hatred and of what such bitter resentment might lead you to do. Elizabeth decided the responsibility was hers: she had to inform her sons for their own protection. Our most fearful enemy was liable to be our own kin. Our own brother."

Vance laughed softly, his eyes glimmering with ironic amusement. "So you are late, *medio hermano*. Does my murderer brother think to taunt me with a truth I have known all along, that he himself has never been able to accept? I pity you, Jaco. You had your chance, but when True sent the messenger to you, you were so eaten with hate you couldn't accept his offer, instead killed the bearer of love and conciliation and sent back his ears and hands to the sender. Your heart is dead and your soul carrion, not fit for the buzzards. I pity you."

Triumph thwarted, Jaco's fury burst. "Pity! You pity Jaco?" he shouted. A cry tore his throat and he lunged at Vance, smashing the gun barrel down on his wounded arm. Vance paled, grimaced as searing bolts of agony coursed through his arm. Struggling to retain consciousness, he sagged to the floor where Jaco kneed him in the jaw and sent him crashing back against the wall. Karen pummeled and cat-clawed the outlaw chieftain, but he shrugged her off, hurling her to one side, out of his way. Desperate, no longer thinking of herself, she crawled between Vance and any further punishment. Jaco paused. His lips pulled back in an animal snarl and his breath came in furious spasms. The gun in his hand rose to point at Vance's head.

The click of the hammer being cocked was deafening in the sudden stillness, in which three bodies stood motionless in strained tableau. A fly buzzed in unconcerned circles, weaving intricate airy patterns between the outlaw and his captives. The sound droned on, subjectively louder and louder before the impending act of violence. Karen closed her eyes, not able to meet the unrelenting stare of the single cavernous eye at the end of the gun barrel. "No," Jaco purred, his face relaxing. "Not yet. The pleasure would be too quick. I have waited too long, spent too much of myself. Tonight my men will celebrate, *señor*. You and your *señora* will provide them with pleasure. This time, you will not interrupt as before—save with howls of rage. No, *Señor* Paxton, *señor campeón*. Tonight you will watch as Jaco and his *vaqueros* take your woman again and again. I would watch you froth at the mouth like a mad dog as you stand tied, close enough to touch her, close enough to hear her struggle and cry out in pain as we take our sport with her. Your rage will do you no good, for as the last man spills his seed in her belly, I shall slit yours. I have waited a long, long time for this, *hermano*. I will be glad to be done with it." He slid the gun into his belt, picked up the whiskey bottle and walked to the door. "And you, *señora*, perhaps, if my men enjoy their sport, I let them keep you. I would have made you a *princesa*. Now, you can be *puta* to the scum!"

Jaco stepped outside where Manuel bolted upright, leaping to attention. The young guard coughed nervously and looked sternly about, an unconscious admission only magnifying his earlier inattention to all but what had gone on inside the *jacalito*. "Manuel!"

"*Si, mi general!*"

"I am not *el general* yet," Jaco replied, nevertheless flattered. "Perhaps in a few days, if all goes well. Maybe you will be a *capitán*, eh, Manuel?"

The youth brightened enthusiastically, delighted with the prospect of assuming rank in the yet to be formed army of

403

the grand revolution. "*Si, como no, señor.* To be *capitán* would be a great honor."

"If you would be so honored, you would do well to keep away from open doors. *Entiende?*"

Manuel paled, nodded vigorously. "I understand completely, *señor.*"

"*Muy bueno,*" Jaco said, smiling as he walked away from the thoroughly cowed young man.

"Jaco!"

The bandit stopped, turned quickly. Behind him, in the doorway of the prison hut, a pale figure stood, barely holding himself erect with the aid of the sides of the door. "Remember what I told you, *chacal.* The hand of peace was extended to you once. You rejected it." Jaco stood with head swaying like a bull confused as the voice drifted eerily across the plaza. "Do you feel a chill, jackal? It is, as they say, footsteps walking over your grave."

Jaco had a choice. He could kill the *gringo* as he stood in the doorway or he could wait. The choice had been made long ago, but he didn't know it. Now, with the ghostly-white figure close enough to kill, the choice came back to haunt him. Stubbornly, he would have his vengeance as he had dreamed night after countless night. Only now the plaguing dream would be made real in flesh and torment culminating in sweet triumph, in vengeance realized for the many years. The Paxton whelp would know suffering as Jaco had known it, would howl, and howling, run screaming to death and out of the dream that would give him no peace. Still . . . hurriedly, he turned and strode away from the voice, away from. . . . Had he felt a chill? He wasn't sure. Maybe only a little one, nothing to worry. . . . "Remember!"

The word caught him from behind, slapped him, lingered, caught in the valley, spun around like a dust devil driven wildly about by capricious winds. "Remember . . ." Jaco was a child, to be bothered by such a man. The whelp's arm was wounded, possibly broken. He had not eaten for a day. He would be bound hand and foot. There was nothing to worry about. Nothing . . . "Ursula!"

"*Si, señor.*"

"I do not see Marcelina. Where is she?"

"I do not know, *señor.* We spoke this morning, then she went with the *gringa* to the river."

"I told *you* to go with her."

"She insisted, *señor*, said . . . "

"Get out of here," he snarled, waving her away. Alone, he turned to stare back at the *jacalito*. The figure was gone. There was a chill in the air, even though the sun was not yet below the mountain peaks. For no reason, he looked up suddenly. *Un zopilote*, a buzzard, circled lazily above him, stirring the dark premonition lodged in the back of his mind. Troubled, he turned away from the *cantina*, sauntered absent-mindedly toward the *tienda* and entered, pausing in the door as his eyes adjusted to the gloom inside the shop.

The interior was empty save for the motes of dust dancing in the bright rays shining through the cracks in the walls and door. A cat walked in from the back room, glanced about and yawned to signal her boredom with the afternoon before settling into slumber. Flores, the diminutive Mexican shopkeeper who somehow managed to retain his girth in spite of the empty shelves, shuffled into the front room from his quarters. "What is it, *señor*?" He fumbled with his glasses, squinting to see who stood before him. "There is little here. I have not felt up to the trip across the divide. San Pedro gets farther away as I become older."

Jaco looked about, puzzled, wondering why he had come to the store. "We leave tomorrow, old man. The *putas*, they will follow. They always follow. You will be left alone, with nothing more than the corpse of a *gringo* for company. Who will spend gold for your goods?"

Flores laughed soundlessly, more like a wheeze than a sound of mirth. "Goods? My shelves are full of dust. Would you buy dust?"

"What will you do?"

The old man stared, his good eye enormous behind the lens, his bad eye milky white and unseeing. "Do? I will die in peace, *señor*."

Jaco scowled sourly, perturbed by the old man's evil eye. He should have made the *viejo* leave with the other villagers when the bandits moved in. He should have gone directly to the *cantina*. He should have . . . the chill again! Angry he should be so affected by old wives' tales, he turned abruptly and stalked out.

"Jaco!"

He glanced back. Again his name from the back! The old man stared into the fading light. "Tell your *vaqueros* . . . no. Tell your *soldados* in the grand army of the revolution I will sell them my dust. Yes. Tell them to hurry—ha ha ha—while I still have dust to sell." He slammed the door and Jaco hurriedly crossed to the *cantina*, still hearing Flores as the old man mulled aloud, over and over to himself, "Dust for soldiers. Yes. Ha ha ha. Dust for soldiers, soldiers for dust."

The old man bolted the door and stared through the cracks until Jaco disappeared around the corner of the *cantina*. His laughter changed to a croaking cough and he shuffled past the vacant shelves to rummage behind the counter, found a brittle plug of dusty tobacco and broke off a section in his mouth. He glanced once more at the bolted door, half expecting to see Jaco again. There was no one there. Alone, he sighed and stepped through the ragged curtains masking the entrance to the back room. Marcelina stepped out of the shadows and returned to her place before the hearth. "You hear?" Flores asked.

"*Si*. I heard. He will leave tomorrow to be a general."

"If you plan to hide here long you had better forget it. *El gran jefe* and the others will surely come to take what little I have left, then again to search for you. And what can one old man do to stop them? Tonight I shall bury that which is most important to me. *Soldados* . . . *!* Ha! When men become soldiers, stealing becomes *requisición*. Do not stay here, *señorita*."

Marcelina shrugged and walked to the back door. Opening it a crack, she looked out at the slowly-cooling hills, dark gray-black shapes against the azure canvas of sky. There was no place to run. Nowhere to hide. *What is the use? Can I hide from the guilt that weighs like* la cruz, *the cross of Christ upon my soul? I have sinned,* Mi hermano, *my own brother.* She fought back the wracking sobs, the overwhelming remorse. *No. I have wept enough. My tears have fallen until there are no more. My eyes are as dry as the sand and the unforgiving stone.* The wind moaned down the North Pass, across the eroded valley floor, a threnody for illicit love and death. *Maruja. Oh, mi madre* . . . the plaintive lament provoked a still deeper response, and suddenly Marcelina knew what had to be done. Jaco had known! He had wilfully, viciously allowed love to flame within her breast, knowing full well the forbidden nature of an alliance between brother and sister. The need to account for her sin and to avenge her betrayal at Jaco's hands grew like a malignant tumor, filling her belly, choking her throat until she could hardly breathe. "Good-bye, *viejo*."

"You return to the *cantina?*"

Marcelina smiled mysteriously. "I return. . . . It is better you do not know."

"If you wish you may stay awhile longer. Sleep, if you like. Later I will have food for you. I will keep watch. When it is dark, you can . . ."

"Forgive me, *Señor* Flores. *Muchas gracias*, but I have eaten that which I should not, and I have slept long enough. Too long. *Adios*." And she was gone.

Vance stared into the gloom, his mind racing. He'd spoken foolishly, angered Jaco all the more. What could he do? Time was short. If only he hadn't passed out, collapsed like a child on the floor. He felt better for the rest, but to what avail? The slightest movement sent waves of pain through his arm, left him weak and nauseated. Sweat beaded his forehead as Karen finished tightening the rags on his splint and tied the sling. Not sure the limb was broken, a bad bone bruise was certain. The splint would help either way. Five minutes later he felt better. Another half hour and he would be able to function.

Karen dabbed with a moistened rag at the swollen lump on Vance's shoulder where he had struck himself when he fell. The afternoon was nearly gone. They would have to try something. Better to die quickly than wait for Jaco to take his pleasure with them. What pain there was, he could live with. "How many guards?" he asked in a flat tone, gesturing toward the door.

"Only one at a time. Arcadio and Manuel alternate. Tonight it is Manuel."

Vance nodded and accepted the dipper of water she handed him, drank deeply and raised his left arm in an attempt to work back some feeling into the stiffened shoulder muscles. "It will have to be soon. We cannot wait for Jaco to come."

"Manuel is armed. What can we do?"

Footsteps sounded outside. Their conversation halted

and Vance melted into the darkness by the door. The moment had come too soon. If Jaco was outside, they were too late. Instead, Manuel appeared in the doorway, his face pale. Crestfallen, he stepped into the room. Karen and Vance stared at him, puzzled by his appearance. As the bandit entered, Vance could see his holster was empty. Why, was evident in seconds, as Marcelina followed him inside, holding his revolver. Karen gasped, shrank back to the tentative safety of the shadows, expecting the worst from the distraught girl.

Marcelina's features grew even more tortured when she saw Vance for the first time. A terrible sadness filled her eyes, and in the darkness, pity welled in Karen, a pity so profound it overrode even her fear of what the girl intended. "I am weary of death, *señor*," Marcelina said to Vance, her voice a hollow echo of the past. "It would be best if you took the gun. I have not the strength to do what must be done."

Vance looked at Karen in surprise. The action gave Manuel his chance. He spun about and lunged for the pistol in Marcelina's hands, wresting it from her grip, trying to turn the gun, to get a finger on the trigger and fire a shot to sound the alarm. But Vance was already swinging his powerful right fist. He caught the youth flush on the jaw. Manuel's head snapped back and the gun jolted from his grasp as he collapsed like an empty sack. Vance, his left arm throbbing wildly, scooped up the gun and glanced at Marcelina, still shaken by his presence. "In the corral are horses. Saddles are in the *granero*, on the other side of the *tienda*," she whispered quickly.

"I don't understand this," Vance said, frowning.

"I have only begun to understand myself, *señor*. There is no time for the telling. Jaco will come soon. Keep to the back of the buildings, and go behind the *tienda*. If the *viejo* sees you he will say nothing. Hurry."

"But you are going with us?" Karen protested.

"No."

"But you must. Jaco will know what you've done."

"Yes." Marcelina smiled. "If he does not, then I shall tell him."

"We can't leave her, Vance."

Vance extinguished the lantern and peered out the door toward the *cantina*. The story was as clear as if Marcelina had spelled out every detail. He turned back to the girl, read the corroboration in her eyes. The invitation he extended was silent, but she understood, answered negatively with a shake of her head. "I am sorry," she whispered. "I must stay." Turning away from him, she picked up his torn and shredded shirt from the cot, held it for him while he shrugged into it. "I am very sorry."

Vance took her arms, held them in a stiff grip. "Marcelina . . ."

"*Vaya con Diós, señor,*" she said, her head lowered. "*Por favor.* Now."

There was nothing more he could say. "*Adios,* little one." He glanced over at Karen. "We'd best get out of here."

Karen frantically grabbed the girl, as if by her touch she could make her listen to reason. "You can't stay here."

Marcelina held out her hand, opened and palm upward to reveal the cameo and chain. "I stole this from you, *Señora* Paxton. My jealousy made me a thief, and worse. Yet I robbed myself of much more. Take it, *señora,* and go. There is much to atone for and little time left in which to do it."

"Karen." Vance whispered, his voice insistent.

Karen took the cameo, handed down from her mother and her mother before. Quickly, she fastened the silver chain about Marcelina's neck, kissed her on the cheek and hurried from the room, her eyes burning from unspent tears.

They crossed unnoticed, keeping to the western edge of the plaza, away from the gradually increasing activity around the *cantina* where two outlaws lurched from the front door, Ursula between them. The bandits were obviously quarreling over the girl and she, her vituperations ignored, was irritated with both of them. Finally, she threw up her hands in disgust and turned back, leaving the two bandits to scuffle together, thoroughly occupied with each other and ignorant of the two figures revealed by the glare of the *cantina's* lights as Ursula opened the door and entered.

Behind the *tienda* at last, Vance began to breathe easier. Now, provided the moon remained obscured, they. . . . The back door of Flores' *jacalito* opened and Karen stifled an outcry as Vance roughly pressed her back against the building. A heavy shape—not the harmless old man of whom Marcelina had spoken—lumbered out. "Arcadio," Karen whispered into Vance's ear. The outlaw staggered off into the night, a burlap sack bulging with goods hung over his shoulder. Vance soundlessly fell in behind him, but a few yards back. Karen glanced into the *tienda* as she walked past, the dark preventing her from seeing the battered, lifeless figure within. Suddenly, fearful of losing sight of Vance, she quickened her pace and stumbled in the brittle dry branches of a tumbleweed.

The noise was enough to break through Arcadio's liquor-befogged senses. "Who is it?" he slurred, wheeling about ponderously.

"Me," Vance answered in a hoarse whisper, leaping the remaining few feet and smashing Arcadio full in the mouth with the barrel of the gun taken from Manuel. The outlaw staggered back, choking, spitting blood and shards of splintered teeth. He held up his hands to ward off further punishment, but too late. Vance bludgeoned him across the skull and the burly Mexican dropped with a groan, so much dead weight. Vance knelt by his side. The sack was full of food, food they would need desperately for their escape. "Let's go," he murmured, heaving the sack over his shoulder and shoving Karen ahead of him.

The horses whinnied nervously as the two made their way across the corral to the shed-like barn. Inside they found saddles and gear as expected, and much more. Uniforms were piled high in stalls. Barrels of gunpowder and boxes of ammunition were stacked against the wall. Dominating the entire floor space of the small structure was a formidable-looking confederate four-pounder cannon which had found its way to Mexico, brought, no doubt, by unreconstructed Rebels who chose exile to surrender, "Jaco's army," muttered Vance. He took a saddle and handed it to Karen, picking another for himself. "Quickly," he said. "You'll have to help."

Outside, he chose two mounts, roped them silently and led them to Karen for saddling. She expertly fell to the task, rapidly arranged blankets, threw the saddles over the horses, tightened the cinches and adjusted the stirrups. The sack of provisions he had taken from Arcadio tied behind his own saddle, Vance grinned. "You have learned," he said. "Let's go. . . . Damn!"

"What?"

"I didn't take his gun," Vance replied, thinking of Arcadio. The supplies had been uppermost in his mind. "No time now. . . . Wait. There's one thing I can do. Get the gate open. I'll be right back."

Her mouth dry with the fear of discovery, Karen ran doubled over, slipped the tie rope and slowly swung open the gate, afraid the creaking sound would be heard in the *cantina.* The bandits who had been brawling were no longer visible, though, and after an eternity the gate finally stood wide. She stiffened as the door to the *cantina* opened and a lone, *serape*-draped figure stepped down onto the worn path leading to what had been their prison. Jaco. . . .

She waited until his back was to her, then ran stealthily back to the barn and was about to call Vance's name when he reappeared in a new shirt, mounted and lashed a bundle to the cantle of his saddle. "Good girl. We'll scatter the horses on our way out."

"Jaco just went out of the *cantina* on the way to. . . . What did you do in . . . ?" Her question died in the asking, for she saw a fiery tongue of flame jut up and lap at the piled supplies inside the barn. Quickly, she mounted and together they bunched the horses and drove them from the corral, as slowly as possible in order to maintain silence. Another minute and they'd be free. . . .

Involved in the task at hand and the urgent need to get away from the barn, Vance failed to notice Arcadio stumble into the flame-illuminated corral, wipe the blood from his eyes, raise the revolver and fire. The outlaw's gunshot spooked the horses and they broke into a gallop as Vance lurched forward in the saddle. Arcadio fired again at the *gringo,* swung his weapon and emptied the remaining four chambers at the woman. Karen winced as something tugged painfully at her sleeve, as leaden death whined harmlessly past. Arcadio cursed and threw the pistol at the retreating figures, then smelled the smoke. Spinning around, he stared in horror at the flames greedily consuming the *granero.*

"The gunpowder!" a voice screamed in the back of his mind. Howling, he broke into a run across the corral. He saw the outline of the *tienda,* where lay the crumpled figure of old Flores, whom he had killed for a sack of food. He saw the figures burst from the *cantina*—his *compadres,* the

411

putas who stole from him and whispered lies in his ears for no more than a *peso*. And as the voice in his mind rose to an uncontainable shriek which spilled from his mouth and filled the valley with an unearthly wail, he saw a child playing in the muddy alleys of his home village. The child was himself. As the boy looked up and his eyes met those of the running man he would become, there was a tremendous flash Arcadio did not see, a resounding explosion Arcadio did not hear. Nor did he feel his massive frame lift leaflike, high into the air and scattered over the countryside, torn limb from limb even as the dream fabric of the child in the alley was rent asunder and lost to the infinite dark.

Jaco whirled, crouched low, gun in hand at the sound of the gunshots. He saw the horses stampede from the corral. Behind them, someone on horseback. No, two. He looked back at the *jacalito* where his prisoners waited, then raced toward the barn and Arcadio's keening cry. The explosion shattered the night and he flung himself to the ground as bits of wood and dust whizzed over his head. The blast was followed by a second, then the riotous chatter from the scattered contents of the broken cartridge boxes. His head pounding, he crawled dizzily to his feet. A woman was screaming in pain, men staggered about crazily in the open. Enraged, he headed for the *jacalito*. His prisoners! Where was Manuel? As if in answer, the youth stumbled from the adobe structure. Jaco raced to the young outlaw, who, only half conscious, babbled meaninglessly, pointing toward the doorway. Jaco jumped past him and into the hut, his pistol drawn and ready, the fear of what he would find tight in his throat. He was met by laughter. Who . . . ? A lurid glare from the fire across the plaza filled the room. Marcelina stepped into the light. "They are gone, *mi hermano*. They are gone and I am responsible."

"You . . . !" Jaco's voice betrayed his astonishment.

"*Señor* Vance, the *gringa*, the gunpowder, the uniforms, the shiny cannon stolen from the *federales*. Your army. . . . Ha! All gone, *mi general*."

Jaco lunged at her, his fingers digging into the coppery shoulders he had lovingly caressed only the night before. "*Puta!* Why have you done this?"

Marcelina stared at him defiantly, accepting willingly the pain in her arms. Her eyes no longer had the capacity for tears. "My brother! You knew! You knew, and we sinned together. We are both damned. What man would look at me without loathing, me, the woman who shared her brother's bed? What man will ride with you, the murderer of his mother and the despoiler of his sister? No *soldado* will follow such a *jefe* as you, not after this night. You have lost all. All! I have done this. Your *puta!* Your sister!" She spat in his face as the bullet slammed her backward into the wall, shattering the silver chain and driving the cameo pendant into her tortured breast. the price had been paid. Marcelina slumped lifelessly to the floor, hate leached from her heart by smiling death. Santa Maria, Madre de Diós...

Jaco walked slowly from the hut. His hand shook from the deed and from the inescapable truth, the irreparable harm done. Manuel backed away from him. "You killed her," he muttered. "Your mother and your sister. Two women.....Your own people....You are *chacal*, as the *gringo* said...." Jaco ignored him, and oblivious to the commotion filling the outlaw settlement of Rio Lobos, headed for the creek. Behind him, Manuel shouted in a broken voice. "You are no *general*. Just *un chacal*, a jackal, killer of women!"

The waters of Rio Lobos carried the ignominious tale downstream as Jaco strode along the bank. There in the brush, the mustang, ground-tethered, cropped at sweet grass, raised his head and shied skittishly as the man approached. Jaco pulled the ground pin free and tried to force himself to calm down. *I will kill them. I will kill them.* ....Unspeaking, he freed the reins, subduing the animal by force, whipping him into quiet submission. Once into the saddle, he guided the gelding along the river and away from the blazing *granero* and *tienda*, away from the bandits searching for their own mounts. He followed the watercourse until it crossed the familiar trail leading to the North Pass, then guided the animal out of the draw and without so much as a glance at the flames that signaled the final fatal culmination of his plans and dreams, rode away forever from the town of Rio Lobos. The *gringo* and his *señora* would be difficult to track at night, but he would continue on, trusting in his hate to guide him...as he had since he could remember.

CHAPTER VI

The smoke from the campfire sought the air with tentative, vaporous tendrils, invisible in the darkness. Great tides of clouds swept across the sky, cumulus barkentines drifting on a sable sea of outflung stars. Somewhere beneath the sparkling depths, like a patch of phosphorescence on the surface of the ocean, small flames of a campfire trembled and danced. Karen had built the fire well within a *cul-de-sac* of huge, barren boulders. She found some scrub cedar, and peeling a strip of bark from one, provided them with a crude vessel for heating water. As long as the flames did not rise above the water level, the bark would not burn. The makeshift pot held enough to bathe Vance's wound and little more. *Vance* . . .

Karen looked at the pain-beset countenance of her husband. She was lucky. The bullet that had tugged at her blanket left only a long reddened burn on her upper arm. She dipped his bandana into the hot water, withdrew it and slid over beside the wounded man. Arcadio's bullet had struck him in the back on his right side just below the belt, plowing a deep bloody furrow through his flesh, glancing off the top of his hip and exiting obliquely, leaving a gaping horror of macerated flesh. Field-dressed with no more than a strip from the bottom of the blanket Karen wore, the bleeding had been arrested for the first few miles, then started again shortly before they made camp. Each mile ridden had been naked, wrenching agony for Vance. Now, the wound exposed and the bleeding stopped again, he winced as Karen applied the steaming compress. The heat soon soothed the ravaged flesh, however, and for the first time since they rode away from the burning town, he knew relief. Twisting his head, he stared ruefully at the wound. "Should have taken his gun. My own damn fault."

415

"It's too late to worry about that now," Karen chided. "What's done is done."

"You're right," he agreed. "And it could be worse." He chuckled grimly. "Look at that. A brand new army shirt, a gift from Jaco, and already ruined. Saving beautiful women sure is hard on a man's clothes." He lay back, serious again in a wash of pain-induced exhaustion. "Good thing True isn't along. He'd have my neck for being three kinds of a fool."

Karen removed the compress. The flesh clean, the extent of the wound could more easily be seen. "How serious is it, Vance?"

"Bad enough. I've got less blood than I ought to have. I'm weak and slow, but I'll hold up. A wound like this isn't dangerous unless it gets infected, or slows us enough for Jaco and his men to catch up with us." He reached out and gripped Karen's arm. "If that happens—or if we run into Apaches—if I get too weak to continue, you may have to go on without me."

Karen's eyes widened, her mouth set in indignant refusal. "No. . . ."

Vance waved aside her protest. "I want you to promise me you will. It's important."

"But I couldn't. . . "

"You can and you will," he insisted, his voice stern and commanding. "When I say 'run,' you run. Fast. What Jaco'll do to me won't matter any more. Hell, I'll probably be past caring. But you've got to get back, tell True and the boys." His head lolled back and he closed his eyes against the jetting spasms of pain defeating his efforts to continue.

"No more talking," Karen said. "I'll check the snare." Quietly, she slipped away from the fire, into the blackness.

Vance forced himself to relax his leg and hip, let the pain have its way and so more quickly subside. What had she said? Snare? He looked around. She was gone. Snare? Of course. Ted would have taught her about snares. *Good old Ted. Should have taught her myself. Man shouldn't be running off all around the country. Ought to stay at home and teach his wife to set snares. . . .* The fire flared to his right and he stared dully at the leaping tongues of orange, hoping the hypnotic dance would lull him. The cedar bowl was on fire. *Better do something about that bowl. Just reach right over there and . . .*

416

Warily searching the night for menace, Karen stepped from the *cul-de-sac* and followed a dry watercourse to a thicket of mesquite, the most likely place for game in the area. The snare, though admirably constructed, was depressingly empty. Disappointed because Vance badly needed fresh meat—anything to build his strength—she picked her way back up the slope, pausing every few yards to listen for suspicious sounds. The night was full of noise, but she could discern no threat. But what specific sounds could she expect an intruder to make? What silences—insects near a man in the dark would fall silent—were the harbingers of pursuit? Would she hear an Indian if he were creeping up on her? The wind sighed around rocks and through crevices, and a soft whoosh told her a bat had passed overhead. She started at the creak of . . . what? The sound came again, and to her right she saw a mesquite branch rub against another. Relieved, she sighed and leaned against a boulder, trying to relax. The moon, gibbous and nearly full, peeped from behind a barrier of fleecy gray and white, illuminating the landscape. Before her eyes the sand, rock and shale slope turned the color of bleached bone. She looked south across the ghostly painting toward the distant broken pass through which they had traveled. Might they not be hunted this very moment? She felt the beginnings of panic, but forced the emotion to subside. Vance had assured her they would have some hours before the bandits could hope to recover their horses and begin the pursuit. Even so, he had turned off the main trail and followed a less likely looking path which would take them through the mountains to a river crossing west of the one they had used two days earlier. There was little chance the outlaws were close at all, especially given the explosion, the burning of their supplies and their lack of horses. Still, Karen felt she knew better. The others might give up the chase, but not Jaco. The bandit leader would find them. Sooner or later he would realize they had turned off the trail, backtrack and find their route. She had glimpsed the fierce turmoil of his spirit, experienced the deep well of his bitterness, cringed from the absolute determination which drove him beyond the bounds of normal men. Jaco would never let them escape. Somewhere in the night he followed, implacable and not to be denied.

Jaco . . . the ferocity of his kisses and the hunger of his

hands as they explored her brought a grudging heat to her body. How powerless she felt against him. Yet despite his contempt for her, she realized he also loved her in a strange and inexplicable way. But such love . . . and such hate . . . fear caught at her heart and she found herself on hands and knees, shivering and staring into the night like a trapped animal. She wanted to be away, to take her chances with flight and the dark, eager pitfalls of the trail rather than wait for. . . . *What can I do against him? What will happen when he finds me?* Alone on the rocky slope, her imagination went wild. *Every rock, every branch, every cactus . . . staring at me?! No! Stop it. Stop. Vance is hurt. He needs me, depends on me. . . . Jaco! No. I'm afraid . . . afraid . . .* The admission helped. *All right then,* she thought angrily, *be afraid. But do what needs to be done! Just start at the beginning and keep on going and doing until the task is finished. The Hampton way. Keep on . . . keep on. . . .*

Clouds were piling up from the south in ever increasing numbers, moving more swiftly now. Overcome by the roiling barrier of scudding gray, the moon quickly fell before their onslaught. Karen got to her feet and continued up the trail, carefully choosing her way back to the hidden campsite.

Vance was asleep beside the fire and she noticed with dismay their bark vessel, the water boiled away, had fallen into the embers and become food for the flames. "Keep on," she muttered softly in an undertone of resignation, more than a little tinged with doubt. Removing her blanket *serape,* she stood quietly and let the cool night breeze lave her naked torso. Thank goodness there was another stolen army shirt in the bundle taken from the *granero.* The wet blanket had irritated her skin, left her itching and red. Suddenly tired, she slipped on the smooth cotton shirt, and wriggling with delight as the soft fabric covered her skin, wrapped herself in the blanket again and lay down to a well-earned rest.

Morning brought only token light, for the airy battlements of the previous night had accumulated in angry, tumultuous proportions that any moment threatened to unleash the fury of a storm on the fugitives. Karen saddled both horses and returned to the fire to find Vance awake and standing up, some color showing in his face. The night's rest had done him good. "Are you sure we should leave?" Karen asked, worried the wound on his hip would open again.

Vance nodded. "It'll rain before too long and wash out our tracks. It's worth the chance, so long as we don't get caught and washed out ourselves. Every trackless mile we put between us and them will be just that much more time we've gained." He unconsciously kicked dirt on the remains of the campfire, stiffening as the simple action rewarded him with searing spasms. Cursing silently, he forced one foot before the other and crossed to the chestnut gelding stolen from the bandits. Karen mounted her gray and watched with consternation as Vance laboriously swung into the saddle, his wounded right side slowly easing over the cantle. A drum roll of thunder from the south punctuated their departure. They topped the ridge below which they had camped, descending immediately into a narrow crevice splitting the next hill. Vance looked up at the walls stretching high overhead. They were riding between the jaws of a trap, and should the heavens choose this moment to . . .

And then they were free. Sloping up a wide saddle to a broad, swayback crest. Karen gasped in surprise, reined in the gray without thinking. Falling away to either side and in front of them lay a barren, hostile vista of trackless land and lowering sky forming a gray and enclosing horizontal void stretching ahead to the north. *I can't . . . I can't . . . there's too much to cope with . . . too much.*

Vance stopped at her side. "One day we'll come back," he said gently. "You'll see then how beautiful all this is." Struck dumb by the vastness, Karen could find no words with which to answer. "We'd best keep on. We'll want to cross the Rio Grande before dark." His brows knotted against the pain, and gripping the pommel with both hands, he nudged the gelding into a walk.

Keep on . . . ? Karen sucked in her stomach, drew a deep breath. *Keep on. . . .* Ahead of her, the chestnut led the way, cautiously picking a path across the slope and down to the empty land before them.

The storm broke. Jagged spears of lightning tore asunder the clouds and loosed a heavy downpour. Karen shivered under the sudden onslaught and pulled the *serape* blanket close around her. Ahead, Vance's outline blurred. Once she

419

lost him completely and experienced a rush of panic. She dug her heels into the gray and the game little steed, anxious for company, trotted forward.

After the first numbing moments the fury of the storm subsided and the cloudburst turned into a steady, drenching rain. Karen pulled up alongside Vance, her gray matching the chestnut's gait. She bowed her head, cringing each time the wind at their backs sent a trickle of water down her spine. Glancing over, she could see Vance's face white with pain and cold against the gray background which surrounded them. He must, somehow, be kept warm. Already suffering from loss of blood and the shock of excessive pain, the cold would weaken him dangerously. She reached out and grabbed the chestnut's reins, brought them both to a halt, and while Vance sat quaking, pulled the ties on the extra blankets stolen from the *granero* and draped them tent-like over him. The steady hiss of rain half drowning her words, she tried to get him to agree to a stop, but he gritted his teeth and gestured to the trail ahead. The horses plodded on.

Time stood still, went unnoticed like the shadows of night. Gray mud, gray sky, the constant droning chant of the rain and the rocking movement of the animal beneath her lulled Karen into a dream world of another time and place, far removed from the wilderness around her. She was in a lurching carriage racing through the streets of Washington, tossed from one side of the interior to the other, the coach door banging open. Details stood out clearly. A button on the seat opposite her . . . a piece of shining brass on the front wall . . . the frozen image of a tree, bent in the wind . . . a leaping figure loomed in the doorway and she glimpsed his face. *The Texan . . . !* One moment he was there, the next atop the carriage and straining to subdue the madly racing team, then standing in the sea of mud at the carriage's side, smiling bouyantly, expansively, his cheeks splashed with mud and dirt. Fading from memory, the city became more a vague recollection of a time, a place and a girl she no longer knew. Far easier to bring to mind the clear scent of sunwashed cedar carried on the wind, or the late night cry of the killdeer winging to her nest. More recent faces swelled from the mists to fill her fantasy. Vance, True, Elizabeth, Maruja, Ted and Jared. Bodine? Yes, he too. And poor Marcelina—what

420

would Jaco do to her? And Marquez, Manuel, Arcadio and . . . Jaco himself. More friendly faces replaced the latter; the men of the PAX. The laconic Harley, gentle Emilio, eager and smiling Billy Harmony, easygoing Shorty. Faces known and cherished, cared for and lost. Lost? *Elizabeth is lost. Maruja is lost. No! No, not lost. Not as long as my heart beats and earth moves.*

The horse bolted forward, jerking her back to reality. Vance slapped the gray across the rump, then spurred his chestnut into a gallop that brought him alongside her. Through a break in the rain, Karen could tell they were in another ravine, broader than the one before. Vance's urgency was apparent, for though she couldn't hear a word, he was yelling at her, his voice drowned out by a dull but ominous roar, gradually increasing in volume. Comprehension struck her with the force of a lightning bolt. She had heard the sound before; the angry forewarning of a flash flood. She peered through the curtain of rain, striving to glimpse a way out of the ravine, but the walls were too steep to offer purchase for the hooves of their steeds. They rounded an outcropping and Vance abruptly reined in. Karen skidded past, fought the gray and turned back toward her wounded husband. Gesturing wildly, Vance pointed at a break in the rocks, no more than a deer trail winding up to a ledge some forty feet above them. Not the best possible solution, the dim trail was the only one available for the wall of water coming down the ravine was gaining despite the game efforts of their ponies. "You first," Vance shouted, dismounting. "Lead him. Hurry!" Karen jumped to the ground and grabbed the gray's reins, and without looking back, started up the precipitous incline. Deftly, she threaded her way, digging the toes of her boots into the mud, slipping, finding support and moving ahead.

Every step was torment for Vance. The wound in his side hurt abominably, was open and had started to bleed again. His left arm felt like lead. The chestnut balked at the ascent. Vance cursed and pulled like a madman. He would have run ahead and left the animal to its fate, but once out of the storm and flood they would need both if there was to be any hope of escape. With a superhuman effort he hauled on the reins until the mustang finally overcame its fear and grudgingly followed. The roar suddenly increased dramatically. Glancing to his left, Vance saw a churning wall of water, mud, rocks and trees round the outcrop and sweep toward him. The chestnut, finally realizing the emergency, lunged forward, all but collided with the gray a half a dozen yards ahead and sent Vance sprawling off the path. He scrambled for a hold, felt a quick breeze as the leading edge of the surging water rushed past underneath him. Half upside down, his hip hit a rock. New and indescribable pain flashed through him, exploding in a single incandescent truth: he had to hold, or die. Time, in emergency, slowed. Pieces of root, or rock, he was able to discern with electric clarity, consider and reject as he went by them. Finally, a crack in the rock face . . . *Now . . . this one. . . .* Moving with a speed beyond normal ability, his right hand reached out, clenched into a fist and jammed into the crack, stopping his fall with a bone-jarring jerk. He lay utterly still, dangling on the face of the cliff, not daring to move lest he plunge into the deadly waters only scant inches beneath his feet.

Having gained the ledge, Karen looked back in relief, only to see Vance knocked off balance and plummet from the slippery trail. She screamed his name, then frantically grabbed a coiled rope from the gray as it gained the comparative safety of the rock overhang. Sliding and falling, she worked her way back down the trail. The downpour increased in fury, blinding her as she groped and searched for handholds, shouting again and again, only to have her cries drowned out by the deafening thunder of the water. Reaching the approximate spot where Vance had lost his footing, she leaned far over the side and strove to see through the deluge. He was a dozen feet below her, splayed against the rock and dangling in thin air. Flood waters raged beneath him. Broken jagged timber juggernauts borne by the rushing current reared from the surface like demented sea monsters, slammed and shattered against the walls of the ravine. Boulders were lifted in place and sluggishly swept away. And if Vance's grip slipped. . . .

She shouted his name again, but he did not—or dared not—stir. Uncoiling the rope, Karen fastened the noose around a jutting stone the shape of a giant tooth, then looped the first few feet a second and third time for strength. Taking a turn around her waist so she herself wouldn't fall, she dropped the free end along the rock face, swinging it until the rope struck against the unmoving form of her husband.

Can't hold on much longer . . . if I could just. . . . Slowly, with infinite care, he moved his right foot along the rock, his toe searching for a hold, however slight. Nothing. He relaxed, rested, sent the left foot searching, found a . . . gently, he probed, touched a piece of stone protruding from the smooth face of the rock. Wiggling the boot to get as much surface contact as possible, he held his breath. *Now. . . .* The tenuous foothold was gone! Disappeared! There was nothing there any more. The pain in his shoulder was easing; a danger signal. *It's getting numb . . . should have stayed where we were . . . damn! To go this way.*

He felt a light slapping sensation on his back. And then again. What . . . ? Slowly, he turned his head and saw the rope, rolled his eyes upward and made out, barely, Karen's fear-whitened face. *Good girl . . . good girl . . .* Now, if he could just grab the rope . . . he'd have to extricate his bunched fist. Impossible, for sudden death would follow. Again the rope slapped against his back. His right hand was numb, his shoulder fast becoming useless. His left arm throbbed dully, but he'd have to take the chance. The pain becoming more acute with each movement, he eased the splinted arm out of the sling and up to meet the rope. Swollen fingers encircled the fibrous line and he tested his grip by taking some of his weight on the arm, grinding his teeth as bone and muscle reacted with unrelenting agony to this latest demand.

Karen watched his hand open and close on the line, noticed the muscles of his body relax, then bunch as he grabbed with his left hand and heaved himself up, freed his wedged right fist and swung toward the rope. For a moment that would forever stretch to eternity in recollection, Vance dangled precariously above the flood, then his right fist closed about the rope and took his weight. With a strength stemming from the wellsprings of love imperiled, Karen hauled on the rope, the rough fibers cutting into her palms as, hand over hand, she pulled, backing around the stone tooth and taking a hasty bight before she lost all she had gained. Teeth grinding, eyes closed with the strain, she hauled again. His weight seemed less than before. Groaning with effort, she staggered back a shuddering step, then another, suddenly fell back completely as the weight left the rope. *No . . . ! Vance, no!* She opened her eyes in horror.

The rope lay slack at her feet, the free end inches from the base of the rock. *No . . . !* She was alone! Vance was . . . in front of her, a form heaved from the mud, lurched toward her. Sobbing hysterically in relief, she watched as he crawled the remaining few feet to her side, using handholds on the pockmarked stone until he reached her and fell, gasping for breath at her side, his arms groping for her, then enfolding her in an unbreakable embrace as her tears came freely to mingle with the rain. *Vance! My darling darling . . .* Her fingers explored his face, unable to stop touching him. Suddenly, their lips met in a hungry kiss. Beyond pain, beyond danger and death, they quaffed the passionate nectar of their love, ineffably sweetened by the narrow escape from disaster. Though their peril was far from resolved, they had met and conquered a frightful challenge. Death had touched their lives, but for now they had denied the dark master his victory. They lay resting on the hard rock, drenched and covered with mud, staring into each other's eyes, each full of the knowledge of each other and life itself.

The rain lessened as they rose wearily to begin their ascent to the horses. Karen gathered the rope while Vance adjusted the cloth compress on his hip, loosening the gunbelt to . . . "Damn!"

Karen spun about, startled. "What is it?"

Vance scrambled past her to the outthrust granite tooth, and keeping a sure grip, looked forlornly over the side.

"Vance?"

"The gun," he muttered bitterly, indicating his empty holster. "When I fell. Now I've lost the damn gun!" The implications of the loss were apparent. With a glance to the south, they turned and headed back up the deer trail, helping each other along the slippery path.

The horses had continued along the trail and moved on past the ledge to the rim of the ravine where they had found a few spare bunches of grass on which they cropped, content to rest for the moment. The rain abated to a drizzle, and though Karen and Vance both needed to dry their clothes, they were reluctant to try to make camp in the open and so close to the scene of the near tragedy.

Exhausted, drenched and hungry, they mounted the stolen horses and headed north for the Rio Grande.

How they managed to cross the rain-swollen boundary between Texas and Mexico, Karen could only attribute to Dame Fortune . . . and the strong swimming abilities of the indomitable mustangs. Born to the harsh life of the wild, broken and trained on the outlaw trail, the horses were used to traveling seldom-used paths, enduring heat, cold, rain and thirst. Karen and Vance joined themselves with a length of rope. If one was swept away, the other might still manage to gain safety for both. But the horses swam with powerful, sure strokes, fighting the pull of the current and reaching the opposite shore with no problem.

The question now was whether to continue to make camp for the night. "Depends on how far back they are," Vance explained. "And if they got out of the storm all right, of course. They'll lose our tracks for sure, but that doesn't prove anything. We're heading north, and all they have to do is cross where you crossed the other day, check out downstream a bit—there's no good places southeast of there—and then head upstream and watch for where we came out. Won't be too hard to find," he said glumly, "with all this mud. Not much sense in even trying to hide our tracks. All told, I suppose we'd better rest."

Karen filled the canteens and both she and Vance drank as much as they could. By dusk they had found a suitable camp within earshot of the Rio Grande's tumultuous churning song. Well-sheltered by a thick stand of scrub oak and mesquite, they were partially hidden by a shallow overhang jutting from a bluff. Warm food and a chance to dry out and, especially for Vance, to warm up, outweighed the risk they took in building a fire. A screen of tree branches draped with Vance's wet clothes served as a shield from prying eyes, and soon a hidden fire blazed cheerily. With the broken knife taken from the *jacalito,* Karen opened two cans of beans found in the towsack and balanced them on rocks by the side of the flames. Half starved after almost three days with no food, they ate slowly but greedily, then washed the cans and put water on to boil for their last bit of coffee.

Vance, wrapped in the one half-dry blanket, lay near the warming fire, watching Karen through the flames as she arranged a latticework of brush, took the homemade, soggy serape from her shoulders and spread it to dry. Her movements were sure and deft, wasting no energy. He sighed, lay back and closed his eyes as the memories rushed through him. How right he had been, in Washington, choosing this woman. How wrong he had been, later, when he failed to allow her the time she needed to adapt to her harsh new home. Was there a woman in the world who wouldn't quail at such an undertaking?

His senses reeled. Giddy from the food, he tried to concentrate. Something he needed to do. Something important before he…in case he… No. Better not to think that. The man who so much as thought of death passed on faster… Passed on. That was it, he thought groggily, forcing his eyes open. "Karen." Had he said it aloud? "Karen!"

She came quickly to his side, touched his forehead with her hand. "Sleep," she said. "You need sleep."

"The amulet." Each word was an effort. "Take it from around my neck and put it on. It's yours, now."

"Vance…"

"No! Do as I say!"

Obedient, Karen unclasped the chain, fixed it around her neck as instructed. Only when Vance saw the dull glow of gold against her flesh did he close his eyes. "Paxton women…an unbroken chain…generations… Mother gave it to me, and I pass it on to you, from her." So hard to stay awake. So hard…"You are a Paxton woman. You are… Keep on. Keep on…"

He was asleep. Remembering True's stories of the indomitable, courageous women who had preceded her and had worn the amulet before passing it on to their first born sons, Karen pulled the blanket to Vance's chin and crept back to the fire. There, the gold cool against her skin, she sat and stared into the flames. She was not alone. The others sat at her side, and kept vigil with her.

The morning sun sent tentative amber streaks of light to pierce the storm-emptied heavens and rout the battling thunderheads, bathed the sky with gold from the east and changed the lofty firmament to a cloud-dappled meadow of the gods. Karen was up at first light to get the fire going. Water bubbling merrily in the empty bean cans, she rummaged in the towsack and found a small brick of tea which, when shaved into the water, filled the clearing with a mouthwatering aroma. The blankets, shirt and jeans had dried overnight and she donned the garments again, feeling

426

ready for anything. Vance groaned awake, uncharacteristically paused to adjust himself to his surroundings, then shoved himself upright and sat with his back against a log. His eyes were red, his face pale and sunken. Karen brought him tea and he accepted without comment, holding the can between two strips of bark, sipping slowly and letting the heat bring him to life.

His wound needed bathing again. Not yet infected, it had opened and bled during the night and was red and ugly. Karen reboiled the bandages and, finding some aloe vera growing nearby, stripped the skin and mashed up the slippery pulp to make a poultice. The cooling pulp seemed to ease the pain some, and though weak from loss of blood, Vance managed to dress alone and eat some hardtack biscuits and jerked meat boiled in water to make a thin soup. By the time the sun was up, Karen had ventured down to the river twice to refill the canteens, each time going a different way in order to better hide her tracks. On the second trip, she brought the horses and carried the bean cans as well. The way ahead would be hot and dry for the spring rains had not yet come this far north and they would need every drop they could carry. Everything full, she was starting back when the distant echoing report of a gunshot broke through the murmur of the river and shattered her sense of safety at being away from Mexico. She held perfectly still, heart beating wildly in her throat, expecting at any moment to see a dozen renegades come charging out of the rocks across the river. Nothing of the sort happened. Only the long, silent creeping passage of minutes. She finally resumed her journey, wasting no time in leading the horses back to the camp.

Vance was standing, braced against the thin bole of a mesquite. "I heard a shot!" Karen exclaimed breathlessly. "I heard it too. Probably someone hunting," he answered optimistically. Karen glanced nervously over her shoulder. "I don't believe it either. We'd best not wait for them." He placed one foot in the stirrup and laboriously swung his leg over, and try though he did to suppress any indication of pain, a groan broke from his lips as he settled into the saddle. Facing Karen, he read the worried frown darkening her face. "I scattered the ashes. Won't do any good. Let's go."

Karen handed him the two bean cans full of water,

mounted and took the cans back so Vance could hold on better, then guided the horses carefully from the thicket. Once in the open, Vance suggested she keep the lead. Karen suspected the suggestion was less motivated by confidence in her ability than by a desire to keep her from seeing just how poorly he fared. Still, there was nothing to be done but comply with his request, so she took the lead north into the borderlands, domain of the vulture, cactus, unrelenting heat and waiting thirst. Behind them. . . . She dared not think of the gunshot, nor the one whose finger pulled the trigger.

One day passed, then another. Hours of endless plodding beneath the baleful stare of an uncompromising sun, then dry camp amidst the chill night air which quickly cooled the wasted land. The water in the bean cans was long gone. Dismounting, Vance stiffly spread a ground blanket and collapsed to earth. Alarmed by his rising fever, Karen forced him to drink, then stripped his bandages to let the wounds dry in the air, replaced the old poultices with new and settled him down to sleep. Later during the night he cried out for more water, and denying her own thirst she gave him the last of the first canteen. If they were to continue, the horses would need most of the rest. Three hours later she helped Vance into the saddle again. The night's sleep had done him little good, but he was determined not to slow them up and insisted they be off before first light.

Could there ever have been rain? Water enough in which to drown? Karen stared into the cerulean madness of a burning sky. She had hoped to retrace the course of the journey south with Jaco and Marquez, but the way had become confused. Their escape from Rio Lobos in the night, the unfamiliar, labyrinthine trails over which they traveled in an attempt to lose pursuit and the more westerly starting place from the banks of the Rio Grande all threw her off and she could no longer ascertain in which direction lay the seep known to the outlaws. Afraid to veer from their set course, there was nothing to do but continue northeast and hope they struck a water hole or at least a party of rangers scouting the border.

There was no water. Nor was there life, save for a slowly circling pair of vultures patiently biding their time in the sky. Sooner or later, they would feed. Karen peered over her shoulder at her beloved. Vance was slumped forward in the saddle, his fingers locked around the pommel in an unconscious and nigh unbreakable grip. The water in the last canteen sloshed invitingly with each step of the gray gelding and reminded her of the dust-choked dryness of her own throat. Her eyes felt parched and grated in their sockets; her blood was sluggish and her brain unresponding. She looked longingly at the canteen and for a moment succumbed to thirsting temptation, but even as she lifted the container to her lips, the chestnut behind her snorted in weary dismay and she grudgingly conceded the animals were more important than the easing of her own discomfort. Reining up in the bottom of an arroyo, Karen half fell from her mount and poured the precious liquid into her bandana, wetting the muzzle and wiping out the mouth of the gray, then repeating the action for the chestnut.

Vance was feverish but still conscious; and he even managed a grim smile. "Could at least stop in the shade," he said, his voice a grating rasp. Karen passed the canteen to him and he let a mouthful roll around on his tongue, then slowly trickle down his throat before handing it back. "One swallow."

"I know," she snapped, feeling guilty immediately. Hands trembling, she raised the canteen and let the water roll in her mouth. *God . . . !* Had water ever tasted so cool, so welcome? Quickly, she corked the canteen, hung it on the saddle. *Don't look at it.* "I'll check the way ahead." Legs quivering with the effort, she climbed to the top of the arroyo, and standing with only her head above the rim, surveyed their surroundings. Nothing looked familiar, though she no longer expected nor hoped for that. The land rolled away in endless, arid repetition. Deceptively flat to appearance, she knew the way they would travel was a tortuous nightmare, mercilessly seamed and wrinkled, sunburnt and. waterless, the product of convoluted generations of centuries. To the north, a vague purple line stretched across the horizon. Hills! *And water . . . water . . .* The trackless distance lying between brought her to her knees. *So far. So far still to go . . . Elizabeth, I'm frightened. I'm not strong enough to make it. What would you have done?*

"What would you have done," she muttered aloud, the words soundless, sucked dry by the oven-like, dessicated air. No gentle breeze from the south came in answer. No green panorama sprung to sight to stretch with lush beauty to the sky. Only stark, unchanging wasteland. Only sand digging into her flesh like tiny granules of glass. Only thirst . . . dully, she lifted her head, searched with bleary eyes the horizon to the south, checking for signs of pursuit. She studied the bitter contours a moment more, stood, swayed dizzily and dejectedly slid down the steep slope to the horses. Seconds later, the diminutive caravan of two moved from the arroyo, avoided a rise and skirted a hillock to keep from being seen against the sky.

A little over an hour later she spied a cluster of scraggly mesquite. Two trail-weary horses, a wounded man and a frightened young woman, both exhausted, drew to a stiff-legged halt, seeking shade and respite from the heat. Disappointed to find neither, Karen used the blankets to construct an umbrella under which they could pass the brutal afternoon hours. The top layer of sand scooped away, she helped Vance lie down on the cooler lower layer. The horses needed tending, too. Karen took a minuscule swallow of water and almost gagged, but managed to keep it down. Working in a somnambulistic stupor, she stripped the mustangs' saddles and blankets and loosely tethered the tired animals. A bandana full of water served to wipe out their mouths and moisten their muzzles again before she reeled into the scant rectangle of shade and collapsed, panting with exhaustion, next to Vance. He was asleep. *Sleep . . . if only I could rest a little while. . . .* Promising herself but a short nap, she stretched back on the blanket, and to the sound of the mustangs stripping meager forage from the mesquite trees, fell immediately asleep.

The sun would not be hurried. Like a brand on the sky, the fierce chariot described a tortuous arc cleaving the dome of heaven and bleaching the cloudless ceiling with pale fire. The blazing fury of its passage notwithstanding, the scalding journey led at last to confluence with the rim of earth where jagged hills loomed deceptively close. The sky was streaked with bands of amethyst, coral and turquoise, followed by even deeper hues of the same until blending into pavonine night. The wandering moon rebuilt the landscape. The lee of every rock and hummock disappeared in darkest night in contrast to the stark white shapes which cast the shadows. Karen woke, chilled. She made a small fire of mesquite branches, and using the final remnant of dried meat, made a broth for Vance, saving the last few ounces of water for the horses. Vance meekly accepted the broth, but only after Karen promised to take some herself. His fever had lessened but his leg throbbed painfully and he was unable to saddle the gelding, although he did manage to climb unaided into the saddle. Karen scattered the ashes of the campfire and returned to the horses, portioning out the last of the water to them. Though as dehydrated as their riders, still the animals exhibited a surprising amount of pluck, appearing eager to be off. The meager rest had done them some good after all and they, almost better than Karen and Vance, knew the way they would have to go to find food and water.

The earth quickly released the captive heat of day, and in the near freezing temperatures which followed, Karen and Vance were forced to bundle up in the blankets as they held their course north. Dreaming of water, Karen nodded, jerked her head to stay awake, mentally scolding herself for being lulled by the gray's monotonous pace. Trying to get her mind away from the almost constant thought of water, she recalled the first leg of her journey, the "agony" of travel from Corpus Christi to San Antonio with plenty of food and an abundance of water, and only the discomfort of the buckboard to plague her. Discomfort? How she would welcome simple discomfort. How nice to feel anything other than thirst. . . . "Water can get mighty precious out here," Vance said from sometime in the dim past. She had heard the words, but paid little attention. And now . . . she forced a painful swallow and stared across the grim landscape until her eyes betrayed her. *Would you like a glass of water, dear? Yes, mummy. Yes yes yes. I want a glass of water. . . .*

She yanked back on the reins in surprise. The moon was gone and the sky brightening with predawn light. The darkness ahead was not of the night but of foothills sweeping up from the plains. The plains they had crossed! Vance's horse drew abreast of the gray. "We made it," he croaked, his voice brittle, tired and proud.

Karen's joy was short-lived. She had kept herself alive with the promise of green hills, but the hills in front of them were brown, as devoid of water as the desert. Her shoulders sagged in dismay. "I forgot . . . how barren they are. I thought there would be water. We've come

431

all this way, but how do we get through the hills . . . without water . . . and food?" The gray strained at the bit but she held him back.

"Give him his head," Vance instructed in a dry whisper. "They'll take us to water." He loosed the reins and the chestnut immediately led off, ears pricked forward.

The slope increased and Vance wound a strip of leather around his hands and the saddle horn, securing himself in place. The fever, loss of blood and dehydration had left him with little strength to cope with the steep trail ahead. Karen searched the rocks for any telltale indications of water. Desperately, she tried to recall Ted's teachings. How like a game her lessons had seemed then, and how serious now when a matter of life or death. Did the horses know where they were going? She had to trust they did. She couldn't last much longer. An hour later, the sun starting to climb, Karen craned her neck to check on Vance and caught a glimpse of what she thought to be a slight plume of dust back across the way they had come. A boulder loomed to obscure the view and when the gray swerved again, the wisp of dust was gone. Illusion, or . . . ?

"There!" Vance exclaimed. His voice broke through her thoughts and she followed his gaze, turning around to stare straight ahead into the yawning mouth of a cave.

The chamber in which they rested was illuminated dimly by a pair of flaming brands, left in the cave's anteroom, evidently by the usual visitors. "More than likely we're at the *Caverna de los Bandidos*. It's a watering stop used by the bandits and Apaches alike," Vance said. "I've heard of it, but never seen it or known how to get here. We were lucky in our choice of horses. They've been here before." He leaned over and cupped another mouthful of water. Karen giggled and luxuriantly submerged her face, letting the biting cold liquid soothe her sunburned, thirsty flesh. "You drink any more for awhile and you'll burst."

Karen raised her head, water beads dancing down her face. "I'm not drinking. Just lying in it. This is the most wonderful water in the whole world. Look. Even you're better."

Vance grimaced. "I'm not dying of thirst, if that's what you mean. Anything's better than that. But I've still got a

432

hole in my arm and a leg that hurts like blazes. Damn it, I can even get around to help you, much less . . ."

Karen put her finger to his lips. "Shhh." She took away her hand and kissed him, pulling back immediately. "You *could* smile."

"That's about all I can do," he grumbled, sagging back to rest again. "Too weak to do anything else."

Karen smiled. "You'll get well. Oh, Lord! It must be noon. I'd better check on the traps."

"Karen . . . you know, you got us through, alone and burdened with me. Ted taught you well."

"Not well enough. He taught me to build the traps, but he left out how to make the birds and rabbits understand their part. They'll be empty again, I just know."

Vance closed his eyes and drifted off to sleep again. Karen studied the face, the form of the man she loved. Gaunt, ragged, his beard scruffy and unkempt. *Even now there is a clean, open handsomeness. A strong face made for laughing, a man with whom I will share my love.* . . . She sighed and headed toward the exit, a long, narrow passage leading to the wide-mouthed antechamber, outside of which the horses had been tethered—after watering—to nibble at the meager forage. They would need more food before taking up the journey, but for the present were happy, and safely concealed from anyone who might pass below. Karen paused well inside the darkness, remembered Ted's instructions. "Never jump out into the open without letting your eyes get used to the light. Otherwise you'll be blinded for the first few minutes." She held back a moment more, her cheek resting against the moist, cool stone. But time was wasting. Reluctantly, she stepped to the mouth of the cave and. . . . The horses were gone! Wandered? No. She had securely tethered them. Then taken. By whom?

"*Señor* Paxton . . ."

The voice reverberated, echoed through the hills, startled her into rigidity, unable to move, to run, to barely breathe lest she open her mouth and scream. That voice . . . that terrible, nightmare voice . . . Jaco!

"*Señor? Señora?*" The taunting call repeated, echoing throughout the chambered cavern.

Karen broke from her trance and fled back to the main chamber . . . to Vance . . . down the corridor. Stalactites, stalagmites, earlier beautiful, intriguing luminescent shapes, became cruel, rending fangs in the mouth of a monstrous beast. "Vance . . . ? Ouch!"

Vance yanked her back against the wall, covered her mouth with his hand. Karen pressed close against him, seeking the security of his nearness. He released his hold and bent to grasp a jutting cone of stone. Bracing his back against the wall, he pushed out until, with a loud snap, the stalagmite broke off near the base, leaving him with a club of stone over two feet in length.

"Ahhh, *Señor*. You have chosen not too wisely. Long and well do I know the *Caverna de los Bandidos*, and when I come upon your tracks, I know the horses will bring you here."

The voice came from every direction and none, surrounded them with echoes. Karen wildly scanned the chamber, searching for the dreaded figure of the bandit. "Where is he?" she whispered. Vance put his finger to his lips and shook his head indicating he didn't know. Five openings led to the interior and Jaco could have been in any one of them, for who knew what other entrances in the surrounding hills led to the pool?

"I applaud your ingenuity. You destroyed my revolution, my beautiful cannon, my handsome uniforms. My men no longer follow me. Once more, Jaco rides alone." He chuckled drily. "Perhaps I should thank you. I am not so sure I wanted the tiresome job of *el general*. All those women and children . . . the responsibility . . . *verdad?* Ah, but no matter . . . "

Karen stiffened. "He can't see us," Vance whispered, pulling her further back in the deep shadows. "Don't make a sound."

"I study your camp and know *mi hermano* is wounded. The *señora* is much woman to bring you across the emptiness. I think I keep her after all. You will be happy to know this, eh, *hermano?* Your *querida* will not be alone after you are gone." The voice paused for empty seconds during which Karen and Vance looked around as best they could, still seeing nothing. Was he changing position? The voice boomed, closer. "No one answers when Jaco speaks. You would insult me, no? Or perhaps the *Señor* is dead. Could that be, *querida?* You are hungry, frightened . . . is this so, *Señora?* I have food. Throw away the *pistola* you

434

have from Manuel. When I hear it splash in the water, then I will bring you food."

Vance whispered instructions to Karen, then shakily made his way from handhold to handhold along the slick cavern wall. Karen hurriedly arranged the blankets in a bundle around their guttering campfire, fashioning the fabric to the bulky shape of a human. "My husband died," she called out, the fear in her voice only lending veracity to the words. "But I have the gun. You have food, but I have the water. Tell me, *Señor* Zopilote, I would imagine this is the only water for miles. Are you not thirsty? Did not the sun scorch your flesh? Does your throat not cry out for relief? Water? Cool, refreshing water is my offer to you, murderer of your mother. Keep your food. I shall be eating soon enough." She forced herself to laugh and then tossed a handful of stone fragments into the pool. The inviting plunk plunk plunk was rewarded with a hoarse, angrily mumbled oath, and then silence.

The waiting. In brooding stillness, the repetitive dripping from the stalactites became a pandemonium, a manic chorus like the ticking of a thousand clocks, punctuating the passing seconds as the tension mounted.

What was that? A pebble dislodged, tumbled as Vance shifted position behind a column of limestone. As well situated as possible, he leaned against the pillar and relaxed, rested until the moment came when he would have to summon the depleted reserves of his strength. His right leg was stiff. His arm felt better. Perhaps, he hoped, the bone was only bruised after all. The whole escapade was poor timing, he thought ruefully. Yet a man could not choose the time nor the place. A man lived, and when trouble came he met it head on. If only Karen wasn't there, placed in jeopardy by his actions, because he'd left her that night . . . that damned cursed night of grief. If only . . . but what had True or Elizabeth ever said about looking back, wishing troubles would go away. Not a word. The way they lived spoke with eloquence enough. They neither were, nor had ever been, "if only" people. He settled himself, knowing the only "if" was in the future, and then dependent on what skills he could command, what abilities he could bring into play. Below him, out of sight on the other side of the chamber, he could hear Karen breathing, the sibilant whispers filling the cave.

"*Señora?*"

"Oh!" Her heart felt about to burst from her breast. How had she not seen or heard him? Jaco stepped from the passageway into the flickering twilight of the torches. His face showed the effect of pursuit. Haggard eyes looked greedily at the water. The fold of his *serape* was brushed back over his right shoulder, freeing the gun closed firmly in his fist. His eyes probed the recesses of the chamber and finally swung back to her, then down to the blanketed form nearby, returning to her and her empty hands.

"I did not think to wait, *querida*. You will forgive me, but I have come far. I am very, very thirsty and have no water for many hours." He shook his head sadly. "It was cruel of you to wish to keep me from water. But the sight of you—and the water—eases my anguish. Do not move, *querida*, please . . . " Eyes swiveling back and forth between Karen and the water, he sidled to his right, closer and closer to relief, finally kneeling quickly by the pool and thrusting his gun in his belt. His right hand plunged into the water, cupped the precious fluid and carried it to his mouth. He sipped greedily and rolled the water around before allowing the first drops to trickle down his throat. "*Me hermano se murió.* How sad. When did he die?" There was no answer. "But no matter. The first drops taste so good. . . . The body asks for more, but we must drink slowly, eh, *querida?*" He stopped, his eyes locked on hers in a burning gaze, piercing the secretive veil of her covert thoughts. Quickly, they shifted to the blankets, then back to her. With a cry of rage he rose to his feet, swept the gun from his belt and spun around.

Vance leaped from his perch, his right leg giving way when he landed. Off balance, he fell into Jaco's arms, knocking the gun aside and smashing his makeshift club down on the weaponless arm. Jaco's cry of rage turned into a howl of pain. The gun skittered across the rock floor and the grappling combatants pitched headlong into the shallow pool. "Run!" Vance shouted, then was lost to the struggle.

"Damn *gringo.* . . . *!*" Jaco lunged upward, his left fist backhanding Vance, who twisted away as his wounded leg buckled again and he went over backward. The bandit pressed the advantage, heaving out of the water and hurling himself on top of Vance, forcing his head under water. "Lying, damn *gringo* . . ."

In his weakened state, Vance was no match for the outlaw. Powerful fingers dug into his throat, a weight straddled his chest and forced him to expel the precious air left in his lungs. His right arm was pinned beneath Jaco's leg, his wounded left feebly clawing in a pitiful attempt to dislodge his attacker. He was dying and he knew it, saw the graves of his mother, sister and brothers, felt the wind against his face and smelled the sweet cedars, their gnarled limbs twisting in a timeless, frozen dance. *At least Karen's safe . . . at least she's safe . . .*

"Run!" The word reverberated off ribbed columns, the spiny ceiling and pockmarked, mossy floor. "Run!" echoing over and over in the mind of the cowering young woman. "Run!" as the man she loved was forced over and back and down beneath the shattered mirror-like surface of the underground pool. "Run!" The word was fuel to her panic. "Run!" and Jaco's roar of triumph filled the interstices of the echo. The gun . . . the gun there before her. But images of bloodless faces, faces of the dead . . . "Run!" came the word, resounding again, ever and ever again . . . "Run!"

"No!!"

The gun fired by accident as her hand clutched the grip, boomed with a deafening roar within the hollow underground cathedral. The bullet ricocheted into the dark, whining angrily and seeking a target. Jaco rolled aside, crawled to his feet, glancing first at the passageway, expecting the worst. No one was there and he turned toward Karen, saw the smoking revolver held in both her hands. She stared in fearful surprise at the gun, then boldly raised it as Jaco took a step toward her. "No," she ordered. "Go. Leave us."

Jaco grinned, hooked his thumbs in his gunbelt. Behind him, Vance, coughing and gasping for air, hauled himself clear of the water. *"Gringa."* Jaco began, stepping closer as Karen backed away. "We have done this before. Do you not remember our dance of death in the magnificent *hacienda?"*

"Keep away from me."

"No no no, *Señora*. I have come too far. With you, perhaps, I could forget all the rest. The Paxtons, their ranch, Rio Lobos . . ."

"Please," Karen pleaded, remembering all too well the

437

storm, the life of the stirring child soon to be torn from her womb, the fear; the sound and smell of gunpowder, Maruja dying, the still, lifeless visages piling one on another . . . *But always death* . . . And always, somewhere, Jaco. "Please?" She took another step back.

"Our dance, *querida*, when first I came to kill you. But no. I see you frightened, proud and beautiful with hair like the sun rising over the desert. I dream of you. A woman to make a man forget. You will be my woman. *My* woman, *querida*. The dance brings us together again, this time forever."

Jaco, his hands stretched before him, palms up. Jaco, his voice soothing, his face arrogant, saturnine, handsome, cruel . . .

"Do you remember when I kiss you? Do you forget so soon the taste, the hunger born in you? Yes, I could tell. A man knows these things, *querida* . . ."

Jaco, the draping wing-like folds of his *serape* slapping wet against his legs . . . swaying with each step. Jaco . . . proud, violent, his reaching hands closing over hers . . . his form and features like Vance's. . . . No. More . . . more like . . . like a looming, haughty . . . bird . . . of . . . PREY!

The gun exploded and flame jetted from the barrel, singeing the front of his shirt and sending a crimson tongue arcing from his back as the bullet carried his life from him and fled away into the miniature cathedral of limestone and water-smoothed quartz. Jaco staggered back from the impact, a look of utter disbelief crossing his face as his legs buckled and he dropped to his knees. He groaned, doubled over for a moment, then with terrible effort straightened halfway to look once again at the smoking pistol and the woman whose cheeks were streaked with silent, cascading tears.

"*Mi querida* . . ." His eyes glazed and as quickly cleared. "*Mi querida* . . . did I not say . . . if you were my woman . . . I would ride after you myself . . . even . . . if . . . to my . . . to . . . my . . ." He slumped forward and onto his side, his eyes staring lifelessly into the stygian void.

" . . . death," whispered Karen.

CHAPTER VII

The climb to the top was easy. A little over a thousand feet in the air and she could see over the jumbled beginnings of the foothills down to the empty desert they had crossed. Somewhere to the south, at the edge of the world, the burning white sky melded with earth in a dim, dancing line arcing from left to right and back again. The afternoon heat was infernal, burning into her with ferocious intent until sweat rolled down her face, trickled down her back and chest and sides, soaked into her shirt and rapidly evaporated. She welcomed such heat for its searing purity: with her own hand she had killed a man. No matter what Jaco had been, he was now dead; whatever else Jaco had done, he had died at her hands. The memory of his confident laugh leaped to mind. The last laugh. The last after all. *You were right, Señor Zopilote. Our last dance has brought us together forever . . . in death.* She sat and stared and stared into the distance, trying to equate her life with his death with Vance's life with anything with nothing. There were no suitable equations. Only the facts: life, the continuation; death, the termination.

She did not remember Vance taking the gun from her hands, nor stumbling up the incline nor finding the boulder on which she sat. She did not remember—she had paid no attention—Vance stopping her at the mouth of the cave, holding her by the shoulders and staring into her eyes. "Are you all right?"

"Yes."

"We'll stay here the night and leave at first light."

"Yes."

Four hours later, the afternoon sun lay across the land, separating light and dark into lines, humps and patches. Shadows yawned openly, shaping and reshaping the roughly-hewn vista moment by moment, moulding the uncompromising panorama sprawled before her. In the foreground, two dirty white lumpy shapes swam in and out of focus. Her hands. Hands with which she had . . . "Everything changes." Who had told her that? "Look twice." The same person. Vance? Yes. Vance. *My hands have changed*. She looked closely. No blood there to wash off. Only the smell of gunpowder. *What? Will these hands ne'er be clean?*

The sun dipped lower, touched a cloud and spilled orange light across the land. The very air suffused with the brilliant color until she felt she was breathing orange, bathed in orange. The cloud was large enough to cover the sun and little more, and from all sides became surrounded with a brilliant orange halo which caught at Karen's spirit, sent it spinning high into the air. As if atop an upflung height, she looked down on herself, small on the boulder, tiny on the hill, smaller yet against the foothills, an infinitesimal speck on the face of the earth itself. Look as hard as she could, she could see no guilt spread about the girl on the rock.

And then she knew. She saw herself against the greater background, saw with new perspective Karen Olivia Hampton Paxton was not the center of the universe. For a single moment she thought the idea infinitely sad, but the sadness fled to be replaced with wonder and joy. For the first time in her life she caught a glimmer of the audacity of man. To walk on the face of the earth was an act of incomparable bravery, and now at last she understood and felt the thrill of such a challenge. There, below in breathtaking complexity and completeness, was the stage upon which *she* played a part in the incredible drama of life. There, hand in hand with fear, pain, deprivation and guilt, there was the ultimate adventure of striving and accomplishment. There, ironic in the face of insignificance, was untold majesty of spirit, the very essence of life. There was continuity and extinction, woven strand by inseparable strand into a durable web of illimitable time. There was peace: the peace of working, of keeping on, of making decisions that would somehow and sometime effect the drama. There was untrammeled beauty in a wild and untamed corner of the earth: the corner she had come to love and understand. There, above all, was home: a man and a woman together,

together in respect, in pride, in protection; in the confident and joyous sharing of self and self.

When, a few minutes later, the sun dropped from behind the little cloud, Karen returned to herself. Still she sat, but now calmly, gazing fondly on the land she had fought. When she heard Vance stumbling up the hill behind her, she slid down from the boulder and took his hand, stood with him as they leaned against the giant rock and looked over the land. "I'm glad we're here," she said, simply.

Vance looked at her, pain forgotten for the moment. "I love this land."

"Yes. I, too." High on the hill, with the sun just barely above the horizon, hand in hand with the man she loved more than the land, a tremendous joy filled her. Her eyes laughing, she turned to Vance. "Do you know what?"

"What?"

"I'm hungry."

Vance laughed. "Come on down the hill, ma'am. I just happen to have some food on the fire."

She patted the dust from her jeans, gave a last glance toward the gnarled, rough-cast hills and started down, helping Vance over the rough spots.

He'd re-made the fire in the antechamber, away from Jaco's body which still lay in the cave. Used as a bandit's hideout for years, it had taken Vance but moments to locate a shelf where lay a cast-iron skillet, a pot, a small pile of spoons and tin plates. When Karen walked in, the odor of beans cooking, bacon frying and coffee boiling assailed her, left her more hungry than ever. Vance filled a plate for her and one for himself and Karen carried them out to their saddles which had been placed side by side on the ground by a flat-topped stone.

She set the plates down, started to turn to call to Vance when a movement caught her eye. She froze. There it was again, barely visible against a high pale wall of granite. "Vance! I see something."

Vance put down the coffee pot, hobbled quickly out to Karen. "Where?"

"Up there," she said, pointing. "There must be a trail along that wall."

"Damn!" he swore, worried she had seen more of the outlaws, angry he hadn't been more careful, wasn't better

441

prepared. "Damn!" If only Jaco had brought a rifle . . . no. If he had, they might both be dead. "Quick. Jaco's saddle bag. There's a glass in there."

Karen ran into the antechamber, rummaged through the saddlebags and found the binoculars, ran back out and handed them to Vance. "They were just beneath the ridge, to the right of that white streak."

"Might be game . . ." Vance muttered, bringing the glass to his eyes. He ranged the length of the cliff. Nothing. Swept across the base and over the ridges to either side. Still nothing.

"Perhaps it was . . . ?"

"Wait!" He focused the glasses on a plume of dust funneling upward from an unseen *arroyo*. Riders . . . it had to be riders. Had Jaco been lying? Had he really brought others with him? He watched the dust drift from farther along the wash. One good thing. At least they were moving away. Suddenly a group of . . . seven . . . horsemen erupted from the draw. Crossing a clearing in the rocks, they were bathed in the reflected light of the sinking sun.

"There!" Karen exclaimed.

"I see them. . . . Damn!" His hand swept down to his holster and the pistol leaped into his palm. Continuing the swinging motion, he fired into the air.

Karen blanched, stepped back in surprise. "Vance . . . ?"

He fired again, spacing his shots. "Turn, damn it!" he shouted beneath the flaming revolver. "Over here. Over here!"

"Vance?"

"The PAX. They're men from the PAX." He fired the remaining cartidige and peered again through the spyglass. "Where . . . ? Christ! They're gone. No. There they are. Heading this way . . ."

"Are you sure it's them?"

Vance grinned. "I better be. Let's move the fire out here so they can see where we are."

The mesquite burned quickly. Vance dripped water on the burning wood from time to time, sending a thin trail of gray smoke into the air. They kept the fire going while the daylight faded and the sun retreated below the horizon, relinquishing its hold on the earth. The moon hovered bright and full, casting diaphanous illumination across the landscape while Vance and Karen rested near the fire, forsaking the comforting walls of the cave and its silent occupant whose final journey had ended in dreamless sleep.

The campfire served a twofold purpose, giving off a sustaining warmth against the chill of the night and providing a beacon for the riders who would soon come. Having eaten well for the first time in days, they kept the coffee pot ready for when the PAX riders got there. More than the food, the coffee put life in their eyes and kept the cold desert air at bay. Side by side, they sat wrapped in blankets, one or the other reaching out from time to time to stir the friendly flames. Vance dozed, drifting awake a little before midnight and noticing Karen huddled nearby, staring across the embers into the cave's impenetrable darkness. "Karen . . ."

She turned and went to him then, hungry for the wondrous comfort of his embrace, weeping quietly as he rocked her in his arms. "It's over," he said. "It's all over."

Of the six who rode into camp the next morning, Vance knew only two; Billy Harmony and Harley Guinn. "We certainly must look a sight," he reflected, noting the grim set to their faces as he hobbled toward them. But soon their would-be rescuers' concern gave way to unrestrained relief at finding the two ex-captives safe.

"You sure give us a scare," Harley admonished after hectic greetings all around. "We would have rode in last night, but the land between here an' where you seen us is pretty wild."

"Who are the others?" Vance asked Harley.

"The lanky one works at the PAX, taken on after you left. Name's Huller. A good hand all the way around. Quiet, but good. The others are rangers."

"I counted seven."

Harley nodded. "That's how come we were riding the high country in the first place. He knew these back trails better than most 'cause he's rode on the dodge. When he was sure it was you two signalin' an' you was safe, he took off for San Antonio. Said he was drawin' to a flush an' had to get back to the game. Funny, by the time he gets back to that game, he'll have been gone at least a week, but I'd almost bet those cards'll be just like he left 'em. Ain't too many folks lookin' for Kania's kind of trouble."

"Kania? The gunman?"

"Same. Come ridin' in hell for leather three days ago an' said he'd heard about Miz Paxton missin', an' that he was gonna string along with whoever was lookin' for her."

"How the hell'd he get to know Karen?"

"Come driftin' through on the grubline when you was gone. She treated him like he was regular folks, an' he took to it, I guess. Said he owed her a favor." He paused, a whiskey-moistened cloth poised to clean out the wound on Vance's hip. "You ready? This is gonna hurt a little."

Karen didn't hear the groan escaping from Vance's lips, for at that moment Billy and one of the rangers came out of the cave, newly filled canteens dangling from the straps looped over their shoulders. Karen handed Billy a cup of coffee. "It's gonna be mighty good to have you back at the PAX, Miz Paxton. It purely is. Why, the place ain't seemed like home with you not bein' there."

"Thank you, Billy. That's one of the nicest things anyone ever said to me." The young ranch hand blushed and looked away, attempting to "seriously" study the campsite.

The ranger gestured to the opening in the cliff face. "That was the roughest of a bad lot. Lucky for you, Miss, Vance was there to take his measure."

Karen, in the act of handing the ranger a cup of coffee, stopped, the scene replaying quickly in her head. She straightened and met his gaze. "Vance didn't kill him. I did."

The ranger took his coffee, looked at her with new respect. "You? You must've . . ."

"It's over and done with, if you don't mind," she interrupted firmly.

"Why, yes, ma'am . . . I mean, no, ma'am," he said, quickly taking a swallow of coffee. "No offense intended."

They spent the rest of the day at the cave and left at first light the next morning. The party could only travel as fast as Vance's wounds would allow, and at Harley's suggestion they took the longer, easier route, heading toward the western pass into the PAX valley. Two days later they were well into the pass and spent their evening at a high, lonely line shack nestled in a fertile break in the hills, graced by a pasture of sweet green grass nourished by three separate underground streams. It was there Karen posed to Harley the nagging question of Vance's health. The trail-wise ranch hand turned his weathered face toward the cabin. "All he needs is rest, plenty of food an' water an' light exercise. He's lost blood, but the wound ain't infected. Them bandages an' herbs'll help speed things up, but oth-er'n that, there ain't nothin' else we can do for him but make him easy 'til he's better. I imagine with some a' your vittles in him, he ought to be up an' around in a week."

"Harley," she began tentatively, "is there any reason why Vance couldn't just stay here with me to care for him until he's well?"

Harley glanced sidewise at her then shook his head, the shadow of a grin flitting across his features. "Ma'am, I reck-on that would just about get a fella healed up an' ready to go quicker'n a regiment of doctors an' a mountain of pills to boot. There's plenty of grub, an' there'll be riders workin' the hills. If you need anything, you can send up a smoke an' someone'll come runnin'."

"A week?"

"Sounds fine to me, ma'am. We'll get you set an' then ride on back. True'll be mighty anxious to see you two." He chuckled softly. "Fact of the matter is, we had to just about hogtie him to a chair to keep him from ridin' out with the search parties. Yeah, he'll be mighty anxious . . ." he smiled broadly. "But I reckon he'll understand."

There were flowers in the hills, bright delicate spots of purple, pale amber, virgin white. For two days gentle spring rains had come, bringing the hills to life with green splendor. Karen Paxton walked down the long meadow be-tween the rocky reaches of the surrounding hills, easily as-cended a gradual incline to the east, topped out on a windy knoll delightfully carpeted with rain lilies and flame-tipped Indian paintbrush and the ever-present statuaries of cedar, lonely against the sky even in the spring. From her vantage point the land fell away in breathtaking decline, sweeping down to a sparkling creek whose dappled waters threaded their way through the hills to the Sabinal. How beautiful this place was, and yet it was but a minute replica of the *Canyon de Uvalde* where the *hacienda* reposed in all its splendor only scant miles to the east. She glanced to the north where the broken ridges lost their cedar crowns. Among those barren summits Ted Morning Sky lay wrapped in silent, final slumber. Was there a Valhalla for the Comanche? Did he once again ride proudly with his people on an endless plain of windswept stars?

"Karen . . .?" Vance's voice drifted up the slope. She turned and waved to him. He was standing by the spring near the cabin, the sun drifting below the hills behind him. The past four days had shown his remarkable recuperative powers. Already he was chafing to be up and around. She started down the slope at a walk. By the time she reached the edge of the meadow she was running.

Deprived of him for so long, the weeks and months of loneliness and hardship left her famished, made overpowering her desperate need. Unbound hair erubescent in the blushing sunset, Karen ran with utter abandonment to the man who waited, whose arms outstretched and clasped her to him, their bodies bending in the ardor of their embrace. They kissed deeply, almost savagely, pausing only long enough to enter the snug confines of the cabin, cozy with the flames in the stone fireplace. Clothes were eagerly cast off and they fell to the bed, bodies meeting, feverishly intertwining at last. Karen covered Vance's muscled torso with teasing kisses until he pulled her to his hungry mouth, then rolled on top of her, his manhood poised at the gate of her passion, probing the tight dark-blond curls. Karen suddenly clenched her thighs together. "Oh, my God, Vance. I forgot!" she said in a saucy, provocative tone.

A look of alarm crossed Vance's face. "What?"

She touched the scars on his arm and hip. "Your wounds. I mean, we . . . well, we . . . can't, can we?"

Vance laughed, remembering their words from a lifetime ago. "If we don't," he answered in mock seriousness, "I'll never forgive you."

It was long into the night before their bodies finally succumbed to the dreamy, languid aftermath of complete and repeated consummation. Karen nestled in the crook of his arm, kissing again and again the burly forest of his chest, musky and sweet. His hand ran down along her back, cupped her taut buttocks and pressed her closer to him. "I love you, Karen."

The words, softer than the crackling conversation of the flames, echoed in the fullness of her heart, filling her with a melody too sweet to be sung, a blending harmony of memory and desire, the secret knowledge of self and self-sacrifice, the give and take and ever-surging tide of sweet-

446

est bliss and headiest ecstasy, and that which defied i. telling because words were simply not enough to capture or hold or define.

"I love you too, Vance," came her whispered reply.

They held each other and did not speak again that night. The last Karen heard before she fell asleep was his heart, pulsing at one with hers, with life and love, the two inseparable.

the
Paxton
Women
saga
continues!

YELLOW ROSE

_____ 05557-3	**YELLOW ROSE**	$3.50
_____ 06324-X	**PAXTON PRIDE**	$3.50
_____ 06325-8	**RAVEN**	$3.50